Belle Dame Sans Merci

Astrea Taylor

~ for my sisters ~

O what can ail thee, knight-at-arms,
alone and palely loitering?
The sedge has withered from the lake,
and no birds sing.

I met a lady in the meads,
full beautiful, a fairy's child:
her hair was long, her foot was light,
and her eyes were wild.

I saw pale kings, and princes too,
pale warriors, death-pale were they all:
they cried, 'La Belle Dame sans Merci
hath thee in thrall!'

Excerpts from 'La Belle Dame Sans Merci,'
John Keats, 1819, lines 1-5, 13-16, 37-40.

~ Prologue ~

Dear Jane,

If you're reading this, it means I didn't make out of the pits of Hell. It's been fourteen days since Lucifer kidnapped me and locked me in this cell, and tomorrow is the full moon. By that time, I'll either turn evil or he'll make me kill again and that will turn me.

I still have no idea why he's keeping me prisoner here. No amount of pleading or banging on the thick wooden door helps.

If I'm turned into an evil beast, please know you've been the best friend I could've asked for throughout all our trials. I love you like my own sister, but I beg you, please don't come anywhere near me if I turn. I will not be myself. Instead, please get me this journal, that I might remember my former self again. I would be forever indebted to you, even if I don't know it at the time.

Thank you for your friendship over these past few centuries. Pray for me when you get to Heaven, and tell my family I love them and hold them dearest in my heart.

Your friend,
Belle

CHAPTER ONE

I stood and made the sign of the cross, my fingertips touching my head, heart, and shoulders. My long skirt brushed the mosaic tile floor as I passed rows of amber-colored pews and stained glass windows on my way toward the door. A few penitent souls glanced up at me. I smiled at their sad faces. Who knew? Maybe I'd answer their prayers today.

Pushing open the weathered wooden door, I squinted at the bright San Diego sunlight. Aromas of *salsa fresca* and exhaust lingered in the dry summer air. Cars honked in a traffic jam, and down the street, a homeless guy rattled change in a cup. I scanned the pedestrians dressed in skimpy clothing and did my best to blend in with them. After walking a couple of blocks, I saw what I was looking for — an omen. A golden ring rotated over the head of a middle-aged man across the street. Of course, he was oblivious to it.

I took out my phone and opened Neutralizer, then captured the omen in the camera view. A dossier popped up.

> Mike Malone. Science teacher at Riverton High School. To be dissipated for killing his student, 16-year-old Beth Wilton.
>
> Accept target?
>
> Yes   No   More Info

A pit formed in my stomach. A teacher? I tapped on **More info**. I needed to know what happened. It was always easier to kill my targets once I had more details.

> Mike Malone met with his student, Beth Wilton, at a drive-in theatre under romantic pretenses. He strangled her in his car, then dumped her body in a marsh. It was found two weeks later by a wetland biologist. Beth Wilton left behind a

mother, father, two brothers, and one set of grandparents. Her karma score was 97% good, 3% bad.

Accept target?

Yes   No

My blood boiled. He'd killed a helpless student — someone who'd trusted him. And she was a good person! She could've been the next Mother Theresa for all he knew.

My eyes phased black, making my vision turn shades of gray and red. I drew in a deep breath. I had to control my demonic features in public. With a little effort, my eyes returned to normal. I ran a hand over my garter belt, feeling the hard steel of my blade beneath my fingertips. Soon, I'd dissipate his soul and revoke his privilege of being alive. I tapped **Yes** and the omen above his head vanished. Beneath his photo, more text appeared.

Demon assigned: Belle Dame

My lips twitched with a frown. I wasn't exactly a demon, but I did demon work. It always bothered me that Neutralizer didn't differentiate between me and the monsters I worked with. But it was a job, and I needed the karma.

I ran across the street, my feet pounding the pavement as I narrowly dodged a taxi. My target glanced over his shoulder at me, but continued walking, his pace unchanged. Even with my strange clothing — long dark gray skirt, black leather boots, and long-sleeved black blouse — he didn't perceive me as a threat. Little did he know.

My phone buzzed with a text. I pulled it out, my eyes flashing over a message from my manager.

```
Lucifer wants to see you
in his office. He
wouldn't tell me why.
Check in with me when
you get back to Hell.
```

My heartbeat rose. I stopped mid-stride to re-read the message, my brows knitting. For a moment, I worried I might be in trouble. Then I laughed. My work ethic was flawless. But, maybe today was the day — maybe I finally had enough karma from killing evil people that Lucifer would discharge me to Heaven. I drew in a deep breath, trying to contain the fluttering in my belly. My fingers flew as I texted back.

Should I come in now?

No, just before the end of the day.

Fine, I could wait. I'd waited centuries, after all. I pocketed my phone and paced down the grimy sidewalk, looking for my marked man. Half a block later, I found him. We passed a couple of dark alleys. For a moment, I thought I might get an easy kill. But, before I could catch up to him, he turned down a highly traversed street lined with ancient mango trees. Their broad green leaves quivered in the cool, salty wind. We were closer to the ocean now. I could smell it.

When my target wandered into a busy coffeehouse, I sighed, glaring at the well-lit tables and benches. Public places were the worst.

I walked into the coffeehouse behind him and felt the frosty rush of air-conditioning. People waited in line to reach a caramel-colored counter. Aromas of coffee and nag champa incense hung in the air. In the other room, the walls held bookcases that stretched from the floor to the ceiling. Newspapers lay on coffee tables nestled between overstuffed leather chairs.

My target turned around for a moment, glancing at me from the line. I took in his deep-set turquoise eyes, his rodent-like nose and mouth, and his scrappy brown hair before he turned around again. He wore a navy blazer over a novelty t-shirt and jeans, marking him as the kind of teacher who thought he was cool enough to hang out with students after class. *Cool enough to press his thumbs against a young girl's throat until she couldn't breathe anymore.* I dug my fingernails into my palms. After I was done with him, he'd never have the chance to hurt anyone again. I'd make sure of it.

The bald eye of a security camera stared at me over a stainless steel espresso machine. I stared back, knowing my face wouldn't register on it. Being a temp in Hell had its perks.

When Mike got to the front of the line, he ordered, paid, and slipped his change into the tip jar along with an extra dollar.

The barista grinned. "Thanks, Mr. Malone."

"Keep it real, Brian, and call me Mike. We're not at Riverton anymore." Mike took his order to a table in the other room.

My jaw clenched. *Great.* I couldn't do it here, not with an innocent acquaintance nearby. I let out a pent-up breath. So much for an easy kill. I'd have to lure him to another place.

The bright-eyed barista blinked at me. "Miss?"

"An Earl Grey, please."

As he poured hot water over the teabag, my senses prickled with the aromatics of herbal bergamot and high-quality black tea, the kind with loads of tannins. I paid and strolled around the bookshelves, waiting the requisite four minutes for a proper steep. When it was done, I dropped the teabag into the trashcan and took the steaming cup to the service table for cream. It was excellent tea. I'd have to remember to come back to this place once the heat from Mike's murder died down.

I walked around the room, pretending to look at the colorful books on the shelves. Mike slurped his coffee and munched on a crumbling scone. I edged behind him, my head cocked to one side as if I were reading the titles of the books. My arm extended for a book behind him, but fell short. I smiled helplessly. "Excuse me."

He gave me a bewildered up-and-down glance.

"Would you mind scooting in a little?" I asked. "I'm trying to reach that book."

"Sure." He scooted his chair forward. "Sorry about that."

"Thanks." I plucked a random book from the case, then held out my hand. "I'm Belle, by the way."

"Mike." He grasped my hand for a moment, then

looked at the book. "What'd you get? Anything good?"

I glanced at the title and shoved it under my arm. *Sleeping Beauty*. Ugh.

"It's a book about fashion design." I tucked a strand of long, chestnut-colored hair behind my ear. "I study fashion at the University."

"Really? The University of San Diego?"

"Mm hm."

His gaze drifted to my floor-length dark gray skirt. "Did you make that?"

I nodded, smiling. I'd special-ordered it from the internet, but he didn't need to know that. In truth, it didn't feel right to wear anything else. Some parts of the 1600's stayed with me. At least I'd updated to a long-sleeved blouse instead of a corset and a shift. I couldn't be *completely* old-fashioned.

He laughed, shrugging. "I thought you might be an actress or something."

I laughed too, and hoped it sounded real. "What do you do, Mike?"

His eyes brightened. "I work at Riverton High School. You're not from around here, are you?"

I shook my head. "No, I'm from Akron."

"Akron, wow! How do you like San Diego?"

"Well . . ." I paused, making a show of examining his ringless left hand. "If you don't have a girlfriend, or whatever, how 'bout I tell you over a drink?"

His brows shot up. "Sure, yeah. It's a bit early, but there's a dive bar nearby." He leaned in close to whisper. "I know the bartender. You won't have to worry about an ID."

"I have another place in mind, if that's okay."

His grin broadened. "By all means. Lead the way."

As we walked out of the coffeehouse, I spun a story about fashion school divas and how hard it was to live in San Diego. He seemed to believe it. He even offered advice about city living and the best food trucks.

After a few blocks, we ditched our drinks. We passed a few dark alleys, but so many passers-by made it impossible for me to eviscerate him there. It was a beautiful day, and with so many people out and about, I doubted I'd be able to make an easy kill. But I had a Plan B.

After a few more blocks, we entered an upscale restaurant called Ophelia. The entire restaurant was decorated in shades of blue, with indigo tablecloths, cornflower walls, and azure carpet. Even the waitstaff wore navy shirts. Almost a decade ago, I'd killed a woman who'd murdered her toddler in those same bathrooms. I knew from experience that they were so far from the dining room that no one would hear him scream.

It was lunchtime, which made it almost impossible to hear anything. People shouted to each other over clashing knives and scraping forks. We waded through the tables and walked toward the long oak bar.

A blonde, mustachioed hipster set sky-colored napkins in front of us. With his tan skin and wisps of sun-bleached hair, he looked like a professional surfer.

"Whiskey, please." I laid my book on the bar as far away from Mike as I could and slid onto a stool.

Mike sidled up next to me. "Make that two."

"ID?" the bartender asked me.

I retrieved my ID from my satchel and presented it.

Mike breathed an almost inaudible sigh of relief. Almost. I had demon ears. When the bartender's back was turned, Mike leaned close to me again. "How old are you?"

"I'm twenty-three," I lied. I was nineteen when I died, but I was so old, I didn't bother counting anymore. Twenty-three was what I passed for these days.

His fingers grazed my leg. "So, do you live in the dorms?"

I was about to answer when my phone buzzed. I glanced down at a text from Nosferatu, the churlish vampire who worked in the cubical beside me.

Hey Belle. I heard
you're in trouble.

I bit my lip to repress a scowl and slid the phone into

my pocket.

"What's wrong?" Mike asked.

"Nothing." I laughed breathily. "I forgot that I have a test tomorrow, that's all."

The bartender set two whiskeys in crystal tumblers before us. "Anything else? Lunch menus?"

"We'll let you know." Mike handed over his credit card. "Keep it open."

We clinked glasses and drank a sip. The liquor tasted of vanilla and toffee, and warmed my belly like fire.

"So you were about to tell me — do you live in the dorms?"

"Yeah." My index finger traced the edge of my lower lip. "You should come over sometime."

"Okay." He guffawed. "I can't say no to that."

I drained my drink and stood, a vicious smile lighting up my face. "Come on, I want to show you something." I nodded toward the bathroom, pulling at one of his hands for a second.

He remained rooted to the stool, his face lined with indecision as he clutched his glass.

I sashayed through the tables toward the back of the restaurant and leaned against the hallway doorframe. My eyes smoldered with a come-hither look. I hoped he didn't see the desperation behind them.

Come on, Mike. I need the karma.

After another moment's hesitation, he gulped his

whiskey and ambled toward me. I led him into the hallway, my fingers grasping the polyester lapels of his jacket, pulling him toward me.

Once we were inside the bathroom, I pressed the lock with a satisfying *click*. The bathroom had been refurnished since I'd been there last, but it was still perfect for my needs. It was spacious, with white stone tile covering the walls and floor, and a droning fan overhead.

Mike's hands ran over my waist as he breathed into my ear, crushing me against the cool wall.

I recalled the details of the student he'd killed. *Strangled 16-year old. Romantic pretenses. Dumped in a marsh.* My eyes phased black again, and my teeth shot out longer and sharper, more like a wolf's than a human's. This time, I didn't resist my demonic transformation. I knew I looked like a monster, but I didn't care. I pulled out my knife through a slit in my skirt and held it against Mike's neck.

He jerked back, his eyes flashing with fear. "What's wrong with your eyes? And your teeth?"

For a second, there was only the hum of the bathroom fan. Then I lunged, my knife swiping toward the tender flesh of his neck. A growl emanated from my throat.

Mike jerked backwards and slipped on the tile. He fell, his head smacking hard against the toilet. Blood ran down onto the floor in big drips from the back of his head. He held up one trembling hand.

I shook my head, a guttural laugh resounding like thunder. *As if that could stop me.* I palmed his head against the floor, feeling a dull thud.

"Stop!" he screamed.

"Mike Malone," I said through clenched teeth. "You've been deemed unworthy of your life for your crimes against humanity. I'm doing this for Beth."

"No! Wait! I didn't kill her!"

I shook my head. "That's what they all say." I slammed his skull against the tile again. A satisfying *crack* echoed throughout the room.

A vision of my death rose before my eyes. The man who'd killed me stood in the crowd of villagers, wearing a dogged determination as the executioner's axe-like blade sliced my neck.

When I came back to myself, no pulse sounded from Mike's veins. No heartbeat thumped in his chest. He was dead.

Colors bled back into my sight as I blinked. My teeth retracted into my gums. I stood and backed against the cold stone tile.

A purple mist floated out of Mike's mouth as his soul dissipated. I held my sleeve over my mouth, barely daring to breathe. The motes floated to the ceiling, then the fan sucked them out, dissipating his soul to the four winds.

I released my sleeve and bowed my head, taking a

moment of silence for Beth Wilton's ghost. The dead girl had to be here, just as I'd been stuck in the material realm after I was killed. I looked around, but I didn't see her. I never did see the deceased, but that didn't stop me from paying tribute. Now that her killer was dead, she could be at peace. She wouldn't be tempted to take revenge, and she wouldn't have to become a temp in Hell, like I had.

I stepped over Mike and walked toward the sink. Violet soap fell in a foamy swirl from the automatic dispenser with a *mmmm* noise. I washed my hands, watching the basin run red, then pink, and finally clear.

After toweling off, I looked at Mike one last time. He lay sprawled on the floor, blood pooling around his head. I jimmied out his leather wallet from his back pocket. Cops didn't look into muggings like they did murders, plus, I needed the cash. Being a temp in Hell didn't pay nearly enough. I pocketed his sixty-three dollars and threw the wallet onto his chest. My fingerprints wouldn't leave a trace — another benefit.

I put my ear to the bathroom door and listened to servers chatting, walking to and from the kitchen. When all was silent, I opened the door. The hallway was empty except for a lone server headed to the dining room. I clicked the bathroom lock from the inside, shut the door, then tiptoed toward the bar. The bartender had his back to me as he muddled something for a happy couple.

14

I retrieved my book and slipped away.

As I stepped outside, a wave of relief rippled down my spine. Sunlight warmed my face, and the smell of the ocean tickled my nose. I'd gotten away with murder again, and I was one step closer to Heaven.

I started walking toward Ocean Beach, eager to see the Pacific Ocean. It'd been a few months since I'd last seen it, and it'd been chilly then. This time, it'd be nice and warm. I'd get to relax on the beach and read for a few hours before returning to Hell and writing up my report.

"Hey!" someone yelled behind me. The bartender leaned out of the door frame, an impetuous look on his tanned face.

I ran, my feet striking the gum-splattered sidewalk. He yelled again, and footsteps beat after me. I rushed around the corner and raced down the street, weaving through the streets.

After a few minutes, the back of my neck still tingled. I turned, scanning the faces of the pedestrians behind me. The bartender wasn't among them, but he'd gotten a good look at me. I cursed under my breath. I'd have to give up hunting in San Diego again. But if Lucifer released me to Heaven today, I'd never miss it.

I walked down a dilapidated sidewalk strewn with litter, toward an old blackened warehouse. A beat-up crimson door glowed with demonfire — the flames only demons and temps could see, marking it as one of the many waystations to Hell.

A meaty man in a biker shirt and bad tattoos on his arms eyed me. "Hey princess, you lost?"

I shot him a sarcastic glance. If he only knew. I was no princess. I'd like to see him try anything. I stepped over a dead rat and opened the red door onto a small cement lobby. The door swung shut behind me with a *thud*. A second later, the doorknob rattled. I shook my head. Stupid mortal. The doors to Hell didn't open for human hands.

Black mold covered the walls, and overhead, fluorescent lights flickered. I held my breath, avoiding a pool of acid-green bile on the floor. I'd learned to ignore the filth in waystations a long time ago. Even if I wrote it in the repair book, it wouldn't get fixed. It was nothing personal — it was just the way Hell worked.

An open shaft loomed on the other side of the room. It looked like an elevator whose doors were missing. The empty space inside was as dark as black velvet. I pushed the greasy red button on the wall, and heard clankings ring out from the depths below. The sounds rose closer and closer.

I tapped my foot as I waited, my thoughts on my meeting with Lucifer. Who knew — maybe Mike would be my last kill ever, and I could leave this dead-end job. Maybe I'd get to see my family in Heaven by the end of the day. Just the thought made my heart a little lighter.

Ping!

```
Everyone's saying
Lucifer wants to see
you because you're
in trouble. Is it true?
```

Adrenaline surged through my veins. I had to resist crushing my phone in my hands. Nosferatu couldn't be right. It had to be another one of his cruel jokes. Stupid demon.

A metal cage arrived with a loud groan. I pushed open the black accordion-like gate and stepped in. The cage shifted precariously with my weight, throwing me forward. Adrenaline spiked in my system, and a cold flush came over my skin. My hands shot out automatically and gripped the bars of the little cage.

After a few tense breaths, the elevator stilled. I'd been in a few bad waystations, but this was one of the worst. I laughed despite it all, shaking my head. It'd be so ironic to plummet to my second death now, just moments before a meeting that might free me from Hell. But if Lucifer's news was bad, it'd be a blessing. I closed the gate and pressed the slimy red button, making a mental note to never use this waystation again.

The elevator dropped, descending faster and faster through soil and bedrock. The room above became a distant point of light as earthen layers zoomed past. It picked up even more speed as it fell, echoing from both hollow ends. For a moment, my body felt weightless. My hair flew up and my skirt fluttered. Then, metal screeched against metal. Vibrant yellow sparks arced over my head. The elevator slowed and jolted to a stop.

I landed in a crouch, then stood and ripped back the black metal gate. Burning sulfur singed my nose, and flickering torches shone on the vaulted brick ceilings of Death's Cross. I glared at an ancient stone plaque covered in cobwebs.

ABANDON ALL HOPE, YE WHO ENTER HERE

Right. As if anyone had a choice.

CHAPTER TWO

My footsteps echoed off the black flagstones as I strode down the cavernous hallway of Death's Cross. Spitting torchlight lit hundreds of ink-dark waystation shafts that led to crimson doors all over the world. Demons and temps passed me, either on their way to, or from, their work topside.

A giant fire imp, twice my height, patrolled the hallway. His dark flesh burned like charcoal, with a faint red fire glowing beneath his skin. His muscles almost burst out of his starched black uniform as he nodded to me and tapped a spiked club against the floor. "The boss wants to see you, Belle," his voice boomed.

I shot him a tight-lipped smile and clutched my book. "Thanks. I'm on my way."

My chest tightened, as it did every time I walked through Death's Cross, but the thought of going to Lucifer's office made it worse. I hadn't been there since I was dragged there as a ghost. I couldn't help but remember how I'd stumbled on these very stones as the demons carried me to him.

It wasn't just the bad memories that made me despise returning to Hell. It was everything — the politics, the gossipers, the stench of brimstone, the evil overlord, the mismanagement, the antagonism of the life-long demons versus the temporary demons . . . I could go on and on. But if today was the day I'd be released to Heaven, I'd never have to see this place again. I shook my head. No. I couldn't get my hopes up. I had to stay level-headed.

I passed under a gothic arched doorway at the end of Death's Cross and into a huge open room packed with half-walled cubicles as far as I could see. The air was filled with the droning sound of demons answering phones, clacking on keyboards, and chatting by water coolers. A golem and a jackal slouched by a copier, their glittering black eyes passing over me. The jackal muttered something under his breath and they both laughed.

I held my head high as I passed them, but I couldn't help but wonder if they knew something about my meeting with Lucifer. They were probably just jealous. I was a temp — my demonic features only came out when I killed. Because I blended in with humanity, I could go topside anytime I felt like it. But they were demons, and their evil nature made their demonic features permanent. To think these demons were once human was chilling. Because they had to keep the reality of Hell a secret, they crept around at night, skulking in shadows and hiding from sight.

I walked through the halls, mindful of the white and gold neon star on the far eastern wall, marking the way to Lucifer's office. Some of the scariest demons worked in that corner.

I didn't see my manager, so I slipped into my little gray-walled cubicle. It was on the way, and there might be a hint about why Lucifer wanted to meet with me. I plopped my satchel onto my desk and logged onto my computer. Two emails popped up — one inviting me to an ice cream social hour, the other reminding me to pin my timecard so my karma would transfer. There was nothing about the meeting.

A housefly buzzed in front of me. I swatted it away before realizing my mistake. "I'm so sorry, sir! It's a habit."

"It's okay — you didn't get me," said a small, thin voice. My manager, McMillan, landed on my monitor and washed his face with tiny black arms. "I saw you coming a mile away!"

"Sir, do you know why Lucifer wants to see me?"

His head swiveled. "No clue. It makes me a little nervous, to tell you the truth. Why would he want to see you? You're just a temp."

"You don't know *anything*?" My insides wilted. Once

again, my manager didn't know what was happening with one of his employees. No big surprise there. I don't know why I expected more.

"Nope, I know nothing. Just don't leave him waiting. Check in with me afterwards, okay?"

I nodded. As he hummed out of my cube, I imagined my blade slicing clean through his little head. He was useless. What could he do if I were in trouble? Buzz in someone's face and annoy them?

A pale, pointy head popped up over my cubicle wall. Nosferatu's lips curled into a mocking smile, revealing sharp, rotted teeth. "Sounds like you're in trouble, Belle."

My nostrils flared as I crossed my arms and glared at him. "Why would you think that? I kill circles around you and everyone else here."

He shrugged. "Lucifer rarely wants to see temps who are doing well."

My eyes narrowed. "Maybe I'm going to Heaven today. Did you ever consider that? Or maybe he wants to promote me. Hey, isn't your manager going to Heaven soon?"

Nosferatu's eyes bugged. He frowned and slunk down the half-wall.

I almost laughed, except he was right. Sometimes, when Lucifer called temps into his office, they disappeared. There were rumors he ate them. I straightened

22

and took a fresh breath, reminding myself I had nothing to be afraid of. I followed orders better than most.

I walked out of my cube and headed through the maze of cubicles toward the baleful star on the eastern wall. The closer I got, the more demons tracked my progression. A cyclops stared at me over his cubicle, his eye as big as my fist. I sidestepped an octopus leaving a slimy trail down the hall and ran into a tall woman with long, golden-blonde hair. *Medea.* I backed away. Her eyes were completely black, marking her as a demon, and she clutched a broomstick. Rumor had it that she'd been in Hell for over two millennia, working off some terrible karmic debt.

"Watch where you're going, temp!" she snarled.

Something slipped into my hand as she sidestepped me and walked down the hall. My palm curled around the sharp edges of a folded note. I started to go after her, but my breath lodged in my throat, and my feet wouldn't move. I tugged against them, but I was immobile. I gasped. What kind of magic was that?

As soon as her black skirt swayed around the corner, my throat opened and I could move. I swallowed nervously. I could go after her, but I didn't want a taste of anything harsher. Besides, Lucifer was waiting. I tucked the note in my pocket. I couldn't read it now, not with the most evil demons nearby.

After a few more turns, I reached the eastern wall.

The glowing neon star emitted a fuzzy yellow light that made my skin look mottled. Beneath the star were two scarlet french doors glowing with demonfire.

Two guards perked up as I approached. A gorgon, with snakes in place of hair, thrust her spear out and hissed. "What do you want?"

I took a steeling breath. "My name is Belle Dame. The Prince of Darkness asked to see me."

Her gray eyes shifted and her mouth turned down, but she moved her spear out of the way. The other guard, a stout orc with leather armor and pervasive body odor, leered at me.

I grasped the doorknob. "Ow!" My hand jerked back when I felt the heat. I glanced down at my palm. It was scorched with a red crescent mark.

The gorgon snorted, doubling over with laughter. The orc shrugged and twisted the doorknob. "Nice knowing you." He pushed open the creaking door.

I walked into a brightly lit room. Before me, a white marble floor shone like spilled milk. An ivory staircase with a decorative iron banister spiraled down beneath a crystal chandelier.

I turned to the guards. "Am I supposed to wait here, or—"

The red door slammed in my face.

I took a deep breath, calming myself. Lucifer's office was downstairs, then. This was some kind of antechamber. I didn't recall this room on the way to his office centuries ago, but I supposed he could've redecorated since then.

I glanced around. There were no cameras, no guards. I was alone. I dug into my pocket and found the note from the witch Medea, then unfolded the creamy, smooth paper and stared at the scrawled handwriting.

Don't trust him.

A chill rippled down my spine. How could she just say that and not explain herself? I wanted to run out of the room, find the witch, and ask her what she meant. I ran back to the red doors and batted at the doorknob with my fingertips. Heat flashed through my hand again. I knocked, but no one answered.

"Guards!"

My fist beat against it, pounding the red wood, but to no avail. The guards, if they heard me, didn't care.

There appeared to be only one way to go.

Down.

I refolded the note and shoved it into the last place anyone would look for it — into my boot. I plodded down the stairs, my fingers trailing along the warm black bannister. Every step echoed on the hard stone, ringing out against the white walls.

At the bottom, I hesitated, gazing with trepidation at a set of french doors just like the ones at the top of the stairs, except these were white, with a golden, five-pointed star painted on them. I wiped my sweaty palms on my skirt, drew in a deep breath, and touched the doorknob. It was room temperature, much to my relief.

The door opened onto a room with high ceilings and the same gleaming-white walls and floor. Four secretaries sat behind burgundy desks: two men on the left and two women on the right. On the opposite end of the room, an oversized ebony door carved with grotesque intertwined animals glowered back at me.

A secretary tiptoed forward, her gait made short by her pencil skirt. Her chin trembled. "Name?"

"Belle Dame."

She tapped something into an IPad. "Ah, yes. The Prince of Darkness is expecting you. This way." She placed her hand on my shoulder, guiding me toward the black door.

I thrashed out of her reach. "Don't touch me."

She flinched, cowering. Every secretary in the room froze. One of the male secretaries jerked his head down, his knuckles blanched white as he clutched his red rotary phone.

I sighed. "I'm sorry."

I'd forgotten they weren't like the rest of us. Lucifer's

secretaries were white-collar criminals who worked in Hell for a few years as temps, then went to Heaven. They never understood what we long-time temps and demons went through. It wasn't their fault, though. We each had our own karmic debts. Mine was to kill evil people, and they were obliged to serve and obey the Lord of the Underworld. In a way, I felt sorry for them. Anyone who had to spend time next to the Beast himself would surely fix their errant ways.

I walked the remaining steps to the towering mahogany door. Carved into it were beasts — goats, snakes, and monkeys intertwined with branches and leaves. I frowned. I didn't remember this door from my last visit either. I looked for a knob or a knocker, but didn't see one. I considered knocking, but there was no place to do so without bruising my knuckles.

A manly voice boomed from the other side of the door. "COME IN."

My pulse quickened. It could only be Lucifer. I searched frantically for the knob, my eyes running over the carvings — bat, monkey, hyena, serpent, sea monster . . . *Where was the knob?*

"COME IN!" He roared.

CHAPTER THREE

My hands shook as I looked for some way to open the massive black door. I glanced back at the secretary for help.

She smirked from behind her desk, as if to say, *'you're not so brave now, are you?'*

I leaned my weight against the door, pushing with my feet. A snake's forked tongue hung near my face. Eventually, it creaked open, little by little.

Lucifer's office didn't look like how I'd remembered it, either. When the demons had dragged my soul there all those centuries ago, it was little more than a cave with red candles dripping on skulls. Crimson velvet curtains had hung from a two-story sepulchral ceiling. Now, the place looked nearly identical to the waiting room. The walls and floor gleamed white, and a chandelier cast spectral light over the marble floors. A huge ebony desk hunkered in the middle of the room. Lucifer sat behind it, a green lamp illuminating stacks of papers in front of him. His muscular, square jaw and strong nose complemented his stylish mop of black curls. He wore a three-piece Italian suit that looked like it was made by the finest tailor in the world. A red handkerchief peeked out from his breast pocket, matching his collared shirt. Except for his completely black eyes, he looked unexpectedly human — perhaps more like the angel he was before he was evicted from Heaven.

The last time I'd seen him, his black hair had been long and unkempt, and his skin was so red it looked like he'd bathed in blood. Obsidian horns had crested his head, twenty centimeters high. I seemed to remember smoke had poured from his nostrils, too.

Even though his horns remained lodged in his skull and he looked like a normal person today, those coal-black eyes were exactly the same. I'd never forget the day he spoke the incantation to recall my flesh to my soul. I'd felt a rush of relief to be corporeal again but also terror. The devil was real! He sliced into my arm with a razor-sharp scythe and dipped a quill into my blood, bidding me to sign an X on his scroll. His bargain was simple. Work as a temp in Hell and have a chance to go to Heaven once my karma built up; or, if I didn't sign, he'd dissipate my soul to the four winds right then and there.

In the end, I couldn't resist his bargain. It was centuries ago, but I could still hear the quill scratching on the uneven parchment — could still see the vibrant color of my blood as I signed my afterlife away. But somehow, in the clean white room, it seemed like another lifetime — almost as if it'd never happened at all.

I dropped into a curtsy. "Hello, Sir."

He looked at me with calculating eyes. "Come closer," he grumbled.

I gulped. I probably should have curtsied lower. I walked toward him, every step bringing back more bad memories. The note rubbed against my foot as I walked. If he found out about it, he could think it was treason. He might dissipate me on the spot. I tried to quell my racing heart and thought about the church in San Diego, so if he read my mind, he'd see that, and not the words hidden inside my boot.

A sheaf of papers fell from his hands. I saw my name on them — they were my most recent reports. More of my reports were stacked in neat piles on his desk. My chest clenched. Maybe Nosferatu knew something — maybe I was in trouble. They say the devil is in the details, and they're right. If the books didn't add up at the end of the week, Lucifer lost his temper, and temps and demons alike lost their heads. But I reminded myself I'd always gotten my reports in early and had killed more than my share. I should be fine.

He motioned to an ebony chair near his desk. On the

armrests were leather wrist-cuffs crusted with dried blood. The smell almost made me gag. "Have a seat."

My heart thrummed. "I'd rather stand, Sir."

"Fine." His voice sounded hoarse, as if he'd been yelling. He rose to walk around his desk, looming over me, then breathed through his teeth. "Your manager doesn't see anything wrong with the way you're working. But I do."

I held my ground, but my scalp prickled with a chill. "What do you mean, Sir? I'm one of your best field agents."

He cocked his head and evaluated me. "Do you really think that?"

I nodded, though the look in his eyes told me I shouldn't be so certain. I prayed this was a cruel joke. It had to be.

He shook his head, his black eyes pinning my soul. "It's a shame you're not aware of your performance, Belle. You're a below average worker."

My mouth fell open. "Excuse me, Sir, but do you have the right information? I— I work harder than anyone else in my department." Barbara, the gargoyle across the hall from me, took months to kill. It took me a couple of days at the most.

"That's true, you do work hard." His fine dark suit creased as he crossed his arms, showing thick muscles beneath the fabric. He leaned against his desk. "The only problem is you're too fast. Your victims don't suffer enough. The p-force of your kills isn't strong enough to raise your karmic debt."

"My . . . *what?*"

"Your p-force, your violence. It's used to calculate karma."

My spine wilted as I gazed into his black eyes. "And it's not good enough?"

He shook his head. "You're in the last percentile of all of the workers in Hell. Even the brownies kill harder than you do."

"But, I thought it was the *number* of kills that mattered, not the violence of the kill." I looked around the room, licking my lips nervously.

"Think of it this way." He opened his hands. "It's like you're catching six hundred mosquitos for dinner when you could be eating one three-course meal."

"But, Sir . . . that's the way I've been killing for centuries. Why hasn't anyone told me about this?"

He sighed, a belabored look crossing his features. "Your manager should've given you a performance review centuries ago. I don't know why he hasn't. He says he's too busy, but I don't know what he could be working on. So, I looked into his employees' work. Did you know your score has barely changed since you arrived here?"

My eyes widened and my face flushed hot. "That has

to be a mistake." *It had to be.* All this time, I'd been working so hard, barely taking a day off, and I'd barely earned any karma? My face scrunched into a scowl. I was going to ream McMillan when I got back.

If I got back.

My heart pounded. "What are you saying, sir?" My voice trembled. "Are you going to dissipate me?"

Lucifer chuckled condescendingly. "No. This is your first warning. And you're going to follow my orders, right?"

I nodded, swallowing the lump in my throat.

"But it begs the larger question," he continued. "You're a temporary worker here. Do you want to be a demon, or do you want to go to Heaven?"

"I want to go to Heaven," I answered without thinking. "It's the only thing that keeps me going, the motivation that lets me kill bad people."

He flattened his lips, his black eyes cold as he stared at me.

I folded my shaking hands in prayer over my heart. "Tell me what to do to make this right. Please."

"Well, you'll need to work smarter if you ever want to ascend. You'll have to torture *all* of your victims from now on. I know you're not the scariest demon in Hell, but anyone can be scary. You just need to try."

I nodded, my mind racing. I wasn't trained on torturing, but I grew up in the medieval era. Plus, I'd seen enough in my centuries in Hell to know what to do. It seemed excessively cruel, but if that was what he wanted . . .

"I can see you're confused." Lucifer settled a pair of spectacles on his nose and squinted at a paper on his desk. "Run me through your last kill. Mike Malone, was it?"

I nodded, a frown forming on my lips.

"Tell me what happened."

I swallowed. "I accepted the target, stalked him through the streets, we went into a restaurant, I lured him to a bathroom, and I killed him."

He blinked. "Please don't tell me this all happened in *one day.*"

"Um . . . yes?" I gulped. I hadn't meant it to come out as a question.

A vein pulsed on Lucifer's forehead. "Tell me how you killed him."

"He slipped and hit his head. Then . . . I slammed his skull against the floor."

Lucifer leaned close, his gleaming white teeth bared. "That's how he died? You didn't even slit his throat?!"

My head bowed. "That's correct."

He snorted in disgust, his skin flushing pink. "You barely tortured him at all. He deserved more than that! That man killed a child and dumped her in a swamp!" He pointed his finger at me. "The way you killed him wasn't a punishment at all. It only lasted, what, a couple of seconds?"

I nodded, realization and dread dawning over me. Lucifer's breathing intensified. Inky black horns rose up through his hair. I cowered and took several steps back.

"You gave him a mercy killing!" His voice shook the room. "That's unacceptable. And they call you La *Belle Dame Sans Merci!* You're supposed to show NO MERCY!"

He swiped the papers off his desk and roared. The heat from his breath scorched my face. I backed away.

"*No more mercy killings!* Torture your next victim for *at least* a week."

"Do you want me to start now?" I trembled. "I will."

"Start tomorrow. I want you to think about it tonight. Make no mistake. This is a warning. If you mess up again, I can't promise I won't dissipate you. Understood?"

I nodded feverishly.

"You're dismissed," he snarled, his voice heavy with revulsion.

I scrambled toward the door, tears flooding my eyes. I couldn't get out of there fast enough. I was stupid to think I'd go to Heaven today. I'd be stuck in Hell forever.

CHAPTER FOUR

The secretaries gaped at me from behind their red desks, their features in fright. They must've heard every single word Lucifer yelled.

"BRICE!" Lucifer roared. "CLEAN UP THIS MESS!"

One of the men jumped up and raced past me, his face a mask of fear.

I rushed past the other secretaries, concentrating on putting one foot in front of the other. Why couldn't Lucifer see it wasn't my fault McMillan never gave me a performance review? A wall of tears pressed behind my eyes, but I couldn't let go — not until I was alone. I ran up the stairs as fast as I could, just in case Lucifer changed his mind about dissipation.

I touched the handle at the top of the stairs, but it didn't burn me this time. The door opened onto the sea of cubicles and the regular buzz of office noise. It was still unpleasant, but it was better than the face-burning roaring downstairs. I tried to keep my face neutral as I walked past the guards.

"Hey, look!" The orc grinned at the gorgon. "She made it out alive. Pay up."

The gorgon rolled her eyes and slapped a bill into his palm.

I hastened into the cubicle maze, eager to get back to my desk. If anyone saw me leaving Lucifer's office with tears running down my cheeks, they'd really have something to gossip about. I prayed Nosferatu was out on an assignment. If he saw me and said one word, I'd tear off his hooked nose and shove it down his throat.

An observant dragon flicked its tongue my way as I plodded through the hallway, my head shielded.

Someone stepped in my path and almost collided with me. "Belle, hey! What do you think of my hair?"

I looked up and saw my roommate Jane. Her long black hair was braided and swept across her forehead and down one shoulder. She pirouetted, her black dress sweeping the floor. Her chocolate-brown eyes focused on mine.

I opened my mouth to tell her how nice she looked, but emotion swelled my throat shut.

"What's wrong?" she whispered, leaning close.

"I just came out of a meeting." A tear escaped my eye. I tried to blot it away as fast as I could. I must've looked terrible. "With the boss," I whispered.

Her eyes flared, then she linked her arm in mine. "Come on, I'm taking you out to lunch."

In Paris, it was already dinnertime. Twinkling stars peeked out of the dusky blue sky, and black streetlamps flickered on, casting a warm light on our little café table. But all the beauty in the world couldn't distract me from remembering Lucifer's vexation. As I recounted my meeting with Lucifer to Jane, she leaned in, shaking her head, her dark brows sloped with sympathy.

"So the end result is," I wiped my eyes, "I have to torture my next victim for at least a week. *Or else.*"

Her face went ghost-pale. "Did he threaten you with dissipation?"

I nodded. "Yes, but as long as I don't mess up my next target, I'll be okay."

"I'm so sorry to hear you went through that. It's terrible! But I don't understand — why didn't your manager tell you about your karma score?"

I slouched back into my chair, my palms turning up hopelessly. "I don't know. Apparently, McMillan has been too busy to give me a review. And worst of all, I've been messing up for centuries. I had no idea. Lucifer said I'm going to have to work for a very long time."

"Maybe I can help." She stroked my shoulder. "I know all about the long kill."

I bit my lip. Jane only had a couple of years left of working in Hell. She'd be gone before I realized it. I'd be all alone again. Despite the candlelight and the good company, I felt as if the ground had been ripped out from under me.

I sniffed back my tears and tried to return to the moment. "How do you do it?"

She smiled. "It's easy. I do it on my shifts at the hospital. I put viruses in their food, or inject poison into a saline drip. You just keep going back and adding more poison."

I forced a shaky smile. Jane had killed hundreds of people with typhoid fever when she was Typhoid Mary, so her karma was to infect evil people with diseases. She'd told me her name in secret one night, even though we weren't supposed to — our real names were the one thing that protected us against Lucifer having complete control over our lives. Belle Dame was suggested to me by my caseworker, who thought it'd make me seem fiercer than I actually was. And to think, Lucifer had made fun of me for not living up to it. My head sunk into my hands.

"I hate to say it, Jane, but my karma is different. I'm not in the Poisoner Division — I'm a Revenger. And I can't exactly slit people's throats in a public place." I shook my head, despair weighing on my heart. "I won't be going to Heaven anytime soon."

"Don't say that." She touched my shoulder.

I stared, glazed-eyed, at my untouched teacup of Earl Grey. Usually, I adored the tea at this restaurant, but now, the rich bergamot essence smelled more like soap than my favorite herb. "It's okay, Jane. I don't think I'd fit in anyway." A lot of demons in the office made fun of the goody-goody angels. Would I become one of them, joking like that because I'd never get in?

She gazed at me. "You're still a good person. You're just being screwed over by a stupid manager."

I looked into her optimistic, hopeful eyes. Did I look like that during my first century of being a temp? Perhaps. But now, I knew better. After centuries of killing, I was weary, especially after my meeting. The light in my soul felt like it was almost extinguished. I rubbed my temples, gazing at the river moving slowly down the banks. "I wish we could just run away from all this. If we didn't have to work, we could do whatever we wanted. No more killing. No more torture. We'd be free. I could start that travel blog I've always wanted to write, and you'd have your own cooking show."

Her mouth turned down. "But you know what would

happen if we left Hell."

I nodded. If we didn't breathe the sulfurous vapors in Hell every twenty-four hours, we'd turn into wraiths, and then dissipate. I hadn't believed it when I first started working there, so I pushed the limit. After twenty-five hours without breathing the air in Hell, my body and lungs collapsed. I couldn't breathe. I ran, then crawled toward a waystation. Once I reached Hell, I took gasping, grateful breaths, and felt myself expand again. One more minute, and I would have dissipated, dead forever.

"I know we can't leave," I said. "It's just a beautiful dream."

My phone pinged.

> **Carlo Dunlap. Banker at HMW Inc., Manhattan. To be dissipated for killing three women and dumping their bodies in the Hudson River: Catherine Jules, Henrietta Role, and Amber Smith.**
>
> **Demon assigned: Belle Dame.**

"Hm. That's weird."

"What is it?" Jane asked, peering over my shoulder.

"The Devil's Office already assigned me someone in Neutralizer. They sent me my next victim's dossier." I shrugged, supposing I should've expected that. It's not often one gets an assignment from the Devil himself.

"Who is it? Anyone famous?"

"No, just a banker, but he killed three women."

She smiled. "Now there's someone you can really get behind torturing."

"Yeah, but where am I going to do it? There are hardly any abandoned buildings in Manhattan — they're all either being worked on or in the process of being sold. And with the population density, someone might hear him scream."

"You could take him to my kitchen." She chewed a hunk of baguette thoughtfully. "It's in Brooklyn, just across the Williamsburg Bridge."

"You have your own kitchen?" I reeled back. "Jane, we've lived in the same apartment since 1923. Why is this the first I've heard of it?"

"I just got it." She blushed and fidgeted with her napkin. "It's stupid, I know, but I'm using it to refine my recipes. I want to make a cookbook someday," she said, her voice small. "I told you, it's dumb."

I blinked. "No, it's not dumb — it's wonderful! I just had no idea. But why don't you want to cook in our apartment?"

She made a face. "The sulfur smell. It's not *that bad* at

our place, but it still interferes with the taste. And I give my food away to the homeless too, so it helps my karma."

"That's so nice of you." I smiled, genuinely happy for her, but I also felt hollow inside. Every good deed she did meant she'd get into Heaven faster. She'd be gone in months, not years.

"Anyway," she shrugged, "I've never killed anyone there, but I don't think it'd be a problem. It's an artist's loft at Berry and South Sixth Street. The walls are thick, and it's sort of a bad neighborhood. The only other tenants are a guy using the place for storage and a punk band who'll be away on tour until the end of the year. The building next door is abandoned, and there's a highway on the other side."

"That could actually work." I let out a huge breath, nodding. "Thank you. I'll keep it clean, I promise."

"Glad to help. I'll text you the address and the key code."

The waiter placed two steaming bowls of soup before us. I dipped my spoon into the creamy potato leek bisque and lifted it to my mouth. Rosemary and cream danced on my tongue. I closed my eyes in bliss.

"Everything looks better after a good meal, doesn't it?" Jane grinned saucily, a hint of her former life as Typhoid Mary shining through.

In spite of everything, I laughed. It seemed as if I

might get through this, that I might be able to start accruing big karma, like Jane did.

"Hey, is that . . ." she pointed at the sky, leaning close to whisper in my ear. "Is that a witch?"

The silhouette of a woman flying on a broomstick flitted between lace-like clouds. She was too far away for human eyes to see, but we had sharper vision.

A chill trickled over my skin. "I guess so."

"You *really* don't know any of the witches in Hell?"

I shook my head, conscious of the note tickling the sole of my foot. I frowned. I sort of knew one, but I wasn't sure if Medea was crazy or not. That note could've meant anything.

Jane's eyes sparkled. "You should have a witch club or something. You have so much in common! Heaven knows, if anyone else had *my* karmic debt, I'd want to hang out with them. To get tips and tricks, you know?"

I shook my head. "They wouldn't want me. I'm not a real witch. I was just killed for being one because it was a convenient way to get rid of me."

I didn't tell her the other reason I was disinclined to befriend the witches, or anyone else in Hell, really. I'd always viewed Hell as a waiting place until my real life started, in Heaven. Jane was the only one I trusted. I'd met her on her first day in Hell, as a cowering, confused temp. We'd been friends ever since. I'd helped her gain her footing, and in return, her perpetual cheerfulness helped me get through the last several decades. I knew she didn't have any ulterior motives — that she'd never turn evil and kill me in my sleep. And in Hell, that was priceless.

Jane tilted her head. "But someone told me anyone who was killed for being a witch had powers."

I huffed. "You shouldn't believe everything you hear. I think I'd know if I had powers."

"So you can't fly on a broomstick?" she teased.

"Not for lack of trying."

"You really tried?"

"Sure. I tried different phases of the moon, crystals, herbs, and what not, but nothing worked."

The witch's silhouette flew between the clouds again, then disappeared from sight. Before long, we were finished with our soup and the waiter set the check down between us.

"My treat," Jane said, snatching it up.

"Thank you for taking me out. I really do feel better. I'll take you up on your offer to use your kitchen. I hope it doesn't mean you'll be behind on your cookbook."

She shrugged, her eyes crinkling with her smile. "Don't worry about that. I'm just glad to help."

I smiled back at her. It was a perfect moment — the ancient streets, the beautiful night, the comforting soup. Jane's optimism had somehow crept into my mind despite one of the worst days of my afterlife. Sneaky girl.

I closed my eyes and breathed deep, feeling my heart crack open. I'd miss her so much when she was gone.

After lunch, I returned to Hell to write up my report. McMillan was lucky I didn't see him anywhere. My blood boiled just thinking about how he'd never given me a performance review. I wanted to tear his eyes off, all five hundred of them. But I'd have to wait another day. It was five o'clock.

I cracked open the book from the coffeehouse and read the story of *Sleeping Beauty* as I walked through Death's Cross toward the apartments. The story was engrossing after all. I could definitely relate to the feeling that I was cursed and sleep-walking through life, waiting for someone to rescue me. But that wasn't the reason why I read books after five o'clock. Mostly, I tucked my nose in a book to avoid the other temps and demons squeezing into the waystations for New York, London, Tokyo, and Sao Paulo. The night shift was a scary lot. The more distance I had from them, the better.

"Hey, Belle," Beelzebub said.

I glanced up at the demon prince with eggplant-colored flesh and black eyes. He was stuffing his enormous bat wings into a leather jacket in front of a waystation with several other demons. His newest converts looked ready to brawl, with shiny new knives and armor equipped with spikes.

"Want to join us? We're gonna start a bar fight in Dubai. It'll be *epic*." His black eyes blazed with malice, and he smiled, revealing pointed teeth. The other demons surrounding him grunted in agreement despite their general human appearance.

The archdemons must've been recruiting again. Part of their training was to pillage cities and go on raids. "No thanks." I tucked my nose back into my book and tried to blend in with the crowd.

"She's such a nerd," someone whispered, just loud enough for me to hear.

"Freak!"

A wolfman thrust his hairy chest at me.

I ignored them and kept walking toward the apartments. I could've defended myself, but they outnumbered me. Besides, I didn't want to anger them. They were literally monsters. The farther I got from them, the better.

At the end of Death's Cross, I walked into a sad lobby with a water-stained, yellow-tiled floor. I was about to press an elevator button when I saw a sign taped on the stainless steel doors.

Elevator broken.
Mgmt has been notified.

Great. Just what I needed at the end of a terrible day. The elevator broke so often you'd think they'd replace it, but demons kept fixing it until it inevitably broke down again. I wondered if it was someone's perverse idea of a joke, or if it was someone's terrible karma.

I opened the beat-up metal door at the other end of the lobby and walked up ten flights of dusty, filthy stairs. My and Jane's apartment was down the hall, around the corner, and at the end. Good old 1132. My keys jangled as I unlocked it.

Once inside, I threw my satchel on the threadbare sofa. I walked past the bookcase, my fingers trailing over the weathered spines of my favorite books. They usually gave me hope when things were bleak, but I didn't feel like reading tonight. I barely even glanced up at my poster of the world, with colorful pins commemorating all my travels. I just wanted to curl up into a ball and forget today had ever happened.

I kicked off my boots and the note from Medea flew

onto my moth-eaten oriental rug. Picking up the creamy paper, I re-read it, my fingertips crushing the edges.

Don't trust him.

I huffed. Who was she to tell me what to do? I didn't know her at all, and she was *evil*. Why should I trust her? All I knew was I couldn't disobey Lucifer — I didn't trust him, but my afterlife depended on doing whatever he commanded.

I went to the tiny electric stove and turned on a burner. When it was pink with heat, I touched the paper to the hot coil and watched the note catch fire. It flared in my fingers until I dropped the charcoal shell in the sink. I ran the water, flushing it down the drain. At least there wouldn't be any evidence now.

I crawled in bed and hugged my book against my chest, overcome with a heavy feeling. I'd worked every day, saving myself for Heaven. Now, I might be alone forever. Or at least, another few decades.

Decades!

I closed my eyes for a second, then forced them open. No. I couldn't be defeatist. I could get through this. I just needed to hold onto what little hope I had, and do whatever I could to get out.

I opened Neutralizer and looked at the dossier for my next victim. He worked in a busy high-rise — probably with heavy security and video cameras. Even if I dressed like an office clone, I might not be able to get in. His workplace was out of the question. I clicked on **More Info**.

> `Carlo Dunlap met his victims through an online dating service. He lives on the Upper West Side at 756 Everton, #45. He eats lunch at Johnny's Pizzeria almost every workday at 12:30.`

Hm. His apartment was probably a highly scrutinized place too. But the pizzeria? If I met him there, I might be able to lure him to Jane's loft.

Carlo's photo revealed a man with cruel hooded eyes, a thick Italian nose, and slicked-back dark hair. He looked like a mobster who'd always gotten everything he'd ever wanted out of life, and what he didn't get, he took.

But the tables would turn tomorrow. He'd never see me coming. My targets never did. I was determined to torture him to within a millimeter of his life, over and over. He'd deserve every cut, every scream, every anguished moment for what he'd done to those three women. I'd make him feel his regret so hard, and then, I'd finally start earning my karma back.

CHAPTER FIVE

The next morning, a gray sky yawned over Glasgow's botanical gardens. I walked the sopping gravel paths, sipping a warm, milky tea. A cool mist drizzled down, making me wrap my coat tighter and hide under my hood.

I needed to start work on Carlo as soon as possible, but I had a few hours to kill before he was due at the pizzeria. Besides, traveling to different cities was one of the only perks of being a temp in Hell. It was my ritual, if I had one.

I walked down a sidewalk and onto a street that shone black with rain. Bells tolled in the distance. After navigating a few more streets, I found myself grasping the ancient bronze handle of St. Lucian's Church. The vestibule was toasty-warm — rows of red candle flames flickered, sending prayers to Heaven. Further inside, the nave rose several stories high, with ivory columns and stained glass windows. I lowered my hood and looked up at the depictions of Daniel and the lion, Jonah and the whale, and other familiar stories. Countless rows of hard-backed pews crowded the room, all facing an altar with gold and white swirls. Only a few people bent their heads in prayer. It was a work day for most people, myself included.

I slipped into a pew in the back row, quiet as a cat, and sipped my tea. The church smelled of incense, old books, and Pine Sol. I breathed it in, taking in the holy atmosphere.

I still couldn't believe Lucifer had said I was an average worker. My jaw ground just thinking about it. But I couldn't fault him. He was just trying to help me get into Heaven, like he did with other temps. The real problem was McMillan. If only he'd managed me properly, I wouldn't be in this mess. His stupidity made my throat burn with anger.

Singing started up from behind the altar — men's voices joined together in Gregorian chanting. It was so beautiful, I felt myself tearing up a little. In my heart, I knew it was better to forgive. I prayed for McMillan until my chest felt a little lighter. He'd get his due one day, but it wouldn't be by my hand.

I went through my usual prayers, starting, as always, with the prayer to deliver my soul from evil. Then I prayed for Jane, for my family in Heaven, and for the victim of yesterday's target. Finally, I prayed for strength as I faced yet another killer. I'd need extra assistance today. Killing was one thing, but torture was an other, crueler punishment. I hoped I was up for it. Lucifer was counting on me. I took a deep breath. I was counting on me, too.

A priest walked down the aisle, his timeless black robe barely making a sound. His green eyes focused on me and pinched, as if he were unsure of me. I wondered what he saw when he looked at me. For all my karmic work, I was still a killer. Was that visible in my eyes? I wanted to follow him, to corner him and tell him it was all for good — that my actions made the world a better place. We were on the same side, the priest and me.

He swept past me, wordless. I remained in my seat. I knew better than to rationalize my work to an outsider. When pipe organ music started up, I drank the last of my tea, pulled my hood up, and walked out of the church.

On the soaked streets, I passed several people with omens over their heads. Usually I'd stalk one and make a killing, but today was reserved for Carlo Dunlap. With every step, I resolved I'd take him down hard. I'd torture him and make it last as long as I could. I'd show Lucifer I was truly *la Belle Dame Sans Merci*.

I walked through the dank hallways of Death's Cross toward the Manhattan waystations, my boots leaving wet impressions on the stone. A smoke-like djinni on guard leered at me, his smile like a knife-drawer. "Any plans tonight, Belle? Or do you want to catch a dirty movie with me?"

I ignored him and pushed the greasy button to a Manhattan waystation. Hell was the worst. When the lift arrived, I stepped on, pressed the button, and closed my eyes for the entirety of the three minutes it took to get topside.

The waystation stopped with a loud *ding*, the door opening onto a luxurious hotel lobby with red and gold-patterned carpet and twinkling chandeliers. I laughed under my breath at the opulence. It'd been a while since I last used this waystation. Did the hotel know they had an elevator that went straight to Hell?

I walked onto a Manhattan city block swarming with people clad in black and shades of gray, all walking as if their destination were of the utmost importance. The air was rife with exhaust, money, and last night's vomit. Sunshine slatted through the towering skyscrapers and warmed the air, making it feel more like summer than early autumn.

I glanced at my watch. I only had a few minutes to get to the pizzeria. I quickened my pace, staring up at the skyscrapers. The city had changed so much over the centuries. I remembered when it was called New Nether-land, in the good old days of 1614, when I was a girl. It was one of my first hunting grounds when I'd first turned. Over the decades, the tall buildings had multi-plied like weeds. Every year, it seemed like another old stone building was torn down, and a huge steel and glass column was built in its place. I missed the old ones. At least they had some warmth. All that metal and glass left me feeling cold.

I turned a corner and recognized my target at the end of the street, walking toward the pizzeria. I ducked back behind the building and caught my breath. No pressure. It was just my life on the line. He didn't have an omen over his head, but that made sense — I was already as-signed to him. I took a deep breath and turned the corner, striding toward the man who'd write me my first big karma paycheck.

Carlo and I reached the pizzeria door at the same time. He shoved through first, mumbling on his phone. I caught the door just before it shut on me, and walked behind him into the steamy restaurant. It smelled of tomato sauce and oregano. I pretended to read the menu on the wall behind the ovens, side-eyeing him.

Carlo's hair looked even more slicked-back in person. Even though he wore a nice suit, he carried himself with a false bravado, like he was on top of the world, but for a reason he was ashamed of. I wondered how many people he'd thrown under the bus on his way up. At least three had paid the greatest price, and for what? For him to make a few extra bucks, or to get away with some deviant act?

My demonic features began to spike. I swallowed and made them subside.

Carlo barked an order into his phone and hung up, then shuffled forward.

"Excuse me." I smiled. "Do you know what's good here? It's my first time."

He looked at me, his brown eyes perking up. "Really? Your first time at Johnny's?"

I nodded. Even his voice sounded slimy. "Yeah, I'm from upstate. I just moved here."

"Hey, Johnny. Get the lady a slice and a soda. Same for me."

A hunched-over teenager dished two slices fresh from the oven. By the register, a plump man with gray whiskery hair rang it up. "Sixteen fifty."

I dug into my pocket and offered Carlo a crumpled-up ten-dollar bill.

Carlo swiped the cash, his sausage-sized fingers lingering on mine. He paid and then pocketed the clinking change. "How about you keep an old man company on his lunch break?"

I resisted the urge to hurl and gave him a *gosh-darn-it* smile. "Sure, why not."

We took the pizza and sodas into a small dining room half-full with old men puzzling over crossword puzzles and parents wrangling young children. Other men in suits sank their teeth into greasy slices of pepperoni while staring at their phones.

Carlo led me to a little table in the back with a red-and-white checkered cloth. I settled onto a retro vinyl cushioned chair. The smell of the garlicky tomato sauce made my mouth water.

He sat down with a satisfied smile, studying me. His brown eyes seemed warmer in real life, twinkling, even. But no matter how nice he looked, I knew what he did and what I had to do. Killers and psychopaths all went the same way when faced with my knife.

"I'm Carlo. What's your name?"

"Belle."

"Hell's Belle," he murmured, a secret smile on his face.

My fingernails dug into my knees. How did he know my nickname? Was this a trap? I glanced around. Behind the counter, the teenager tossed a disk of dough into the air while the old man sprinkled mozzarella on an unbaked pizza. Nothing seemed out of place. There were no demons waiting to take me down. None of the customers even looked in my direction.

Carlo wagged a finger in the air. "Nah, you're more like that girl in *Beauty and the Beast*."

I laughed, my heartbeat slowing down a little. "I wish." A provincial life was exactly what I imagined Heaven to be like. But I couldn't talk about myself — I needed to change the subject. "What do you do for a living?"

I bit into the stringy pizza and my eyes rolled into the back of my head. It was the best I'd ever had. No wonder Carlo ate here every day. I made a mental note to tell Jane about the place. She was always looking for good restaurants.

"I'm a banker. One of the big ones." His eyes lit up with pride. He leaned close, his bulbous nose hovering over my plate. "I don't like to brag, you know, but between you and me, I make eight figures."

"Really?"

"You bet. But I'm humble, you know? I support the little people." He lifted his palms up, as if to say he meant the pizzeria, then took a big, messy bite and chewed with his mouth open, smacking loudly.

I nodded, adding another detestable detail to my mental dossier. The concept of 'little people' had always bothered me. Carlo wasn't a bigger person just because he had more money. It was probably that kind of thinking that made him rationalize killing a few 'little people,' and not worrying about the consequences.

He took a sip of soda. "What do you do, Belle?"

I smiled. "I just graduated with a degree in business, and now I own my own bakery."

"Whoa, you're a businesswoman?"

"Yeah, but I don't have a lot of clientele just yet."

"Why not? Ain't your stuff any good?"

"It's great, but business is hard. I have a lot of competition. I'm afraid I might not make it."

"That's too bad. You should find an investor. Someone to make connections and take a little off the top."

"Um . . ." I grinned. Maybe this would be easier than I thought. "Are you interested? I can show you what I have. My bakery is just over the bridge."

He leaned back and blinked at me uncertainly. "How old are you?"

"Twenty-three."

His mouth twisted into a smile, but his eyes remained hard, uncertain. "I don't know. I got some stuff back at the office that needs my attention."

"Please? I just iced a whole batch of red velvet cupcakes back at my kitchen. Don't you want to try one?"

He looked uncertain.

My heart sank. I knew what I had to do. Be the *Belle Dame* — use my looks and pretend I was interested in

60

him. I leaned forward and cupped my face in my palm, gazing up at him with doe eyes. I hated doing it, but it got the job done more often than not. Someday, maybe I'd meet someone who thought of me as more than a pretty object, but today was not that day.

"Please?"

Carlo's gaze softened and his eyebrows rose. "Well, I guess I have a little bit of time. Where to?"

CHAPTER SIX

We took a taxi to Jane's loft. I insisted on paying, and Carlo let me, the cheapskate. I told him it was for his time, but really, it was so there wouldn't be a record of his last known location. If the authorities ever figured out he was missing and being tortured in Jane's kitchen, there'd be a messy showdown. Killing an innocent cop would turn me evil in a heartbeat.

"That's a lot farther from Manhattan than I thought." Carlo trailed behind me, his hands dug deep into his suit pockets. His head sunk a little into his suit jacket even though it wasn't cold.

"Sorry." I bit my lip. "I just moved here not too long ago. I'm still figuring out how long it takes to get places."

"Well. These cupcakes better be good. And I might take one for the road, too."

Jane's kitchen was in a slim building made of gray stone. I traipsed up concrete steps to the reinforced glass door. "You're going to love my cupcakes, I promise." I smiled back at him.

On the other side of the street stood a tall man with a pale face and dark hair. Sunglasses obscured his eyes, but he was watching us. My lips pressed together. Was this one of Lucifer's spies? I inhaled deeply, sniffing for his scent, but didn't detect the telltale sulfurous vapor on him, but the wind was blowing in the wrong direction. I tried to read his facial expression, but it was neutral.

Carlo was also fixated on the man across the street. He stared at him, unease clouding his face.

"Is he a friend of yours?" I asked.

"I thought maybe he was with you."

If that was one of Lucifer's spies, I needed to get started, and fast. I punched in the key code as fast as my fingers could manage. "He's probably waiting for the bus." The lock clanked and the door creaked open.

Carlo and I stepped onto the scratched granite floor of the lobby. Along one wall was a series of brass mailboxes overflowing with mail, and against another leaned a dying palm tree. Staircases covered in worn blue carpet led up and down. In the corners, dust bunnies stirred. I smiled. The place was barely used. It'd be perfect for the task at hand.

Carlo hesitated, his brows drawn. "This looks more like an apartment building. You really have a bakery in here?"

"Yeah, it's just up the stairs. Come on, I'll show you." I tugged at his hand, smiling.

He held his ground, his mouth a thin line as he glanced back through the window at the man across the street. "I should get back to the office." He smiled an apology and tried to pull away from me.

The smile slipped from my face as I clamped his hand in mine. He wasn't going anywhere. I had him, and his time was up.

He tried to jerk his hand away, harder this time. It didn't move. "Damn, you're pretty strong for a lady."

Three women murdered. Dumped in the Hudson River. My teeth grew fierce and my vision phased dark. Transforming, I took a step forward, fury rolling off my body like a heat wave.

"Jesus Christ!" He backed against the wall, knocking his head against the mailboxes. "What the hell are you?!"

He tried to reach the door, but I held tight. He was used to getting away with everything, including murder, but there'd be no mercy today. I latched onto his forearm and dragged him up the stairs, one by one. He squirmed, but I held tight.

"Let me go, you evil bitch!"

I laughed. If he only knew.

At the top of the stairs, I punched in the second key-code to Jane's bakery. The stainless steel door squealed open. I threw him inside. He landed against a cement wall, making a dust cloud rise up. He fell to the floor in a heap, groaning.

The walls, ceiling, and floor were made of unfinished cement. The room felt like a basement, even though it was on the second floor. Two tall, smudged windows illuminated the room with a dim, dirty light. Through the window, cars zipped by in a blur on a highway off-ramp. If what Jane had said about the thickness of the walls was right, it was an almost-perfect place for torturing.

Whiffs of roasted garlic and honey-baked ham hung in the air. I glanced at Jane's stainless steel sideboards, refrigerator, oven, and a sink stacked with clean pots and pans. Near the windows, a thin white door led to a pink-tiled bathroom. Several cookbooks were spread out over a battered wooden desk, with bookmarks and post-it notes sticking out. A rusty radiator clicked and gurgled.

Carlo staggered up from the wall. "Lady, I gotta go."

"Not gonna happen." I pulled handcuffs from my satchel and approached him. They jingled with every step.

Desperation glinted in his eyes. He bolted for the door, but I was ready for him. I shoved him back against the wall. He landed with an *oomph* and stood up again, a crazed look in his eyes.

"You gotta let me leave. Now! You can't keep me here!"

I blocked his exit, daring him to try again. "Sorry, I can't let you go."

"Get outta my way! I ain't afraid to hit you!"

I nodded, crouching. "Now we're getting to the meat of the matter."

My fingers tingled as I fought the impulse to reach for my knife. This was the part where I usually killed my victims — a slit to the throat or a stab through the ribs. Now, I was venturing into new territory. I needed to make it hurt.

He feinted left but dashed right. I was one step ahead of him, and pushed him down to the floor again.

He shook his head. "Why're you doing this?"

"I'm doing this for the three women you killed!" I growled.

"What?!" He straightened, his features scrambling in confusion. "I didn't kill no one!"

I narrowed my eyes. "Lucifer says you did."

His pupils dilated. He looked as if he might crap his pants. Then, he ran toward me, his fist swinging up in a hammer-hook. I ducked and plowed my shoulder into his soft belly. He fell against the wall with a giant *oomph*. He tried to get up, but I slapped a cuff around one of his wrists. His other fist swung up, clocking me hard in my jaw. It ached with a piercing pain, but I seized his free arm. He grunted as we wrestled against each other — I pushed harder, leaning into him, struggling to loop the handcuffs under the bulky radiator. With a final squeeze, the cuff clicked into place. I stood back, relieved and panting.

He jerked against his cuffs, his face maniacal. "You're freaking crazy! You know that?"

I snatched his phone from his breast pocket. It dangled teasingly from my fingers.

"Give it back!" He flailed toward me, but the handcuffs kept him at bay.

I laughed at the rage on his face, then dropped his phone to the floor. It clattered before I smashed it with my boot and kicked the pieces into the far corner.

"Why are you doing this to me?" He was near tears, his eyes bloodshot. A trail of snot dripped from his nose. "I didn't hurt no one."

I was used to this part — the denials, the pleading, the promises. I opened my mouth, about to tell him I'd heard it all before, when a dark figure passed near the window. I turned just in time to see the shadow of a man outside.

I cursed. There must've been a fire escape. My sense of smell hadn't alerted me to any nearby mortals.

"Help!" Carlo shouted. "She's got me chained up in here! HELP!"

My fist connected with Carlo's jaw, knocking him out against the wall. I couldn't have him yelling, even if there were thick walls.

I shook my fist out, unsheathed my knife, and rushed to the window. Maybe the guy on the fire escape would have a beacon over his head, and I could make it a two-for-one. But when I looked out the window, there wasn't a fire escape or a balcony, only a vertical drop, the highway, and more buildings in the distance. Directly below the stone exterior of the building squatted a small backyard, with patches of dirt and struggling grass.

I strained my ears, trying to hear the spy. Pigeons cooed on electric lines, and a couple argued down the block, barely audible above a car alarm and the traffic in the distance. But the interloper, wherever he was, was silent.

I ran to the second window and looked outside. Nothing. I checked that the windows were locked, then kicked the bathroom door all the way open. The hinges splintered, and a *bang* echoed off the pink tile. But no one was there with us.

My hands pressed against my eyes. I was certain I'd seen something. Stress must've gotten to me, or maybe it was a pigeon. I needed to focus. What if it was the spy who was watching us from across the street? If that was the case, I needed to do something to Carlo, and fast. I couldn't have Lucifer thinking I wasn't working quickly enough.

I stomped back through the room to Carlo, still unconscious and slumped against the wall, his hands cuffed to the radiator. My blade hovered above his thigh. I took a breath, channeling the energy I needed to begin. I thought of seeing my parents again, and brought the knife down, stabbing his leg.

He screamed awake, disoriented and shaking with fear, straining against his handcuffs.

"Stop it, please!" Tears slipped out of his eyes. "I didn't kill anyone."

"Say it again, murderer." I sliced another line on his leg. "Say you didn't kill anyone again!"

He howled in pain, doubling over into a fetal position. "You lunatic! You'll get caught. The police will hear me and–"

"About that." I pulled a rag out of my satchel and stuffed it into his mouth, then tied it around his head. His words became unintelligible. "What were you saying?"

I wiped the blade on his fine suit jacket and slipped it back into my garter sheath, turning away from him to walk to the window. I didn't see anyone there, but surely anyone reporting back to Lucifer would see I was serious. I could torture, and I might even be good at it.

As I gazed at the cityscape, a black pit curled in my stomach. Something about torturing Carlo felt barbaric, wrong. It didn't make sense — I'd killed thousands of people. But somehow, this felt more inhumane. Maybe I just wasn't used to the long kill. I glanced back at Carlo.

He trembled, his puppy dog eyes silently begging for release. Tears rolled down his cheeks and mingled with the blood pooling on the floor.

I turned back to the window and held my belly, wondering if I might get sick. Why did this feel so wrong? Why did it feel like I was hurting someone I cared about? It was his eyes — they weren't flinty or dead like the people I usually killed. They were creepy, that was for sure, but there was something kind or warm about them, as if his soul wasn't tarnished beyond repair.

I swallowed and reminded myself that I'd been assigned to do this, and that he should be in pain, especially after what he'd done to those women. He should feel every nerve in his body cry out to pay for what he'd done. Carlo deserved his punishment. I just had to be strong enough to dole it out, slice by slice. I imagined my karma accruing from my actions and felt a little relief. It would be hard work, but well worth it.

I sat against the wall, pulled out my phone, and read a text from McMillan.

Belle, we need to talk.
It's about your last
meeting with Lucifer.
I'm afraid I have some
explaining to do. Let

```
me know when you're back
in the office.
```

A wry smile grew on my face. *Some explaining to do?* So he did get reamed by Lucifer. Good. He deserved it, though nothing would make up for the fact that I'd be working for decades longer due to his incompetence.

Another text popped up, from Jane.

```
How's it going?
```

I grimaced and typed back.

```
               This is harder than
                     I thought.
```

```
Did you hurt him yet?
```

I closed my eyes, trying to block out Carlo's cries of pain.

```
                                          Yes.
```

```
I'm sure you're fine.
Just do something every
so often. Take your time.
Remember, it's a marathon,
not a sprint. :)
```

I ran my hands over my face. The cement walls felt like they were crushing me. I couldn't stand to be in the loft any more. I plugged in an old boombox in the corner and turned it on. Bon Jovi's "Livin' on a Prayer" jangled out. I almost laughed. Nothing like a little rock music to hide pleas for help. I cranked the volume, walked into the hallway, and pulled the door shut.

I stood there a few minutes, my heartbeat slowing down. Eventually, Carlo yelled through the gag, but I could barely hear him over the music. My shoulders relaxed a little. It'd probably be okay. I walked down the carpeted steps and pushed open the cold glass and metal door into the bright sunny day. Once outside, the polluted city air calmed my nerves. The familiar sounds of trucks idling and cars honking made me feel more in the moment.

My feet carried me toward the nearest waystation, and

I let them. I needed to be away from Carlo's sobs. Torture was hard — I understood why it earned more karma now. It took so much more time and effort. I frowned as I walked on the dull sidewalk. If this were one of my usual kills, I'd be back at my desk already, pounding out my report, oblivious to how little karma I'd earned. At least now I'd be earning big karma. Heaven would start to get closer. I just had to make it through these next few decades.

I stopped at a crosswalk, pulled out my phone, and re-read Carlo's dossier.

To be dissipated for killing three women

I was doing the right thing, despite the fluttering in my belly.

Back home, I found myself staring again at Carlo's dossier. In his photo, he had the cold, shark-like eyes of a killer, but in real life, his eyes were warm, if a little condescending. I zoomed in on the picture. Something about it looked wrong — the edges of his irises were a different shade of brown. I gasped. Someone had photoshopped his eyes. The longer I looked, the more obvious it was. Someone had put matte brown discs where his irises were, making them look cold and dead, more like the killers I usually went after! But who would do such a thing? None of my other targets were ever photoshopped. They looked exactly like their photos.

I lay back on my bed, my mind spinning. Maybe someone did it as a joke, or maybe there were copyright issues with using the photo, though I doubted Hell would care about infringement policies. I texted Jane.

> I think I'm losing
> my mind.

I stared at the little screen, hoping she'd answer, needing her to answer. But she worked odd shifts at the hospital. She might not get my message for hours.

I opened a book and tried to read, but my mind wouldn't let it rest. What did the photoshopped eyes mean? As the night dragged on, my eyes winked shut and I fell asleep beside my book.

I awoke in a sweat, my heart thundering. I dreamed the NYPD broke down Jane's door and rescued Carlo. I tried to catch my breath and calm down — it was just a dream, even though it had seemed so real. The flashing lights had blinded me, and the siren had pierced my ears.

It was just a dream.

Maybe so, but my gut told me something was wrong. I grabbed my jacket and ran for the door.

CHAPTER SEVEN

I ran through Death's Cross, all thoughts on Carlo. My legs jiggled nervously throughout the three-minute waystation ride to Brooklyn. What if my dream was right, and he was gone? What if he was telling the police about me right now?

When the Brooklyn lift finally stopped, I threw open the red door and ran toward Jane's kitchen. I ran past sheets of plastic flapping in the wind like specters, over sidewalks covered in gum and brown stains, past structures made of steel and stone, and by foggy bakery windows with plump men sifting powdered sugar. I passed a church with a steep oxidized copper roof and a resounding bell, marking the time. Five am. Something pulled within me to go inside, but I had to get to Carlo.

Birds chirped from stunted city trees as I turned onto Jane's street and punched in the code. I launched inside, breathless, wary of any signs of police activity in the lobby, but the palm leaned against the wall and the brass mailboxes stood patiently. I crested the top of the stairs and found Jane's door closed, locked, and intact — just as I'd left it. I breathed a sigh of relief. Carlo hadn't been discovered. My stupid paranoia was almost laughable. I tapped in the key code and turned off the stereo in the middle of a Joan Jett song.

The savory smells from yesterday had been replaced by something more fetid. Carlo half-rose from the radiator, moaning behind his gag, his handcuffs clinking as he tried to stand. When he saw me, he slumped back down to the floor, sobbing. He seemed like a shell of a man. I was barely able to meet his eyes. I'd hoped torture would get easier, that I'd get used to it just as I'd gotten used to killing, but it wasn't happening. Maybe one day I'd get there, but in the meantime, it was playing tricks on my mind.

I stumbled toward the windows and checked the locks. They were still in place. No one had been in here. My nightmares were just paranoid delusions. Outside, massive gray clouds tumbled in a tumultuous pre-dawn sky. Lightning sparked in the distance.

I rested my hand on my dagger and evaluated my work from yesterday. His cuts had scabbed over, all except for the deep stab in his leg, which still oozed crimson. I could barely look at it. I still couldn't meet his eyes.

When my phone pinged with a text from Jane, I turned away gratefully.

```
Sorry, didn't see your
text until now. Just
got off my shift. Are
you at the loft? I can
come over if you'd like.
```

```
                Yes. Please hurry.
```

I sat against the wall, watching the storm build. She'd know what to do.

Before long, I heard the door downstairs creak, and then the loft door sprung open. Jane walked in, her hair damp from rain and her cheeks flushed.

Carlo made a commotion through his gag. He groveled toward her, his eyes begging her for release.

"Hi." I stood and embraced her. She smelled like the mounting storm outside. "Thanks for coming."

"Of course. Let's see your vic." She crouched low to examine him. "So, I see a stab, a couple of slices and bruises . . . Anything else?"

Carlo moaned through the gag, trying to speak.

I racked my brain, trying to think of anything else that could qualify as torture. "He hasn't eaten since yesterday. Oh yeah. He wet himself."

"Good." She nodded sagely, then stood up. "I don't know what you're worried about. He's in pain and he's scared. You're doing great."

Carlo shriveled against the wall, his eyes wide. His breathing was ragged, and he started sobbing again.

"You just need to torture him again. Keep it fresh, you know?"

I swallowed and took Jane's arm to lead her into the bathroom. I closed the door. The pink walls gleamed in the bare-bulb's light.

"There's a problem," I said. "He doesn't seem like the other people I've killed."

"What do you mean?"

"I feel like there's something different about him. And someone photoshopped his dossier photo to make him look like a psychopath." I showed her the picture. "Jane, what if he didn't kill those women?"

Her eyes narrowed. "You think he's innocent based

on a photo and a feeling?"

I sighed. "I don't know. Maybe. The thing is — if I kill an innocent, I'd accrue so much karmic debt, I'd turn evil at the full moon and never get to Heaven. Does he look like a killer to you?"

"Belle, they all look like that near the end." She *tsked*. "Maybe his photo just uploaded weird. You can't risk disobeying Lucifer. He said he might dissipate you!"

I hung my head, my eyes not quite focusing on the floor. "I know, but I still feel weird about torturing him."

"Listen." She grasped my shoulders and looked into my eyes. "My first time torturing bad people was hard too. It goes against that tiny part of us that's still human. But this guy is a murderer. He deserves it. Neither of us came up with this system — we're just caught in the middle, taking orders from all the higher-ups for karma. The archangels must've had a reason for doing things this way. Belle, please follow Lucifer's orders. I can't risk you being dissipated." She clasped me in a hug.

I lifted my heavy arms and hugged her. My throat felt dry. "You're right." I laid my head on her shoulder, a deep breath escaping my lips. "I'm just tired, that's all."

"Don't worry. This'll all be over soon. And then you'll be a professional."

I drew back, staring at her warm face. How did she always see so much potential in me? "How do you get through the hard times of torturing?"

"I think about Heaven when I do it. It's the only thing I've ever really wanted. Well, besides having a family, when I was human."

I nodded. I could do that.

Footsteps fell outside the bathroom door.

I froze. "Someone's here!" I unsheathed my knife and slammed the door open, my eyes darting around the room.

Carlo remained in a ball on the floor, but his eyes were lively, looking around. I crept past the steel side-boards, knife gripped in my fist.

"Belle, there's no one here."

"*Shh!*"

My eyes darted left, then right. He had to be behind the fridge. It was the only place out of my sightline. Knife raised, I whipped around it, but only saw dust bunnies stirring. There was no one else in the loft. My shoulders sank. Had it been my imagination? My knife slid back into its sheath with a soft metallic *clink*. I felt ridiculous. I could barely torture, and I'd just hallucinat-ed an intruder. I should've been stronger, better at my job. What was wrong with me?

Jane approached, her head tilted to one side. "I have to go — I'm feeling a bit woozy. Too long away from Hell, I think. Do you want me to come back later tonight?"

I nodded.

"I wish I could help you more."

"It's okay. I'll figure it out."

We embraced, then she wandered out.

Carlo lie slack against the wall, his head hung. An unpleasant odor permeated the room. I put my hand over my nose. If that wasn't torture, I didn't know what was. But I knew I had to make it worse. I took out my knife again.

His wet brown eyes bore into mine again. They seemed to ask 'why?'

My stomach turned, but I let my knife fall through the arm of his suit jacket, slashing his skin.

He gasped. Blood rose to the surface of his sleeve. He tucked himself into a ball, as if he could hide from me. When he blinked, his puppy-dog eyes flashed at me through his wet lashes.

I hesitated, my heart in my throat. *Those eyes!* But I had my orders. I raised the blade high, determined to earn my karma back.

"Stop!" a man's voice called out.

I startled back. My eyes darted toward Carlo's gag, then to the windows. One of them was open a crack. I searched the room, but I didn't see anyone. "Who's there?"

Something knocked into me. I fell, my shoulder slamming against the cement floor. My knife clattered away toward the bathroom.

Carlo half-stood above me, hunched like a beast as he

strained against his handcuffs. A wild gleam raged in his eyes. His foot kicked out toward me and struck my shin.

I backed away from him, rubbing my leg. *That would leave a mark.* I'd thought he was weak with pain and hunger. It looked like he'd been saving his energy for a moment like this. And to think, I'd been letting him off easy! I was a sucker for his stupid eyes. Now they looked animalistic, fierce, determined to take me down. *There* was the killer I needed to see. *There* was the man who'd murdered three women. How could I have been so blind?

A fury overtook me. My anger boiled until it over-flowed into a raging bloodlust. I picked up my knife and started toward him. My eyes phased black and my teeth shot out like razors. My fingernails grew sharper, claw-like, and tufts of hair rose from the backs of my hands. I stopped for a fraction of a second, glancing at them in confusion. That'd never happened before. But I had no time to ask questions. Carlo had to be put down.

I slashed at his neck, aiming to make a small cut. Before I could, he caught my hand between his elbows and twisted his body. My arm was pinned. My nerves flashed with pain and the knife fell from my hand. I cried out, trying to wrench my hand away, but it was held tight. My newfound claws slashed his cheek and I bit his throat, tasting the warm metallic tang of blood.

He screamed, releasing me, but one of his broad

shoulders caught me in the face, knocking me backwards.

My inner fury raged. *How dare he?* I wanted to destroy him. It was all I could do to not tear off his arm right then and there. I shoved it hard, and relished the sound of his shoulder bones popping. He howled and fell to the floor, whimpering.

I pressed my lips together. He wouldn't be trying any surprise attacks again anytime soon. I picked up my knife and looked around the loft. If someone really was here, I had to brace myself. I doubted I'd survive an attack from a demon, but at least I'd go down with a fight.

"Who's there?" I shouted.

Silence pervaded the room except for the din of traffic noise and the rumble of the approaching storm.

"Answer me!"

A tall figure stepped out from behind the fridge, his fingers spread in the air. "Please don't hurt him any more."

What kind of demon would say that? Was this a trick? I strained to see him in the shadows, but all I could see was his silhouette. I tensed, listening for an attack from behind, all my nerves wired.

"Come out from that corner," I said.

The man walked toward me. High cheekbones rose from a pale, moony face splattered with freckles. His deep-set Mediterranean-blue eyes contrasted with his

84

black, shoulder-length hair. He wore a gray button-up flannel shirt and white cotton pants, which made him look like he ran a winery in Napa Valley. I frowned — there was no beacon over his head. That meant he was a do-gooder, and I couldn't kill him. But there was something strange about him. I felt as if I'd seen him before. Then it hit me — he was the man watching me and Carlo from across the street, the man in the sunglasses.

"Stop where you are," I growled. "Who are you?"

"I mean you no harm." He ventured another step closer.

"Don't move!" My fingers tightened around the handle of my blade.

Carlo shouted from the floor, his voice muffled behind his gag.

"Shut up, Carlo, or I'll kill you right now!"

The stranger's mouth turned down in a grimace. "Please don't kill him."

"You shut up too!" I surreptitiously inhaled, trying to pick up his scent. But he smelled like nothing; or rather, only dust, or snow.

He looked at me with those intense eyes. "You won't be able to smell me. I don't have a scent."

I took a few steps back. "What? What are you?"

"I want to help you." He offered a shaky smile.

"Yeah, right." I huffed. "Are you an archdemon?"

Fear flickered behind his eyes. He shook his head.

"I'll tell you who I am, but will you please release that man? His name is Carlo Dunlap, son of Adam and Grace Dunlap."

"I know who he is," I snapped. "Why do you care?"

He ducked his head. "He made some bad decisions, but he's still a good person."

I shook my head. "No, he's not. He killed three people."

"He didn't kill them, and he doesn't deserve this. Please let him go."

My fingernails itched to attack the intruder. It was all I could do to not claw his eyes out. I growled. "Why should I believe anything you say?"

"Because." His sad eyes bore into mine. "I was once like you."

I scowled, a bitter laugh escaping my mouth. "You don't know anything about me."

"I do." He swallowed, glancing at the floor. "I used to be a temp in Hell, too."

I blinked. *Used to?*

CHAPTER EIGHT

I felt as if someone dumped a bucket of ice water onto my head. "Are you an . . ."

He nodded. "I'm an angel. I do the same kind of work as you. Just on good side."

I stared at him. Could he really be an angel, or was this a trick? I tried to remember everything I'd heard about angels. All I could recall was they didn't have a scent, they had wings, and Lucifer couldn't hear their thoughts — they were outside his realm. And while he didn't seem to have a scent, that didn't prove anything. Where were his wings?

Thunder shook the room, making the lights flicker. Carlo cowered against the radiator.

The man took a tentative step toward me. "I'm not going to hurt you, I promise. I just want to talk."

"Stop walking. How do I know this isn't a trick? I'm under orders to torture and kill this man."

He shook his head. "If you do anything else to him, you'll become evil."

I searched his face. "Why should I believe you?"

"I ran your calculations myself."

I raised my knife again. "Now I know you're lying. Only Lucifer can do that."

"I can do it, and I did." His dark brows pulled down over his grave eyes. "Lucifer and God were the only ones who could calculate karma for a long time. But we don't trust Lucifer. Some people think he has an alternate agenda. It took us a few decades, but we figured out how to calculate karma."

"Why didn't you just ask God for help with the calculations?"

"It doesn't work that way." He shrugged.

I drew back. How did it work, then?

"Anyway," he continued, "we made an app, and we're going to distribute it to all of the temps and demons, so you all know where you stand."

I recoiled. If everyone in Hell knew their karma, that could mean trouble. There could be riots.

"When I checked your score a couple of days ago, you were almost eligible to go to Heaven. Then you started torturing Carlo."

My eyes widened, but I fought to hide it. He had to be wrong — surely my karma was getting *better*, not worse. "That can't be true. This man is a murderer."

"It's true," he said, "and I can prove it."

I bit my lips, weighing the earnesty in his eyes. "Prove to me that you're an angel, and I might believe you."

He cast his eyes to the ground, his posture stooped. I waited a few seconds, but nothing happened. I smirked. He was a phony. This was just a stupid joke from Nosferatu or some other demon, trying to twist the knife with what was already a hard job for me. I raised my hands. "No proof, huh?"

A loud *rip* of tearing cloth came from behind him. Pristine white-feathered wings whooshed out from behind his back, stretching out almost all the way to the walls. He thrust them with enormous beats until his feet lifted off the ground.

I shielded my eyes and backed against the wall, my mouth open. Each beat of his wings felt like a hurricane wind against my face. My demon features retracted in fear and humility. A real angel! I'd prayed for centuries for salvation, and finally, it was right before me. I peeked from behind my hand at his snow-white wings, marveling at their beauty and strength.

He smiled a little, as if he enjoyed the show. His feet hit the ground with a thud and his wings folded back behind him. "Thank you for transitioning back. It's easier to look at you like this. I take it you believe me now, Belle?"

I gasped. "You know my name, too?"

"Yes, I know your name because I'm assigned to stop you. I also know your birth name, Babelin."

I crumbled, crouching against the wall, breathing through a sea of sickness overcoming me. I hadn't heard my name spoken aloud since my execution. It nearly incapacitated me. But I shoved my emotions down. I had to know more.

"Now that you believe me," he said, sliding a smartphone across the floor toward me with a skittering noise. "Type in your name."

I picked up the phone with trembling hands. Black text appeared on a cream-colored screen.

```
Demon
Angel
Human
```

"We put all the temps under demons." Donovan shrugged apologetically. "Sorry."

"It's okay."

I selected Demon. Another page loaded with a blinking cursor. I typed in my name and hit enter.

```
Belle Dame, 99.6% bad. 0.4% good
```

I stared at it, my chest tightening, my hands shaking. "That's not possible."

"I'm sorry, but it's true. I can take some of it away right now, if you allow me to. May I touch your hand?"

I bit my lip. All this time, I'd dreamed of seeing a real angel, and now one was before me, offering me salvation. I held my hand out toward him, breathless. As I approached him, something buzzed between us, like bees crawling all over me. I backed away. "What's that feeling?"

"Dissonance. I'm good, you're bad. Are you okay?"

I nodded and approached him again. When my fingers touched his, a strong vibration jolted through me, from my scalp to the tips of my toes. He clasped my fingers into his large hands while my entire body trembled. I tried to resist falling to the floor, and was only stabilized by his hands wrapped around mine.

The angels' flesh sizzled, his face contorting in pain. He appeared to suppress a scream. Aquamarine light flashed between our hands, throwing him back several feet onto the floor.

I ran toward him. "Are you okay?"

He glanced at his blackened, burned hands, and smiled. "I will be. Stupid safeguard. It only lets me take so much at a time." The skin beneath his eyes looked darker than before. "Check your score now."

I typed in my name again.

```
Belle Dame: 99.3% bad, 0.7% good
```

"That's it?" I asked. "Just a few tenths of a percentage?"

"Sorry. That's all I can handle at the moment." He cringed as he rose.

"No, it's . . . I really appreciate it. It just looked like you took so much, and—"

I couldn't speak. The weight of my nearly evil soul clogged my throat. Everything I had done was to go to Heaven, and it was all for nothing. I swallowed a lump. If McMillan had helped me, like he was supposed to, none of this would've happened. Instead he was complicit. He'd just sat back and let it happen. He was the reason Lucifer looked into me in the first place. My fingers itched, imagining slicing his tiny body into fillets and feeding them to the pigeons outside.

"Belle," the angel winced. "I'm troubled by your thoughts right now."

I glanced at him. *He could read thoughts too?* That might've been nice to know. "If you can read my thoughts, you know someone else is responsible for the situation I'm in."

He cast weary eyes to me. "Please be careful. You can't do anything hurtful from now on. One step into the darkness isn't just one step. It's more like *fifty-thousand* steps. Once you venture toward evil, it's hard to find your way out. The darkness surrounds you. You don't know where you stop and where the darkness begins. And the darkness begets more darkness."

I narrowed my eyes at him. "How do you know so much about this?"

"I just do."

I looked back at my score. It crushed me to think I was so close to being evil. I wanted to deny it, but deep down, I had to admit I'd felt something sinister stirring inside me lately. That would explain my fingernails transforming into claws too.

"So, all this is because of what I did to Carlo?"

Carlo murmured through his gag.

The angel looked infinitely sad. "Yes."

I stood and brushed the dust from my skirt. "I can't be faulted for this. Neutralizer told me he was evil—"

"He's not. Look him up on Cloud."

I sighed and leaned against the wall. "I don't need to look him up. I believe you. Some part of me knew he wasn't." I hung my head. My gut had been right about him. He was innocent. And he'd only attacked me in an attempt to save his life, not because he was a monster —

he'd attacked me because *I* was the monster. But even though my intuition had told me to be merciful, I'd tortured him anyway. A few more cuts, and I dreaded to think what I would've become. "I didn't mean to torture an innocent. I was just following orders. Doesn't that count for anything?"

The angel shook his head. "I'm sorry, but it doesn't work that way."

"Why not?!" My voice echoed off the walls. "That's not fair!"

His hands splayed in front of him. "It's a rule to protect Heaven from temps who might be under evil influences."

I swallowed. I wanted to throw the phone across the room, but I clenched it tight. "So what now? Can you help me?"

"Yes, I can, but now's not the time." His eyes darted back to Carlo. "I must get him to a hospital. Can I remove his gag?"

I nodded, the pit in my stomach swelling until I felt sick again. Poor Carlo.

The angel crouched, speaking softly to him. "I'm going to remove your gag, but you can't make a noise. As long as you obey my commands, I'll help you. Is that clear?"

Carlo nodded wildly, tears coursing down his face.

"I'm sorry, Carlo." My voice squeaked.

The angel untied the knots. The gag fell from Carlo's mouth. He worked his jaw a little and glared at me.

"I know, Carlo." The angel placed a finger over his lips. "But not one word. I'll deal with her later." He extended his palm out toward me. "The handcuff key, please."

I bit my lip. "Only if you promise to take me to Heaven." My throat was thick with hope.

He sighed. "I can protect you, but I must take Carlo to a hospital first. Give me the key."

I took a deep breath. "Do you promise?"

"Yes! Give me the key."

Thunder crackled, and rain slashed against the windows. The lights dimmed for a second. I looked into the angel's eyes and at his outreached arm, and my resolve melted. I believed him. He would take me to Heaven. A weight fell from my shoulders. I'd never have to go to Hell again. Centuries of killing and torturing would fall off my karmic debt. I'd be free again.

I bent over and opened a leather pocket on my boot, then pulled out the silver handcuff key. I extended my palm to give it to him.

When his fingers brushed the key, another vibration startled me. I pulled away, frightened, the key clenched in my hand.

"It's okay." He stepped closer, then drew out the key from my hand, his fingertips tickling my palm with vibrations.

Carlo's lower lip trembled as the handcuffs fell away. The angel lifted Carlo like he was a baby.

"Wait." I held out a hand. "What's your name?"

"Donovan."

I squinted at him. "Did we meet before? When you were a demon?"

"No. I was killed in the Welsh Revolt, in 1412 and left Hell before you arrived. But I've heard of you, of course. Did you know the poet John Keats? Or did he just hear about you?"

"It was a long time ago." I turned to the wall and took a moment before regaining my composure.

"I'll be back soon. Stay here." He swept toward the door and left.

I watched them hunker down the hallway and stairs, then out the door. My heart expanded with relief. One more cut and I could've turned evil. I'd been so close. But if Carlo was an innocent, why did Lucifer assign him to me? He must've known I'd turn evil. Was this another case of mismanagement in Hell? Or was it something else?

None of it mattered now. I'd finally be going to Heaven. I could almost dance with joy. I'd miss Jane, but she'd be coming to Heaven soon enough. I laughed out loud, my voice echoing against the walls.

My phone pinged. I looked at it and saw a message

from the Devil's Office.

*Karma calculators are not
demon-supported software.
They contain misinformation
and inconsistencies. If you
have any of them on your
device, delete them
immediately. Violators will
be dissipated.*

I drew in a sharp breath. Donovan was right about
the software — it had begun. Of course, the Devil's Office would say the app has misinformation, but there had
to be some truth in it. They wouldn't threaten dissipation otherwise.

That reminded me — Jane would be back soon. She'd
have questions about what happened to Carlo. I debated
telling her about Donovan, but the less she knew, the
better. I had to keep her safe. I hoped lying didn't count
against my karma.

Thanks for your help
earlier. I'm going

home for the night.

My phone pinged with her response almost instantly.

Okay. See you later.

I breathed a sigh of relief. It'd all be over soon enough.

My phone chimed again. I looked at it, anticipating another message from Jane. Instead, it was a text from McMillan.

Get to my office. Now.

CHAPTER NINE

Chills raced up my spine. McMillan never took that tone with me. Maybe he knew I freed Carlo to an angel. Or maybe he knew Carlo wasn't actually evil. I couldn't tell if he was on Lucifer's side or if he might be trying to protect me. For all I knew, it could be a trap. One thing was certain — I couldn't reveal anything about my situation. If McMillan suspected me of releasing Carlo, I could be dissipated, but as long as he didn't suspect anything, I might be able to escape with Donovan to Heaven. I just needed more time.

My fingers trembled as I typed a reply.

```
                        Hi. I'm tied up at
                        the moment. Can we
                           talk tomorrow?
```

He responded immediately.

```
No. NOW.
```

I swallowed. If only there was some way to know whose side he was on. Something silvery-gray glinted from the corner of the room. I went toward it and picked up Donovan's phone. I bit my lip, hesitating. I supposed he wouldn't mind if I used it.

```
            Demon
            Angel
            Human
```

I selected Demon and typed in McMillan. A long list of McMillans appeared, ranging from 1,574% bad to only 6% bad. I scrolled through it, cursing. Why had I never asked McMillan what his first name was? There were no pictures either, which made sense, because demon images couldn't be captured. But that meant I had no idea if he was on my side or not.

My phone chimed with another text from him.

Where are you?

I grimaced. With any luck, I'd never have to see him again.

I'm on my way in.

I silenced my phone and typed in more names to distract myself until Donovan returned. Lucifer was 421,332% bad — far into the evil realm. Jane was less than 5% bad. I sighed. She was so close to Heaven! Donovan had said I was almost eligible for Heaven before yesterday morning, too. My karma score was probably about the same before it was ruined by Lucifer.

My eyes phased and a hard pit formed in my stomach. The darkness in my soul stirred again, like a sickly creature rolling around inside my body. I didn't like this feeling. I pressed my eyes shut and tried to take a clearing breath, but the worst-case scenario played over and over in my mind. What if Cloud was wrong and I was actually over 100% bad? What if I turned evil at the next full moon and became a monster, forgetting everything about who I was?

I shook my head. Donovan said he would help. Maybe he could take away more of my bad karma. I took a couple of deep breaths, and after a few moment, my eyes changed back.

I backed out of the demon tab and selected `Angel`. Of course, Donovan was 100% good. I typed in my parents' names and felt my soul lighten at their 99% good scores, but my elation was temporary — they were as good as I was bad.

I almost didn't want to look up Carlo, but curiosity got the better of me. I had to know who I'd tortured. I scrolled through numerous Carlo Dunlaps until I found his picture.

`Carlo Dunlap: 25.1% bad, 74.9% good`

I gasped. Not evil — definitely not a murderer! Why had Lucifer lied about him? What could he gain by turning me evil? I stared out the window at the street, watching for Donovan. I hoped he'd have answers, and soon.

After the storm rolled through and I received several more frustrated texts from McMillan, someone buzzed into the kitchen. I ran down the stairs. Donovan stood rigid on the porch, watching the cars on the street. His hair dripped with rain. Something about his body language made him look on edge, as if he had bad news.

"Are you alone?" I shouted through the door.

He turned and looked at me through the glass. His lips twitched up into a smile. "Yes."

The low vibration thrummed in my body again. I shifted. "Unarmed?"

"Yes," his eyes strained, "though you probably can't say the same."

I opened the door and let him in. His gray shirtsleeves had been rolled up, revealing muscles and crimson splotches from where he'd carried Carlo.

"I didn't know if you'd come back," I said, closing the door behind him and locking it.

He stared at me. "I told you. You can trust me."

"I know, it's just . . . what you said was so strange. I wasn't sure if you were just saying those things so you could rescue Carlo. Then I used your phone to look it all up, and I saw it's true."

We walked up the stairs and into the kitchen. I shut the door, my eyes avoiding the red stain on the floor by the radiator. Carlo's screams still rang in my ears. I pressed my thumb into my temple and rubbed. "Please tell me he's okay."

He nodded. "He will be. He's at the hospital getting stitches and being treated for dehydration. I gave him a near death experience. He won't remember anything that happened. But, Belle, now that he's taken care of, I can speak frankly." He grimaced. "We think you're being prepped for a role in Hell, and we can't allow that to happen."

My stomach churned. "A role? Like what?"

His frown told me I might not want to know. "All we know is Lucifer is trying to turn you evil. Maybe he thinks you'd make an excellent guard."

"A guard?" I shook my head. "If that's the case, he has a crappy recruiting method."

"Has he mentioned anything about that to you?"

"No." I sighed, gazing at the floor.

He moved closer. "What's wrong?"

I frowned. "My manager won't leave me alone. I think he knows I'm on the run."

"Don't worry. I'll help you."

I looked up into his calm eyes. They seemed to tell me he understood my darkest fears. Perhaps he was once afraid of them too. I felt myself smile a little. "I'm exhausted. Can we just go to Heaven now?"

His expression drooped. "Not exactly."

"What?" I drew away from him, a sour taste on my tongue. "Why not? You promised—"

He walked toward me, his hands animated. "I'm sorry, but it doesn't work that way. We can't risk having someone with your score there. You'll have to work on bettering your karma first. And—"

"Don't you understand? Lucifer is going to *dissipate* me for helping you." I shook my head, unwilling to believe what I was hearing. "Please, just take me to Heaven. I'll be good, I promise."

"That's what the halfway house is for — to prove it to us."

"But Lucifer can read thoughts. He'll find me!"

"He won't. He can't hear prayers or anything that happens there. Only angels can. Don't worry — we have a plan for you. After a few years or decades, or however long it takes, there'll come a time when you're good enough. And then, I'll take you to Heaven, I promise."

A few years or decades? My eyes threatened to phase again, but I controlled myself, my jaw set. "I thought we made a deal for you to take me there *today*."

"I'm sorry, but this is the way it has to be."

I huffed, throwing my hands up. "What would I even do in a halfway house? Knit mittens for the poor?"

"I can't say what tasks you'll be given, but they'll be good deeds designed to lower your karma. And you'll pray every day — that helps your karma too. You'll just have to be careful not to harm anything until your score is a more reasonable level. You can't even kill an insect."

"Not even an ant?"

"Don't even think about it. You're too close. Even harming a demon could turn you evil."

"What if it was in self-defense?"

"I'm afraid that still counts."

My mouth fell open.

"Look, I don't make the rules about karma. I just know how it works."

I gazed at the ceiling, my gut contracting against my spine. Killing was what I did, what I was good at. I'd have to re-learn how to live my afterlife all over again. Worst of all, I felt like I was trading one life sentence for another.

But he was right. It was a better deal, and I'd finally be free from Hell — away from the stink, the mismanagement, the lying Beast, and everything else I loathed.

I considered him. "What about breathing the vapors?"

He smiled sadly. "You won't need them if you're under our protection."

Under our protection. Something about the way he said it made me feel calmer. I finally realized what he was offering — the angels would protect me from Lucifer. I wouldn't have to live in fear anymore. A whole new world would open up, one in which I could be good and do good work. I wouldn't have to kill anymore. I could retire my knife unless someone needed me to chop vegetables for a soup kitchen.

"Okay." I let out a big breath. "I can work with that. Let's go."

BANG!

I jumped. Someone pounded on the kitchen door so hard the room shook. Donovan and I locked eyes.

"Belle!" A mischievous voice shouted from the other side of the door. "Come out, or we'll break the door down!"

Donovan backed away, his eyes wide. "Demons. Four of them!"

I gasped. "How'd they get through the other door?"

"Come on, let's go." He caught my arm.

His touch buzzed my skin, making my knees almost buckle. My whole body tingled and I couldn't move. He caught me in his arms and dragged me toward the window.

CRACK!

A spiked club splintered through the door. Another *crack* resounded, and a hole appeared. A thick green arm reached in, feeling around for a doorknob.

Donovan pried open the nearest window, climbed onto the sill, and leapt into the air. A microsecond later, he rose back up in front of the window, reaching out for me, his broad ivory wings thrashing. "Come on!"

I reached for him just as the loft door slammed open.

Footsteps struck the floor, closing the gap. When my hands touched Donovan's, another surge pulsed up my spine. I almost fell, except he held onto me. He pulled me up and flew higher, lifting me until my feet nearly cleared the window.

Except, someone yanked my boots back toward the loft. I slipped a few centimeters from Donovan's arms. I grasped his forearms tighter, but several hands clamped onto my legs and pulled me down.

He strained to keep me in his arms. "Hold on!" His wings beat harder, faster, but the demons pulled back. I tried to resist looking down. The ground below looked dangerously far away.

My legs stung as the demons dug their claws into my flesh and pulled. I wanted to scream — it felt like they were tearing me apart. I started to slip.

"No!" Donovan cried.

But my fingers slid from his. I fell, feeling the hard smack of the windowsill on my belly, knocking the air out of me. Large hands pulled me inside the kitchen and threw me onto the hard cement floor. My back ached, but I sprung up and ran toward the window.

Two ogres stepped between me and Donovan, their massive green flesh blocking my way. Each of them held a deadly weapon. An orc approached me from the other side. I sunk into a fighting crouch and growled at the three of them, ready to take them out.

"Don't fight them!" Donovan shouted from outside. "You could turn evil!"

Another orc leaned out the window, swatting his gargantuan mitts at Donovan. "Come here. Angels taste like chicken."

Donovan shrank back. His apologetic blue eyes met mine for a second before he zipped away, flying across the sky. Then he was nothing more than a tiny shadow, lost amongst the roiling gray clouds.

I stared at the colorless sky, a sudden coldness hitting me at my core. Where was he going? He'd left me with some of the strongest demons in Hell. He'd said I was important and *he'd left me*.

Someone took a handful of my hair and yanked, jerking my head back. I growled at my assailant, but my rage died in my throat as I gazed at the cold, black eyes of Mephistopheles — Lucifer's errand boy.

CHAPTER TEN

Mephistopheles tightened his grip on my hair. "The Prince of Darkness demands your audience, Belle."

I shrank away from him, my heartbeat thrashing in my ears. I'd seen him march demons to Lucifer's office — I recognized his leather jacket and black hair, slicked into a greaser style. The demons he handled were never heard from again. I'd always thought they'd deserved it, but now, it looked like I was next. Lucifer must've heard my thoughts about the angel. Why didn't I leave with Donovan to take Carlo to the hospital? A feeling of dread surrounded me, numbing me to my bones. All my hopes of a better life were extinguished, snuffed out like a moth too close to a flame. I knew I couldn't fight the demon guards, but I wasn't going down without an argument. Donovan might bring back reinforcements — he might still save me.

"Did I do something wrong?" I asked.

He shrugged, sneering. "I'm pretty sure conversing with an angel isn't in your job description." He pointed at the orcs. "You two. Restrain her."

They clenched my arms, their claws digging into my flesh. Heavy mouth-breathing resounded in my ears, and the smell made me gag. Or maybe it was their body odor.

I pulled away from them, my eyes darting to the window. "Let me go! What right do you have to treat me like this?"

An ogre near the window observed me dully, his massive gray hand resting on the handle of his club. "Looks like we got a screamer, boss," he said, his baritone voice filling the room. "She could be trouble outside."

"No matter." Mephistopheles reached into his leather jacket and produced what looked like a piece of red chalk. He approached one of the cement walls and drew a horizontal line up as high as he could reach, then vertical lines leading down to the floor. Finally, he drew a line where the floor met the wall, making a door-sized rectangle. He stepped back just as the lines burst into crimson flames. The room lit up with a bright red glow, so glaring it hurt my eyes to look at it. My cheeks burned from the heat.

After a few seconds, the light and warmth subsided. The last of the flames leapt feebly around the edges. Black smoke smoldered from the rectangle. Then, molten lava oozed out, sizzling. It all caved in and fell backwards, revealing a dark pit leading down. A little metal platform stood level with the floor.

Ding!

I stared at it, my mouth gaping. I'd only ever heard about means-stations — I never knew they were real.

One of the orcs sniffed my hair. "What does he want with her, anyway? Don't seem so important."

"Who cares?" Mephistopheles glowered at his crew. "If Lucifer wants this spawn, we bring her in."

I tried to squirm out of their grasp. "Let me go! I'll give you anything if you say you never saw me or the angel here. I can pay you." I bit my lip. It was a lie, but I had to try it.

"Sorry, no can do." Mephistopheles motioned to the guards. "What are you waiting for? Stop standing around and shove her in. That thing doesn't last long."

The orcs picked me up. I craned my neck, watching the window for Donovan, but they loaded me onto the lift and set me down between them. It wobbled precariously as Mephistopheles and the last ogre squeezed in. I looked for something to hold onto, but it didn't have a metal frame — just the platform.

Mephistopheles' crabbed fingers pushed the red button mounted on the floor, and we began to sink. The windows vanished from sight, along with all the promise they held.

The familiar pull rose within me as we travelled through the earth. I glanced at my captors, swaying as we plummeted down further and further. Donovan had told me to not hurt them, but maybe I could reach the button — that might reverse the elevator. Maybe Donovan would even be back at the loft with a pack of angels to rescue me. My toes twitched. If I could just slip my leg between the ogres. . . I edged my foot forward.

Mephistopheles turned around from the front of the elevator, his eyes watchful. He sneered and stepped between me and the button, as if he could read my mind.

My mouth went dry with fear. This couldn't be happening. There was no escaping Hell now. Donovan wouldn't be able to help either — we were in Hell's territory. I turned my gaze to the floor grate.

Instead of the usual trepidation I felt upon returning to Hell, an even greater dread grasped my soul. If Lucifer knew I released Carlo, he'd dissipate me. No questions asked. I closed my eyes and said a prayer.

We landed with a thud. The orcs grabbed my elbows and wrenched me out, walking me down a dark hallway.

"Hold her tight," Mephistopheles said. "Can't have her trying to escape."

The orcs glommed onto me even more, their rough hands burning my skin. But I walked down the dusty hall with my head held high, determined to retain what little dignity I still had.

At first, I didn't know where we were, but then the flagstones and red brick arches of Death's Cross started to look familiar. We were on the far side of the waysta-tion bank, at the very end. After a minute, we reached the more well-traversed waystations. Several demons and temps passed us, casting curious glances as they used the waystations or walked toward the office. The djinni on guard gazed at me with questioning eyes, but I couldn't look at him.

We reached the end of Death's Cross and walked under the huge gothic archway and into the cubicle maze. I'd hoped we might be able to slip through with-out making a scene, then Mephistopheles shoved me forward. I fell onto the floor, the contents of my satchel rattling loudly.

"Come on, princess! We don't have all day." Mephistopheles sneered.

Several heads poked up from their workstations and eyed us. Nosferatu, the little vampire, clutched the edge of his cubicle and stared boldly, a livid smile on his face. A centaur crossed her arms and smirked as a golem whispered something to her, his eyes wide with delight.

I got up and walked, mindful of more and more demons looking our way, their heads popping over cubi-cle walls like jack-in-the-boxes. I recognized the look in their eyes — that'd been me once. I recalled the thin voice of a mothman who'd whined, *'I'm innocent! I didn't do anything!'* He'd twisted against the guards so hard that Mephistopheles decked him out cold and made the guards drag him to Lucifer's office. I'd glanced at the mothman and returned to writing up my report, certain he'd done something terrible to deserve his treatment and subsequent vanishing.

But now that it was me being marched through the office, it was different. I wanted to say something about how I didn't deserve this, but I knew it'd come off as false. I hung my head, my heart thudding painfully with every step. Every twist and turn marked the arrival of new demons gaping at me.

After what felt like an eternity, we arrived beneath the glowing star on the eastern wall. The guards on duty opened the scarlet doors, and we walked inside. The all-white room seemed ominous now. Between the marble tiles on the floor, the mortar was stained pink, as if someone hadn't cleaned up a pool of blood well enough. I hadn't noticed that before.

"You can let her go." Mephistopheles watched me, his face almost apologetic. "There's nowhere for her to run now."

The guards released me. Blood dripped down my arms, the puncture wounds from the orcs' claws burning with infection.

I managed to trudge down the stairs with them. In the

antechamber, the secretary who'd helped me before turned her back to us, pretending to be busy at the copiers, her shoulders hunched almost to her ears. One of the men stared at the papers on his desk, his head sunk low. The other two secretaries barely looked at us. I wondered if Lucifer had been on a yelling rampage again. Or maybe they knew what was going to happen to me, and it wasn't good.

"Hey, Poindexter!" Mephistopheles shouted.

One of the male secretaries put down his papers and faced Mephistopheles, trembling.

"Tell the boss we have Belle Dame."

"Yes, sir." His voice quavered. "Just a moment."

He lifted a red phone and murmured into it, then set it down. "You can bring her in." His frightened eyes met mine for a moment. He seemed to be worried for me. I wondered if he remembered me from a couple of days ago.

"Move," the bigger orc said to me.

I walked toward the big black door at the end of the room. Mephistopheles opened it with one huge push.

Lucifer looked up from a computer screen and removed a pair of reading glasses from his gleaming black eyes. He stood up slowly and walked around his ebony desk to stare at me. His face was pale and neutral — there was no sign of his demonic angry self. But my heart still hammered. Did he know I'd released Carlo? About my plotting with an angel? My only hope in hiding this lay in the fact that Lucifer couldn't hear prayers.

Please Donovan, give me strength. Let me survive this.

Lucifer's eyes constricted as he looked at me. "You may release her." His voice was a growl, powerful enough to shake my bones even though it was little more than a whisper.

The guards backed away, side-eyeing each other as Lucifer circled me. I swallowed, trying to keep from running. It wouldn't do me any good. Mephistopheles was right. I was trapped.

"What have you been up to, little one?" Lucifer asked.

"I— I was torturing the banker, just like you ordered."

"And how has *that* been going?" He enunciated every word as he paced the room.

My mind raced. "Torturing is harder than I thought." I tried a smile, but it fell from my face. "Quick deaths are much easier. But I'm learning a lot."

Lucifer bent low, so close that I could see every pore on his reddening cheeks. With strong fingers, he lifted my chin so his black eyes stared into mine. I prayed to Donovan to cover my thoughts.

"You have nothing else to say to me?!"

I shrugged in what I hoped was an innocent gesture.

He wheeled around the room. "How about," he roared, "you tell me how the banker escaped?!"

I shrank back. My mind reeled with how to spin the

truth. "It's true. . . My target got away. But he attacked me. I think fear for his life gave him strength. And I'm not used to torturing—"

Lucifer clicked his fingers in a loud *snap* that echoed off the white walls.

Two lizardmen came forward, dragging a man hanging limply between them. My heart stopped as I recognized Carlo — his brown eyes were red and swollen, as if he'd been sobbing for a long time. His white hospital gown didn't hide the black stitches on his legs and arms where I'd cut him. When he saw me, he shook his head and wailed.

I shrank back in horror. Donovan had given him a near-death experience, but those didn't work in this realm. That meant Carlo remembered everything. But there was something else even more disturbing. Humans weren't allowed in Hell: it was strictly forbidden. Lucifer didn't seem to care that he was breaking the rules.

The lizardmen threw Carlo on the floor. One of them raised a baton and smashed it over his back. Carlo crumpled and fell forward.

"So tell me," Lucifer barked, his horns poking up. "What happened here?"

I shook my head. I didn't know what to say.

His onyx horns shot up higher. "Did you fail the orders I gave you? Answer me!"

"Yes. I failed." I dropped onto my knees, my head

bowed. "I'm sorry. I'll do better next time."

I prayed that losing my victim was all he knew about. Maybe he'd take mercy on me.

"Stand up, Belle. Make it right. Finish him. Now."

I blinked, not knowing what to say. My breath was ragged as I looked at Carlo. I couldn't kill him. "Sir . . . that man might be an innocent."

Lucifer's demonic teeth extended, revealing the giant maw of a beast as he stared me down. His horns were fully extended now, and his skin was redder than blood. "This man killed three women!"

"Sir . . ." I cowered, my breath lost in a sob. "Not according to the app I saw, Sir. And I have it on good information that I was eligible for Heaven before you assigned me to torture that man!"

"Belle, need I remind you you're not supposed to have any karma apps? And for good reason. They're wrong!"

I kept my face a mask, my prayers running through my mind on repeat. *Donovan, help me. Please.*

Lucifer grasped my chin with his sizzling-hot fingers and glared at me. He was so close I could smell the sulfur on his breath. "If I say he's guilty, he's guilty. If I say you're damned, *you're damned.*" He released my face roughly and paced across the room, looking disgustedly at me. "Does she still have her blade?"

Mephistopheles nodded from his stance at the ebony door. "Yes, sir."

"Good. Belle, kill this mortal for his crimes against humanity. Now." Lucifer breathed through his mouth, animalistic.

My stomach twisted as I looked at Carlo, sputtering and crying on the floor.

"Please don't kill me!" he whimpered. "Please, I'll do anything."

"BELLE! THAT'S AN ORDER!"

I looked at the Beast's vile transformation, my stomach heaving. All my life, I'd tried to do the right thing, and I'd been punished. But no more. I wasn't going to play his game. I was done. "No." I unsheathed my blade and threw it on the floor. The knife clattered between me and Lucifer. "I won't kill an innocent."

Lucifer snarled, crossing the room at a clip. He placed his hands on my neck. "You know what could happen if you disobey me!" His coal-black eyes bore into mine.

I gasped for breath. His hands burned my neck like acid. I clutched them and stared at him, detesting everything I saw. I'd worked for him for hundreds of years. I'd killed, striving for Heaven, and he'd lied to me and denied my ascension. Now he was ordering me to kill an innocent. I saw him for who he truly was, finally. I couldn't trust him at all. It was a wonder I ever had. "I'd rather be dissipated," I gasped for breath, "than follow orders from a maniac."

He released my throat and snapped his fingers. "Bring

forth the mortal."

I breathed deep, rubbing where his hands had been. I watched, unable to move, as the guards dragged Carlo toward us. I wanted to tell him how sorry I was, but there was no hope for either of us. We were both in this terrible place together.

"This can't be real." Carlo laughed in a high-pitched delirium, glancing at the guards holding him. "Lizard people! The devil! This has to be a dream. I'll wake up and everything will be fine."

My heart beat so hard with adrenaline, I could barely hear his lunatic rants.

Lucifer picked up my knife and slammed the handle into my hand. "DO IT. KILL HIM."

"No." I held my hand open, refusing to hold the knife.

Lucifer growled and pressed his steaming hand over mine. He forced my fingers to loop around the handle, his hand closing over mine. He lifted my hand and forced the blade up in the air over Carlo's chest.

I shook my head, a lump swelling in my throat. I closed my eyes — I couldn't watch.

"No, no!" Carlo screamed.

Lucifer forced the knife down hard. I tried to hold him back, but I couldn't. The knife went down and met resistance in flesh.

Carlo's scream pierced my mind. I tried to wrench my

hand away, but Lucifer dragged the knife down further, deeper. The crack of Carlo's ribs reverberated in my palm.

Through slitted eyes, I saw Carlo's soul float out of his mouth in a purple mist. My stomach dropped. An innocent was dead, killed by my knife, and by my and Lucifer's hands. Would that count against me? I was so close to being evil, I couldn't take even the smallest infraction of karma.

Lucifer released me and my legs gave out. I caught myself on the marble floor and looked up at him, ready for him to take my life, to dissipate me for disobeying his orders.

He grasped my face again and peered deeply into my eyes. I stared boldly back at the black-eyed, horned monster who'd sacrificed an innocent, indignant. If he was going to kill me, I wanted him to see my defiance, my hatred for him.

He released me with a *harrumph* and motioned to the guards. "Get rid of the body, and lock her in the cell. Her transformation will happen soon enough."

"What?" I whispered. A cell? I stood up and looked for a way out, but all of the doors were blocked by guards. "No!"

"YOU WILL DO AS I COMMAND." Lucifer wiped his hands on a white handkerchief and strode back to his desk.

122

"Let me go!" I screamed.

Demon arms gripped me, and a hypodermic needle appeared before my face. The wolfman in front of me barked, "Hold her still!"

I fought against them, but I could barely move. I felt a prick on my shoulder, then all of my fight drained away. I shut my eyes, praying for an angel who would never come.

CHAPTER ELEVEN

I turned over in bed, burying my face into my pillow, but the sulfurous stench didn't go away. Why was it so much stronger, and what was that dripping noise? I blinked and sat up, my heart racing. Something was wrong. I glanced at my bedroom furniture — dresser, nightstand, coffee table — everything was off by a few centimeters. And in place of my bedroom door was a wall made of gray stone. Instead of the Eiffel Tower nightlight on my nightstand, a lone candle flickered.

I cowered back against my headboard, bunching the sheet in my hands. Some twisted demon, or a team of demons, had moved my entire apartment into this stone cell. The only thing missing were my books. I touched the gray wall, hoping it was a dream, but it felt rough and warm beneath my fingertips. My heart sank. I could only be in the pits of Hell.

I threw off the sheet and ran toward a heavy wooden

door. The iron handle twisted in my palms, but the door didn't budge. I pounded my fists against it.

"Is anyone there? Open the door!"

I gasped at the scabs and purple bruises blooming all over my wrists and arms. A chill went up my spine. I didn't want to think about what had happened the day before. I just wanted out. I slammed my shoulder into the door.

"Help! Anyone! YOU CAN'T KEEP ME IN HERE!"

It barely moved. I struck it again with my fists, but no one answered.

I noticed a slender white door at the back of the room. I ran to it and wrenched it open. A porcelain claw-foot bathtub, sink, and toilet sat under a low ceiling. Water dripped from the ceiling onto the floor. A shiny silver plate hung in place of a mirror, and all of my toiletries were strewn here and there, just as I'd left them at home.

I backed away from it all, shuddering. Who'd done this? Who'd collected my belongings and arranged them in exactly the same manner as how I'd left them? Just thinking about someone else's hands on my personal objects made my stomach curdle.

But this confirmed it — Lucifer wanted to make me evil. Otherwise, he would've killed me last night. *Last night.* A crusty red stain ran down the front of my blouse. I covered my mouth as the memory resurfaced. My hands ached, recalling the feeling of cutting through muscles, tendons, and bones. I'd lost the fight against Lucifer, and Carlo had died by my knife.

My knife! I patted down my garter belt and pockets, hoping to feel the firm metal beneath my hand, but only felt the cotton of my skirt. I cursed and clenched my fists, my fingernails digging deep into my palms. The guards must've taken it.

But did they know about my stashes? I'd hidden knives in my belongings every time I upgraded. A secret knife might help me if I got the chance to use it.

I ran my hands under my bed, feeling for the steel tucked into the underside of the mattress. Nothing. I opened my nightstand drawer, then rummaged at the bottom of my dresser. Nothing. They'd all been taken. If only they'd brought my books too. I had a knife tucked in the hollows of *Practical Magic*. But then again, I couldn't use it. If I attacked, cut, or killed anyone, I could turn evil.

I yanked against the bathroom fixtures, looking for anything I could use as a weapon, but nothing came loose. The demons who'd moved me in had been smart. They probably suspected I'd fight my way out, given half a chance, and they were right. I wanted to make them pay for it, to rip their throats out and disembowel them with my new claws. The darkness inside of me burned with anger. My teeth burst longer and sharper, and my

126

eyes phased. It would feel so good to stab Lucifer the same way he'd killed Carlo. I'd slice into him, cut through his heart, see him bleed out, and watch his soul dissipate. Pleasure rippled down my spine. The dark ooze inside me felt like a creature beneath my skin once again, crawling around, longing to break free.

No. That wasn't me. I took a deep breath and stabilized myself. I clenched my eyes shut and took control. After a few minutes, my demonic features recessed. Transforming into my demonic self was too easy. I sat on the bed. I knew what the sludgey feeling inside of me was now. I'd thought it was my dread of torture, or my fear of torturing an innocent, but it was the part of me that was bad, the animalistic part that wanted to hurt others. My urges had been so strong lately they'd been hard to ignore. *Darkness begets more darkness.* As far as I could tell, it didn't seem to have grown since last night, but it wanted to. It certainly hadn't shrunk. As far as I knew, I hadn't reached 100% bad. I hadn't really killed Carlo — it'd been Lucifer's hands that did all the work. He'd just forced mine along with his. Surely any supreme being would know I didn't want to do it. I was trying to do the right thing, as I always have. My mood brightened a fraction, but I knew my options were limited. I couldn't go half-cocked on anyone, even if they deserved it.

On the other hand, if Carlo's death was added to my karma, I'd become evil by the next full moon, in less than two weeks. I'd become a different person — my worst self.

I shook my head. That couldn't happen. I believed I was still good underneath it all. If only there was some way to know. If only I had a phone to look up my score. I ground my teeth. The phone wasn't in my possession. It'd been taken along with my knife and my freedom.

I gasped. Lucifer could hear my thoughts. I instantly prayed to Donovan. I didn't know if he could hear me, but that didn't stop me from trying. He'd said he wanted to save me. I wondered if it extended to the pits of Hell. Did he have any temp friends? If only there were some way for him to reassure me. I closed my eyes for a moment, but no voices or visions came.

My eyes flashed open to the gray ceiling. Just as well. I was used to being on my own.

The metallic reek of dried blood on my shirt made my stomach turn. I plodded to my dresser and grabbed fresh clothes. At least the bathroom door locked, though I was certain that little bit of privacy wasn't guaranteed. Guards could remove the lock or bust down the door anytime they wanted. Nothing was mine anymore.

I winced as I disrobed. The dried blood on my shirt stuck to me. Countless purple bruises marred my body, from my face to my ankles. Lucifer's fingermarks were visible on my throat, in violet lines. His hands had been so strong when they'd grasped me. I'd been powerless. A sea of sadness rose into my chest, choking me. I swallowed it back, hating him more than I could bear.

But those weren't the only bruises on my body. Carlo's well-aimed kick caused the discolorations on my leg, but those were nothing compared to the thick reddish-purple bands all over my arms where the orcs had held me. My arms looked stained, and ached as if someone were still pressing upon the bruises.

I remembered the last time I had bruises like that, from the men who'd dragged me away from my family home. I could still smell the rot in the cell they'd kept me in, could still hear the children's whimpering as we awaited judgment. From time to time, throughout the centuries, I felt their grubby fingers touching my arms and legs in the dark. The songs I sang to the children still haunted my dreams.

I took a deep breath and glared at the bathroom walls. They reminded me I was under someone else's thumb once again, that I was being handled and judged again. I was powerless.

I ran the bathwater and sat in the tub as it filled, my arms wrapped around my knees. As the warm sulfurous-smelling water rose, a little bar of sandalwood soap knocked against my legs. I almost laughed. The demons who'd moved all my stuff had even taken my little scrap of soap. I'd bought that at a Moroccan bazaar a couple of months ago on one of my travels, just before killing a slave-trader. I used the soap to wash the dried blood off my skin, but I didn't feel any cleaner. I felt stained to my soul.

I leaned back in the tub. It'd be so easy to slip under, to give them the ultimate *goodbye*. My darkness would never grow any larger. I'd never turn evil, never have to face Lucifer or his demons ever again. My soul would dissipate to the four winds, and I'd be free for the first time in centuries. Heaven wouldn't be waiting for me, but it'd be better than serving Lucifer for the rest of my afterlife.

I sank low. The water rose above my nose and mouth, and the sound of rushing water filled my ears. I held my breath, then emptied the air from my lungs. Seconds passed. My heart beat hard with every crushing moment without oxygen. My head pounded until I couldn't take it anymore. Water flowed into my nose and ran, slippery, down my throat and into my lungs.

My head jerked up above the water. I coughed, gulping in air, holding the edge of the bathtub as I sobbed shattering tears.

This wasn't like me — I'd survived worse than this, and I just might survive this too. This was the darkness talking. I needed to talk back to it. I couldn't give up so easily. I hadn't fought against the men who'd taken me before, because I believed that they knew better. I thought that they had a link to Heaven. But this was different. Lucifer was the embodiment of evil — he'd lied to me, made me torture, and ordered the killing of an innocent. And now he was waiting for me to turn evil so he could use me further.

I couldn't let that happen. I vowed right then and there to end him. I'd do anything — I'd risk turning evil and even face dissipation if I could take him down with me.

I walked out of the bath and met my gaze in the silver platter that hung in place of the mirror. My blue eyes were red-rimmed from crying, but they never looked so purposeful, so steady. Before this week, my afterlife had been about killing evil people to get into Heaven. Now, I'd kill the most evil being ever — the devil himself. I was good at killing. I was one of the fastest killers in Hell. This would only be a little different. I'd almost certainly turn evil, but dethroning Lucifer would be worth it.

My fingers curled around one of my makeup brushes lying on the sink. I twisted the applicator brush off, then ran the blunt wooden edge against the stone wall. Fragments of wood came off. I scraped it again and again until the makeup wand became a sharp point. When I pressed it against my arm, a drop of blood rose to the surface of my skin. It was a crude shiv, but it might work.

When I walked into my cell, fully dressed and packing three shivs in my garter belt, something glinted on the coffee table. I walked closer and found a silver platter with a hunk of brown bread, fat sausage links, and a blush-red apple.

I glanced around at the shadows of the room, but no one was there. My heart nearly stopped as I looked at the tray. Of all the breakfasts in Hell, why this one? When I was human, it was what my family ate every morning. Was this Lucifer's way of saying he knew where I was from — that he knew my name, too? No, it couldn't be. If that was the case, he'd be able to control me even without turning me evil. He wouldn't have to make me kill Carlo, and he certainly wouldn't have to lock me in a cell.

Someone banged on the door. I backed against the wall, dreading whoever was on the other side. Whoever it was knew far too much about me.

CHAPTER TWELVE

"Are you decent, princess?" asked a manly, sneering voice through the door.

The clanking of iron keys in the lock sounded from the other side of the door, then it creaked open. A dung-colored ogre peered at me from behind the door, a heavy-looking sword hanging from his belt. My hopes of overpowering the guard crashed and burned. Ogres weren't the brightest creatures, but they were as strong as five demons.

Mephistopheles sauntered in with a smug smile, his hands clasped behind him. He wore a crimson collared shirt, black dress pants, and fine Italian leather shoes. He had the air of a spoiled prince, but he wasn't one of the archdemons. He was just a lowly guard. I hadn't noticed it before, but without his leather jacket, he looked like a younger version of Lucifer.

I scowled at him, my arms crossed. "What do you

want?"

He shut the door in the ogre's face with a loud *thud*, his smile growing. "I've been assigned to watch over your transition. What do you think of your new room?" He threw out his hands.

"Why am I being kept here?"

His black eyes were unreadable as he walked in and looked at my tray of food. "You didn't eat your breakfast."

"I'm not hungry."

He *tsked* and shook his head. "Belle, you gotta eat."

I shrugged. "Why do you care if I starve or not?"

"Fine, if you want to throw away the breakfast I made for you, go ahead." He threw the apple up in the air and caught it, then strolled a few lazy steps in my direction. "But no one in Hell cooks like I do."

For a moment, I thought he'd offer the apple to me. Then he bit into it, studying me as a rivulet of juice ran down his chin.

I huffed. At least the apple wasn't enchanted. I couldn't say the same for the rest of the food. But if he'd made my breakfast tray, did that mean he knew who I was and where I was killed? No, that was impossible. No one knew my name — no one but Donovan.

I cleared my throat. "Are you going to tell me why I'm being kept here?"

His brows rose. "Why do *you* think you're here?"

134

I rolled my eyes. "I don't know. Lucifer wants me to be a guard or something?"

His smile broadened, and he walked in a circle around me. "Do you *want* to be a guard?"

"No. But do I have a choice?" I turned, keeping my gaze on him.

He bit into the apple again, then pitched it into a wastebasket with a *thunk*. "Of course you do, only I don't think you'll like the alternative."

I scowled. "What? Dissipation?"

He nodded, then sat down on my bed and ran his hands over my quilted lavender blanket. He lay down and laced his fingers behind his head. "Why don't you just give the old fart what he wants? What's the harm in that?"

My blood burned. I didn't want his dirty fingers touching my things. I bit back my anger, trying to let it simmer instead of boil. "Are you serious? You really think I'd make another pact to serve him, this time for all of eternity?"

"You don't have to serve him. You can serve *yourself*." He winked. "That's what I do."

I recoiled from him. He shouldn't be talking like that. "Aren't you worried Lucifer will hear you?"

"He can't hear me." He sat up. "Watch this. Lucifer is a dick! He's the dumbest demon who ever walked in Hell!" He shrugged, his eyes dancing. "See? Nothing."

I blinked. "How is that possible?"

"I have a thought charm." He toyed with a tiny quartz pendant on a silver chain around his neck. "Highly illegal, but Lucifer doesn't know I have it. You're a witch. Don't you have one too?"

I froze, my thoughts flying. I'd heard of witch tech and thought charms, but I thought they were just rumors. And I wasn't really a witch, but he didn't seem to know that.

I smirked. "Of course. But I didn't think *you'd* have one. Who gave it to you?"

"That's a secret. Where's yours?"

I glanced down at my chest. No necklace. "It must've fallen off when I was captured. It's too bad I don't have my spell book to make another."

"Ah." He scooted close to me, his fingers hovering near mine. He was so close I could feel his body heat.

I drew away from him. "What are you doing?"

"He can't hear your thoughts if you're within two feet of a thought charm, remember?"

I nodded. I didn't trust him, and I knew it could be a trap, but I didn't have anything left to lose. What really interested me was that he was talking. Was he that lonely, or was he trying to get me to confess? If I could keep him talking, he might help me. At the very least, I could learn more about my situation, and possibly find a way out.

"You work with Lucifer almost every day," I said. "Doesn't he ever wonder why he can't hear your thoughts?"

"Sure, but I take it off sometimes, when I'm feeling *good*." His mouth curled around the last word as if it tasted bitter.

I studied his face, uncertain. "Why should I believe anything you say?"

He shrugged. "Why would I lie? I don't care what happens to you. But I did do you a favor. I got rid of your phone." He shook his head. "Pretty clever, buying a burner phone to download the karma app. You know, you could have been dissipated for having that."

I pressed my lips together and stared at the floor. As much as I appreciated the favor, I still didn't trust him. But I wanted to keep him talking. "Is this how you were recruited to be a demon? Kill an innocent and turn evil at the full moon?"

"Something like that."

"Do you like taking orders from him?"

"That's part of being a guard — it's my job. But most of the time, I'm lying on a beach in the south of France, working on my tan." He flexed his bicep. "Gotta keep up appearances, you know."

My instinct was to back away from him, but I needed to stay within the charm's radius. I edged closer.

"What happens if I don't want to be a guard?"

He laughed. "I don't know why you're resisting. It's the same job you have now, only you'd get your own office, amazing benefits . . . and you'd get to work with me." He grinned, his eyes playful.

I glared at him. "But I'd lose all my memories, and I could never go to Heaven."

"Belle, you don't want to go there. If you only knew how boring that place is! Besides, you'll have to work for centuries to make up for your bad karma, anyway. And for what? Just to hang out with some prudes?"

The darkness coiled inside me again, ready to strike. I wanted to tear his eyes out. But it wasn't just him — I was angry about everything — my situation, my helplessness, Lucifer's lies, and the fact that Heaven had once been so close I could almost taste it.

"Don't get me wrong," he grinned. "I think your score is great! You're one of the fastest assassins in Hell. Everyone thought you were gunning to be a guard."

I crossed my arms. "Well, I wasn't."

"Right. And I can see you haven't turned evil yet." He scooted away from me. "Lucifer will be *very* interested in that."

"Wait." I leaned toward him, eager to stay in the thought charm's radius. "What happens if you tell him I'm not evil?"

He stood and stretched, his mouth turning down. "He'll make you kill again. Only this time, he'll make

138

sure it's done right. I hope you don't have any friends, because . . ." He slashed his fingers across his neck.

Jane. No. I couldn't let that happen.

"Later, princess." He started walking away.

"Wait!"

He raised a fist to pound on the door.

"Mephistopheles, *wait!*"

He stopped but didn't turn around.

My heart beat fast. I racked my brain, desperate for anything to help me. "I think something is changing inside of me. I might be turning evil."

He looked down his nose at me. "Yeah, right. If you're evil, I'm the Easter Bunny."

I ran across the room until I stood within the radius of the thought charm. "No, I mean, *that's what I want you to tell Lucifer,*" I whispered.

His face twisted in malevolent pleasure. "You want me to *lie* for you?"

I nodded.

He took a step toward me. His dancing black eyes and hungry mouth took up my entire field of vision. "Why would I do such a thing?"

I swallowed, my thoughts calculating. "I can help you."

His dark eyebrows flickered. "I'm listening."

What could he need? I was willing to bargain anything if I could survive this and keep Jane out of trouble. I glanced at the charm hanging near his collarbone.

"I'm a witch. You know what we can do. Charms, spells, potions." I hoped he didn't notice my increased heartbeat, my panicked eyes.

He stroked his chin. "Okay, witch. Maybe there is something you can do for me."

I nodded feverishly. "Anything. Just name it."

He leaned close, his breath hot in my ear. "Make me a love charm."

I took a quick breath. Which demon had caught his eye? And what would happen when the love charm turned out to be a dud?

"What's wrong?" His eyes searched mine. "Can't do a simple love charm?"

"Of course I can. I just need a few things."

"Like what?"

"My books. And . . . a hair from the person you love." I'd heard that somewhere — I hoped it rang true.

"No problem. I'll bring them to you tomorrow."

I caught his sleeve. "So you'll tell Lucifer I'm turning evil?"

He nodded, his eyes trained on me. "Yes. But if you mess this up," he tapped his finger at my chest, right over my heart. "I'll tell him everything — and not just that you're a goody two-shoes. I'll tell him your mortal name."

I froze, unable to move or think. "You know my

name?" My voice squeaked.

He nodded. "I sure do, Miss Babelin."

I swallowed nervously, too shocked to respond. It was my worst fear come true. All I could do was hold out my hand to shake on it. His hot hand sizzled against mine.

"Until next time, little witch." He smirked and rapped on the door.

A metallic lock clanked, and the door swung open. He walked through, holding my gaze until the ogre shut the door.

I strode back to my bed and threw my quilt on the floor, as if that could stop me from remembering his hands running over it. I didn't trust him, but I had some time — a little less than two weeks, if I played my cards right. It might be enough time to learn more about where I was and to learn what Lucifer expected of me. And maybe even time to kill Lucifer.

Help me Donovan, I prayed, desperate now more than ever to keep my thoughts silent. *How am I going to come up with a love spell when I'm not really a witch?*

CHAPTER THIRTEEN

Pounding on the door awoke me. I sat up, nerves racing, and pulled the sheet around me. Muscles tensed, I clutched a sharpened makeup wand in my hand.

"Belle! You awake?"

"Who is it?" I shouted.

"It's your favorite demon," Mephistopheles' voice sang from the other side of the door.

I groaned, thankful to be wearing a concealing dressing gown. "Come in."

Iron keys jingled, and the door swung open. Mephistopheles carried in another breakfast tray. The ogre locked the door behind him.

When Mephistopheles set the tray on my little table, I scowled. It was the same food as yesterday, as if to remind me of what he knew. He sat on my bed beside me, his crystal pendant gleaming in the candlelight.

"Looks like you just woke up."

I smoothed down my hair and swallowed my morning breath. "What time is it?"

"It doesn't matter. But this does." He reached into his pocket and produced a roughly polished topaz stone set in gold prongs. A strand of hair was wrapped around it, knotted several times.

I held it near the candlelight to look at the hair. It was light-colored — red or blonde. Not mine. I breathed a sigh of relief. "Whose is it?"

"Not telling. When will my love charm be ready?"

I gave him a flat smile and set the pendant inside the drawer on my bedside table. "I can only forge a love charm when Venus is in the right aspect. Otherwise, it won't work. I'll need to consult the heavenly bodies and get back to you. Bring me my books and a timepiece."

"Why do you need your books?"

"I need my astrolabe to know where Venus is. The spells for the love charm and the thought charm are there too." My knife was hidden in one of my books too, but he didn't need to know that.

His face scrunched up, his eyes flickering with disbelief. "What sign does Venus have to be in for you to make the charm?"

I blinked. I had no idea what sign Venus was in. "Scorpio." I hoped it was months away.

"Very well." He leaned back and stretched out on my bed again. "Need anything else?" he asked exasperatedly.

I made a sour face. "Only my freedom."

He laughed loudly. "So you do have a sense of humor! I knew you had it in you. But seriously? We both know you won't be freed anytime soon."

I frowned. "How much longer will I be stuck in here?"

"It all depends."

"On what?"

"On how well you play the game. Let him think you're evil. Transform in front of him. Take the position he offers. You'll be freed to roam around his quarters in ten minutes."

I made a disgusted sound.

He reached out and grabbed my shoulders, pulling me close. His breath smelled warm and sweet, like fennel. I froze as our faces hovered.

"You were outside the radius of my protection. It only goes so far."

I shrugged my shoulders where he'd touched me, but I stayed close. I was too much myself around him, too free with my thoughts and words. Did he have another charm? One that made me say whatever I thought?

I glanced at the breakfast tray. The smell of fresh bread made me salivate, but I was eager to learn more. "Who told you my name?"

"I was reading witch lore on the internet a couple of months ago, when I came across a passage. It was about a maiden who was supposedly the most beautiful girl in the whole village. And I thought of you." His fingers brushed the tips of my hair.

I pulled my hair away from his fingers and glared at him. "Don't touch me." He had to be lying. That was too easy. He must have another source.

"And the name Belle — it's so close to your real name. You didn't really put a lot of imagination into that, did you? And you look like a German."

"I was born in France."

"You look French too."

I rolled my eyes. "I'm supposed to believe that, of the thousands of people persecuted in the name of a few sociopaths, you came across someone, and thought it was me?"

"Don't lie. I know it's you."

Something cold stirred inside of me. If he could find my name in some dusty old records, that meant Lucifer could too. Perhaps he had, and it was just a matter of time before he used it against me.

Or maybe it was a lie. He was older than I was — could he have walked through the streets of my village? Had he been one of the faces in the crowd? I evaluated him, backing away ever so slightly. My chest heaved. "You were a demon when I died, weren't you?"

"I was, yes. It was a dark time." He steepled his hands.

I swallowed a sob. "Why didn't you stop the executions? You could've killed the evil people who were killing innocents like me. You could've saved thousands of people. You — you could have saved *me*."

His angular jaw set. "I wasn't assigned to kill them."

I crossed my arms and glowered at him, the ooze within me agitating. "What *were* you assigned to do?"

"I'm sure you've heard about my friend, Dr. Faustus."

"Of course I've heard of him." Faustus had made a deal with Lucifer through Mephistopheles, but that didn't answer my question. What kind of demon was he? What was his karma? Making deals — wealth for souls? "So you were assigned to make a deal with Faustus and you were so busy you couldn't stop genocide?"

He stared me down, his eyes sharp. "I had to follow orders. It was something assigned to me for my karma. I'm sorry, princess."

"I'm not a princess," I spat, teeth bared.

"Yeah. Keep telling yourself that." He rolled up from the bed and headed toward the door. "I should get going. But before I leave, you might want to dress up tonight. Lucifer expects to see you for dinner."

"What? Why?"

He threw his hands up. "Don't kill me. I'm just the messenger."

I stomped across the room toward the thought charm, resenting every step he made me take to get closer to the thought charm. "I don't want to have dinner with him. He disgusts me."

He shrugged, shaking his head. "It doesn't matter what you think of him. He's the Prince of Darkness, you're in his kingdom, and he wants to have dinner with you . . . Unless you'd rather experience the wrath of the embodiment of pure evil, you'd better go."

I crossed my arms. "What does he want?"

"He probably wants to ask you about being a guard. It's too bad you don't have a thought charm. I hope you can keep your thoughts civil until I can get those books to you."

My breath quickened. "Let me borrow yours."

He stared at me. "No."

"I need it. Please. Otherwise he'll hear me thinking about making your love charm."

He swallowed, weighing the matter. After a moment, he sighed and took it off. "Fine, but you owe me."

I took it from him and dropped it over my head. Relief spilled over me like a thousand feathery touches. "Thank you."

"When you make my love charm, I'll be the one thanking you. You'll forget all about me once you're evil. They always do." He gave me a wistful glance.

I drew back. The way he'd said it made it seem like I wasn't the only one Lucifer had done this to. "What do you mean?"

"Nothing." His lips clamped and his eyes grew cold again. He slid out the door, a miserable look crossing his face.

A slippery feeling of dread rose over me. Lucifer must've done this to other women before for Mephistopheles to have said that. How many had there been? What kind of evil person would do this to someone else?

I rolled the crystal between my thumb and forefinger, the sharp edges piercing my fingertips. No matter how many women Lucifer had abducted and held against their will, I decided it would end with me. I had a little bit of protection, and I still had my own thoughts. I just had to kill the beast.

CHAPTER FOURTEEN

I stared at my reflection in the silver plate mirror, the possibility of victory trembling in my eyes. Mephistopheles' words rang in my ears.

Lucifer expects to see you for dinner.

My hand ran over three sharp points tucked into my garter belt. Tonight, I'd try to either kill Lucifer or escape Hell. Maybe both, if I was lucky. If I succeeded, everything would change. I'd be free — out from under Lucifer's thumb. If I didn't succeed . . . Well, dissipation was sort of like freedom.

Now that I had the thought charm, I could think freely about killing Lucifer without worrying he'd hear my thoughts. I practiced tearing out my shivs and stabbing him. I reveled in my fantasies of ending him once and for all. It'd cause riots. Hell would change — maybe Heaven would even take it back. If I was successful, I'd end the terrible reign, and something new would happen

— anything would be better than Lucifer.

I glanced down at the dress I'd chosen for dinner. Golden fabric fell to the floor. It was my ugliest gown, but that's not why I chose it. A hidden slit ran up the side. I could run, fight, and roundhouse a demon — or hell — even the Beast himself.

I tucked the thought charm behind the neckline of my dress. The fact that Mephistopheles and I weren't dissipated for using it was proof enough that it worked. It was refreshingly nice to allow my thoughts free reign without having to stand so close to Mephistopheles. I shuddered with disgust just thinking about it.

Heavy banging reverberated on my prison door, making me jump.

"Come in." I hunched over, pretending to be weak. A clump of hair fell before my eyes.

A minotaur opened the door and bowed under the doorframe, swinging a trident with razor-sharp points in my direction. He was followed by a three-foot-tall goblin with pointed teeth. A giant keyring and a baton dangled from his belt.

The goblin strode toward me with heavy iron handcuffs. "You've been ordered to appear before the Prince of Darkness," he said in a reedy voice. "Hold out your wrists."

I held out my shaking hands, hoping for a front-cuff. It'd be much easier to escape if the cuffs were that way.

The demons exchanged a look. I thought I saw the minotaur shrug. The goblin cuffed the hot shackles onto my wrists.

I repressed a wicked smile.

The minotaur's sharp trident swung out, coming dangerously close to my stomach. "Walk," he grumbled, his bovine eyes glowering.

I let him march me out, but not before feeling another surge of hope. Whenever he blinked, his eyes closed for half a second. My chances of escape just got better.

We passed through the wooden door and stepped out into a warm red-bricked hallway. A green ogre picked at a half-eaten meal of what looked like an enormous roasted turkey leg on a silver platter. A knob of bone stuck out, looking remarkably like a femur. He sucked his fingers noisily before pushing the door closed. One of the leather armor plates covering his rear was crooked, revealing a patch of stained underwear. A perfect place for my shiv to plunge into, if I needed to wound him.

"Prisoner," grouched the minotaur. "Turn around and follow the goblin." His trident jolted into my back.

I leapt, my flesh stinging. He'd probably drawn blood. I faced forward, even as I thought about removing a wand and lodging it in his eye. My demon teeth shot out in anticipation of a fight.

No. I couldn't let the dark side win. Not yet. I clamped my razor-sharp teeth back, tight-jawed, until they were normal.

The goblin lifted a sputtering torch from a wall sconce. He held it high, lighting the ink-dark passages of red brick arches, not unlike Death's Cross, only these looked older, more crusted-over with water stains.

I barely saw where my feet fell, and only narrowly dodged heaps of grime and cobwebs. A large brown rat scurried along the corridor toward us. I lurched back, but the guards ignored it.

We turned right, then right again, down a corridor with several passages leading off to one side. We took the second one, then walked past five paths that smelled like they led to bathrooms.

I tried to remember the order of the turns we took. There were so many I was losing track. I'd hoped there'd be exit signs or direction markers, but the walls were bare.

We passed into a wider, well-lit hall. Two torches illuminated a sleeping beast. As we neared, it stirred, waking, and I saw it was a three-headed dog. Cerberus. He rose to his massive forelegs, all six eyes shining with malice as he growled and drooled at me. Behind him, a waystation's hollow corridor loomed, a slight breeze lifting the hairs on my arm. Inside, a lift waited, the red button visible.

My pulse pounded. That waystation could be my way out. Maybe Heaven was within my reach after all. I inhaled, relishing the clean, earthy scent of the air, mixed with the smell of wet mongrel.

"Hey puppy," I whispered. What had I heard about him? I racked my brain, but all I could recall was that he guarded the way to and from the underworld, and that he liked food. If my dinner with Lucifer had any kind of meat, I might have a chance to escape.

The towering dog whined and stretched, bowing low. A giant chain around his neck rattled against the stone floor. One of his heads panted and seemed to smile at me. His middle face yawned, a pink tongue curling, before he closed his chops and regarded me with sleepy eyes. The last head bared his teeth, almost growling. He flashed vicious yellow eyes at me. That would be the one to feed.

"Face forward," the minotaur grumbled.

I straightened and kept walking, determined to memorize the next several turns as best I could. I felt almost breathless with hope.

After a left, a right, and another right, we arrived at a blue door with spirals of black metalwork. The goblin set the torch into a wall sconce, then fumbled with the giant keyring on his belt. The minotaur muttered, keeping one eye on me while thumbing his phone.

I took a cool breath and assessed the situation. This must be the dining room — I could even smell bread cooling on the other side of the door. If I timed it right,

I could run into the room, grab some food, and run back to Cerberus. I might have to fight, but I'd been praying so much that it might be okay. Besides, it wasn't like I'd kill the guards — I'd just maim them enough to keep them from running after me. Maybe once I was topside, Donovan could take away my excess bad karma.

I drew in a deep breath. My muscles tensed, ready to run as soon as the goblin found the right key.

"Belle," a loud voice boomed. A torch bobbed toward us, slowly revealing Lucifer, his broad chest strained into a tuxedo jacket and a pressed white shirt. His ivory skin gleamed in the torchlight, and his well-coiffured black hair revealed no horns. When he smiled at me, his teeth were shiny, white, and normal. Only his eyes spoke to the deadly deeds he'd performed and his evil nature.

I clenched my jaw and scowled. I needed him to believe I was on my way to becoming evil so he wouldn't make me kill again.

"I'm so glad you decided to come," he said, smiling.

"Did I have a choice?" I snapped.

The minotaur watched me, his brows drawn. I glared at him. I didn't care what he thought now.

"Touché." Lucifer laughed a little. "Mephistopheles was right. You're on your way. Only, I don't see it in your eyes yet. But I suppose that'll change with this full moon. How beautiful you'll look with your eyes phased black all the time."

154

I seethed, my fingers aching for my sharpened wands.

The goblin finally unlocked the door. It squealed open onto a grand banquet hall with high ceilings and a chandelier set with twelve cornflower candles. A long table glittered with silverware, goblets, and a crystal vase, which held a bouquet of blood-red roses. It looked like something out of a magazine. I glanced around, looking for food, but didn't see any.

Temps in starched aprons lined the other end of the hall, their eyes crackling with fear. Some of them wore chef's hats. I squinted at them. Hell had its own chefs?

"Take her handcuffs off," Lucifer said to the guards. "There's no need to be uncivil, right Belle?"

I stared at him, unsure of what was happening. Where was the omnipotent manifestation of evil I'd seen at our last encounter?

The goblin unlocked my cuffs. I rotated my wrists and flexed them, determined to be ready for whenever I could strike.

"Wait outside," Lucifer said to the guards. "I don't need you."

"You want us to leave?" the minotaur grumbled, uncertainty in his eyes. "But she—"

"Leave us, you idiot!"

Lucifer reared his hand back as if to slap him, his face flushing red. The minotaur and goblin bowed and scurried backwards until they exited the room. The door closed behind them.

"Now, then." Lucifer approached the table and pulled out a tall wooden chair with a magenta poof on the seat. "Belle, please sit."

I sat, my eyes trained on him, wary of his every move. I wouldn't let him strangle me again. Food or no food, I'd attack him right then and there, rather than let him touch me like that again.

But he made no such move. He walked toward the other end of the table and sat on a chair like mine, some ten feet away. The candlelight made him look softer, like less of a beast, but I wasn't fooled. He was a madman. Behind the thin veneer of civility, his bestial nature burned in those raven-black eyes.

A violinist emerged from the back door, his face ashen. He shifted his gaze around the room before raising his bow and playing a few sad notes.

My fingers itched to reach for a sharpened wand as I evaluated Lucifer, visible just beyond the roses. I couldn't stab his heart — his suit looked too thick. No matter. The carotid artery was one of my favorites. My victims bled out in mere seconds. His was exposed — I saw the artery pounding on his thick neck.

He stared at me, his eyes unreadable.

Was he trying to read my thoughts? The thought charm felt heavy against my chest. I swallowed.

Lucifer raised a hand. "Come on already," he barked

at the chefs. "Serve the first course."

The chefs scrabbled, ladling orange-colored soup from a cauldron into two bowls. Servers set the bowls down in front of us simultaneously, along with a plate with tiny pieces of toast, topped with a swirled gray paté.

"Try the foie gras," Lucifer said, crunching into one and spilling crumbs all over the tablecloth.

I frowned. The ironic parallels of being served a captive, force-fed duck's liver didn't escape me. I could barely stand to look at it. But tendrils of steam rose from the butternut squash bisque. Against my will, my mouth watered. Mephistopheles hadn't given me lunch.

Lucifer attempted to smile, but it was too wide, too toothy. Certainly false. "Has Mephistopheles taken good care of you?" He dipped his spoon into the soup and slurped it.

"Why are you keeping me prisoner here?"

He stared at me, his brows tightening. "Mephistopheles said he spoke with you about it, that you understood."

"What makes you think I'd be interested in that position?" I shook my head. "And why'd you lock me in a cell?"

He set down his spoon and shook his massive head. "I apologize. You must be so confused. Let me explain: evil develops over the course of a moon cycle, reaching its apex when the moon is full. When people become evil, they don't change at all, while others go on killing sprees. Some become so depressed, they try to take their own lives. Locking you away is for your own protection as well as ours. I'm sure you've noticed your cell doesn't have any sharp objects."

My breath caught — the thought had crossed my mind in the bathtub. Did that mean I was becoming evil? I blinked back my emotion as he continued.

"If your transformation to the dark side is complete, as Mephistopheles believes, we can talk about your future here in Hell — what you want, what I can offer . . ." He held out his open palm, then closed it, one finger at a time. "But if you're not transformed yet, you'll have to stay in the cell until the full moon brings it out, some ten more days. Please don't hesitate to let me know if there's anything I can do to make your stay more amenable."

I recoiled. Why was he being so nice? He'd forced me to kill, and now he was trying to make me feel better about being locked in a dungeon? It didn't make any sense. "Why were all my belongings moved here?"

He frowned. "This is your new home. I want you to be comfortable."

I bit my tongue to keep words from coming out. I had to be careful.

"Are you not hungry?" he asked. "Is the food not acceptable?" He glared at the chefs, who exchanged anxious glances.

I swallowed. What would he do to the chefs if he thought I didn't like it? I'd have to eat to get to the next course anyway.

I dug my spoon into the soup and raised it to my lips. Surprisingly, it was delicious. The addition of freshly ground nutmeg was refreshing. I ate another spoonful, then another. When it was gone, I dropped my spoon in the bowl and glowered at Lucifer, letting my eyes phase black.

Lucifer smiled. "I must say, this is a treat, Belle. I never thought you'd want to eat dinner with me. You were always so . . . *good*. But now, I see you're so much more." He set his spoon down beside his bowl and dabbed his mouth with a white cloth napkin. "Bring the next course!"

The servers leapt into action again. One of them cleared my bowl and plate, and another positioned a fancy fork and a serrated knife before me. I tried to not look too happy, but it was perfect. I could go for his heart after all.

Two more servers carried in a large silver platter covered with a lid, and set it down on the middle of the table. One of them removed the lid while the other carved a hunk of roast beef decorated with aromatic sprigs of rosemary. A smile crept over me. Cerberus would be very happy — happy enough to get out of the way while I took the waystation topside.

The servers plated the sliced meat with a smattering of roasted potatoes, then set them before us. I picked up the heavy knife and sliced, eating a few bites while watching Lucifer from the corner of my eyes. He kept his eyes on me too, staring at my every move.

The moment he glanced down at his plate to cut his beef, I surreptitiously stole a slice of meat and slipped it into my boot. It felt warm and squishy against my ankle, but it also felt wondrous. It'd be my ticket out of here. I repressed a smile. The dinner was going so well. My opportunity to escape seemed more possible than ever. I inhaled deeply, recalling what topside smelled like. The leaves would be turning colors in some parts of the world by now. I wanted to be up there on earth, safe with Donovan, feeding the poor or making clothes for babies, or whatever he wanted me to do to make up for my karma.

The violinist ended his song and started playing another. I recognized it immediately. *Clair de Lune.* It had crept from every music house before the turn of the century, when gas lamps lit the cobblestoned streets in a wash of warm light. I'd hunted those streets, drunk on music, happy to dispatch the errant souls amidst such beauty.

A strange twinkle gleamed in Lucifer's eyes. "This is one of my favorite songs. Shall we dance, Belle?"

My breath latched. This was my chance to kill him. I remained absolutely still as he set his napkin on the table.

"Clear the plates," Lucifer said.

Before I could reach for the knife, the servers whisked everything away, knife and all. I watched them go with longing, my disappointment heavy. But at least I still had my shivs.

My heartbeat rioted as Lucifer crossed the room and drew close. He extended an arm toward me.

"Belle, may I have this dance?"

I swallowed and stood, then cursed internally when I realized that traditional dancing positions forbade me from hiding my weapons in my hands. I'd have to weigh my attack carefully. My left hand went to Lucifer's shoulder while the other clasped his pale, sweaty hand. His hand rested on my upper back.

We moved to the sweeping notes. He stayed a respectable distance from me, his hand never traveling farther than it ought. Maybe he knew I was from an older time, or maybe he was trying to be a gentleman. Whatever it was, I wasn't buying it. I saw through him.

He swept me across the room, his feet as light as air. I could barely keep up with him.

"You're quite good at this," he chuckled.

My teeth ground. "I'm good at a lot of things."

When he twirled me at the climax of the song, I saw

my opportunity. It was now or never. I reached for my shivs and drew two of them from my garter, breathless. I wound my hand back, and in one swift motion, brought the sharp points down on the artery pulsing in Lucifer's neck.

The points glanced off his skin as if they were rubber, leaving no trace of blood or puncture. I gasped. They fell from my hands, rattling a staccato on the floor.

Lucifer stumbled back and looked at the shivs, his eyes wide in shock. His hand rose to touch to his neck.

Why hadn't they worked? I ripped the other shiv out and tried to plunge it into his femoral artery on his leg, a banshee cry in my throat.

But Lucifer was ready. He caught my wrist and held it, his eyes electric, watching me with an undecipherable look as we struggled.

The violinist stopped playing, his last note a screech before he ran toward the back of the room. The servers ran out too, dishes and trays clattering to the floor and shattering.

I pressed harder toward his artery, summoning all the strength I had. But it didn't move at all. We were in a deadlock. His face reddened and his horns grew tall, but I didn't let that intimidate me.

"This is a different kind of dance," he growled, pushing against me. "But I can appreciate it for what it is."

I pressed forward with all my might, desperate to stab

him. This was my last chance. I had mere seconds of my miserable life left.

The door shrieked open and footsteps ran toward us, armor rattling. Strong hands pulled me off Lucifer, crushing my bruises. Needles of pain ran up my arms, but I squirmed in their grasp as they dragged me away from him. I had to kill him! It was the only way to end it, once and for all. I wrestled against them, thrashing, then twisted my arms and freed myself from their grips.

"You idiots!" Lucifer yelled. "Capture her!"

The guards brandished their weapons at me. It was an unfair fight — eight against one. But even more unfair was the fact that I couldn't fight. If I did, I risked my karma score maxing out. My only hope lay in the open front door that appeared to be unguarded. If I could get out, I could find my way back to Cerberus, give him the meat, and take the waystation topside.

"Be careful." Lucifer roared. "I want her alive!"

The guards lowered their weapons slightly, their expressions confused as they crowded around me, backing me against the wall. I faced them, growling, calculating their weaknesses. I saw the wolf man's limited flexibility, the minotaur's moment of blindness whenever he blinked, the goblin's short stature and his hands holding the handcuffs, and the fire imp's slow reactions and burning flesh that would hurt anyone else who touched him.

When the minotaur blinked slowly, I ducked under his arms, then pushed the fire imp into the orc. I ran around the goblin and faced the wolf man's ready claws. I feinted left but zagged right, avoiding him. I raced away, my steps frantic. The door was in sight! I sped up, glancing behind me. They struggled to run after me.

"SIEZE HER!" Lucifer roared.

I turned, my heart light, only to run right into another orc in the doorway. She grasped my arms, pressing hard on my bruises. Sharp pain jolted through me. I groaned as she twisted my arms behind my back. The goblin trotted forward and clamped the hot iron shackles around my aching wrists with heavy *clicks*.

I hung my head. It was all over now. I prayed to Donovan for my soul, for anyone or anything to rescue me.

"Bring her to me." Lucifer's skin was a faint pink, which slowly cleared as his composure returned. He stared at me, his black eyes unsettling, his horns only halfway up.

The bottom of my stomach panged. I'd failed. What would become of me? Would he make me kill again? I wouldn't do it. I wrestled against the shackles, but it was no good. They were locked tight. My moment of opportunity was over, and I hadn't even hurt him.

Lucifer stood before me. A surly smile played on his lips. "I can see you're still in the violent stage of your transformation. I'll give you more time. But it was a

164

marvelous dance while it lasted." He reached out and pinched my cheek.

I twisted my face away, rage boiling inside of me. "Let me go!" I snarled like a rabid dog, threatening to bite his fingers, only chomping at the air.

"What a bark!" His black eyes slid over me with admiration. "I can only imagine how fierce your bite is. I suppose we shall see at the full moon." He motioned to the guards. "Lock her in the cell. Station two guards at the door at all times. Nobody goes in or out without my permission."

His smile was sickeningly sweet as they hauled me away. "I do hope we have another opportunity to dance, Belle."

CHAPTER FIFTEEN

I sat on my bed wringing my hands. I'd attacked Lucifer, and yet he'd reacted as if I were a mewling kitten. Why hadn't I been dissipated? My head lowered into my hands. My plans had crumbled. Now, there'd be no chance of escape, no chance of killing him again. After that performance, he'd make sure of that.

Clanking sounds came from behind the door. Mephistopheles loped into my cell, his eyes wilder than usual as he ran to my bed. He scrambled in and reached for my neck, lifting his necklace off me with burning, hot fingers.

I pulled away from him. "Ow."

He threw the necklace over his black hair and onto his neck, then breathed an unburdened sigh. "You don't know how hard that was."

"Yes, I do." I crept closer to him, already missing the reassuring feel of the thought charm near me.

"How'd it go tonight?" he asked. "Dinner was okay, I trust?"

I glared at him. "You haven't heard?"

"What? Did you accept the position?"

I snorted. "No. Quite the opposite. Apparently, I shocked him."

"*You* shocked *him?*"

I glared at him. "Yes. Why are you so incredulous?"

He laughed. "Belle, you're a killer, but he's the Prince of Darkness. He's been around a long time, and he's done some evil stuff."

"Yeah, well, maybe he's growing soft. He freaked out over a little animalistic behavior."

His eyes went cold. "What did you do?"

I crossed my arms and leaned against my pillow. I didn't want to talk about it, but he'd hear about it soon enough. "I attacked him."

"You *what?!*"

"I tried to kill him."

"Oh, ho, ho!" He laughed nervously, dipping low to stay close to me so I'd stay in the charm's radius. "Are you serious? With what weapon? The guards took everything away."

"I made my own weapons out of makeup brushes."

". . . And you *attacked* him?"

"Yeah."

"Wh- what did you do?"

I shrugged. "I tried to stab him in the neck. But it didn't work. It didn't pierce his skin."

Mephistopheles held his head as if it were about to explode. "Holy crap. First of all, I can't believe you'd do something like that. Props to you. I mean, for all my time here, I never had the balls to do that. And you just went for it! I seriously underestimated your crazy. But . . . you know he's a fallen angel. Only a mystical weapon would actually pierce his skin."

I huffed. "This is very useful information. I wish you'd said something about this *before* I attacked him."

He laughed. "I didn't know you were going to try to kill the Prince of Darkness! I mean, even his name should tell you that you can't kill him with a couple of pointy sticks."

I rolled my eyes. "Rub it in. I failed."

"No, I don't mean it like that." He gazed at me, serious. "The cool thing is that you tried."

I raised my eyebrows. So he really didn't like Lucifer. And the enemy of my enemy certainly was a friend.

He shook his head. "But it could've gotten you killed. What happened after that?"

I swallowed, conjuring the memory. "He ordered me to be locked away until my 'transformation was complete.' I think it convinced him I was turning evil."

He shrugged. "Maybe that's for the best. You'll have plenty of time to make a thought charm of your own."

He wagged a finger at me. "After you make my love charm, that is."

"About that." I glanced down at the bed. "I'll need to borrow your thought charm again. Otherwise, he'll hear me making the love charm."

He grimaced as if in pain. "Can you do it with me in the room?"

Something clenched in the pit of my stomach as I tried to think of an excuse. "I can't. I need to concentrate."

His eyebrows twitched. "Are you saying you can't concentrate with me in the room?"

I sighed heavily.

"Fine," he said. "As long as you make the love charm. But if what you said is true, I can't keep coming here." He glanced at the door, frowning.

"Are you in trouble?" I asked. Even though I didn't trust him and he disgusted me, I'd actually started to look forward to his visits. The break in monotony was refreshing.

"I hope not. I don't do well in solitary confinement."

I huffed. "Me neither."

"Right. Sorry. But," he reached in his pocket and passed me a brown plastic oval, roughly the size of my palm. "There's another way for us to talk. Since you owe me the best love charm ever made, I'm lending you this."

I shot him a questioning glance.

"Open it."

I pried the plastic disk and it hinged open. I gazed at a circular mirror, expecting to see my reflection, but the mirror was black.

A high-pitched chime sounded from his pocket.

"I have the other one." He dug it out, opened it, and showed me. The mirrors were no longer dark — they reflected our faces in each other.

"Think of it as a two-way radio, only in mirror form. When my charm is finished, this is how you can let me know."

I swallowed and nodded. "I'll need my—"

"I know. I'll get your damn books."

"Thank you."

"And keep the mirror close." He shot me a fleeting smile, then walked toward the door.

I half-smiled, starting up my prayers again. Soon, I'd have my books, and with them, a knife. And with that knife, another chance at freedom — at killing the guards or ending it all if I became evil.

Later that day, someone else began making and delivering my meals instead of Mephistopheles. A barely heated microwave dinner was slid under the door slot without silverware or napkins. I gazed at the mashed potatoes, gelatinous saline-rich gravy, freezer-burnt vegetables, and mystery meat, and banged on the door. "You have to be kidding me. I can't eat this!"

There was no response.

"Come on. What can I do to get some fruit or chocolate? Please?"

The guards grunted in amusement, but otherwise, ignored me.

Eventually I gave in and picked at the mushy food with my fingers. With the first bite of potatoes, my palate felt brined. I flung the food off my fingers. I wondered if I'd ever have fine food again. I missed traveling so much. I'd kill for a cup of perfectly brewed Earl Grey and a flaky cheese danish, a wide sky above me as I walked to a cathedral. But this was my life now.

I dug my fingers into the peas and crinkle-cut carrots, determined to eat something healthy. My fingers touched something hard beneath them. I brushed the peas off a piece of parchment wrapped in plastic wrap. My fingers trembled as I opened it.

Hold tight, Belle

I gasped, staring at the ornamental script. It couldn't be from Donovan, unless he had someone on the inside. Could it be Mephistopheles? Was they planning to break me out? My heart fluttered in anticipation and a smile crept over my face. I knew Mephistopheles was a good guy. All his bravado was just a mask. Somehow, through this awful situation, I'd made a friend. He'd figure out how to free me, and I'd be free to run to Donovan's safehouse.

I walked to the candle and held the note over the fire until it caught, then dropped the flaming paper onto the stone floor. I didn't want any trace of it in case anyone searched my cell. Then I packed my things into my satchel and slung it around my shoulder. I wanted to be ready as soon as he came for me.

Two days later, on my sixth day of imprisonment, Mephistopheles burst into my cell. I ran across the room to be close to him, within the charm's radius, grateful for a break in my prayers. My heart hammered as my thumb ran over the strap of my satchel. It must be time — he was rescuing me, just like his note said. I ventured a peek around the cell door. Two fat orcs asleep on the flagstones, faintly snoring.

"I gave them Ambien milkshakes," Mephistopheles said, his dark eyes lit up. "There's enough in there to knock out a whale."

"I can't believe this is really happening." I grinned, taking a step forward.

He pushed me back into my cell, his eyes wide. "Get back. If the patrolling guards saw you out, we'd both be skinned." He hauled an armful of books from the hallway and set them on the floor of my cell.

I blinked at him. "But— Is now not a good time?"

"No. Is it ever a good time around here?" He hauled in another armful and drew close to me, breathing heavily as he blocked the exit.

I searched his eyes but didn't find anything besides his usual business-like demeanor. No sign of conspiracy or camaraderie. Something inside me wilted. Maybe the note wasn't from him. But if not him, who sent it? Who else had access to my meals? Who would risk everything to give me a little bit of hope?

"I couldn't fit all of your books in one trip." He panted, his breath hot against my cheek. "Please tell me I brought the book you need for the spell."

I looked through my books, my heart sinking. Not only was I not leaving Hell today, but neither *Practical Magic*, nor my hidden knife, were among the books he'd brought. I shook my head. "You didn't get the right one."

"Damn it!" He kicked the pile of books, sending some skittering across the room. "What color is it? Red? Blue?" He scratched his head, beads of sweat forming on his brow.

"Um . . ." I turned away from him, drifting as far away as I dared while still being near his thought charm. I could see the book in my mind — the black cover with Sandra Bullock and Nicole Kidman on the cover, but I couldn't tell him about it. I didn't want him to know what to look for — he might find the knife stashed inside. I ran my hands through my hair. "I can't remember."

"You really don't remember?"

"No. Just please bring all of them the next time."

"Whatever, princess." He bowed mockingly before sliding through the door, his eyes watchful until he was out of sight. The metal locks clinked in place behind him.

I plopped on my bed and gazed at my pile of books. Normally, they were my best source of escapism, but now, I couldn't bring myself to read any of them. One of them stood out, though. A green one with embossed

BELLE DAME SANS MERCI

flowers lay on top, a black pen in the middle where I'd written my last journal entry. I picked up the book and let it fall open to my neat cursive handwriting.

> I'm so excited to go to Heaven!
> Maybe I'll get released tomorrow.
> I hope I get to go there with
> Jane. I can't imagine Heaven
> without her. But then again,
> I'll be so happy, it won't matter.
> And seeing my family

I closed the book and slumped in my bed. I'd been so optimistic. So stupid. I'd trusted that the system worked, that Lucifer had good intentions. I was so naive. Not anymore. Now, I knew the system was rigged. Lucifer didn't want to release anyone to Heaven because he'd have one fewer demon to boss around. It all came down to control for him — control over karma, control over who was killed, control over what I could and couldn't do.

I hunched forward, opened the book again, and un-capped the pen. My hand hovered over the page, then my words poured out of me like a waterfall. I wrote down everything that had happened to me, from the day I got the message to go to the Devil's Office to my orders from Lucifer. I wrote about killing Carlo, about Lucifer's meaty hands around my neck, and my 'dance with the devil.' I wrote and wrote, until the candlestick burned out, and I had to replace it with a fresh one. I wrote for hours, until my hand cramped, and still, I kept writing.

I wanted some kind of record, something to remind me of my former self if I became a monster. I might never look at my journal again if I turned evil, but it could help me one day, if I ever came out the other side of it.

Finally, I wrote a letter to Jane and put it in the front of the book. She might be the only one who'd care enough to help me. I needed all the help I could get.

The next night, the panel at the bottom of my cell door opened with a groan, only instead of an MSG-laden meal, a stack of books scraped across the floor. I jumped out of bed and ran to the door, crouching low, hopeful that tonight was the night.

"I only have a moment." Mephistopheles grunted, shoving more books in. "I gave the guards tainted chocolate. They'll be in the bathroom for a while, but I can't do anything like that again. They're not complete idiots." He shook his head and drew a deep breath. "I can't stay, but I checked your astrolabe. Venus is in Scorpio in two days. That's what you need, right?"

My heart thumped harder. "Right."

"Call me when it's done." He stood, his black wingtip shoes visible through the flap.

"Wait!" I called out.

He bent over. "What?" His frown was barely visible in the dim hallway light.

I bit my lip. "Open the door. I want to talk with you." I thought about the hunk of meat I'd saved from lunch. Cerberus would have to take it. It was my only chance.

Mephistopheles made a face. "I can't. The guards have the keys, and they're not here."

I bit my lip, trying not to let disappointment show in my eyes. "When can you get me out of here?" I squeaked.

He laughed and stood. A moment later, his steps echoed down the hallway.

I got up, crossing my arms, my prayers starting up again. Of course he wouldn't free me. What had I been thinking? The more I thought about it, the less likely that note was from him — the handwriting was too neat, too eloquent to be his. His handwriting probably looked spidery, or it'd be illegible — if he even knew how to write.

I moved the books inside, scanning them for the black cover of *Practical Magic*. My heart leapt when I found it, right in the middle of a stack. I jimmied it out, my fingers caressing the soft golden pages. When I flipped the cover back, I expected to see my trusty snakeskin switchblade in the carved-out hollows. It wasn't there. There was, however, something about the size of my thumb wrapped in red paper. I unwrapped it. His quartz thought charm fell into my palm, cool and sparkling. Written on the paper were tiny letters.

FOR THE LOVE CHARM
~ M

I took a deep breath and leaned against the headboard. He wasn't going to rescue me — his handwriting was different from whoever had slipped the note in my food. Even worse, Mephistopheles had said that Venus would be in the 'right sign' in two days. Just my luck. I'd guessed the wrong sign.

I rolled over and tucked into a ball, a sinking feeling hollowing me out. I'd thought my lies had given me more time, but the moon would be full in three days.

What would he do when he found out I wasn't really a witch?

CHAPTER SIXTEEN

I ran my fingers over the symbols on the golden pages of my astrolabe. It told me the moon would reach its apex tomorrow morning at 7:14 am. By that time, Lucifer would either think I was fully evil, or he'd find out I hadn't turned. If what Mephistopheles had said was true, he'd make me kill Jane to ensure I went evil this time. My throat closed up just thinking about it. I'd rather stab myself than kill her. Maybe I could beg for her life. If only I had more weapons, more resources, more time.

I sighed, my eyes glazing over at the stone walls surrounding me. Maybe it was inevitable that I'd become evil. Would the evil me enjoy being a demon and doing Lucifer's bidding? I doubted it. I wondered if I'd ever enjoy anything again, or if my existence would become even more hellish.

I prayed to Donovan and God and anyone who'd listen. There was no response. Tonight was my last night.

There'd been no more chances to escape — no more candlelight dinners with Lucifer, no more walks in the labyrinthine hallways. Mephistopheles had been my last hope to escape, but he didn't look promising, either. He hadn't visited lately, preferring instead to communicate through the mirror. I still kept hope up, though. Something in my gut told me there was more to him. He'd seemed so nice at times — friendly, even, and no one in Hell was nice. I thought Jane and I were the only ones until I got to know him. But maybe he was nice because he wanted something from me.

I wrote in my journal until a chime from the magic mirror rang out. I opened it with trembling hands.

Mephistopheles' black eyes twitched in the mirror, and the veins in his neck looked strained. "It's almost the full moon. You'd better be done with my love charm."

I rolled my eyes in mock frustration and sighed. "You just interrupted me. Now I'll have to start all over again."

His fist banged hard onto a surface. "Damn it, Belle! How long does it take to make a simple love charm?"

I held up my diary, opened to the page I'd just written on.

Break me out of here, and I'll make

all the charms you'll ever need.

I lowered the book and glanced at him cautiously.

"I'm beginning to suspect," he narrowed his eyes at me, his jaw set, "that you can't make anything at all!"

I blinked, grasping for anything that might endear me to him. "Do you feel nothing for me? I thought we had a connection." It was the last straw, the one I didn't want to use. The damsel in distress. *La Belle Dame.*

He breathed through clenched teeth. "If I wanted *you,* why would I ask for a love charm for *someone else*?!"

Tears flushed in my eyes, hot and desperate. "Is there anything I could give you? What about my soul? You could have it."

His face hardened. "It's already damned. You have nothing to offer me except for that charm." He shook his head, his eyes turning colder. "You know, I feel sorry for you. Killing your best friend tomorrow morning will be really hard. And who knows — maybe right after you slit Jane's throat, you'll turn evil, driven mad by the deed. Or maybe, you'll lie around in a cell until the next full moon, waiting twenty-eight more days to turn evil . . ."

I stared at him, unwilling to let myself think about that.

He cracked his knuckles. "Only, if you screw me over,

I won't let you off that easily. I'll tell Lucifer your name. That way, he won't have to wait for the next moon cycle. He'll be able to command your soul like THAT." He snapped his fingers. "Unless you finish that charm TONIGHT."

The thought of being trapped in my cell for another moon cycle weighed on me like a leaden blanket, but it might mean another chance for escape. Only, I'd be evil for sure at the next full moon. But Donovan might be able to help if I got out. He could take some of the bad karma away.

My best chance for escape was still with Mephistopheles. I gazed at his angry eyes. "I'll finish it tonight."

"Midnight." He glared at me coldly. "Not a minute later."

The mirror went silent and dark. It fell from my hands and onto the blanket as I slumped against my pillows. He wasn't the ally I'd hoped for, but I couldn't blame him. I'd lied to him about being a witch. I could only imagine what he'd think when he found out my love charm was nothing more than a trinket.

I pocketed the mirror and clutched my diary against my chest. I hoped it would remind me of my former self when I turned evil. At least then I could look back at my life and know who I was.

Shuffling and grunting noises sounded outside the door. The *clang* of a sword on a shield rang out. I sat up, muscles tensed. I shoved my journal into my satchel and threw it around my neck, just in case Mephistopheles changed his mind. I crouched, ready to fight, in case it was anyone else.

A metallic clattering of a sword falling on the flag-stones outside my door jarred me. My breath caught. Voices argued. Then the door sizzled and hissed. Smoke trailed into my cell. I coughed.

BANG!

My cell door exploded off its hinges. I shielded myself as shrapnel whizzed over my head. My ears rang with a high-pitched noise.

A shadowy figure jumped over the door, ran through the smoky room, and clamped his fingers around my arm. I tried to make out who it was, but he wore a black ninja mask. He was too short to be Mephistopheles. I pulled back, but he was strong. I aimed a kick at his stomach and my foot struck his belly. He reeled back, bent over. Another figure materialized from the smoke and grabbed me around the waist, hauled me onto his shoulders, and took off running.

"Wait!" I squirmed in his grasp. "Let me go!"

But his strong arms held me tight, his collarbone digging into my ribs. A quiver of arrows jostled in my face. He ran over the door and into the hall, dodging something dark on the floor. A giant green ogre and the orc who'd guarded me lay sprawled out on their backs, immobile.

"Set her down," a feminine voice said.

My captor bent over and my toes touched the stone floor. In the flickering torchlight, I saw a tall woman, her honey-colored hair falling around her angular face and onyx-black eyes. I gasped. It was the witch who'd given me the note weeks ago, Medea. Surrounding us were women of all ages and races. Some wore hoods, others wore masks that covered everything but their eyes. Every one of them brandished a weapon. Knives, shields, and hunting bows glinted in the wavering light.

A jolt ran through my body, from my toes to the top of my head. I'd been rescued!

One woman stepped forward and pulled back a brown hood, revealing cotton-white hair and a face with more lines on her papery skin than I could count. "Can you run, Belle?" Her voice creaked.

"Yes. But who are you?"

"Not now." Medea said, glancing over her shoulder. "The means-station is going to expire soon, and it's our only way out. You have to trust us."

"Come on!" the woman in the ninja mask shouted. "We're losing time!"

We ran through the hallways, around damp corners and cob-webbed halls. Beside the ninja, another woman wound a red string into a ball as we ran.

After a couple of minutes, we reached a means-station. Its ominous red borders cast a vermillion shade on the halls.

I paused in front of it. "Where does it go?"

"Topside. Get in."

A petite woman with short brown hair frowned, her eyes focused on her watch. "I don't know," she said in an Irish brogue. "The station expires in three minutes."

I gaped at her. "But that's how long it takes to—"

"GET IN!" shouted Medea, her black eyes panicked.

We squeezed in and shut the doors. Medea stomped on a red button on the floor. The lift rose and picked up speed. Gravity pushed down on my head and shoulders. I tried to make eye contact with the group, but no one looked at me. My heart beat irregularly as I thought of the unthinkable. "What happens if the shaft closes before we make it to the top?"

The woman in the ninja mask pulled it off, revealing a pile of curly orangish-red hair and a pale, heart-shaped face with a snub nose. "Do you really have to ask? By the way, do you always kick people who rescue you?"

"Quiet, Kelsey," Medea said. Her black eyes flashed at me, almost liquid in the low light. "Now that we have a moment, I can answer some of your questions. My name is Medea and this is my coven. We rescued you because we heard about your predicament."

"But . . . how did you know I was there?"

"An anonymous tip." She brushed dried blood off her

tunic. "Apparently, someone thinks you're worth saving."

I drew in a quick breath. Donovan must've told them I'd been captured. Maybe he'd be waiting for me when we got topside. But what if the worst-case scenario came true? My rescuers deserved to know about the possibility of my turning evil, just in case. I gazed at the floor grate, my heart beating faster as I tried to find the words. "There's something you should know."

"Not now," Medea said. "Let's just get through this and get to the safehouse. Then we can talk." She turned her black eyes to stare intently at the door.

I nodded. We still had a few hours before the full moon.

We sped through the earth, higher and higher. I tried not to count the seconds, but I couldn't help it. The minutes ticked by, and still we climbed through more and more layers of earth.

When the brake sparks finally leapt over our heads, my heart burst into light. Every nerve in my body pulsed as the elevator slowed, then stopped with a loud *ding!*

"Hurry! Get out," someone yelled. "It's about to expire!"

The women started running off the lift into a dimly lit, wide room. I peered between them, waiting for my turn. At last, it was just me and a woman with blue hair in front of me. She ran over the blue and white flickering flames, but tripped and fell on her long skirt. Her face was on the ground, her fanny was in the air, and her leg was cocked up at a strange angle, blocking the way out.

"Get up!" I shouted.

"I can't. My ankle's twisted!"

I couldn't make it over her. I shot desperate eyes at the women beyond.

The sound of rocks and earth slamming together echoed throughout the chamber. The flames around the means-station border flickered lower.

Medea's eyes grew large and she ran toward us. "Belle! Get out of there!"

The banging came closer and closer.

I heaved the woman's legs up and threw them on the other side of the lift, then leapt from the station. The walls crunched as they closed behind me.

Fire and lava consumed the means-station in a molten black mass. After a few seconds, it died down into a gray rectangle with blue flickering flames that faded away. In the elevator's place was a normal-looking beige-tiled wall, matching the surrounding walls exactly. The only traces of the means-station were the lingering wisps of smoke.

"Sorry." The woman with the blue hair shuffled up to stand on the lacquered wooden floor. She adjusted her skirt and shrugged. "I didn't mean to bungle the landing back there. I'm Helga, by the way."

"It's okay." I breathed deep and stood. "We made it

out."

Every bone in my body hurt. I strode in the direction the witches had run. Two basketball hoops stood like sentinels at either end of the room. The smell of rubber and sweat stung my nose. "Where are we?"

"A high school in Sweden." Helga limped down a fluorescent-lit hallway lined with more beige tiles. "But we aren't staying here. We have to keep moving, or we'll be caught. Come on." She waved at me.

"But—"

"Are you deaf?" Kelsey sneered at me, her red hair gleaming, even in the dim light. "We have to move. They can trace means-stations. Come on."

I hustled down the hallway after Kelsey and Helga. They pushed through heavy metal doors and walked outside down a flight of concrete steps.

Outside, eight women stood in a parking lot a few yards away, each of them holding a broom as they evaluated the starry black sky. The Irish witch glanced at her watch and pointed to the sky. "We'll travel east, about two hundred kilometers from here."

Medea held a broom out to me. "You'll be wanting this, Belle."

I took it from her, the rough pine branch scraping against my palm. It looked just like the brooms made in my village centuries ago, with braided straw bound with string at the end. I swallowed. Surely they knew I wasn't a witch. "What am I supposed to do with this?"

"Have you never flown on a broom?" Her eyebrows rose.

I shook my head.

She sighed. "You'll have to learn tonight."

I drew back from her. "But I can't fly. I'm— I'm not a witch."

"Humor me and get on the broom," she said.

I acquiesced and sat on it side-saddle, my legs on the same side. My hands wrapped around the top of the branch.

Kelsey laughed at me, her voice tinkling with glee. "Are you trying to fall off your broom? Because that's how you fall off your broom."

I pressed my lips together but lifted a leg over it and sat astride on the hard wood. The bark scratched against my thighs. If only they'd given me enough time to change into pants.

"Hold it like this." Medea placed my hands lower, thumbs up. "Now arch yourself forward. Flying is about willpower — the *will* to move forward. Try it."

I leaned forward, but I knew what would happen — the same thing that'd happened countless nights as I tried to fly from the multiple rooftops all over the world. Absolutely nothing. I shook my head.

"Try again."

I tried again, but only felt silly.

Kelsey eyed my lack of progress with cruel brown eyes. "I told you she wasn't one of us."

Medea sighed. "Fine. Since you're such a smartass, she'll ride with you."

Kelsey glared at her, then turned to me, scowling. "Better not fall off. I won't come back for you."

Medea pointed her finger at Kelsey, her expression severe. "You'd better not let her."

Kelsey muttered.

"Time to fly!" shouted the Irish witch. "They're coming."

"Scoot back." Kelsey shooed me, then sat on the broomstick in front of me. "Hold onto my waist, like you're on the back of a motorcycle."

I put my hands lightly on her ribcage.

"Not like that!" she barked.

I huffed. "I've never ridden on a motorcycle before!"

"Oh gods, you're one of those!" She tossed her flame-colored hair over her shoulder. "Just put your arms around my waist and—"

"They're here!" the Irish witch shouted.

The school doors flew open. Shadowy figures darted down the steps.

The witches soared into the sky, as quick as dragonflies. One of them shot lightning from her palm, making the streetlamps explode with a cascade of sparks.

"Clasp your hands around me!" Kelsey shouted.

"NOW!"

I clenched my hands. She kicked off and we catapulted up, into the air. I slid backwards, toward the earth. A spike of adrenaline rushed into my nerves as I tightened my grip, my muscles clenching hard. The ground grew smaller and smaller below us.

Demons glared up at us, Lucifer among them. Even at that height, I could see his fuming black eyes and his horns, extended to their fullest height.

"BELLE!" he called out. "YOU CAN RUN, BUT YOU CAN'T HIDE!"

His voice rattled in my ears as if he were three feet away instead of three hundred.

Kelsey swooped higher into the crisp night air into a sky as dark as velvet. More stars shone in the darkness, twinkling and pulsating. The other witches surrounded us, leveling out at the same height. We flew together toward the cratered, ivory moon.

I spit out a piece of Kelsey's hair that kept flying into my mouth. "Where are we going?"

"Somewhere safe." Her voice was hard, bitter. "You're a fugitive. I hope you like running, because that's your life from now on."

CHAPTER SEVENTEEN

My arms wrapped tightly around Kelsey as we flew. The sky was so silent, so pure. I'd never seen anything like it before. Clouds whipped by like bits of lace, and our only companions were a flock of geese making their way south in a V-formation.

I was free again! And flying in the air on a broomstick with a coven of witches! My heart took flight, and tears ran down my cheeks, crystalizing in the chilled night air. I breathed it all in with gratitude. Even my shivers from the chilly air felt wonderful compared to the cell I'd been locked in. I prayed to Donovan, glancing around the sky for any sign of him darting between the clouds, but he was nowhere to be found. Maybe once we were on the earth again, I could call him.

Without warning, Kelsey tipped the broom down, in synchronicity with the other witches. We plummeted, zooming toward a circle of towering pine trees and a grassy clearing. I tried not to scream, clasping Kelsey and pressing my face into her red-gold curls. I slipped forward and tried to squeeze the broom as tightly as I could. Kelsey leaned back into me and then something rumbled under my boots. We stopped.

I stood up tentatively, my legs wobbly. I felt dizzy, as if I'd been on a spinning top the entire time. I wondered if I'd get sick.

Kelsey stood and looked back at my boots, caked with mud and grass. Behind us, the lawn was ripped-up with two tracks where my boots had dug in.

"Noob." She laughed.

The others dismounted in a run or hovered a couple of feet above the ground before jumping off their brooms gracefully. They started walking down a path. I stepped over the broom, too stunned to respond.

"You're okay," Kelsey said. "Just catch your breath."

I bent over and breathed in wet earth, dew-sparkled grass, and pine sap, and started to feel better. The circle of pine trees swayed, brushing the sky as they tossed in the gentle wind. Above them was an almost-translucent purple net swaying along with the trees. It looked like it was made of interlocking circles that formed flowers.

"What's that?" I asked.

"Ultraviolet protection."

"Protection from what?"

"You know, from Lucifer hearing our thoughts and

from demons finding us. Come on." She wandered down a path, her shoes crunching on the pea-gravel.

I looked for Donovan in the sky again but only saw the nearly full moon. I wondered if the ultraviolet net was keeping him out. I couldn't blame the witches for that, though — they needed to have a safe space.

An owl hooted from the tree nearby, possibly as spooked of me as I was of it. I ran to catch up with Kelsey. Around the corner, in another clearing, sat a two-story log cabin bordered by gnarled juniper bushes and rocky herb gardens.

I followed Kelsey up three cement steps and through an oak door. When I shut it behind me, I was stunned to see ten different types of locks jingling. Kelsey set her broom against the wall among the others, beneath a sign.

Witch parking only.
All others will be toad.

Women lounged in a living room stuffed to the brim with couches, sofas, and armchairs, all covered with colorful afghans and a fine layer of dust and cat hair. Cobwebs spun over the white walls, connecting the framed needlepoints to the ceiling. A broad bookcase stuffed with weathered tomes took up almost half of one wall. Some of the spines were so deteriorated, they were falling off. A brunette witch knelt in front of the fireplace, blowing on lit kindling, while another held pieces of wood. A long counter and a stove were visible in the next room.

But the most striking feature about the cabin was the cats. There must've been a dozen or so, striding over the stained rag rug, brushing against ankles, and jumping on laps. A husky orange tabby head-butted the hem of my skirt with a throaty, "*mrrrrow.*"

Medea held a black-and-white kitten against her lavender sweater. "Ah, that's better," she sighed. When she looked at me again, her black eyes seemed more invigorated. "Do you know how to draw energy from them?"

I reached down to stroke the marmalade cat's thick fur. "You can draw energy from cats?"

"Mm hm. The Egyptians figured it out long ago." The mewling kitten jumped onto the floor and scampered away. Medea nodded to the hallway beyond. "We have a lot to talk about. Let's go somewhere private."

She led me into a small bedroom with a rocking chair, a dresser, and a double bed with a blue quilt. I sat on the bed as she closed the door. There was something severe about her expression, and it wasn't just her black eyes. She had a weight about her, like something sad was pulling her down. She sat in the rocking chair.

I fidgeted with my hands. "Who lives here?"

"None of us live here, but we use the place from time to time. It's a safehouse, spelled with cloaking mechanisms. A neighbor takes care of the cats, but she won't bother us now." She stared at me, her mouth turning down. "Belle, do you have any reason to believe you might turn evil at the full moon?"

I took a deep breath, grateful she'd brought it up, but not knowing where to start. "I don't think so, but . . . Lucifer did make me kill an innocent. Sort of — *he* stabbed him, not me. His hands were around mine when it happened."

She nodded solemnly. "I see."

"Do you think it'll count against me?" I bit my lip.

She glanced at a ticking clock on the wall, then back at me. "Do you feel evil? Tell the truth."

The black coiling thing inside me leapt up. I shrugged. "I'm not sure. I have bad urges sometimes, but it passes."

She nodded. "Time will tell. But better temps than you have turned evil." She pulled out a burner phone and showed me the screen. I leaned close to read it.

```
Belle Dame: 99.1% bad, 0.9% good
```

I grimaced, though it could've been worse. It appeared my prayers had worked after all, and kicking Kelsey didn't count too much against me. But still, it was pretty bad.

"Belle, you'll have to be very careful. If you went evil in our safehouse, you might try to kill us all. We'd have to put you down. Do you understand?"

"Yes, of course." The thought of killing my saviors made me feel sick. I took a few deep breaths.

"We'll also have to watch you to make sure you don't turn before the full moon. It's nothing personal."

I nodded. "I understand. I'd do the same thing in your place."

"Good. I can see you have questions for me," she said, her voice clear. "Go ahead."

"Um . . . Yeah. So, you said this is your coven?"

"Yes, but every witch who's here wants to be here. You have that right too. You can walk out of here and forget all about us. But if you leave our protection, I have no doubt the demons will find you, and I don't think you want to go back to Hell."

"No. I really don't want to be a demon. Um, so, is this the way Lucifer recruits all his guards?"

Her brows furrowed. "What do you mean?"

I cleared my throat and swallowed. Someone laughed in the other room. I tried to find the words. "Why couldn't he just ask me if I wanted to be a guard? Why go through all this — kidnapping me and trying to make me turn evil, just to be a guard?"

Medea stood and ran a hand over her face as she paced. "That's not why he kidnapped you, Belle."

I stared at her. "Why else would he lock me up? He made me kill an innocent to try to make me evil."

"Yes, but that wasn't to make you one of his guards." Her voice was hard. "He has plenty of those."

My mind raced. What else could he want? To make me an archdemon? But those demons worked for millennia before they were promoted. Not even Mephistopheles was one of those.

"Are you really that naïve?" She leaned forward, her head tilting. "He wants to make you *his mistress*."

I sat back, my mouth falling open. So that was why he'd treated me so well, and the dinner and dancing — so he could rip my personality away when I turned evil and make me fall in love with him by being the only 'nice guy' around. And all this time, Mephistopheles allowed me to think he wanted me to be a guard! I wanted to punch his smug face in, the liar. My inner darkness roiled. I felt my eyes turn black.

"Belle, you're changing. Come back."

I shook my head. My eyesight cleared.

She leaned forward, her eyes fierce. "You cannot let yourself go like that."

"I'm sorry. I got angry. Someone lied to me."

"You need to resist giving into your demonic form." She sighed. "An outburst like that could take over, and you could turn evil. You need to learn control. This is why we can't let you have a weapon right now. I hope you understand."

I nodded. "I won't let it happen again."

Medea nodded and held up her hands. "But . . ." she evaluated me, "am I right in assuming you weren't interested in becoming Lucifer's mistress? You can tell the truth."

"No," I sputtered. "I could never be with him. Not after what he did, the lies he told. I still want to go to Heaven."

She laughed. "That's about as likely as finding a unicorn on Antarctica."

I looked at her. With her coal-black eyes, she couldn't go to Heaven — they marked her as someone who was evil or once evil, and barred her for life. But my eyes were still human. I might still have a chance.

"There's something else I have to tell you about," I said, fidgeting with my hands in my lap. "An angel tried to save me before I was caught by the demons who took me back to Hell. We almost escaped to a halfway house."

She paused, her eyes wide. "You spoke to an angel?"

I nodded. "He was the one who told me about my score, and that my last target wasn't really bad. If it wasn't for him, I would've killed an innocent unknowingly. He saved me. He might still come for me." I glanced at the window.

"Belle, I don't want to be a downer." She looked at me pityingly. "But your angel probably thinks you've gone to the other side. Hardly anyone escapes the pits of Hell. Have you seen him since we broke you out?"

"No, but would the ultraviolet net keep him out?"

She shook her head. "It just keeps out demons and temps in Hell, unless we speak the words to let them in. He could've found you at any time, especially when we were flying. Did you pray to him?"

"Yeah, I did." I swallowed. I'd prayed *a lot.*

"Don't tell anyone about him. I mean it. Angels aren't exactly on the same side, even though we have the same enemy."

"Okay." If what she'd said was right, Donovan was too good to be true after all.

"So, do you want to stay here with us while we figure out a plan?"

"Stay here in the cabin? What about the vapors?"

"We stored a few canisters here. You should take one of the vials in the closet, and keep it on you, just in case we have to flee."

"But those canisters will run out."

She nodded. "We'll go back for more vapor."

"Wait. You're going to go back to Hell? After breaking me out?"

"Yes. We must keep up appearances so they don't think we stole you. We're not the only witches in the world, you know."

I gaped at her. There was so much I didn't know about them. What else could she say to surprise me?

She cleared her throat. "If you stay, and if you're not evil, we'll protect you. We'd need you to increase your karma score, of course. That means doing chores around the house and the garden. After we know you're not evil, we might teach you a few spells, and flying, of course."

"But I told you before. I'm not really a witch."

Something sparkled in her eyes. "I think you might just be. Why don't you try to prove me wrong?"

My chest tingled. I'd always wanted to learn magic. It'd been my dream ever since I was a child. "As long as you're sure I won't hurt anyone."

"We'll save the offensive magic for a later time. When your soul is less . . ." Her mouth twisted.

I nodded. "I understand. I can't bear to think of what I would've become had you not rescued me. I can't thank you enough."

"You're welcome. I only wish someone had saved me when I was in your position."

My mouth fell open. "You were his mistress?"

She lifted her haunted black eyes to meet mine. "For twenty years. I detested every minute of it. He was cruel."

I wanted to reach for her hand. "I'm so sorry. But

you're not evil anymore."

"No."

I hesitated, but I had to ask. The full moon was so close, and I had to know what I might turn into. "Do you mind if I ask what it felt like when you were evil?"

She gazed out the window thoughtfully. "I remember those days almost like a child trapped in a well, looking out and seeing things happening, with no control over them. I reacted with anger to everything. I didn't know who I was, but I didn't love him. He told me if I tried to love him, he'd give me my memories back, of who I was before he did that to me. Of course, he never followed through. We fought every minute of every day. After what felt like a lifetime, Persephone returned and made him drop me. By then, it was too late. My soul was tarnished."

"How'd you come back from being evil?"

She shrugged sadly. "I did whatever I could. I worked for centuries at more soup kitchens than I can remember, and helped the poorest of the poor, all the while wearing a mask to hide my evil features. I know I'll never get into Heaven, but at least I'm not an animal anymore. And all my old features have returned, except for my eyes."

I shook my head. "What did he think would happen? That you'd love him?"

She nodded, sniffing back tears. "He expected me to

fill the void Persephone left. I was his prisoner. I couldn't escape. There were demons behind every door, guarding my every move." Her moist black eyes focused on me as she gave me a sad smile. "It's in the past. But four months ago, Persephone left him again. That's when I noticed him looking into you."

"Where'd she go?"

"Back to her mother's realm, Olympus."

"Is that the same as Heaven?"

"No, it exists independently."

"But aren't there legends about her going back there every year?" I asked.

Her shoulders sank. "Maybe that happened in the beginning, but Persephone is a demi-goddess and Lucifer is a fallen angel. They've lived so long that a calendar year is nothing to them. Or maybe their concept of a year is just longer now. In any case, she stays away until she finds it in her heart to forgive him. I don't blame her. He's a beast."

"Help me understand something." I smiled nervously. "I see why Lucifer would want you. You're a powerful witch. But why would he want me? I'm nothing. I can't even do magic."

"Belle, I had no magic when he took me. All of that came later. But I think you underestimate yourself. When you stalk your victims, you exercise a bit of charm over them."

I shook my head, but something gave me pause. The *Belle Dame* thing I did — it'd always worked. I'd gotten my way and made the kill. I looked at her. Could it be true? All this time, I'd thought my success with those conquests had been because of a pretty face. Had I been wielding an enchantment all along?

"It's crass compared to our magic, of course," she smirked. "But it's still magic."

"Really? Are you sure?"

She nodded. "You don't know how powerful you are, Belle." She hesitated, eyeing me hopefully. "I've just given you a lot of information. What do you say? Do you want to join the rebellion against Lucifer? We can protect you."

"But what help would I possibly be to a bunch of witches who are more powerful than I can even imagine? I can't fight. I'm too close to being evil."

"I still think you can help us. If you join us, you'd be part of our sisterhood."

I bit the inside of my cheek. They'd taken a huge risk, breaking me out of the dungeons. It was a brave act, and I owed them. Plus, I needed their protection. It wasn't like I could run from Lucifer and all his guards — they'd follow me to the ends of the earth. But something still nagged at the back of my mind. I knew Lucifer would probably kidnap someone else and do the same thing he'd done to Medea, the same thing he'd tried to do to me. I couldn't accept that. He had to be stopped, no matter what the price.

"I appreciate the offer of protection and sisterhood, but I want more than that."

"What's that?"

I gazed steadily into her dark eyes. "I don't just want to join the rebellion. I want to kill the Beast."

CHAPTER EIGHTEEN

"You want to take down Lucifer?" Medea stared at me, her eyes wide. "But we don't know the consequences. You might turn evil! You might be barred from Heaven forever."

"I know." I gave her a weak smile. "I'm willing to take that chance. When I tried to kill him last week—"

"Wait. You already tried to kill him?!"

"Yeah, but it didn't work. My shivs didn't pierce his flesh. Mephistopheles even made fun of me because he said that kind of weapon wouldn't kill Lucifer."

"Ugh, that creep?" She frowned. "He checked on me when I was Lucifer's prisoner, even after he told him to stop."

"He's definitely a creeper. But what he said got me thinking. If we could get our hands on something magical, we could make a weapon to end Lucifer once and for all."

She shook her head. "Magic can't kill him. Witches from long ago tried. There was a war — it was before my time, but it raged for many years, and they were very powerful. In the end, he wiped them all out, leaving almost no traces of their culture. There are spells we don't even know about because of the widespread destruction that happened there. You may have heard of the ancient civilization of Crete?"

I nodded. "So, maybe not a magical weapon, then. But maybe there's something else that would kill him. I can ask the angel."

She pulled back slightly. "Also, I can't promise the witches here will want to help you. You're asking them to risk their lives. Some of them have gotten used to the way things are."

"I know. I wouldn't ask them to help if it wasn't so important. We can't let him do this to anyone else."

"Yes, I understand the importance more than anyone else, I think." Her eyes watered for a moment before she blinked the tears away. "I'll stand with you, even if no one else does."

I smiled at her. At least I had one person to help me, and she was even a real witch.

She grasped me in a hug. "I'm glad to have you in the rebellion. Come on. Let's go celebrate your freedom."

We walked into the living room. Laughter and chatter rose above mesmerizing harp music. Some of the witches danced, while others sat on couches and chairs, stroking cats and lifting glasses of wine or tea to their lips. Candles flickered on coffee tables, and a rope of white Christmas lights glowed from a mantle strewn with Goddess figurines and statues. A fire crackled in the fireplace.

One of the dancing witches extended a hand toward me. I waved her off, my exhaustion overcoming me, and sat down heavily into a nearby sofa. I was happy to be safe, at least for the time being.

The older witch beside me finger-combed her long white hair with a liver-spotted hand. "Flying always gives me such terrible tangles," she said in a creaky voice.

The Irish witch, sitting in a nearby armchair, ruffled her pixie-cut brown hair. "That's why I keep mine like this." She smiled at me. "By the way, my name's Iona." She poured a goblet of garnet-red wine and handed it to me.

"Thank you." I lifted the glass and drank. The dark, oaky taste made me swoon, and after another sip, my belly warmed. Relaxation slid over my tense muscles.

The ancient witch gave me a gap-toothed smile. "I'm Claire."

"Nice to meet you," I said.

"You too," she crowed. "But, to be honest, dear, I feel like I've known you for a long time. We've been watching you for years."

I drew back. *Years?* "Really?"

She nodded. "Aye. Just in case the Beast took an interest in you. You're his type, you see. But now look at you — you're one of us!" She elbowed me, a grin lighting her lined face. "It's ironic, isn't it? When we were human, they accused us of working for the devil, but it's only *after* they killed us that we actually did!"

"Lucifer is a tool," Iona said. "But it's not really his fault. It's those damned big horns taking up so much room in that noodle of his! There's no room for anything else! By the way, we have three minutes."

"Three minutes," the witches whispered to each other.

Claire smiled and drew out a long, sharp knife from the sofa. Medea pulled a bow and quiver from the fireplace and nocked an arrow, drawing her arm back and aiming for my chest.

I looked around the room. Countless knives pointed at me. The witches had gathered in a circle around me, every single one of them holding a weapon except for Iona.

"What's going on?" My pulse raced.

Iona glanced up from her watch. "Two minutes until the full moon crests. Surely, you expected this, Belle. It's nothing personal."

"But . . . I thought I had until tomorrow morning."

"It already *is* tomorrow morning, just not here, where we are. We went ahead a few time zones. But trust me."

She looked at her watch again. "The moon is less than two minutes from being full."

Claire shrugged. "It's one of her powers."

I gave them a shaky smile, my eyes glazing over at the witches surrounding me. I supposed if I turned evil and had to be taken out, this would be the way I'd want to go. I bowed my head, my hands in my lap. "I understand. Do what you must."

I closed my eyes and thought of Jane, of her bright eyes and kind heart. What must she think of me now? That I was dead? My eyes flew open. "Wait!"

The witches stared at me, alert, on guard.

"One minute!" Iona called out.

"What is it?" Medea asked from behind her bow.

I blinked back tears. "Could one of you give my journal to my friend Jane if I turn evil? She's in the Poisoner Division. She'll want to know what happened to me. It's in my satchel."

Medea nodded. "I'll see that it's done."

"Thirty seconds!" Iona shouted.

I held my breath. A vicious smile lit up Kelsey's face. She looked as if she might lunge toward me with her hunting knife at any moment. I gazed at the floor, hoping I wouldn't turn evil. I thought of Jane, of Donovan, and my family in Heaven.

"Five. Four. Three. Two . . . *Happy full moon!*"

I slumped back with a sob of relief. All this time, I

hadn't known what would become of me, but I'd been saved. Maybe there really was a supreme being who saw that Carlo's death wasn't my fault, that I didn't deserve to be evil for all eternity. Maybe they were even rooting for me.

A collective cheer rose around the room.

Medea un-nocked the arrow and slid it back into her quiver. The witches put away their knives and weapons. Only Kelsey scowled in the corner, knife still drawn.

Medea tapped a fork against a wine glass. "Belle has decided to join us in this coven. She's our sister now, so make her feel welcome."

The magical harp music started up again, and more of the witches danced, holding hands and snaking around the room. I laughed, leaning back so they could weave around the sofa.

Iona reached out to hug me, a sweet smile on her face. "Good job, Belle."

Claire reached across the sofa and enfolded me in a light hug, her white hair soft against my face. "Congratulations, dear. You resisted the dark side!" She glanced at Kelsey, hovering nearby. "You can put that knife away now."

Kelsey's lips twitched down. She sheathed her knife into her belt, but kept her fingers on the handle. "There are some of us who believe people can turn evil after the full moon has crested. In my old circle, we counted the full moon as the day before, the day of, and the day after the full moon."

Claire's head tottered. "What are you trying to say?"

"I'm on house-guard duty, and it's late." Kelsey looked at her exasperatedly. "I think she should go to bed now."

"*Pssht!* No one believes that silly nonsense about 'three days of a full moon.' Not with people turning evil, anyway." Claire's hands made a shooing motion toward Kelsey. "She should celebrate her freedom. What do you care if she stays up talking to a couple of old witches?"

Kelsey's eyes bordered on mania. "I care because she could kill us all," she said through gritted teeth, "*and I want her to go to bed.*"

I sank back into the sofa, my lips pressing into a line. Why was she being like this? I didn't want to go to bed. I wanted to talk with the magical women I'd just met. I glared at Kelsey, knowing I couldn't trust everyone here. I'd have to watch her.

Claire set her wine goblet on the coffee table and stood up faster than I would've thought possible. She poked her finger in Kelsey's face. "Listen here—"

Iona stepped between them. "Kelsey, listen to your elders. We'll handle Belle for the time being. There you go, run along."

Kelsey's mouth twisted, but after a pause, she shot me a dirty look before throwing open the front door and walking out into the dark night. The door slammed shut behind her.

"Huh," Iona huffed. "Fire elementals!"

"We're not all like that." Claire made a face.

"Don't mind Kelsey." Iona chuckled. "She's just mad she's not the baby of the coven anymore."

I reached for my glass and took a big sip of wine. I didn't know if I believed them. There was something about Kelsey that was too edgy, too sharp. Just being in her presence made me nervous.

A white cat with sparkling green eyes jumped onto my lap. I ran my hands over its soft luxurious fur and it began to purr. One day, I might be able to take energy from a cat like the other witches did. I'd be able to learn magic, do spells, and maybe even even ride on a broomstick. My heart felt light looking around the room at my new friends.

Medea brought a new bottle of wine around and topped everyone off. Then she held her glass high and gazed at me, a small smile curving her lips. "A toast! To Belle."

"To Belle!" Everyone raised their glasses high and leaned in to clink them. The sound rang out through the little room.

I grinned. It was all so wonderful, so magical. I felt at home for the first time in centuries. The little cabin felt so warm, and I never wanted to go anywhere else ever again.

But I had a mission — to take down Lucifer, so he could never again do to another what he'd done to me and Medea. The thought of my cramped cell and Carlo's sacrifice made my determination stronger.

I stood up, glass in hand. "I have another toast. One I hope you'll join me in."

Some of the witches nodded. The dancers stopped twirling and turned their attention toward me.

My heart clenched as I tried to find the words. After everything I'd been through, all the threats and all the torture, I barely knew what to say. I took a deep breath.

"I'm tired of the way things are in Hell. We've been living too long at the mercy of a fascist dictator. If Lucifer can hold Medea prisoner for twenty years, kill innocents, hold me against my will, and turn heaven-track temporary demons evil, I say that's an abuse of power. I think he no longer deserves to be in charge."

Some of the witches nodded, while others stared at me, wide-eyed.

My heart pounded hard in my chest, but I raised my glass even higher. "To taking down Lucifer. Are you with me?"

Silence pervaded the room. Then, Medea stood and raised her glass. "To taking down Lucifer."

One by one, the witches raised their glasses, their steady gazes meeting mine.

"To taking down Lucifer!" they roared.

We clinked glasses one more time, and fresh determination sparked up within me. I drank, reveling in the taste of the velvety wine. I knew killing Lucifer might be impossible, but I also knew I'd do anything to make it happen. I just had to figure out how to kill the most powerful being in Hell. And of course, I'd truly have to earn the name *Belle Dame Sans Merci*. This time, I'd show no mercy. I'd make sure of it.

CHAPTER NINETEEN

The next morning, I lay in the narrow twin bed, effervescent with elation at the sunshine streaming in through the window. The voices of people carrying on with morning routines was music to my ears. Everything about my new situation in the safehouse felt like a miracle after my weeks in the dark dungeon. My head pounded from a little too much wine, but I didn't regret celebrating last night. I'd even danced after a while.

My shower last night was marvelous. I hadn't realized it at the time, but a reddish dust had clung to my skin the entire time I was imprisoned, making me feel slimy and clammy. Now, I felt fresh and optimistic, even though I could've slept for days longer. I didn't want to miss what smelled like a killer breakfast.

Something about last night bothered me. Despite our boisterous toast to take down Lucifer, I had no idea how we could kill him. All I knew was I was willing to do everything I could to try. Maybe I'd find something if I looked on the internet, or if Donovan ever came back, perhaps he could help me.

I opened the bedroom door and found Kelsey leaning against the wall, knife drawn, her mouth jerking into a frown. I hadn't seen her since she'd stormed out, when Claire and Iona had told her to relax. She didn't appear to have taken their advice. Something malicious flickered behind her eyes.

She pressed off the wall and strode toward me. "There she is. Feeling alright? You don't look so good."

"I'm fine." I walked around her.

The kitchen was lit with beams of sunlight filtering in through huge, smeared bay windows. It was easily the largest room in the cabin, with a round dining room table, several cupboards, a stout gas range, and a vintage blue refrigerator that gurgled and clicked from time to time. Bundles of dried herbs hung from nails all over the room, and an oversized farm sink held dirty dishes from the night before. Even though the ivory-tiled floor was dingy with stains and debris, the room was still magnificent. Jane would've loved it. I took a deep breath, hoping she was okay, and made a mental note to ask one of the witches to check on her.

"Morning, Belle!" In front of the stove, Iona cracked eggs into a heavy skillet sizzling with melted butter. "How many eggs?"

"Two, thank you."

She slid two over-easy eggs onto a plate with several pieces of sausage. I inhaled them along with a thick slice of whole wheat toast slathered with bilberry jam. "Where is everyone?"

"Back to work. No rest for the wicked," she sang, smiling.

I laughed. "Is there any tea?"

"Cupboard to my left." She took the frying pan to the sink.

"Please, let me wash up," I said, taking it from her. Washing dishes was a quick way to raise more karma, and my deficient soul couldn't be picky.

She laughed. "You won't hear an argument from me."

I searched the cupboard and found a rusty tin of stale black teabags — it wasn't Earl Grey, and it certainly wasn't Twinings, but it'd have to do. I boiled some water in the kettle and added a bag to a chipped cup. While it steeped, I ran the water in the sink, eagerly awaiting the tea. But after steeping, it tasted old and musty. I took only two sips before leaving it.

The sink soon filled with bubbles and I started washing. After finishing all the dirty dishes in the kitchen, I gathered the empty glasses from the living room, collected the trash, and scrubbed the spots on the kitchen counters. Kelsey surveilled my every step, arms crossed.

The house was in worse shape than I'd thought. I

couldn't help but notice mouse droppings on the floor and stains inside the cupboards. But I could gain back a lot of karma by cleaning it.

When I reached for a foul-smelling orange afghan in the living room near Kelsey, she sneered, refusing to move.

"Excuse me," I said.

"Am I in your way?"

My eyes darted around. Everyone else was in the kitchen. I gingerly picked up the blanket, eager to retreat back to them.

"Go ahead, Cinderella," she said. "Clean the house."

I threw the blanket on the floor, anger flaring up in my lungs. "What is your problem?"

"*I* don't have a problem." Her mouth twitched. "*You're* the one who might turn evil and murder us all."

"Yeah, well, you'll feel really silly for mocking me when that doesn't happen."

"We'll see." She brushed past me, her shoulder jarring against mine. "Better safe than sorry."

I wheeled around, my eyes phasing black.

She turned back to me, a sadistic grin on her face. "There you are! I knew you had it in you." She pushed me, her hands thrusting me back several feet toward the front door. "Come on! Let's go."

A growl started in my throat, but I swallowed it down. I took a deep breath and made my eyes phase back to normal. "No. I'm not going to fight you. I'm not evil."

"What's wrong? Are you afraid of what you really are?" She unsheathed her knife and crouched in front of me.

I knew she was just trying to protect her sisters, but she seemed wild, unruly — maybe even evil, though her eyes weren't black. I took a deep breath, watching her, wary of her next move.

A witch I hadn't met yet walked into the living room and stoked the fire in the fireplace. "Getting cool in here," she said with a strange accent.

Kelsey slunk to the edge of the room, her eyes following me.

I whipped up the blanket, bunched it into a ball, and stormed into the laundry room. At least that confrontation was over. Things could've gone a lot worse. If I'd let that darkness spin up inside me and unleash itself, I could've turned evil. I needed to not react to her, although the thought of slitting her throat made my angry inner coil throb with immense pleasure.

An hour later, after I was finished scrubbing the kitchen floor, Medea drew me aside into the living room. Her honey-colored hair was freshly washed and smelled of sunflowers. "Look, it's working." She showed me the burner phone.

I held my breath and blinked at the screen.

Belle Dame: 98.9% bad, 1.1% good

I laughed, effervescent joy rising within me. Cleaning was working. I just had to resist Kelsey's antagonism and keep my head down with good, hard work.

"I got you something." She handed me a brown paper package.

I unwrapped the hard paper and gazed at a knife with a smooth birch handle. The stainless steel blade was smaller than what I was used to, but it was beautiful, and perfectly balanced. I embraced her.

"Thank you so much."

"You're welcome. Now, I want to tell you the house rules. You can use the laptop and the burner phone, but you can't contact anyone from the outside. No logging onto email accounts or social media, if you have any of those."

"Okay."

"I'm setting up a schedule to help guard the house. There'll be a minimum of one witch on perimeter control and one on guard in the house. This is for your safety and to get to know the others in the coven. Shifts will change at breakfast and dinnertime, so if you want to feed people and get that karma, those are good times for it. Follow the commands of anyone on guard. They know our ways. Kelsey and Fern have volunteered for the first shift."

"Um. About that . . . I don't think Kelsey likes me very much."

Medea tilted her head. "She just takes some warming up to. That's how she was with me at first, too. Give her time."

"Okay." I glanced at my lap, uncertain if I believed it. But I'd give her the benefit of the doubt.

"Iona and Claire will take the second shift tonight. I have to go back to Hell."

"Would you mind checking on my friend Jane? I'm a little worried about her."

"Sure. You said she's in the Poisoner Division, right?"

I nodded. "Thank you so much for everything."

"Of course." She donned a violet robe and grabbed her broom from the bunch by the door. "And let me know if you see *your other friend*."

I watched her walk outside from the window. She sat on the broom and gracefully flew off — she made it look as easy as breathing. I wondered how easy it'd be for me.

Iona sat down on the sofa. Claire sat nearby, a mug of steaming coffee in her hands.

"So," Iona started to say, her eyebrows expressive. "I know we talked a lot last night, but you must still have some questions."

"Yeah, I do, actually." I sat down into an armchair and smiled at her. "How did you know? Are you

223

psychic?" I laughed, though I shifted uncomfortably when I remembered the magic mirror in my satchel. If they found out I had a line of communication with Mephistopheles . . .

"No." She waved an arm. "Nobody's psychic here. You just have that look on your face. And everyone has questions when they first join us. So go on, come out with it."

There was something about her sparkling brown eyes and moon-like face that reminded me of my mother. I felt as if I'd known her for years. I took a deep breath. Now was as good a time as any to tell her and the other witches the truth.

"I actually have a confession. Medea thinks I may have used magic to get my targets to go with me, but I don't think it's true. The truth is . . . I'm not really a witch. I was only killed as one because I pissed off the wrong suitor. I'm about as magical as a doorknob."

There. It was out. No more hiding. I glanced at their faces, wondering what they'd do now that they knew I wasn't really one of them. Would they still stick with me and my plans to kill the beast? At least Kelsey wasn't anywhere nearby to gloat.

"Belle, listen to me." Claire's watery blue eyes focused on me, her voice creaky. "I can clearly see you have magic in you, dear. Maybe the people who killed you did too. You should at least *try* to use it."

"But I've tried for centuries." I shook my head, thinking of all the 'magic' books I'd read, all my nights spent clutching a broom on a rooftop – all for nothing.

"*Psshhht.*" Claire waved her hand in the air. "You didn't know the first rule about magic. It doesn't work unless you're in a coven or a crone teaches you. Luckily for you, you have both now." She wriggled her eyebrows. "You're a witch, Belle. That comes with a lot of power. It's time you learned magic, if you feel up for it, that is."

My eyes teared up. I blinked back the emotion, nodding. "Do you mean it? You really think I might be able to do it?"

She nodded, her wispy white strands flowing. Iona beamed.

"I'd love that." I dashed a tear from my cheek.

"So, what's your next question," Iona asked, "now that *that humdinger* is out of the way?"

"I guess I was wondering how magic is allowed to exist. I mean, I'm sure Lucifer wouldn't allow it, so that means he can't stop it, right?"

"Exactly, and a good question." Iona nodded. "Magic is wild, something even the old red devil himself can't control."

"Aye," Claire said. "We don't know what it is exactly, whether it's the language of the old gods or the music of the universe, but it lets us do amazing things."

"Was there a first person who used magic?"

Iona shrugged. "We don't know — if so, it must've been several millennia ago. Maybe it was even a god or a goddess. All we know is that magic has spread far and wide, all over the world." Her hands floated in the air as she spoke.

Claire leaned forward. "Can you imagine the first witches, trying out spells, not knowing what would happen?"

Iona laughed, slapping her knee. "I dare say they had a lot of accidents! Especially with fire elementals like you!"

"That's another thing, Belle," Claire said. "We all have different elements that resonate with us. I'm fire, Iona's water, and Medea's air."

"Elements?" I asked. "What does that mean exactly?"

"It means," Claire paused to cough. "Some of us can cast spells that others can't. For instance, Iona is a water elemental, and she's in touch with the moon. That's how she knew when it was full. I couldn't do something like that, even if I wanted to."

Iona smirked. "Yeah, but she can light a fire with her mind. How cool is that?"

"What about the earth elementals?"

"They deal with physical things," Iona said. "Most of them can communicate with animals, and some can make plants grow. And they can summon things they've never touched."

Claire nodded. "All the other elementals have to own an object before we can control it. Like our brooms."

"Does every witch have an element?" I asked.

They nodded.

"What do you think mine might be?"

Claire shrugged. "That's for you to discover. But we'd love to teach you magic — if you'll have us, that is." She glanced at Iona. "I dare say we're more patient than some of the other witches here."

"Or all of them combined!" Iona laughed.

I nodded eagerly, breathless. "I'd like that very much."

Iona patted my arm. "Good. But don't let us stop you from your housework. I know how important it is for you to raise your karma, and this old house needs it, that's for sure. The cat box won't clean itself! We'll be here when you have a moment."

I got up, a giddy laugh bubbling inside of me, determined to work even harder than before.

CHAPTER TWENTY

Later that day, the last load of towels and dishes ran in the machines. Scrubbing pots had made my knuckles raw, and my knees throbbed from scouring the tile, but after an entire day of cleaning, the house looked nicer. Afternoon sunlight shone on the gleaming countertops and floor, and the cabin seemed bigger without all the cobwebs dangling from the ceiling. I rearranged a bouquet I'd made from the herb garden. The smell of fresh lemon verbena and lavender filled me with a sense of accomplishment.

I went to the bookcase in the living room and ran my eyes over the titles. Reading always let me escape into another world, one where things made more sense, and happy endings existed. Claire sat in an armchair, dozing, an open book on her lap. Her white hair was backlit from the afternoon sun streaming through the window. Iona lay on the couch, one arm over her eyes.

I plucked out *Stardust* and sat on a couch beside a black and white cat curled into a ball. After reading for a few minutes, the words became fuzzy. I yawned, recalling the lackluster sleep I'd gotten the night before. A good cup of tea would sort me out, not that it was available.

Claire roused, blinking heavy eyelids. "Belle, you look worn out."

"I'm okay." I smiled.

"No, you're not." She frowned, sliding a bookmark into the pages and closing the book. "You need to keep your energy up in case demons find a way through our protection. How about we teach you how to draw energy from a cat? It's easy. Go ahead and pet her." She indicated to the cat beside me.

My fingers sank into its downy black and white fur. The cat yawned and stretched a clawed arm. I didn't feel anything magical happening. "Is it working?"

"You'll know when it works, believe me. Some witches draw energy through their fingers, some breathe it in, some take it through their hearts. Give it a try."

My heart plucked with trepidation. "Will it hurt her?"

"'Course not." She shot me a gap-toothed smile. "I drew energy from old Missy there just last night, and she looks fine, doesn't she?" She limped across the room and sat next to me, placing a gnarled hand on the cat's spine. "Yep, she's fully charged. As long as they have food, water, and time, they'll replenish whatever you take. And

229

you can't kill them — they shut off the flow when it's too much and go to sleep. Think of them like batteries. Go ahead, take some energy from her. Imagine she's giving it to you. Her energy is filling you up with each breath, healing you."

I petted the cat, trying to bring her energy into my heart. The cat felt warm, and she purred, but nothing inside me felt different. I tried to absorb the energy through my hands, but it all felt the same. I glanced at Claire.

"Keep trying." She picked up her book again. "It'll feel all tingly on the inside."

I turned my attention back to the cat and closed my eyes. I imagined her energy going into me. Something stirred in my stomach where the dark coil usually pulsed. A tingling swept over my insides. Could that be where I drew my energy? I breathed in from the depths of my belly and felt a wave of pins and needles crest into me, filling me up. My eyes flew open as the tingles surged down my arms and legs.

I gasped. The room shifted into focus. I felt as if I'd just awoken from a full night's sleep, or like I'd just drank the best cup of tea ever. I saw dust motes dancing in the air that I hadn't seen before, and through the window, saw Kelsey kicking the dead leaves outside on guard duty.

"Good," Claire said. "What element do you feel closest to?"

I raised my brows. "I don't know."

She sighed and cocked her head. "You have a lot to learn. See those books on the shelf over there?"

I nodded.

"Those have spells from every witch that's come through this house." She hobbled toward it and clawed off a book, then held out Grimm's Fairy Tales to me.

I turned it over and flipped through the pages. "I don't see any spells. It just looks like a regular book."

She sat down onto the couch next to me. Her wizened hand waved over the cover where the title was. Green glowing text appeared to rise off it. My mouth fell open. It was beautiful, like the northern lights.

"Now you try."

My hand hovered over the book, just as hers had. Nothing happened.

"Try again."

I concentrated hard this time, willing the green print to appear with everything I had.

Claire touched my arm. "You're trying too hard. Try softer."

I let my concentration fall away and trickled my fingers over it. A couple of letters appeared on the cover and then vanished.

I gasped. I'd actually done it! I'd commanded the energy within me and made something change. Claire was right. I actually did have magic in me. It was proof.

She flashed kind eyes to me. "Find me when you can maintain it for a few seconds. Until then . . ." She sat back in her chair and closed her eyes.

I tried to work the book a little bit longer, but it didn't happen again. When Claire started to snore, I tiptoed into the kitchen. I didn't want to disturb her slumber, but I also had another responsibility.

Opening the laptop, I searched through everything I could think of, including, "weapon to kill Lucifer," "how to dissipate an angel," and "fallen angel death." I read Bible verses, sermons, meditations, new age websites, and more, but I didn't find anything about how to kill him. I began to wonder if it was even possible. What if I never found anything about a weapon? What if he kidnapped another girl? I sighed and slogged ahead, making notes in my journal with whatever details I could find.

The next morning, I washed the sleep from my eyes and padded into the kitchen. Iona sat at the round mahogany dining table, eating fragrant blueberry pancakes.

"Good morning, Belle. I left some for you on the counter."

"Thanks." I pressed my hand against my temple. "I still can't believe all of you are helping me. No one has ever done so much for me."

"You're quite welcome," she said. "I wish I could stay longer today, but I have to go back to Hell. Not that I want to. But I'll be back before you know it. Claire's already left."

Two women walked through the front door and set their brooms by the threshold. I recognized them from the party two nights ago. Hazel and Lovetta, if I remembered correctly. They were quiet, but their faces were warm.

"That's my cue," Iona said.

"Okay, be safe. I'll make breakfast one of these days."

"Sure. We thought you needed the sleep today. Don't forget to study. Claire and I will be back soon enough."

She opened the door and walked outside into a light sprinkle. I heard her faintly say some words, and instantly, the rain appeared to fall around her and not hit her. I laughed. Would that be normal for me someday? Perhaps . . . But only if I could master the method to see the spells first. My heart sagged at the thought of all my sleepy hours last night, spent trying to make more text appear on the cover of Grimm's Fairy Tales. I hoped

233

today would be different.

I drew the tea tin from the cupboard, determined to make it work today. When the water boiled, I made my cup and added a few sprigs of bergamot and lavender from the bouquets I made last night. The tea still tasted flat, but it was balanced by the aromatic herbs. It was better, at least.

I made breakfast for the two new witches, then cleaned all the dishes until they sparkled. I took energy from a friendly tabby, marveling at the tingling, refreshing sensations, then sat on the sofa and focused. My hand floated over the book as I attempted to command the energy at the pit of my stomach. Something like my inner darkness spiraled up within me, flooding my senses. Green letters sparkled into sight, hovering before me. I laughed out loud.

The text faded away, but I wasn't deterred. Now that I knew how to channel my intentions, I could do it again. I flexed my energy spot, concentrating. The words appeared again, incandescent and glowing stronger than ever. I barely breathed, trying to maintain them. My chest buzzed with light as I read every word.

karnicia jamais far heinke
for making the hair grow faster

The following day, when I showed Claire the spell, she shrugged. "Don't bother with that one, dear. Your hair's already as long as days!"

"What about that one?" I pointed to a Dr. Suess book with swirling colors.

She made a face. "That's dark magic. Not for you. Try this one." She handed me a dusty leather-bound book. On the cover was a painting of a friar riding a horse. *The Canterbury Tales.*

I blew a layer of dust off it and settled into a chair. After a few minutes, words jumped up at me, electric.

clemit pro sequious
for transitory protection

I smiled. I had no idea what transitory protection was, but I was thrilled nonetheless.

Claire looked up from her book. "You're getting faster."

"What's this spell?"

"It's for protection. It's one of the most powerful ones we have, even though it's not that hard. Try it."

I swallowed and cleared my throat, drawing on my inner depth. "*Clemit pro sequious.*"

I glanced around, anxious to see what would happen, but everything looked the same.

"Again," Claire said.

"*Clemit pro sequious.*"

She pressed her lips together. "Keep trying kiddo."

She turned the pages of her book as I spoke the words over and over. I took energy from two cats, refilling my weakened stores.

After an hour of trying, my voice nearly going hoarse, something changed. Dozens of lightning-blue comets spun around my body. My shoulders tingled with what felt like a sugar rush. I gazed at a crystalline sphere around me, marveling at the magic I'd created.

Claire closed her book. "Now you're cooking!" Her arm reared back, and she lobbed her book at me. I flinched, but the book hit the bubble of light and crashed back toward her. She caught it awkwardly, bending the pages a little. "See? Protection. Try and pick something up."

I reached for a cat lounging on the rug, but a firm jelly-like boundary prevented me from touching it. "Huh."

"Sort of like a bubble, isn't it?" she asked.

I nodded.

"Notice you can still touch anything on your person, though."

I opened my satchel and touched the top of my journal, feeling the ribs of paper on my fingers. No jelly there.

"But that's not the best thing about it," Claire continued. "Anyone who attacks you when you cast the protection spell will be repelled just like that book, and if it harms them, the karma doesn't go onto your score."

"Really? How do you know that?"

"Who do you think found it out? I've used it so many times. If it counted against me, I'd be evil a long time ago. Anywho," she stood and stretched. "Practice it and learn some more spells. Nothing that might hurt anyone, though, you hear?"

The bubble around me burst and my hand plunged into the cat's soft fur. She grunted and turned to wink open one sleepy eye at me. I laughed. I'd never dreamed I'd be wielding this kind of power. I recited the words in my mind, committing them to memory.

"I have to get going." Claire walked toward the door and slipped into black Mary Janes. "Reporting for duty."

I craned my neck to look at her. "Before you go, can show me the thought charm spell? I really want to learn that." It was a lie, which I hoped didn't count against my karma. I really wanted a love spell, so I could make the charm for Mephistopheles, but I didn't think she'd teach me that.

Claire gave me an inquisitive smile. "You're not in danger here. We spelled the grounds against Lucifer hearing your thoughts."

"I know, it's just . . . Medea said we'll be leaving for another place eventually, and I'll need it then. I can't exactly count on charm-proximity when we're twenty-thousand feet above the ground."

She nodded. "Good point. But we won't be leaving anytime soon. Plus, it's not a beginner's spell. Object charms take hours of work, and if you stop, you'll have to start all over again. Tell you what. Practice the easy stuff for now. I'll be back soon to help with the next level." She patted me on the shoulder and ambled out of the room.

I nodded in acquiescence, swallowing my pride and looking at the hundreds of books on the bookshelf. If she wasn't going to help me find a thought charm spell, she wouldn't help me find a love charm spell, either. But if a protection spell was here, a love charm spell might be too. I could go through the books. It'd take energy and time, but once I made the charm, I'd be free from Mephistopheles. I'd never have to see his ugly face again.

I had mixed feelings about making the charm for him — I knew he wasn't an ally, but he had helped me, and a promise was a promise. I knew he hadn't told Lucifer my

238

name yet, otherwise, he would've been able to control me — he would've made me run ragged to the nearest waystation back to Hell. But Mephistopheles could tell him my name at any time. I needed to get him that charm to ensure he wouldn't share my name.

Lucifer's black eyes seemed to burn into mine the last time I saw him, as he stood on the parking lot, becoming smaller and smaller as I sped off with the witches. His words still rang in my ears.

"YOU CAN RUN, BUT YOU CAN'T HIDE!"

I pushed it out of my mind and picked up an armful of books from the bookshelf, sitting down on the couch with a deep sigh. There were so many books! Why couldn't she have taught me what I wanted to know?

Cats prowled in the windowsills and brushed against my legs. At least I had a supply of energy. I took a deep breath, waved my hand over the first book, and concentrated, hoping to make the green letters rise again.

CHAPTER TWENTY-ONE

On my fourth morning at the cabin, the weather got significantly cooler. I looked out the frosted kitchen window and blew on my hot tea. Swirls of bergamont steam rose to my face. I held my breath as I waited for the karma app on the burner phone to load my score. The reception was terrible in the woods, but at least we hadn't been discovered.

Finally, a score appeared.

```
Belle Dame: 97.9% bad, 2.1% good
```

I was below 98% bad! I leapt up, wanting to dance. It was about time!

Maribeth looked up at me from her book, her brown eyes cautious. Her umber face still carried baby fat — I figured she was about the same age I was when I was killed. I'd caught her glancing at me through her long black braids from time to time, but she rarely spoke. The only thing she'd ever said to me was her name, when she'd introduced herself to me on my first night at the cabin.

I smiled at her, deciding to bridge the gap between us. "I just checked my karma score, and it's getting better. I guess all this cleaning is working. What element are you, by the way?"

"Um, earth." She stared down at her book and swallowed, her shoulders hunched.

"Where are you from?"

"Congo," she murmured, her mouth drawn.

I repressed a gasp — I'd heard about the killing of young women and children in that country, under fear of witchcraft. It still happened to this day, despite attempts to educate people against it. I shifted uncomfortably. "Are you a revenger, too?"

"Look . . ." Her brown eyes met mine. "To be honest, I don't feel comfortable talking to you, but I promised Medea I'd take a shift."

My brows raised and I drew away from her slightly. Apparently Kelsey wasn't the only one who was afraid of my score. Thinking back, Marianne hadn't been part of the crowd to raise a glass with me to take down Lucifer. Maybe she was on patrol.

"No offense," she continued. "I just don't feel good

about this. I feel like something bad is going to happen."
She shook her head and walked out of the room, her
book dangling from her hand.

A flush of embarrassment deflated me. I couldn't
blame her for feeling that way, but surely she had to see I
was still a good person. Or maybe she was one of those
people who had to 'see it to believe it.'

I gazed at the pale ceiling. Actions spoke louder than
words. I could prove it to her, with enough time and
dishes.

Through the window, I saw Medea, in a black great-
coat, patrolling the grounds with her bow. Her boots
rustled the russet leaves near the ancient junipers, and a
quiver of arrows hung over her shoulder.

She'd be happy to hear about my karma score. I
opened the door and slipped out, my boots crunching
the leaves as I ran.

Medea turned and notched an arrow, drawing it back
faster than I could blink.

I stopped mid-stride, frozen with fear. My hands
raised in the air slowly. "It's just me."

She lowered the bow, her mouth twisted. "Don't
sneak up on me, Belle."

"I'm sorry. But I wanted to tell you the good news.
I'm finally up to 2.1% good!"

"That's nice." She smiled, but her eyes remained alert
on the perimeter. "Have you discovered anything about a

weapon?"

"No, not yet." I sighed. Even though I'd scoured through over three hundred pages on the internet, I hadn't found anything about a weapon or how to kill the beast. "I did find something that might explain why Lucifer wanted us — why he targeted us instead of others."

She stopped and stared at me, concern in her eyes. "Go on."

"There's a Bible passage in Revelations that talks about a beautiful temple priestess riding a beast — that's the original translation anyway. It got me thinking. You're obviously beautiful. Persephone is too, and my name is Belle . . ."

"You think there's something more to the *Beauty and the Beast* story?"

"Yes," I frowned, "but it gets worse. According to the scripture, the woman and the beast are supposed to bring about *the end of the world*."

She leaned forward, her brows drawn. "The end of the world? Are you serious?" One hand flew up to cover her heart.

I nodded, gazing into her liquid black eyes. "I'm afraid so."

"If humanity crumbled . . ."

"I know." My head fell forward and I shut my eyes, not wanting to think about it. So many would die. Innocent lives would be lost all over the world, and a new era would rise, one ruled by cruelty and blood. It'd be another dark age.

"We can't let that happen." She reached for my hand. "We have to keep you safe, for all humankind, no matter what the cost. If that's his plan, it means he believes what's in the Bible. Are you studying magic with Claire and Iona?"

"Yes."

"Good. I would've volunteered to teach you, but nothing in my routine can be different. The archdemons are watching me closely. I already look guilty enough of kidnapping you, merely because the same thing happened to me. Keep looking for a weapon. There has to be something."

"I will."

She smiled sadly and laid a hand on my shoulder before striding away.

I walked to the garden and knelt in the damp earth. The smell of the last green tomatoes made me feel a little better. I picked a few and put them in my pockets, as well as some hardy squash for dinner.

Even though the sunlight was diffuse behind a sheet of clouds, it still felt good on my face. I stood and lifted my face to the gray cloudy sky, then opened my arms wide and inhaled the pine-scented air.

A crisp breeze began to blow. I shivered, pulling my

sweater closed.

The breeze stopped just as quickly as it had started up. I looked around, curious to see if another witch was playing a trick on me, but it was only me, Medea, and Maribeth at the cabin today. Maribeth had said she was an earth witch, so she wouldn't be able to do that magic. And I didn't think Medea seemed in the mood to do something like that.

The breeze had started to blow when I held my arms out. *Could I have made the wind whip up? Could I be an air elemental?* The ghost of a smile formed on my lips.

Over the next couple of days, when I wasn't cleaning or searching the internet, I worked my way through the bookcase, one dust-covered book at a time. I uncovered spells and wrote them in my journal so I could reference them without expending energy to find them again. I still hadn't found the spell to make the love charm for Mephistopheles, but I'd learned a few new ones, much to my delight. My favorite new spells included *manus illumino lux*, which made my palm light up with a glowing orb (helpful for finding things in the dark), and *pelluminbestil-lia*, for making a piece of leather turn into an equivalent-sized animal. The little brown bunnies I made from the floppy loafers in the closet sniffed and hopped, tickling my palms with their whiskers and pink noses. I almost didn't want to turn them back, but after one of them bit me, I was no longer enchanted by them. I read the spell backwards, and watched as they froze, mid-nose-twitch, and morphed back into shoes.

One of the most useful spells I learned was making myself invisible. The spell cast a white sparkling light around me, though it didn't work as well as I thought it would. When I tried to steal a chocolate chip cookie from Iona's cooling rack, she looked directly at me.

"Looks like it might frost tonight," she said.

I froze. "You can see me?"

"Go ahead, have one." She waved her spatula at me. "You deserve it."

I munched on the cookie, savoring the warm, gooey goodness even as disappointment crept over me. "But how can you see me? I saw the sparkles."

"*Camarquat heroses* doesn't work on other witches from your own coven. It's so we don't bump into each other." She flicked her spatula at me, an impish grin on her face. "You still have a lot to learn."

"I know." I sighed. "It's a little overwhelming."

"You're doing great," she smiled. "Don't worry.

There's a learning curve. You'll find your way. Have you ever heard of *per aspera ad astra*?"

I sucked the melted chocolate off my fingers. "Is that another spell for invisibility?"

"No, it's an ancient Latin saying. It means you have to travel over a steep and rocky road if you want to get to the stars. That's what you're doing. You have a hard path, and I dare say none of us would trade with you, but you're weathering it well."

I smiled. At least my efforts hadn't gone unnoticed. "Thanks."

"Go ahead and take another cookie. I have to get the rest of these to St. Brigid's for the bake sale, but there's no reason why I can't share some with you."

I pulled a ten dollar bill from my satchel and laid it on the table before swiping another cookie.

"Belle, you don't have to—"

"I want to. Good luck with the bake sale."

That afternoon, after Iona left and my chores were done, a storm rolled through. Thunder rumbled and wind whistled through the trees, making the cats scrabble under the sofas and beds. Freezing rain tapped on the windows, and it looked as dark as dusk outside. Fern, a New Orleans witch, tromped about outside in a big Rasta hoodie.

I sat on the sofa with Claire, who was knitting an

oddly shaped tube with multi-colored yarn. A fire crackled and snapped in the fireplace.

"Isn't Fern cold out there?" I asked.

"Nah. There's a spell for warmth."

I passed my hand over the worn cover of *The Count of Monte Cristo*, focusing my energy. After a minute, green writing appeared.

xerceus stomanium que grashna
thought charm protection from the devil
requires physical object

Finally, the thought charm! It wasn't the love charm I'd been looking for, but at least I'd be protected from Lucifer when we left this place. I rummaged through my satchel until I found a copper penny with a Queen's head on the front and a maple leaf on the back. It was perfectly inconspicuous — I could take it anywhere I went and no one would know.

"What'd you find there?" Claire asked.

"The thought charm spell."

She reached for a glass of water on the table. "Can you draw energy from a cat while you're doing something else?"

"I don't know. I've never tried."

"I'm asking because it's useful for this spell. It takes a lot of energy, and with those physical object charms, you can't stop the spell, otherwise, you'll have to start all over again. Are you sure you're ready for something like this?" Her eyes gleamed with a dare.

"I don't know." What she'd said gave me pause, but I wanted to try it. The sooner I mastered it, the sooner I'd be able to produce the love charm.

"Go ahead. Don't let me stop you."

I held the coin in the palm of my hand and focused. "*Xerceus stomanium que grashna.*" The energy rose from my belly and out of me. I repeated the spell, over and over.

After a minute, I felt weak — spots swam in front of my eyes. But nothing happened to the coin. I drew from the cat and felt my energy rise again. "*Xerceus stomanium que grashna.*" I pushed it out from my belly, through my hands, and into the coin.

After about an hour and a half, the coin grew warm and glowed with an apple-green light. A coppery smell infused the air.

Claire peeked at me over her knitting. "Nicely done."

Lightning sparkled in the dark sky, followed by a giant boom of thunder. I thought of the last thunderstorm I'd been through — when Donovan had begged me to stop torturing Carlo. It seemed like an eon ago. Had it really only been a few weeks? With the next crash, the lights flickered a little.

Fern came in from outside, completely dry, and plopped into an armchair. She fluffed her long wavy hair and drank some apple cider. Her green eyes stood out against her warm brown skin. Freckles dotted her nose.

"How much longer do you think we'll be at this cabin?" I asked.

Claire shrugged. "Who knows? Why?"

"No reason." I couldn't tell her why — because I needed to have the love charm ready whenever we left so I could drop it for Mephistopheles.

"For what it's worth," Claire smiled, "I hope we don't leave anytime soon."

"Me too," Fern said. "I don't know if you can tell, Belle, but it's been a while since we got a new coven member. Everyone's been having a great time. You'd think you were a celebrity."

I smiled at her, my chest lightening as the fire sizzled with rain.

My new thought charm felt so nice in my hand, and even better, I now knew I was ready to make a love charm. I just needed to find the spell. I was more than halfway done with the bookshelf. It was only a matter of time.

I needed to tell Mephistopheles, too, to quell his anxiety. But if I was being honest with myself, contacting him was for me, too. I'd feel better if he knew I planned on keeping my promise. It didn't stop me from being angry with him, though. He'd lied about Lucifer's motives.

I slipped into my bedroom and closed the door. My fingertips tingled as I pulled out the magic mirror from my satchel. When I opened it, it was dark.

After a few seconds, Mephistopheles snapped open his mirror, breathing hard. His black eyes bulged and his mouth twisted, revealing fangs. "Belle! Where are you?!" he growled.

Footsteps creaked on the hallway floorboards. I froze, glancing at the closed door, listening, my heart pounding until whoever it was walked away. I regained my composure and narrowed my eyes at him. He didn't scare me, and he certainly wasn't holding all the cards this time.

"I'm somewhere safe, no thanks to you. Why did you tell me Lucifer wanted me to be a guard? He wanted me to be his mistress. There's a huge difference!"

He recoiled. "*I* never said he wanted you to be a guard. *You did.* I merely didn't correct you."

"You're an asshole," I scowled. "But at least you haven't told him my name yet."

"Yeah. Unlike some people, I keep my word." His voice strained. "Even *after* the deadline to produce the goods has passed."

I took a deep breath. "I keep my word. The spell just wasn't in the books you gave me."

One of his eyebrows arched. "Oh really? You're not

going to flake out on me again?"

"No." I watched him through guarded eyes. "I'm working on your charm, I promise."

He inhaled through his nose and smiled. "Excellent. Just tell me where you are—"

I shook my head. "When it's done, I'll reach out to you."

"Belle," he snarled, his eyes clouded. "I don't know what lies your new friends have been telling you, but—"

I closed the mirror and threw it into my satchel. I was tired of him calling the shots. It was my turn.

CHAPTER TWENTY-TWO

The next day, I crouched over an enchanted broom. Cool wind whipped through my hair and shook the pines encircling the grassy area just down the path from the cabin. The sky was mercurial — brown and gray clouds tumbled overhead, moving fast. Every now and then, a pocket of blue sky shone through before being swallowed by the roiling clouds again.

"Attention on the broom," Sarah snapped in her American accent. She walked around me, her posture taut, her long blonde hair and paisley dress rustling in the wind.

My muscles strained with intention. I'd been at it for three hours as she barked orders and critiqued my form, but I remained earth-bound. I cursed, wanting to throw the broom into the bonfire pile. Only I couldn't. The witches expected me to fly to the next safehouse with them.

My hair streaked across my face. I tucked it behind my ear for the fourteenth time and took a breath to steady myself, then leaned forward, my core engaged.

"Go up on your tiptoes," Sarah said.

I raised up onto the balls of my feet.

"I said tiptoes! Now, lift off!"

I struggled to fly, but remained on the ground as firmly as if I were planted there.

"You must have some crazy kind of earth magic," she shook her head, "'cause you're grounded as hell. Are you an earth elemental?"

I released the broom and stood up wearily. "I don't know. How can you tell?"

"There are tests, but I can tell you one thing — you're not air. Air signs don't need to be taught to fly."

I grumbled, staring at the ground. I'd wanted to be air, but I supposed I'd have to find another element. "How long did it take you to learn to fly?"

She shrugged. "It doesn't matter. Everyone's different."

"But you're an air sign like Medea, right?"

"Yeah, we're both air, but she can do weather magic. I can do a little of that, but I'm more of an etheric stars-and-space kind of girl."

"So," I frowned. "You flew on your first try, right?"

She nodded. "Pretty much."

I took a deep breath. So that's why I felt like a cat

taking swimming lessons from a fish.

"Tell you what," she said. "I'll ask the others if they had the same problem. Maybe someone else can shed some light."

I watched her walk down the path toward the cabin. When she was out of sight, I smoothed my hand over my forehead and tried to calm my breathing. My lack of progress disgusted me. I'd been knocking out the spells lately, but flying eluded me. If I really was an earth element, I supposed that would explain my trouble. I remembered what Iona had said about the learning curve and felt a little better.

A shadow moved near the pines. Kelsey's flaming red hair flashed between the boughs. She snickered before continuing to walk the perimeter.

I gripped the broom tighter. I wouldn't let her win. I'd show her I could fly.

The roiling sky parted for a second, and a tiny fleck of rainbow peeked through. Somewhere, the sun shone, but I was stuck on the ground. I was about to turn away when something flickered in the corner of my vision. Was it my imagination, or did I see a man flying through the clouds?

Donovan, is that you?

I waited, praying, my heart in my throat as I scanned the gray clouds. Was he avoiding me? He had to be able to see my score, to know I wasn't evil. And yet, he stayed away.

I trudged inside and stacked the broom against the wall with the others. Clanking and conversation came from the kitchen. The witches had volunteered to make dinner, since it was the new moon. Fern stirred an alfredo sauce, and steam rose from a pot of boiling pasta on the burner. The smell of herbed chicken in the oven made me salivate.

"I just don't know what to do." Sarah faced Fern, her back to me. "I've never seen anyone so bad at it. It's like she has bricks in her panties!"

Anger boiled within me. I consciously swallowed my demonic features.

Fern laughed a little, but when she saw me, she shook her head. She walked toward me, her green eyes apologetic. "Belle, you must be thirsty after all that hard work. Let me get you some water."

Sarah whirled around and cringed when she saw me standing there. "I'm sorry, Belle, but it's the truth. I don't know what to do." She shrugged and walked out of the room.

Fern held out a glass of water to me. "Don't listen to her. You just haven't found your way yet."

"Thanks." I took a sip, then swept into the living room, eager to get away so they wouldn't see my watering eyes. Dirty cups and plates cluttered every surface. No one else had cleaned the cabin to allow me to make up the karma, but I was getting tired of it. I was beginning to wonder if there was anything else I could do to make up karma.

I tried not to feel inferior, but I wondered if I couldn't fly because I wasn't a real witch. Even though I'd learned a handful of spells, I was terrible at them. It took hours of trial and error before they worked. I wasn't like Sarah, who'd probably flown when she was two years old.

I sucked some energy from a black-and-white tomcat seeking my legs and started to feel better. He head-butted my ankles, purring and meowing in a funny way. I laughed.

Fern leaned against the wall, her arms crossed. The green from her jacket picked up the green in her eyes. "If you think you're an earth witch, I might be able to help you."

I picked up the glasses and plates and carried them to the farmhouse sink. "Why? Are you an earth witch?"

She nodded, trailing behind me a couple of steps. "Flying is harder for us, but not impossible. Do you want to try again in fifteen minutes?"

I ran the water in the sink and gazed at the bubbles. My inner resistance softened. I was just afraid of failing again. Fern's warmth was charming after working with Sarah, but I wasn't convinced anyone could teach me how to fly. I shrugged. "We can try, but—"

"Okay. See you in a few."

After I washed the dishes and recharged again from an affectionate Persian kitty, I slogged outside, a broom hanging limply in my hand.

Fern walked toward me from one of the ancient pines. She waved to it, as if she'd been talking with it, then squinted at me. "Sarah's right. You're too grounded. Exactly how I was when I was first learning. Let's try something different. Close your eyes."

I obliged, feeling a little silly. I was certain Kelsey was making fun of me from her post on the perimeter.

"Can you feel the breeze?" Fern asked.

I nodded. The cool wind played with my sweater and hair.

"Tune into it. Feel how the speed of the wind increases and dies down. Feel how it changes direction."

I felt the wind play on my arms and face, and took a deep breath.

"Now, feel the weight of the air. It's heavy with water. Can you feel that?"

The air surrounding me did have a weight to it. I felt it on my face, pressing down on my shoulders. "Yes."

"Keep your eyes closed and mount your broom. Now, empty your mind until you feel as empty as the air. No thoughts. Let the air enter your mind."

I took another breath of the cool air, crouched over my broom, and felt my spirit grow lighter, as if my burdens were only an illusion or only a confused thought.

258

"Tip forward," she whispered.

I leaned forward on my toes, my muscles taut, but I didn't feel anything. I sighed and opened my eyes. "Now what?"

But Fern wasn't there. I looked down — she waved from the ground, some twelve feet or so below me, a broad smile on her face. I panicked, clutching the broom, my breath hitched. For a second, I was afraid I'd fall, but I hung there, suspended. Before me, the sky stretched out wide, the clouds like a gray ceiling.

A duck flew near me, wings beating, its liquid brown eyes focused straight ahead. I watched him pass, marveling. No one had taught that creature how to fly — it'd come naturally to him, and in baby steps, too. I focused on his tail feathers and leaned toward him. The broom scuttled forward, picking up speed. The duck quacked and flapped harder, desperate to get away from me. I laughed, a light feeling radiating from my heart. How surreal everything seemed.

"Try to aim upward," Fern called out. "But don't go over the net!"

I tilted the broom up and soaring through clouds that passed over my face like wet cotton. I crested over the clouds and stopped, suspended. The blue sky stretched out as wide as I could see. A rainbow shimmered over some faraway green patch of earth. The air smelled rich, like ozone and sunlight. I felt giddy. I'd done it, finally, after hours of trying! It was like I had my own queendom right there. I almost didn't want to go down. Part of me was afraid I'd never fly again if I did.

The ultraviolet net blew in the wind above me like a giant parachute, covering more area than I'd previously thought. Donovan wasn't anywhere to be seen in the clouds, like I'd hoped. But then again, I'd given up on him. He was too good to be true. Besides, I'd already been rescued. I didn't need him.

After a few minutes, I tipped the broom down a few millimeters and shot down, dropping below the clouds. I pulled up and hovered again. From that height, I saw the little cabin, the plump orange pumpkins in the garden, and the long path winding out.

"Belle!" Fern called. "See if you can go in a circle. Lean in one direction!"

I tilted to the right and flew in a wide circle around the cabin. I saw the witches in the kitchen through the steamy windows. Soon, I was back where I started.

"Come back down!" she yelled. "I don't want you to get too tired."

I dipped the broomstick a little and began to hurdle down. The ground sped faster and faster toward me. I cranked the broom up just before hitting the ground, then collapsed in a heap on the grass.

She offered a hand, smiling, and yanked me up and into a warm hug. "Belle, you can fly! I'm so proud of you."

A huge smile broke over my face. "Thank you so much. You don't even know — I've wanted to fly for centuries!"

She put her hand on her hip. "And they said you couldn't be taught. What did they know?"

I laughed, still feeling weightless. It was like I had a new space in my heart.

"You need to practice as much as you can. And make your own broom, too. Nobody likes to share."

Sarah applauded from the cabin door. "Nicely done. Now, come and get some dinner."

After dinner, Fern approached. "I have to leave soon for Hell, but did you want to try some earth magic? I can give you the test."

"Sure." I brightened, hoping I might be in her elemental clan. "If you think I'm ready."

I'd give anything to have such a kind and patient teacher. I didn't want to admit it, but I longed to be taken under someone's wing. I felt like a loner — I missed my heartfelt conversations with Jane.

"We'll see. Come on out back."

The garden was heavy with white and orange pumpkins. Fern stopped in front of a patch of barley.

She stared at me, and for a moment, I thought I saw her ears go long and pointy.

"Belle," she whispered, "do you sense any animals nearby?"

I looked at the silent vegetable patches and the fenced-in herb garden, straining to hear any animal-like sounds. The night was still.

She pointed at a pine tree in the distance. "There's a raccoon in that tree. Can you feel him?"

"No, how do you do that?"

Her eyes had a faraway look. "It's like we share a mind. A lot of animals do it, and trees and other plants too."

I toed the ground, my heart dropping. "Does that mean I'm not an earth witch?"

"Not necessarily. Come with me to the herb garden."

We walked through the gate and knelt beside a branching rosemary shrub and a mass of creeping thyme.

"Focus your energy on the plants," she said. "See if you can make them grow."

I inhaled their herbaceous aromas and gave them energy from my solar plexus. I expected the plants to vine out longer, or bloom, or grow bushier, but nothing happened. I tried harder, using energy from my entire body. After several minutes of straining, I sighed. "Should I be saying a spell or something?"

"No. If you were an earth witch, you'd be able to do it naturally, without any spells. One more thing." She pulled out a small white rock from her pocket and placed it on the ground before me. "Can you move it?"

I stared at it, trying to nudge it, imagining it moving across the earth.

After a minute, she picked it up, then straightened and brushed the dirt off her knees. "Sorry, Belle. You're not earth."

I picked myself up, feeling low again. I'd failed the test. I'd wanted so much to be an earth witch, especially because Fern was so nice. Would I ever belong to a group? My heart pounded in my ears.

"What kind of elemental do you think I might be?" I asked.

She winced. "Do you have an affinity for water?"

I shrugged. "Not particularly."

"What about fire?"

My skin crawled. I shook my head.

Her eyes were sympathetic. "You'll find your path. I'm sure of it. Let's go inside."

I took one last glance at the heavens before following her in.

CHAPTER TWENTY-THREE

The next morning, after I finished all my chores, I walked down the pea-gravel path toward the clearing, inhaling the fresh air. Sunlight diffused through the pine needles, and the ultraviolet net bounced in the breeze, its interlocking-circle pattern almost invisible. A few rabbits poked their heads out of their burrows to gaze at me, and an elk rustled in the dried leaves somewhere far away.

I was still amazed by this place. I thought I'd been all over the world, but being in rural Sweden in autumn reminded me there was still so much to see. The forest was so different compared to the bustling cities I usually frequented. Although I missed the churches and teahouses, just smelling the clean, fresh air did wonders for my soul. The natural wilderness was like its own kind of sanctuary.

Around the next bend, something moved between the

trees. I stopped in my tracks. Was it the elk? I dashed behind a tree and peered out. A man's silhouette formed, walking down the path toward me. His dark jeans, white sweater, and hiking boots marked him as a native Swede. Maybe it was someone on a walk. Or maybe it was a demon who'd found a way through the net. Come to think of it, Hazel was always somewhat distant with me, her eyes always on the fearsome side. Had she sold me out?

I fumbled for my knife and dropped it on the path with a clatter. I snatched it up, clutching it in my trembling hands, and inhaled through my nose. There weren't any sulfurous vapors, but the wind was dead. I cursed, knowing I might have to run rather than fight — unless I wanted to risk turning evil.

I peeked around the corner. He walked down the path, coming closer.

"Belle?" a gentle voice called out.

I blinked. It wasn't a stranger, but that voice didn't belong to a demon. Then who . . . ?

The tight feeling in my chest relaxed when I recognized Donovan's dark hair and strong, freckled cheekbones. I gasped. I thought he'd forgotten all about me. I re-sheathed my knife and ran toward him, crunching over the gravel.

He rushed toward me, stopping when we were arms' length apart. His cerulean eyes churned with joy and relief. His mouth trembled, as if he had so much to say, but didn't know how to begin. "Belle! How— how are you?"

"I'm good." I almost laughed when I saw his downy white feathers folded on his back over a white sweater. I ventured a glance around. No one else was nearby. If Maribeth was watching me from her perimeter patrol, she didn't make herself known. I smiled, glad to have a somewhat private conversation. "I thought I'd never see you again. How are you?"

Donovan's eyes teared up, and he breathed hard. His throat made a noise that sounded like a sob. "I never thought you'd make it out after those demons captured you. I thought . . ."

I swallowed, my smile fading from my lips. So Medea was right — he *had* given up on me. He'd left me to rot in a cell. But I couldn't blame him. He couldn't do anything about me, except tell the witches. And he had. That alone had saved me.

I reached toward him and brushed a lock of his hair out of his eyes. "Don't cry. I'm okay. And you helped me escape. I can't thank you enough for telling the witches about my imprisonment. They said it was an anonymous tip, but I knew it was you." I smiled up at him.

He shook his head, bewilderment in his eyes. "It wasn't me. I don't have any connections to Hell, besides you."

I blinked, stunned. If it wasn't him, then who'd told the witches about me being in a cell? Moreover, what *had* he done? Had he just given up on me and cried on a cloud for a couple of weeks? What kind of angel abandons the person he was assigned to rescue? I took a tiny step back, feeling my heart wall itself off from him. It hurt worse than any dagger, almost as bad as seeing Carlo killed. I glanced back at the little cabin, my mind churning, searching for an excuse to leave.

"I wanted to do something!" He swallowed roughly, his eyes watering. "I just didn't know what to do. I thought you were dead. I didn't hear your prayers for weeks. I mourned for you, Belle."

I pressed my lips together. I wanted to comfort him, but my own pain was too immense. I was the one put through the trauma, so why was I the one comforting him? He seemed less like a guardian angel and more like my incompetent manager. And to think — I thought I'd really knew him, that he was my knight in shining armor. But did I even know who he really was?

I shrugged, letting go of my resentment as best I could. "In the end, I suppose it all worked out for me. The witches got me out, and I'm not evil, despite the terrible things Lucifer made me do."

His brows furrowed. "I'm so sorry for what happened. If we'd only left earlier that day—"

"It's okay." I touched his forearm. My fingertips

buzzed, and the feeling trickled up my arm to my shoulder. It wasn't as strong as before, but it was still palpable. It was funny — our touch felt like magic, only weaker. With him, I was less in charge of myself, less able to do anything — my body turned to jelly; whereas with magic, I was powerful. I could change matter and do the impossible.

Donovan's tears eased up as he gazed down at me. "I'm so glad you're okay. Do you want to go to a halfway house? I can fly you to one right now. There's one not too far from here."

I glanced at the blue sky and the white clouds. It'd be so much fun to fly through them. I wanted to feel the moisture of a cloud wrap around me and then burst through it to feel the sun on my back. But not with him. I wanted to fly on a broom, and then return to my friends and work on my karma. I didn't want to live in a halfway house with borderline-evil demons, not when I had a whole house full of mostly supportive people. And I definitely didn't want my only friend to be someone who'd abandoned me.

"I really think you'd like it there." Donovan's hands splayed as he spoke. "They run a coffeehouse and make pastries and soup. All the proceeds go to the poor and homeless."

I took a deep breath. "I'm going to pass on that."

His eyes popped open and his neck bent forward.

"What? Are you serious? Belle—"

"Donovan, these people have been kind to me. I can't leave them. They feel like my family."

"You know," his head waggled a little. "You can have other families. New ones." He reached for me, his hands running over my arms until he touched my shoulders, then my back, where my heart was. "I could be your family."

The buzzing sensation shot through my heart and nerves. Bliss cascaded all throughout my limbs. For a moment, I saw what my life would be like if I went with him. I saw us traveling to foreign cities, walking on a beach, our hands entwined and our feet in the surf; dinner at luxurious restaurants, and my secret smile when I picked a feather from his tuxedo jacket . . .

He pulled me close, embracing me, his hands smoothing down my back.

I saw my life in the clouds with him, in Heaven, a house, my parents visiting. I saw us adopting a little baby, swaddled in white. Tears rose up to my eyes. A *baby*.

I pushed Donovan's arms off me. He didn't deserve to touch me. It was an unfair trick, making me see that. Those were his dreams, his plans; not mine. And all this time I'd been out of Hell, he could've visited. I'd prayed to him — I'd begged him for help! Maybe he hadn't responded because he was afraid I'd turn, or maybe he'd heard me and still abandoned me to whatever fate I had in store. It was selfish of him. More than anything, I knew he didn't have my best interests at heart. He was only thinking of himself and what *he* wanted.

His eyes searched mine. Nearby, a bird chirped, and a breeze rustled the trees.

"I'm staying here," I swallowed. "I know you don't understand, but no one should be able to hurt anyone else the way Lucifer has hurt me. He's done it before, and he'll do it again."

"But . . . what on earth are you going to do to him? He's much more powerful than you."

I took a deep breath, knowing I could trust him enough to tell him our plans. He might even have information for me. I leveled my gaze at him. "We're trying to find a weapon that'll kill him once and for all. Have you ever heard of such a thing?"

He staggered back. "Belle, you don't really think you'll survive an attack against him, do you?"

I shrugged. I had survived one, though I couldn't tell him that — he wouldn't understand. "Look, I know I might die, and even if we did manage to take him down, Heaven might deny me, or be a long way away. But I have to try."

His face was taut, his eyes emotional. "Belle, I know all about rebellions. When I fought in the Welsh Revolt, I was killed in battle. At the time, I thought I'd died for a noble cause. But now I see it was a waste. People like us
270

can't take down someone that powerful. And I was just rebelling against a king. You're going up against one of the original angels!"

"But—"

"Listen to me." He pointed a finger at my chest. "That kind of person will always be in charge. Even if the impossible happens, and you actually do take him down, some other monster will rise to his place. And who's to say he won't be just as bad or worse? Think of your soul, Belle. Think of me. You don't have to die."

"Help me not die." I gritted my teeth. "Help me kill him!"

He shook his head. "I can't fight, not again."

"Well, I have to do this. With or without you."

He wheeled back, his hand touching his head. Sob-like breaths came from his mouth again.

I looked into the emerald woods, hoping to see anything to distract me — a sign of life or a rustle of branches in the breeze — but it was as if the forest was holding its breath too. I tried to control my voice to keep it from shaking. "You didn't answer my question. Have you ever heard about a weapon that could kill Lucifer? Or anything that could pierce his skin?"

He shook his head, mute.

"At least tell me what you know about him. It might help."

He raised his hands helplessly. "I don't know

271

anything."

"Just tell me what you do know."

He sighed and rolled his eyes. "He's the Prince of Darkness. He lives in Hell. He was kicked out of Heaven. That's it."

I considered his words. "When you say kicked out, what do you mean?"

He shrugged. "The archangels made him leave."

"Yeah, but how?"

He mused, biting his lip. "They cast him out of Heaven, to Earth. They cursed him so he couldn't stay on Earth for too long because that wasn't his home — it was for God's earthly creatures. So he created Hell with his other fallen angels."

A crow flew overhead, wings wide. It let out a *caw* before disappearing from sight.

"What happened to Lucifer's wings?" I asked.

Donovan's eyes searched the air. "I . . . don't know."

"Where did he land when he fell to earth?"

"Well, the rumor is that he aimed for the Atlantic Ocean, but he landed in what's now southern Germany. But what does that matter?"

I looked at his downy wings folded over his shoulders. "Your wings mark you as an angel. They're part of being good. And since they were once a part of him, they might be able to pierce his skin. If we can find his wings or a feather, and make it into a weapon, it could kill him. Or maybe neutralize him."

He cringed. "What if his wings let him get back into Heaven?"

"It wouldn't be enough, not with his karma score. He's evil — Heaven has safeguards against that."

"Belle, I don't want you taking a chance. If you hurt him, you could turn evil. Your karma score is too close."

I shook my head. "Being evil isn't the end of the world. One of the witches who rescued me came back from it. It just takes a lot longer to earn back the karma."

He pouted. "How long?"

"A hundred years or so."

"That's a long time." He looked forlorn, his eyes haggard. "And she may not be truly evil anymore, but she lost her memories, and she's been marked. She can never go to Heaven. That's what I'm afraid of for you." He shook his head. "I saw your parents in Heaven yesterday. I wasn't going to say anything to you, but . . . don't you miss them?"

My brow furrowed. The thought of my family burned a hole in my chest. How dare he? Of course I yearned for my mother's embrace, for my father's steady gaze as we talked about our day over dinner. I glanced at Donovan's imploring eyes. "Of course I miss my family. But this is my life now, and it's been this way for centuries. Can't you see that?"

"Rethink this." His fingers curled around my hands,

making vibrations travel up my arms to the base of my skull.

I closed my eyes as his warm hands enfolded mine completely. He took a step closer, his breath fluttering against my forehead, then his cheek leaned close to mine. Everything tingled and felt light, as if I were made of dancing points of light. But it wasn't real. I took a step away from him and gazed into his crystal blue eyes.

"If I survive this, come find me."

"Belle, no . . ."

I turned and walked through the silent forest back to the little cabin, and didn't look back.

CHAPTER TWENTY-FOUR

A few days after seeing Donovan in the woods, I walked down the dirt path leading toward the woodshed, eager to see Medea. After weeks of not seeing her, she was finally on the schedule again. I needed to tell her about Donovan and what I'd discovered. If it meant what I thought, we might have a chance to kill Lucifer once and for all.

Birds sang, and pine needles snapped under my feet as I walked on the path. The weak afternoon sun was barely visible through the dense layer of clouds covering the sky. My breath came out in a cloud too, and I drew my coat closer, grasping the pale willow basket tighter in my stinging fingertips.

I followed the sound of splitting logs and saw Medea through the trees near the woodshed. Despite the rural surroundings, she was dressed in her usual long black silky skirt, only now, instead of a heavy sweater, she wore a navy tank top with a decoration made of rhinestones. Her arms were bare as they flowed in a dance — it looked as if she were conducting an orchestra, only she was *chopping wood, with magic.* As her arms moved, a tree trunk flew onto a chopping block. She brought her hands down and the trunk was torn in half with a loud chop, halving the pieces again and again. When she swept her hands toward the shed, the logs flew inside, stacking themselves into a neat pile. She swept her light hair back from her face and moved another trunk to the cutting block.

"Medea!"

She startled when she heard my voice and turned to me, her cheeks flushed.

I glanced back at the cabin. No one had followed me. "Can I talk with you about something?"

"Sure." She grabbed a canteen hanging from a nearby branch and took a swig. "Everything okay?"

I ventured a smile at her fathomless black eyes and nodded. "Remember when I mentioned my special friend? The one we talked about on my first night here?"

Medea glanced around, wary. *"Obsuratia nebula,"* she mumbled. A black cloud of mist churned in the air and swarmed around us.

The flavor of licorice tickled my throat. I coughed. "What . . . ?"

"It's a privacy screen. Are you talking about the *angel?*"

"Yes. I spoke with him the other day. He came here."

Her eyes widened for a moment.

My palms began to sweat. "I would've told you sooner, but you weren't on the schedule."

"Go on."

"He didn't know about any weapon to kill Lucifer, but he did tell me where Lucifer and the other fallen angels landed when they fell to earth. I looked it up online and there's a huge crater there."

She nodded. "I know all about the Ries Crater. I looked at it centuries ago. There's nothing there."

"Exactly — there's nothing at the Ries Crater because there's another place where they actually landed. Or three, to be exact. Lucifer and his angels were ejected from Heaven so forcefully, they skipped over the surface of the earth, like a smooth stone over still water." I pulled out a map from my pocket and pointed to the Ries Crater and the two smaller craters to the east. "It's only in the last fifty years or so that scientists matched the date of the Ries impact to the two other locations. One of the craters is in Germany, and the others are in the Czech Republic."

"Okay. Wow. What's there?"

"There are crystals called moldavite at those secondary craters that aren't found anywhere else on earth. I've been trying to figure out what that means, and I think I got something." I took a deep breath. "There are

277

paintings of Lucifer leaving Heaven. Some of them show him with angelic, white, feathery wings; and some show him with bat wings, but we both know bat wings are a demonic manifestation. One of the basic rules of Heaven is that no one evil can exist there, so he couldn't have demonic features. So when he left, his wings had to be angelic — feathers, to be exact."

Her eyes narrowed at me. "What are you trying to say?"

"I was thinking — maybe when he fell to earth, his wings crystallized and shattered. If I'm right, these crystals are a supernatural artifact."

Medea drew a deep breath, realization dawning over her black eyes. "You think those crystals might actually pierce his skin and could kill him?"

"Right. There's only one problem. There are three different locations where they're found. I don't know which one he landed in."

She grasped my shoulders, her eyes dancing with hope. "You might be onto something. Don't tell anyone else about this, not until we have a chance to look into it more." She wound her hand in little circles, gathering the black mist like a wool skein. When she released it, it slipped onto the ground and formed her shadow. "Keep looking for answers."

I nodded, a sense of joy almost lifting me off the ground. I slipped a few logs into the basket and trotted back to the little cabin, eager to do more research.

Over the next few days, after my chores were finished and a casserole or a roast was cooking in the oven, I sat at the kitchen table with the clunky old laptop and read everything I could about the crystals at the craters. The bottle-green crystal called moldavite even looked like a shattered feather.

When I tired of my internet research, I uncovered more spells written on the books. I was still hunting down the love spell for Mephistopheles, but the bookcase was dwindling. I was getting a little worried. Day after day, I went back to the bookcase for more spells and cracked them, one after another. Some were easy to reveal, like the one to repel mosquitos, but some took an hour or more to sparkle to life. I began to draw energy from the cats so often it was almost as easy as breathing.

Kelsey wasn't around the cabin as much, but whenever she was, she managed to treat me as if I'd still turn evil, even though her 'three days of the full moon' were long gone. It confirmed my suspicions that she just didn't like me. But I decided I could deal with that. Iona was probably right — she was jealous of the newest member.

One night, after the dinner dishes were washed and put away, I walked into the living room for the last few books on the bookshelf. Deep moonlight poured in from the windows, illuminating Claire's white hair as she drowsed in an armchair.

I picked up one of the remaining stacks of books and went to my room, hoping the spell I needed was in there. After a couple of duds and one cat later, I ran my hand over *The Wizard of Oz* and read the sparkling green letters that rose up.

herandomun amorindum gargaoa erophina
to bind in love and devotion
requires a physical object

A love spell! I almost laughed out loud with relief. At last, I'd get Mephistopheles off my back. For the past couple of weeks, the thought of the magic mirror, sitting in the bottom of my satchel, made my heart heavy with dread. I hadn't opened it since the last time I'd spoken with him, and it hadn't chimed lately either. I didn't trust him, but he hadn't told Lucifer my name yet. He couldn't be all bad. When I'd looked up his score a couple of days ago, it was more good than bad. For the first time, I wondered if the Devil's Office was right about Cloud having an error. Could he really be partially good? Then again, maybe he wasn't as bad as he seemed. It would explain why he never did any of the dirty work. Maybe it was an accident.

But I didn't have time to wonder about his karma score. I had to make that love charm. I closed the door of my room. The two cats lying on the bed blinked at me sleepily. I stroked the gray one and drained her, reveling in the almost-instant energy boost. I wound the hair around the topaz pendant and spoke the words of the spell, imagining it imbued with power. Drawing on my solar plexus, I felt my energy trickle out into the stone.

After an hour with nothing happening, I sipped on the white cat's energy, then repeated the spell again until my energy was so low I could barely speak. I tried sipping from the gray cat again, but I'd already taken everything from her.

I needed to continue the spell — if I didn't, I'd have to start all over again, and I had no idea when we were going to leave the safehouse.

I chanted until my throat was hoarse, concentrating even more, flexing my inner magical muscle. I inwardly begged for it to work. I pressed my body against the charm, until I was past empty, drained, the words barely registering on my mumbling lips. The sky outside my window grew light, with pink hues of sunrise peeking through the pines, but I kept going, blinking wearily.

At last, the pendant glimmered with rosy sparkles. I thought I was hallucinating from lack of sleep, but the sparkles grew bigger, and the pendant felt warm in my palm.

I tucked the pendant into a slender pocket in my satchel near the burner phone and fell back onto the bed, exhausted and relieved. My last thoughts before I passed out were imagining a place I could leave it for Mephistopheles to find when we traveled to the next safehouse.

I paid the price for that magic the next day. Not only did I sleep past breakfast, but I aroused Claire's suspicion. The cats had mewled and clawed at the door until she'd let them out. At the sight of me lying on the bed, she placed a bony hand on my forehead.

"Are you feeling well?" she croaked.

"I'm fine," I said, every word scorching my sore throat. I looked into her blue eyes, hoping she didn't suspect me. "I just tried to do too many spells last night."

She shook her lined face. "The spells that brings this kind of exhaustion . . ."

"It was a thought charm."

"Hm." She looked as if she didn't believe me, then

sighed. "You shouldn't push yourself like that, dear. You're still in training. You could've died."

She brought in the massive orange tabby, who purred and kneaded the bed. I petted his soft fur, drawing his strong energy into me until I couldn't draw any more, then I fell back, still exhausted. She brought in another cat, and I took from that one too before it scampered away.

"Magical fatigue is worse than being tired. Promise you won't do anything like this alone again?"

All I could do was grumble an apology and nod. Sleep was overtaking me, and I couldn't keep my eyes open.

"We'll talk about this again." Claire stood and closed the door.

When I awoke, it was dusk. The witches on duty had eaten leftovers for dinner. Their dishes and silverware were set in the sink, even though they were nowhere to be found. I ate some leftover quiche from the refrigerator, still feeling like garbage. For the first time since I'd arrived, I had a day off, though it didn't feel like it.

But the thought of the topaz pendant in my satchel made it all better. At least my spell had worked. I had a love charm for Mephistopheles, and soon, I'd never have to worry about him again.

CHAPTER TWENTY-FIVE

The witches kept a closer eye on me after that day. They made a new rule that I had to check in with them if I wanted to do serious magic or leave the house. It was demeaning, but I had to play by their rules. I didn't want to arouse suspicion that I'd worked on a love charm for a demon. Truth be told, I deserved the punishment. I wondered what they'd do if they found out about that — flay me? Kick me out of the group? I wore my satchel, determined to never be without it.

I did everything I could to keep them happy, but they still side-eyed me whenever I closed the door to my bedroom or left the house to gather herbs or firewood.

One chilly afternoon, while cleaning the litter boxes, I heard a knock on the back door. I looked through the glass and saw Fern, her dark hair blowing in the wind. In her hands, she clutched two metal hell-air canisters like suitcases. Someone trailed behind her, with black hair and sparkling dark eyes peering over the grocery bags she was carrying.

I dropped the scooper and threw the door open. My insides beamed with light. I could hardly believe Jane was here, at the cabin, in front of me. She set the bags on the counter, then I drew her into a giant hug. I felt some part of my insides relax — something I hadn't even known was knotted. We broke apart and smiled at each other. Tears rose to my eyes, but I laughed and dashed them away.

"It's so good to see you, Belle," Jane blustered. "I was half-afraid you were dead!"

Fern smiled and set the canisters on the kitchen table. "I figured you deserved to see her. She swore she could keep a secret."

I beamed. "Thank you so much, Fern. You don't know how much this means to me."

She winked before heading out for a perimeter check.

"Belle, I was so worried. You were missing for weeks, and my kitchen was trashed! I asked around, but no one knew where you were. Nosferatu, that little shit, he said Lucifer probably dissipated you!"

I shook my head. Typical Nosferatu — he didn't miss me at all. The feeling was mutual. "I'm sorry about your kitchen and that I didn't reach out. They forbade me from contacting anyone, just in case it could be traced. But I'm in good hands now."

I looked over my old friend for any strange enchantments or pendants. I wouldn't put it past the witches to spell her so she wouldn't be able to talk about the location or the people who kept me secret. I couldn't think of any other way the witches would let an outsider here. But I didn't see anything out of the ordinary.

Jane's eyes darted around the cabin. "Are they treating you well?" she whispered, despite the fact that we were alone.

"Yes. They're teaching me magic!" I began to unpack the groceries into the cupboards and the vintage blue refrigerator.

"That's wonderful!" She shook her head in astonishment. "You're finally a witch, like you always wanted! After all these years."

"I know. I can even fly on a broom! Well, sort of. I'm not very good yet."

"Wow. Can't say I'm jealous, not with my fear of heights. I'd make a terrible witch, wouldn't I?"

I shook my head. "You'd be great. You might just be more of an earth elemental."

"An *earth elemental?*" She grasped my hands, her eyes lighting up. "You have to tell me everything!"

I smiled weakly at her. "Did Fern tell you what happened to me?"

"No, she said it's for you to tell. Why?"

I drew in a deep breath. "It's a really long story. And

you must be tired from your journey. Do you want some tea? Something to eat?"

"You know me — I always want something to eat. Oh, I almost forgot." She rummaged in her purse then held out a yellow tin with a gold banner. "I brought you some tea."

I squealed with delight and took the box of *Twining's Earl Grey* from her. It'd been ages since I had a decent cup of tea. I hugged it to my chest, smiling. "You know me so well."

I set the kettle on. Soon, bergamot aroma saturated the kitchen. I sliced some bread and unwrapped a block of sharp cheddar onto a cutting board. A tabby brushed against Jane's legs and a black cat jumped onto the counter to sniff my progress.

"My, someone likes cats here." She reached down to stroke the tabby. "I can't believe the security you have here, too. It took three protection gates to get here."

"It's a pretty secretive place. But it has to be."

"But why?"

"Let's go in the other room. I need to sit down." My arms felt weak from dusting the new spiderwebs off the ceilings, but in truth, I needed to restore my energy.

We brought the teaset and platter of food into the living room and set them on the coffee table. Jane munched while I grabbed a black shorthaired cat and set him on my lap. As we waited for the tea to steep, I breathed a deep sigh, drawing energy. I didn't know where to begin, but I supposed I could start at the scores.

"Jane, have you ever heard about Cloud?"

"No, what's that?"

"It's one of those karma calculators outlawed by the Devil's Office, only it's not just for people. It's for demons and angels too."

"What?" she asked. "Is that why they outlawed it?"

"Most likely."

I unlocked the burner phone and loaded the app. As I typed my name in, a fluttery feeling rose in my stomach. It'd been a few days since I'd last checked. Checking my score every day was like watching a pot boil — it felt like it took forever. I held my breath as the screen loaded.

```
Belle Dame: 95.9% bad, 4.1% good
```

"Jane!" I exclaimed in disbelief. The cat leapt off my lap. I showed her the phone, my heart in my throat. "I'm at 4.1%!"

Her hand rose to her chest and she drew back. "Goodness, can that be true?"

"It's good!" I smiled, bubbles of laughter rising within me.

She paled. "What?" She took the phone in her hands

and frowned at it. "But that's terrible! How on earth—"

"Sorry. Let me explain. It was a lot worse. I was so close to being evil."

"Evil?!"

"It turns out Carlo was an innocent."

"But — you were assigned to torture him!"

"I know." I gazed at my hands folded in my lap. "Even though I was only following orders, it still affected my score." I met her eyes, pleading for her to understand. "I didn't know any better, I swear!"

"Oh Belle, that's horrible. I'm so sorry." Her eyes watered. "I feel like I should've known somehow."

I made a dismissive gesture with my hands. "I know what you mean. I feel like I should've sensed it too. And maybe I did, in a way. I felt like there was something about Carlo that was different."

"I remember." She looked at me with sympathetic eyes. "And I talked you into torturing him! I'm so sorry."

I reached for her and smoothed her back. "It's not your fault. We were all fooled."

"But, wait. How do you know that karma calculator works? The Devil's Office said there are problems with them."

I poured the tea into delicate cups, avoiding her gaze. I couldn't tell her about the angel. The best thing would be to keep her in the dark about it, as much as it hurt me.

"I looked up a lot of people. It checks out."

She picked up her teacup and blew, making big curls of steam rise. "What happened to Carlo?"

"I . . . let him go. And somehow, I guess word got around to Lucifer, because demons showed up to your kitchen and took me to Hell." My stomach churned just thinking about his face, his hopes raised when he was released only to be dashed again when my knife plunged into him.

"What did Lucifer do?"

"Lucifer had Carlo in his office. And. . ." My heart plummeted. "He made me kill him so I'd turn evil."

She gasped. "*He made you kill an innocent?!*"

I nodded.

"No!" Jane set down her teacup and lifted both hands to cover her mouth. "Say it ain't true!"

I nodded, a pain in the back of my throat as I fought to keep the tears from rising.

"You poor thing!" She reached out and enclosed me in her arms.

I leaned into her embrace, feeling my struggle over the last few weeks melt. I hadn't realized I'd been on edge for so long.

"But why would he want you to be evil? You're just a temp, and you're on the Heaven-track."

I ground my jaw, my face tight. I didn't want to say the words. They seemed ridiculous. What Medea had said resonated with me as true, though, and Mephistopheles had pretty much confirmed it when I'd asked him.

I took a deep breath and released it out slowly, gazing into Jane's kind eyes. "He wanted me to turn evil so I could become his mistress. There's some legend about Beauty and the Beast in the Bible, and he thought it would bring about the end-of-days. He locked me in a cell, but I was rescued by these women." A swell of relief made my heart heavy. "They saved my life. If they hadn't rescued me, Lucifer would've made me kill you."

Her mouth opened but no words came out.

I glanced at the black cat purring in my lap and thought of Medea. "The worst part is I'm not the only one he's done it to. There's another woman here who wasn't rescued. She lived through it for twenty years. She saw the signs, and that's why she and her coven rescued me."

Jane was silent, her eyes wide.

"The worst thing is there's no stopping him from doing it again with someone else. We don't want to see anyone go through that ever again — that's why we have a plan to kill him. We've been doing some research, and we might have a way. But," I swallowed and drew back, looking into her moist brown eyes. "You're endangering yourself by coming here. I don't want you tangled up in this mess. If anything ever happened to you, I'd never forgive myself."

"You're my best friend." She waved my concern off. "I'd do anything for you."

My chest constricted. "You'd even go up against the Beast himself?"

"Yes. Don't worry about me." She smiled, dimples burrowing into her round cheeks. "I can take care of myself."

I smiled at her, the tension inside me releasing its death grip a little more. There were so few people in my life that I was close to. Her support meant everything. "You know, Jane, your score is really good."

"Really? What is it? Tell me."

I typed her name into the app.

```
Jane Black: 1.6% bad, 98.4% good
```

"Oh my goodness," I gasped. "You're eligible to go to Heaven!"

"Heaven?" She gazed at the score, her lips parted, then a smile spread over her face.

"How'd your score get so low?" I asked.

"It must've been . . . I saved three good people's lives at my hospital last week. But I didn't realize . . ."

I smiled at her. For as much as I appreciated her support, I knew she shouldn't be here. She needed to get to Heaven or a safe place as soon as possible. I wondered if Donovan could take her to Heaven. I said a silent prayer to him and resolved to talk with Medea about it too.

"Belle, if you kill Lucifer, you might just become an archangel!"

I shook my head and gazed at the spiral rag-rug on the floor. "I don't know about that."

"Well, I'm sure you'll make up your karma in no time."

I smiled weakly at her. "If our plan doesn't work, I'll never get to Heaven, and I'm okay with that — I want you to know. I'm finally standing up for myself instead of letting other people make all of my decisions."

She took my hand in hers. "When I get to Heaven, I'll ask them to grant you a pardon. They'll have to see the logic in it. You'll be singing hymns with me in no time."

I bowed my head. "I don't think it works that way. I'll probably have to earn it, just like everyone else did."

Her head tilted and a wry smile played on her face. "Never underestimate how much I can wear someone down by talking to them."

I laughed.

"Tell me more about your life here. You said you do magic now. Can you do spells?"

"Yeah. I can't do much, but I'm working on it."

"I'm so happy for you. Finally, you're a witch." She

grasped my hand. "If you need to raise your karma, maybe I can help. We can make dinner. I brought everything to make a magnificent lasagne."

"Okay." I slipped the phone into my satchel, and we went into the kitchen. We put some music on and chopped vegetables and sausage. Soon, noodles boiled in giant pots, and sauce simmered on the stove. Aromas of garlic and basil filled the house.

An hour later, Jane pulled from the oven a bubbling dish with melted cheese. It was so delicious that Medea joked they'd make her an honorary witch. Maribeth even thanked us and smiled. Jane poured a round of wine and toasted my saviors. It was a perfect night, if there ever was one, and I appreciated it as if it were my last.

CHAPTER TWENTY-SIX

The next day, I caught Medea in the kitchen before she left for Hell. The smell of waffles and syrup still hung in the air.

"Can I talk with you?" I asked.

She slipped a band around her blonde hair. "What's up?"

"*Obsuratia nebula.*" I pushed the energy out of my gut, and a black misty cloud formed around us. Even though no one else was around, I didn't want to take any chances.

"Belle, you can do a privacy cloud? I'm impressed. You're a quick study. This must mean you have something good for me."

I gave her a crisp nod, breathing in the wonderful licorice aroma of the spell. "I did some more research and I wanted to run something by you. I'd mentioned that crystal, moldavite, is found in three locations. I think I know which one has Lucifer's wings."

"Tell me more."

"There were two impacts at the Ries Crater — one larger one, and then a smaller one after that. They both bounced off to the other locations I mentioned last time."

"Do you think Lucifer made the first or the second impact?"

"The way it reads in the Bible, he was ejected first, so he had to be the first, bigger impact. But that's not what's important. The bigger 'asteroid,' as the scientists are calling it, bounced to a secondary location in the Bohemian part of the Czech Republic and made a crater there too. And guess what? The moldavite crystals there are light green. The moldavite at the secondary asteroid impact sites are much darker — brown and black."

"And Lucifer means light-bringer," Medea murmured, nodding.

"Right." I pulled out a map and pointed to the region. "Here's where the crater is. It's near the city of Ceské Budojovice."

She gave me a tiny smile. "Belle, this is huge. All this time, I thought we might never be rid of Lucifer, that we'd have to live our afterlives on the run, or pretending to obey."

"I hope I'm right." There was one more thing I didn't want to think about — even if we pierced his skin with the crystals, there was no guarantee he'd actually perish. But I pushed it out of my mind for the moment. "Before you go, there's one more thing I wanted to ask you about."

"Mm hm?"

"Jane is eligible for Heaven, and I'd like to get her in. I don't want her to have to return to Hell."

"I see." She glanced at her watch. "She can stay here, but you'd better do everything you can to get that angel of yours back here. She's not a witch, and our resources are already spread too thin."

My heart expanded, and I breathed deep. The sooner Jane was safe in Heaven, the better I'd feel. "Thank you so much."

"You're welcome. Now, if you'll excuse me, I have to keep up appearances." She summoned her broom from the foyer, walked out the back door, and drifted into the sky.

That evening, Jane and I made dinner again. Word had gotten around about the meal from yesterday, and more witches showed up. It was the full moon, too, so almost all of the witches were there enjoying themselves with wine and tea.

"That smells amazing," Sarah said, poking her head into the kitchen. Her pale nose wrinkled as she sniffed the air. "What is it?"

I surveyed our dishes. "Roasted quail, herbed potatoes, and green beans."

"Actually," Jane said, pulling a heavy dish from the oven, "they're *haricot vert*." She removed her oven mitts and stirred a steaming pot on the stovetop. "You should know that, Belle, you're French."

I picked one up and bit into the soft, sweet flesh. "I never saw these when I was in France, or Germany, for that matter."

"Whatever they're called, they smell delicious." Sarah smiled.

Jane and I plated the meal and brought them out to everyone in the living room. We joined them once everyone was served. Burgundy wine flowed into glasses and mugs. Everyone marveled over the tenderness of the meat and the evenly browned potatoes. Even Kelsey ate a full plate, though she skulked away without a thanks. For dessert, we served quivering slices of lemon meringue pie alongside tiny cups of espresso.

After the meal, Sarah leaned back on the couch, holding her belly. "That was amazing. I'm so full I can barely move. But we'll clean up, Belle. You've earned a night of respite."

"Especially after that meal." Iona drew a finger over her dessert plate, picking up the last crumbs. "Simply scrumptious."

I petted a cat and debated telling them not to bother until Jane cast doe eyes in my direction.

"It sure would be nice to see the land, Belle. Care to show me around?"

"Well . . ." I bit my lip. There was something I needed to do. The witches had been after me to make my own broom, and tonight was a full moon. Any magic I did tonight would be stronger. "Do you mind if I do some magic?"

"*Do I mind?*" Jane laughed. "Of course not. I'm curi-ouser than ever."

"Alright," Sarah got up and tied an apron over her prairie dress. "Who's going to help me with all these dishes?"

Jane and I grabbed our coats and walked out the back door. The sun was setting in a smeary mass of orange and pink on the horizon. We picked sprigs of lavender and sage from the herb garden, then strode down the path through the pine forest. After a few minutes, we came across a field with tall golden grass, swaying in the night breeze. Each stalk was tipped with seeds, pods, or tiny wildflowers. I unsheathed the knife Medea gave me and sighed. The last time I'd used a knife like this was to kill Carlo. Its blade glinted in the dying orange light. For a moment, it looked like it was covered in blood. I dropped it. The knife landed in the dark soil.

"Are you okay?" Jane asked.

I nodded, sniffing back suffocating tears. I told myself it was a different knife — it had a different thickness, a different weight. I couldn't believe I'd tortured him. I could almost still feel his hot blood run over my hands. Carlo's death seemed like it was a lifetime ago, but it'd only been a few weeks. So much had changed since then. I'd gotten closer to my new family, and it was so much better than anything I'd ever known my entire life.

"What's wrong?" Jane reached a hand to draw my hair away from my face.

"This place, this life . . . it's all so magical. I didn't even realize how much I'd gotten used to the stress of everyday life in Hell. It was so cruel, so merciless. I hated every moment of it. And now, it's all gone. For the moment, anyway."

Jane knelt beside me and picked up the knife. She brushed off the soil, then held it out to me. "I've always believed there was a plan for us — something better, even though we may not know what it might be."

I looked at her kind face and smiled. I didn't know if I believed in a bigger plan or not — I just needed to survive this day, and then the next, and the next. And someday, if things went to plan, I'd confront Lucifer and take his life, and face whatever happened after that.

I cleared my mind with a fresh breath of prairie air and curled my fingers around the wooden handle of the knife. With my other hand, I gathered a bunch of grass and pressed the knife against it, severing the stalks from the roots bound in the earth.

"What's next?" Jane glanced around at the indigo sky and darkening woods. An owl hooted in the falling night.

"Manus illumino lux."

I took out my journal, then shined the light from my palm onto the bookmarked page where I'd written the spell for enchanting a broom. "The next item is *'a pine branch felled not by human hands.'"*

"Where are we going to find that?" Jane asked.

"I'm sure there's one in the forest somewhere."

We walked back to the forest path. I shined my palm on the ground, exposing roots and needles. After a few minutes, we found a fallen branch. Jane held it as I stripped the branches and needles off with my knife. She then held the long grass and herbs while I braided them to the bough with hemp rope. We consecrated the broom by burning dried wormwood and sage around it. The sweet smoke tangled in my nose, and I felt heady after inhaling it.

It was adorable — a little smaller than the others, and

301

a little more rustic-looking, but it was perfect for me. I especially liked the herbs in the grass.

I took a deep breath and spoke the words to enchant the broom, feeling a river of energy flow from me. "*Ingar volatum.*"

"Did it work?" Jane asked, her eyes excited.

"Not yet. Enchanting objects takes a while."

Jane ran her hands over her arms. "Can we go inside and do it? It's getting chilly."

"No, it has to be where the branch fell." I glanced around, mindful of how far away the cabin and the cats were. I wouldn't be able to take their energy from this far away. I hoped I was up to the spell. I should've told the other witches what I was doing, but I had Jane with me. If I passed out, she could get help.

I looked at the broom and wondered how long the enchantment would take. The other magical items I'd created had each taken at least an hour. "It might be a while. You can go inside if you want."

"No, it's okay. I'll keep watch over us. Are we still under the protection thing?"

I glanced up. Bats flew through the nearly invisible net shimmering above. "We're safe."

Jane's eyes slid over the dark forest. "Maybe I'm just paranoid."

"You know, we have guards in addition to the net."

"That makes me feel better."

"Here, take my knife." I handed it to her. "Just in case."

I took a deep breath and chanted, pushing the energy out of me, watching with half-closed eyes for a sparkle or glimmer. There was nothing but my chanting and the dark night.

After several minutes, something rustled in the forest. I looked around, but didn't stop chanting.

Jane startled up to her feet, and I heard the *ching* of my knife being drawn. She walked toward the noise, her footsteps snapping branches. I hesitated, almost stopping the flow of magic. What was out there? Would she be able to defend herself?

She returned, shaking her head. Whatever animal had crossed our paths stayed out of our way.

My chanting increased. I went into a trance for what seemed like an eternity. My vision blurred and dimmed. My glowing hand became nothing more than a faint glow in the strange shadowy world. Still, I chanted on, feeling a pit of emptiness carved within me. I chanted even when I had nothing else to give but the deep chasm of nothingness, my voice nothing more than a hoarse whisper.

Somewhere deep inside of me, a reserve of energy burst forth, renewing my words. I pushed it all out into the broom until my energy was exhausted again. My throat grew scratchy, and still, words and energy trickled out from me.

After what felt like two hours, crystalline white and blue sparkles spun around my little broom. It glowed like a beacon in the velvety night.

Jane startled back. "I never knew magic was beautiful!"

The sparks absorbed into the rough bark. I held the broom in my hand, admiring the sage and lavender and the braided grass.

"So, does it work now?" Jane asked.

"It should work, yeah."

She grinned. "Wanna test it out?"

I hesitated, uncertain. I hadn't practiced enough, and I didn't want to embarrass myself by remaining on the ground. A couple of cool raindrops fell onto my head, ticking off the boughs around us. I raised my hood just as a volley of more rain began to fall. "Tomorrow. Let's go in."

"Fine with me." She ran her hands over her arms again. "Someone said there's juniper vodka back at the cabin."

I nodded, exhausted. I wouldn't be much of a drinker tonight, but I'd keep her company as long as I could stay awake.

We walked over the uneven ground toward the path, my palm lighting the way. The path glowed in the moonlight. The little cabin, with its smoke from the chimney, looked so serene.

The broom felt both heavy and light in my hands. I didn't know what I had expected, but it felt like a huge accomplishment and an even bigger challenge. Someday soon, I'd have to try to fly on it. I hadn't flown since Fern had helped me. I knew I should've practiced more, but I'd been too busy trying to create Mephistopheles' charms — I'd been distracted. But now that his charm was made and I had my own broom, I had no excuse. I'd try first thing tomorrow morning, as long as the skies were clear.

Once we were inside, I leaned it against the wall beside the others, a bit of pride sinking into me. In the kitchen, music thumped and witches laughed. I petted a giant white cat and sat down to take some energy from it.

Kelsey walked into the living room and leaned against the doorframe, her arms crossed as she glared at my broom. "Can that thing fly?"

I barely looked at her. "Yeah, I'm pretty sure it will."

She huffed. "But you didn't check?"

"Not tonight." I rose and walked toward the kitchen.

She caught my arm, her grasp keeping me.

"Why don't you try it out now, Belle?" A teasing smile lit Kelsey's face. "You won't know if it works unless you try."

"I said *not tonight*." I wrenched my arm back in disgust, fighting back the anger inside. My demonic

305

features itched.

"What's the matter? Afraid you're going to stay on the ground again?"

I sighed. Usually I'd brush past her, but I had to know why she hated me so much. It was one thing to make fun of my lack of skills, but this felt personal. "What do you have against me?"

She stepped in front of me, entering my personal space. Black splotches surfaced in her eyes, only to disappear.

Two of the cats near us growled and bristled. They arched their backs, their ears twitching.

I froze, a cold wash falling over my spine. Had I turned evil with this little exchange? It couldn't be. I couldn't have.

Footsteps sounded from the porch. Through the window, all was dark except for the shadow of pines moving in the wind. Then a silhouette darted between the trees.

The cats hissed at the window. More cats ran into the living room and hissed or snarled.

Kelsey came at me, pinning my arms to my sides.

"What are you doing?" I kneed her in the groin and broke free, running into the kitchen. Her fingernails scraped my back.

The witches laughed, wine glasses in their hands. I glanced behind me, but Kelsey didn't follow me.

"Fern!" I shouted. "Who's on guard?"

Fern set a glass of wine down onto the table. "Hazel and I are, why?"

Beside her, Hazel set down her glass of gin and tonic and smiled.

"What's wrong?" Jane asked.

My heartbeat clamored in my ears. Who was outside? Had demons figured out where we hid?Could they have discovered a way through the protection spells?

"What is it?" Sarah asked.

"I saw a shadow through the window outside. Maybe it's nothing . . ."

Fern walked into the front room, her eyes strained on the window outside. When she whirled around to face us, her eyes were wide with fear. "Demons!"

CHAPTER TWENTY-SEVEN

"Obserae!" Fern extended her arm, locking all eight of the locks on the front door with a purple light.

Iona threw a bolt of violet energy at the back door. *"Obserae!"*

Other witches repeated the spell, locking the windows.

The sound of something hitting the front door reverberated through the room. "I know you have Belle!" Lucifer's voice rang out. "Send her out and we'll forget this ever happened."

Jane glanced at me, her eyes wide. I knew what she was thinking. If we hadn't gone inside when we did, we'd be captured again.

We all converged in the living room in the eerie quiet. Even Kelsey looked frightened as she backed against the wall.

Fern's eyes peaked with fear. "Lucifer is out there with

at least seven demons. I can feel them out there, creeping around, trying to find a way in."

"Why aren't they attacking the house?" I asked.

"It has extra protection besides the locks," Fern said. "But how could they have gotten through our gates?"

"Someone here must've given them a key." Medea looked around sternly. "Who betrayed us? Answer me!"

No one spoke. Jane's lips trembled and her eyes filled with tears. "If I led them here, Belle—"

"No. This couldn't have been you." I looked around at the others, my heart rattling in my chest. Some of the witches unsheathed their knives while others bent over to power up with a cat. None of them looked particularly guilty. The magic mirror in my satchel felt heavy on my shoulder. I adjusted the strap.

Jane ran from the room into the kitchen.

"Jane!" I shouted after her. Someone placed a hand on my chest.

"What's she doing?" Medea's eyes were cold.

"I don't know. But she's good, I promise."

From the kitchen, a metallic noise rang out. Medea and Fern stepped in front of me and crouched in front of the doorway. They each whispered something, making red crackling balls of energy sizzle in their palms like lightning.

"Stop it!" I pulled at their shoulders. "She's not the one who led them here!" I wanted to tell them it was the magic mirror, but I couldn't get the words out. I couldn't admit to my new family that I'd betrayed them.

"Quiet!" Medea hissed.

Kelsey twitched in the corner. Rings of sweat circled her armpits and her chest. Her face was flushed and her breath shallow, as if a panic attack was taking hold.

I approached her, hands reaching out to still her jerking motions. For all our differences, I still didn't want her to suffer. "Are you okay?"

"Get away from me," she scowled, drawing back. "I'm fine."

"Jesus and Mary!" Jane shouted. "I only got a weapon, in case I have to fight the demons!" She returned to the living room, her dress sleeves rolled up, a meat cleaver clutched in her hand.

"It can't be Jane," Fern said. "She doesn't know the spells."

"Unless she's deep undercover," someone said.

"No!" I shouted. "I met her on her first day, over a hundred years ago. She's fine."

Medea kept an eye on her, but closed her hand, absorbing the red ball of energy into her palm. She walked through the room, glancing at us. "There's no time to talk. There's only one thing we can do — fight our way out." She turned to face me. "We have to keep Belle safe. The future of humanity depends on it. We'll provide cover to let Belle make a getaway."

My stomach knotted. They were all risking their lives for me. "I'll fight with you."

"No. You're still too close to being evil and you need to flee."

Iona frowned, drops of sweat forming on her forehead. "There'll be casualties." Her eyes had an other-worldly look that raised the hairs on my arm.

Medea shrugged. "We don't have a choice. They've seen our faces through the windows. They know who we are, and we can never go back to Hell."

Someone banged on the door, making us all jump. I exchanged a look with Medea.

"They figured out how to breach the magic protecting the cabin," she whispered.

Kelsey ran for the door and started tearing the locks open.

"What are you doing, child?" Iona pulled her away from the door.

"Come on, you heard him." Kelsey's jaw clenched. "Let's give her up."

Medea's eyes opened wide. She stared at her, slowly circling around her. "It was you, wasn't it?"

"Of course not!" Kelsey slunk against the door and laughed. "I'm just saying that none of us have to die if we just give them what they want!"

"*Virtona sanctum!*" Medea launched a white glowing orb that struck Kelsey in the mouth. She gasped and reeled back.

I recalled that spell — it was to make someone tell the truth.

The orb jiggled down Kelsey's throat. It glowed, visible through her skin. Her hands flew up to her neck, and she choked for a moment until the ball travelled lower. It stopped at her stomach, where it expanded and glowed. She spasmed and fell to her knees, then fell forward, stomach heaving, and lay still.

"Is she dead?" Jane asked.

When Kelsey lifted her head, her eyes were black, her skin jaundiced. Her hair hung in clumps and strands.

Everyone took several steps back.

"What happened to her?" I asked.

Medea's eyes were large. "It's her demonic self. She's evil! She must've hidden it with charms. How did I not see this?"

I stared at Kelsey, repulsed by her demonic features. I'd known there was something wrong about her, but I had no idea it was this bad. Worst of all, that could've been me, had I let her jeers get to me.

Jane ran to shield me, the stainless steel cleaver held up menacingly.

Kelsey brushed back a plait of stringy hair. "You have it all wrong." She struggled to stand up by the door. Her yellowed hands turned a brass lock with a click.

"Kelsey, stop!" Medea shouted. "You can fight this."

Sarah's hands rose to her open mouth. "I can't believe she's evil!"

Kelsey cackled, a manic smile lighting her face. "Little prissy prude can't believe I fell for the devil, huh?" She laughed and twisted open another lock.

"*Obserae*," Iona whispered, her eyes tearing up. Violet light sprung from her hand, locking it again.

Medea stepped forward. "*Misanae volgam*." Red, spiky energy crackled in her palm. "Kelsey, stop. I'm warning you."

Kelsey twisted another lock. "Lucifer wants me, not her. Who would want a powerless witch? She can barely fly!" She slid back a bolt.

Iona threw another locking spell, zapping the bolts back in place.

"Someone lied to you." Medea walked closer to her, one step at a time. "Don't do this!"

Kelsey's hands jerked, unlocking the locks faster.

Iona chanted to close the locks as soon as they opened.

Kelsey screamed. She hunched over and drew her curved knife from her belt, brandishing it in the air.

"STOP!" Medea shouted.

At first, I was afraid Kelsey would charge us with the knife, but she plunged it down into her pale forearm. A stream of blood poured from the cut onto the floor. She dragged the blade up her arm, cutting a wide gash into her sallow skin.

I gasped, drawing back. "Is she killing herself?"

"No, worse." Fern shook her head, her brow creased with worry. "It's dark magic — it requires blood."

A river of blood ran onto the floor as words bubbled from Kelsey's lips. Her fierce black eyes bore into mine as she chanted.

"STOP IT KELSEY!" Medea shouted, the red fire in her hand growing larger and brighter, swirling angrily. It was so bright it blinded me, hurting my eyes.

But Kelsey didn't stop. She chanted louder. A strong wind rose in the cabin, rocking the curtains and raising the hairs on my arm.

I wanted to do something, anything. But my mind was blank. I didn't know what to do. I couldn't think of one spell I knew. Jane shuddered closer to me, a worried expression on her face.

Kelsey splayed her hands, releasing a torrent of white light at the door. The locks exploded in a cacophony of metallic pinging.

We ducked, covering our faces as bolts and screws flew across the room.

Medea reared her arm back and threw the red star at Kelsey, and then another. They landed on her chest, ran down her flesh, and sliced deep gashes from her shoulder to her hip. I thought I saw the white of her bones appear before more blood spilled out of her. Kelsey struggled, reaching up toward the door knob. She gasped a horrifying rattle and fell forward, collapsing onto the floor into a puddle of blood.

"I'm sorry." Medea whispered to her. She lifted her palm and shot another electric red star into Kelsey's head.

Kelsey jerked, animated for a moment, then she lay still.

Iona cupped her hands over her face and turned away. Fern chanted something, and the metal pieces of the locks flew up from the floor and reassembled themselves to lock the doors.

The other witches gazed at each other in shock. I swallowed hard. I'd seen the darkness inside Kelsey long before they had. I knew there was something wrong with her. That was why we'd fought — my bad nature was stirred by hers. I stared at her limp body on the floor. A heavy sadness flowed over me.

From outside, something heavy slammed against the door. I jumped.

"Don't worry," Fern said. "The house is still spelled against them."

Medea faced the group, dashing away tears. "It's our duty to protect Belle at all costs. Belle," she took me aside. Her liquid black eyes bore into mine. "You have to get to that place we talked about."

"To—"

"Keep it secret until you're absolutely certain you're safe. You need to get there one way or another, okay?"

I nodded feverishly.

Medea faced the group. "We may be surrounded, but we still have the advantage of flight. Iona, prepare the chimney. We're going out like it's Christmas Eve."

Iona raced to the mantle and fiddled with the plume.

"*Adprendo!*" Brooms flew through the air and into the hands of the witches who summoned them. I tried to summon mine, but it remained stationary against the wall. I strode over to it and clutched it, feeling the rough bark beneath my palm. There'd be no testing to see if it worked now. Either it worked, or I'd be grounded. I hated to think what would've happened if I had tested it, like Kelsey wanted me to. I would've sailed straight into Lucifer's hands.

The witches donned capes and coats. Iona handed me Kelsey's black peacoat. It didn't feel right to wear it, but I didn't have anything else.

"What about me?" Jane asked, donning a green cloak. Fear had turned her features cold. "I can't fly."

I wanted to reach for her and say something reassuring, but I had no words. I barely knew how to fly myself. We were both liabilities. I only hoped the witches would keep her safe, if they could. I shot an imploring glance to Medea.

"You'll ride with Iona," Medea said. "She'll keep you

safe."

Someone pounded on the door. "Open up!" Lucifer shouted. "Or I'll burn the house down!"

Iona stood up before the chimney and brushed her hands together. "It's ready."

"Go straight up in the air," Medea said to everyone, "and hover a hundred feet above until everyone is out. Fire at any demons on the roof until we're all out."

Fern tucked her broom beneath her and flew up the chimney. More witches followed.

The pounding on the door was replaced by another noise. The demons were slamming against the back door.

Jane gave me a concerned glance, her face ashen as she drew the broom into position, the cleaver still clamped in one hand.

Iona threw her leg over the broom and sat in front of Jane. "Hold on tight."

Jane nodded. Iona leapt into the air and flew up through the chimney.

Other witches left. Something crashed. Bolts of orange and green lightning lit up the lawn and shots rang out. Someone was screaming. My heartbeat thundered in my ears. The war had begun.

Then it was just me and Hazel standing by the fireplace.

"You first," she said. "You can do it."

When I turned to face the chimney, the air pulled on

me, rustling my hair. I almost laughed — *a magical chimney*. I let the air pull me up, my shoulders hunched together as I jostled through the narrow brick passageway. I rose toward the tiny rectangle of dark sky, then popped out of the chimney and hovered several feet over the cabin, clutching my broom. Witches swooped over the lawn, firing bolts of light at the demons. Bullets and arrows flew in the sky from all directions. Hazel appeared out of the chimney and immediately plowed into the demons on the lawn.

Sarah shot silver spells at a trio of demons who kept changing into animals and changing back into demons. Claire was in a duel with a bat-like creature who flew around her, its giant jaw snapping shut near her broom. Medea channeled a storm, lightning and thunder rumbling behind her in the sky. Wind thrashed against me, and cold rain fell in huge drops. I held on tighter to my broom. Iona fired orange bolts at demons, darting around them, toting a petrified Jane around on the back of her broom.

There were too many demons. We were outnumbered at least five to one.

Lucifer stood amidst the battle, his arms crossed over his tailored suit. His horns were out and his skin was a bruised red. He barked orders out to his minions, but he hadn't seen me yet. My breath came hard as I remembered how I'd tried to stab him in the throat. It wasn't fair that he could get away with everything he'd done and be impervious. I wished I could kill him now and stop him from hurting anyone else.

Standing next to him was Mephistopheles' lanky figure, his black shirt and jeans almost blending into the darkness. I tried to catch his eye. After a second, his black eyes turned toward me. I dug in my satchel and grasped the cool faceted stone, then dropped it on the chimney top and pointed at it.

Mephistopheles nodded as if he understood, then, he elbowed Lucifer. "There she is!" he shouted, pointing at me.

I gasped — I'd thought he was on my side!

Lucifer turned his glowing red eyes to me. "Get the girl!" he roared. "NOW!"

Demons scrabbled toward me, some of them climbing the trees. A slime-green swamp monster leapt toward me, fingers outstretched. I was so shocked, I forgot to fly, but I tightened my muscles, leaning forward, and flew out of reach. The monster dropped to the ground in a puddle and reformed, jumping toward me again.

I glanced at Jane, but the angle of her flight didn't look right — she had slid to the back of the broom. She tried to pull herself forward from the straw, but with the cleaver in her hand, she strained. I shot toward them to help, but before I could reach her, she slid back, over the straw, falling head over heels. She screamed as she plummeted to the ground.

"No!" I yelled.

Iona raced after her in a blur, but she wouldn't make it in time. Jane fell too fast.

I gritted my teeth and wrenched my broom down, tearing through the sky. I wanted to scream too. I couldn't lose my best friend. I knew I couldn't fight, but I had to go after her.

A jackal ran toward the direction Jane was falling and caught her. The air was forced out of her lungs, then I heard her scream as he ran off with her into the forest.

"Stay safe!" Iona shoved me back, my broom twisting like a top. She arced down and sped after them, zipping through the pines and disappearing from sight.

A volcanic fury raged inside of me as Jane's screams echoed through the forest. My eyes phased black and my teeth became daggers. If anything happened to her . . .

"Belle! Fly higher!" Fern called out. "You're too low!"

I picked myself up again, determined to keep my concentration on flying. But it was hard. My thoughts were on Jane and whether she was okay or not.

Giant *whomping* sounds erupted from below, and I turned just in time to see Lucifer, his leather-like wings unfurled and pumping, lifting him in the air as he flew toward me.

Fern took hold of my broom and rushed upward with me. We rose into the night sky, then she shot into the

320

sky above without me.

I hovered in the air, reaching for her. She glanced back, bewildered, then her eyes grew large. Something pulled on the back of my broom. I whipped my head around.

Lucifer sat behind me, hunched on my broom like a corporate gargoyle. I jerked back in surprise, clabbering to hold onto the handle. His glowing red eyes sent a jolt of dread through me. My broom sunk lower and lower. I fumbled with my knife, unsheathing it. I brandished it at him, trying to channel my courage.

"That's it," he said. "Give into your dark side. You want to, don't you? Come to me. I command you." He reached for me with one clawed hand.

I swiped at his arm, but my hands shook so much, I dropped the knife before it made contact. I watched it fall to the ground helplessly, then reeled back to kick him in his smug face.

"No!" Fern shouted. "Belle, don't! You could turn evil!"

Blazing green fire appeared out of nowhere and leapt over Lucifer's wings. He screamed in pain. His claws clutched the broom, but he lost his balance and fell, shouting, to the ground.

I pulled up into the sky just as more shots rang out. A bullet soared over my shoulder. I ducked closer to the broom, speeding into the sky.

"Faster!" Fern shouted as we raced up near the cloud cover.

My heart ached. I kept thinking about Jane. I wanted to fight, but I couldn't, not without taking the chance of becoming evil. It was too dangerous. I fought the urge to turn my broom around and shoot whatever spells I could at the demons. It felt so wrong to be so high up when so many were fighting.

More shots rang out. One of the witches below us clutched her chest and fell off her broom. Another witch dove after her. I couldn't tell who it was — it could have been any of them.

Medea appeared before us, her black eyes wild with magic, her hair tossed by the wind. "Get her out of here. Keep her safe. I'll meet up with you at the location we talked about." She tipped her broom down and charged into battle with the demons. I saw her clash with an ogre, a volley of sparks coming between them.

As we sped higher into the sky, my tears crystalized in the cool air. I didn't want to leave. I wanted to help, but I couldn't do anything. I said a prayer for them as we rose through the clouds.

"Fern, we need to go back. I know I can't fight, but I could do something!"

"No. We have to keep you safe."

I shook my head. "I don't want to be safe. I want to help them." My broom sank a few feet.

Fern grasped my handle. "Please don't make this any harder than it already is. I have my orders. We're leaving."

As she flew us out of there, I pressed my mouth shut, not letting the tears come. I wanted to believe the witches could win against all those demons, but I wasn't confident.

"BELLE!" Lucifer's voice rang out, magnified in the foggy air. "Turn yourself in. Your friends don't have to die!"

I looked back, but all I saw were green and gold crackles of battle spells. My heart went out to the witches fighting for me. I felt so bad to be flying away. I should've been on the battlefield, helping.

"You can't escape us!" Lucifer yelled. "Wherever you go, I'll find you!"

We vanished into a cloud and came out into a clear dark sky dotted with stars.

Donovan, I prayed. *Please help my friends. Please! Jane never should've been here, and she's eligible for Heaven. Please, if there's anything you can do!*

I glanced around at the bluish sky, hoping against hope to see him or a battalion of angels coming to our rescue. But there was no one there, only dusky clouds and cold, twinkling stars. If Donovan heard my prayers, there was no indication of it. I had to face the facts. We were alone, fighting this war by ourselves. Heaven had given up on me.

CHAPTER TWENTY-EIGHT

We raced upward through the dark sky, away from the whoosh and crackle of magic below. Fern clung to my broomstick, leading me higher and higher. The witches screeched battle spells as they fought the demons. From time to time, a gunshot or a scream rang out. I glanced back, seeing the green and golden beams of lights illuminating the clouds, and felt as heavy as a rock.

"Fight against your emotions, Belle!" Fern yelled, her hair flying in her face as she looked back at me. Her indigo cape fluttered in front of me. "Fly, damn it!"

Tears ran from my eyes. I felt like my heart was being ripped out of my chest. We'd left Jane and our friends behind. Worst of all, they were fighting for me, *dying for me*. It took everything I had not to yank the broom away from Fern's grasp and help them.

"That's high enough," Fern said. "We should wait to see if anyone else is coming."

We hovered, breathing in the ozone-rich air. Above us, the night sky was wide open. The stars were so close and bright they seemed to be affixed in front of me like floating diamonds.

"Are you going to be okay if I let go of your broom?"

I nodded, though I doubted my ability to fly. It took all my concentration to remain aloft, to keep that 'air mind,' like she'd taught me. Sarah had been right. I was no air spirit. My arms shook with the constant reassertion every time an air pocket shifted, and my hair flew around like a wild creature, sometimes blowing in my face, usually whipping behind me. But worst of all was the bark of my broomstick. It felt rough against my legs, no matter which way I turned it.

I tried not to think about the battle below. Tears sprang into my eyes as I replayed the image of Jane falling to the ground, her fingers grasping for Iona's broom. Losing her had been my greatest fear. I shuddered, my heart heavy. There were things worse than death and Jane deserved better. She was all that was good — she'd been so close to going to Heaven. I should've sent her back to Hell the moment she arrived at the safehouse. I'd never forgive myself for the mistake.

Then there was how useless I'd been. Even though I'd learned a few offensive spells, I couldn't cast one for fear of how close I was to becoming evil. But I could've given her a protection orb. I'd just sat there and watched it happen.

I gripped my broomstick until my knuckles turned white. I hoped what Fern had said was true, that the witches we left behind were strong enough to fight the demons. Hopefully, they'd meet up with us at the impact crater. We could forge the weapon, and Jane might be able to ascend to Heaven. But what if they didn't survive?

My air pocket dipped and I fell, dropping through the air. I screamed and clamped my hands around the handle, pulling the broom back up. A bolt of adrenaline coursed through me as I started climbing back up through the sky. I'd been so distraught by my emotions I'd almost forgotten I was thousands of feet above the ground.

Fern swooped by my side and clutched my broom again. "Are you okay?"

"I'm fine." I swallowed hard, my breath ragged. I'd almost fallen 20,000 feet.

She glanced at the clouds below, where the battle rampaged, then met my eyes. "Keep your focus. Don't let your sadness consume you."

"How do you do that?" I gave her a mirthless laugh.

She smiled sadly. "I think of puppies."

"Puppies? Not kittens?"

"Not for me. Always have been more of a dog-lover."

I imagined puppies with blue ribbons tied around

their collars, playing and rolling over each other, but my mood didn't brighten. I kept thinking back to Kelsey, lying on the floor in her own blood. "What happened to Kelsey back there?"

"She was tempted by the dark side. She was evil, and we didn't know it. She hid it well."

"But why would she do that?"

"I don't know. I suppose Lucifer made her feel special."

"I can't believe she cut herself."

"When witches bleed, it increases the power of their spells. It's basic self-defense. Black magic requires it, and it comes with a heavy price."

I didn't know what to say. All I knew is that would never be me. I'd never go to the dark side if I could help it. I'd seen too much, and I had true friends. I wasn't fooled by Lucifer's mind games. I cringed, wondering if he'd groomed her the same way he had me. Fern's tight lips made me think she didn't want to talk about it.

"Where are we going?" she asked.

I bit my lip, unsure if I should tell her. "South."

"Thats it? That's all you're going to tell me?"

"You heard Medea. I can't say it until we're safe."

She shrugged, but seemed to accept the answer. Crystalline snowflakes swirled around us. My eyes burned with the wind, and I shivered, hunching close to my broom.

Fern shot me a concerned glance. "*Calidus corpore,*" she murmured, gesturing with one hand.

My skin glowed for a moment before warmth spread over me. My shivers stopped.

"I keep forgetting you're so new," she said. "You don't even know the basics. What is this, the third time you've ridden on a broom by yourself?"

I swallowed hard. "Second."

She rolled her eyes. "If you fall, Medea will have my head."

I stared at her. She seemed certain Medea would come out of the battle, but I wasn't so sure. What if Lucifer took her again? I closed my eyes, my stomach rolling.

After a few minutes, three witches rose from the clouds. I squinted and saw Claire and Maribeth toting Sarah, propped up between them, her eyes barely open. As they came closer, I saw blood staining her prairie dress, a red splotch covering most of her chest. They hovered beside us, the metallic tang of blood hung in the thin air.

"What happened?" I asked.

"She took a bullet." Claire's lined face trembled.

I closed my eyes, my mind spinning into more darkness. It surrounded me, pressing in upon me from all sides. I was thankful that Fern was holding my broom. I was in no state to fly.

"We need to take her to a hospital." Maribeth stared at Sarah, her dark braids whipping around wildly in the wind.

"We can't." Fern shook her head. "It's the first place the demons will look for us. They have workers there."

"But she needs medical attention!" Maribeth's eyebrows drew together and she leaned over her broom. "She'll die if we don't take her to a doctor."

"We'll give her healing spells until we're somewhere safe," Fern said. "Somewhere the demons can't find us."

"What, the safehouse in Norway?"

"No, we can't go there, either." Fern sighed, her voice a carefully controlled tone. "Kelsey probably told Lucifer about all of our safe-houses. No, we're flying to the east coast and taking a ship across the Baltic Sea. It'll take some pressure off of us flying, and it'll be safer than staying on earth."

I nodded. It was a good plan. There were no waystations over the ocean.

"No!" Maribeth said. "She needs a hospital!"

"We can't go to a hospital — they'll definitely find us. I'm sorry, but I have my orders." Fern's face was stern even as her eyes were wet.

Sarah struggled to raise herself up on her broom, her lips trembling. "She's right—" She whispered, her face scrunched in pain. "We can try for a hospital a little farther away."

330

Maribeth clutched her. "You can't be serious. You might not make it!"

"I have a plan," Fern said. "There's a village nearby. I've flown over it before, and I sensed a lot of cats there. We'll fly low and take as much energy as we can to heal Sarah. Then we'll go to the shore and heal her properly."

Maribeth sighed, but gave her a small nod. "If it's what you want?"

"Yes," Sarah whispered. "No hospital."

Fern turned to me. "Will you be okay if I let go of your broom, Belle?"

I nodded. Just seeing how bad Sarah was hurt changed my perspective. Besides, Medea and I were the only ones who knew about the possibility of the weapon to kill Lucifer. He was the reason all of this started in the first place. If it weren't for him, Sarah would be fine. Jane would be safe. The spirit of revenge flowed through me, reenergizing me.

"Yes. I can fly."

In strained silence, we flew toward the full moon, over picturesque rolling mountains, following train tracks peeking through the clouds. After a while, I saw a train chugging along, a plume of vapor wisping behind it. It was so small it looked like a child's toy.

After half an hour of flying, Fern called out. "The village is below us! Follow me."

She plummeted through canyons and ridges of ominous dark clouds. We followed her through the roiling gray masses. Clouds whipped past my vision, moistening my cheeks.

Suddenly, the clouds were gone and a church steeple was directly in my path. I turned my broom up, narrowly avoiding it, and steadied out over a little village built around a lake. Cobblestone roads led to crafty gift shops and tourist locations. I recognized it to be Mora, a village I visited sixty years ago. But if that was the case, we were still several hundred kilometers from the coast.

I caught up to Fern and flew beside her. But, when I opened my mouth to speak, she cut me off.

"Sip from the cats while you can. We don't have much time."

I sipped the cat energy as we flew over the rooftops and was gratified with a small tingle of rumbling in my belly. It didn't satisfy me completely, but it gave me a little more spark. I wanted to ask her about what she thought was happening to the witches we'd left behind, only I didn't have the words to talk about it yet. It was too fresh, too raw of a wound.

"The clouds are thinning out." Fern pointed her finger up. "Time to go up again." She gave me a tight smile, a tear tracking her cheek as she disappeared into the white clouds above.

I followed her. For a moment, I couldn't see anything except a pervading white aura filled with diffuse moon light. The dense vapor was close, cloying. I held my breath and pulled the broom up with all my might, then crested out of the clouds and into the starry night. Fern flew a few hundred yards away, her dark-moon face turned back to me. We hovered, watching.

After a minute, the other witches burst through the clouds. But they didn't look too good. Sarah looked as if she had passed out. Claire struggled to keep her upright.

"I want to heal Sarah," I said. "I have enough energy."

"No, it's out of the question. We'll see how strong you are when we reach the coast. Then you can do whatever you want." She mumbled something and shot a white light at Sarah, then turned haunted eyes to me. "We have to go. Come on."

We flew for hours. My hands blistered and my muscles ached with the continued effort. I managed to put the night behind me by keeping my sights on the full moon as we flew, but over time, it rose over our heads and before long, was behind us. The night was so different from the last full moon, where we'd drunk wine and danced at the party where I was declared 'not evil.' When would I ever dance again? I couldn't conceive of it.

From time to time, a burst of white light flared up behind me — another healing spell. Sarah remained bent over her broom, clutching her wound.

I rode closer to Fern, but I had so many questions, I didn't know where to start. I looked back at the women straining to keep up with us. Their spells cost energy, and it looked like Sarah still wasn't any better.

"You're getting pretty good at flying," Fern said with a sad smile.

"Do you think we'll make it to the shore in time to help Sarah?"

"I hope so." She blinked back tears for a moment before she flew ahead to navigate the landscape.

I willed myself onward, into the dying night.

CHAPTER TWENTY-NINE

"We made it!" Fern pointed to the horizon, where the land sunk into a dark mercurial harbor. Golden street lamps shone on a dock with several piers, where boats rose and fell.

"*Camarquat heroses!*" An invisibility spell sparkled over Fern. She descended, flying over the fishermen milling on the docks, and jumped off her broom onto an old-fashioned white yacht. Porthole windows dotted the sides, and a captain's helm perched in the rear. Two tall masts rose from a wide, wooden deck. Fern cast a spell, making orange light spark from her hands, then she opened a door that led to the innards of the ship.

The other witches and I hovered in the sky beyond the clouds, waiting for her sign. Below us, through cracks in the clouds, the fishermen looked as small as ants. They prepared their boats and hauled supplies, oblivious to us. Some of them even had omens rotating over their heads, and another time, I'd be tempted to kill them and gain the karma. Not today, though, not with Sarah so injured. All I wanted to do was help her.

Fern ran up the deck of the yacht and waved at us to come in.

I'd just started to cast my invisibility spell when Claire touched my elbow. She looked older, her face even more wizened than before. Dried blood covered half of her gray sweater and skirt. "Give an old witch a hand, dearie. Cast an invisibility spell for the three of us, would you? We barely have the power to stay upright." She smiled weakly at me, her arms straining with the effort of holding Sarah and controlling her broom. Sarah looked unconscious — her head rolled toward me. Maribeth's face was tense, as though she were barely holding on to an ocean of tears.

I nodded, hoping I could perform the spell. I knew it would cost me a lot, but I wanted to do it for them. I channeled my energy, felt it crest inside my core like a huge tingling wave, then pushed it out to them. "*Camarquat heroses.*"

It worked — they glowed for a second. Claire's eyes crinkled in thanks, then they dipped down toward the boat. When they were close, they hovered, and Fern helped Sarah off the broom and laid her onto the deck.

My eyelids began to droop. I dropped a couple of feet before jerking my broom upright and flying higher. I blinked through an immense exhaustion, fighting to stay awake. Breathing hard, I tried to muster the power to cast the invisibility spell on myself. *"Camarquat . . . heroses."*

I looked at my arm, expecting to see it glow, but nothing happened.

The yacht's motor gurgled and roared to life. Claire stood at the helm, checking gears and flipping switches, while Fern unlaced the ties. The boat drifted away from the dock and coasted into the rocking waters of the harbor. Still more fishermen arrived, unpacking equipment and loading materials onto the other boats. The clouds were thinning. I had to make myself invisible. I couldn't let them see me, and I was running out of time.

Fern waved at me, urging me to get on the boat.

I had to go. It was now or never. *"Camarquat heroses!"*

Beautiful, glowing magic flashed over my skin. I took a grateful breath. It had worked, but it'd be a hard landing — I still didn't know how to land properly. The last time I'd tried, I'd fallen onto the ground, and then, I didn't have to worry about a moving target.

Leaning forward, I started to hurtle toward the boat, my heart thundering in my ears. I zoomed over the dock, and then the water, and soon, the boat was beneath me. I tried to match its speed, but it was difficult. I tilted the broom down and fell, crashing and rolling onto the deck, my broomstick beneath me.

I cursed, rubbing the area on my lower back where I knew a bruise would form. But I'd made it onto the boat. I grasped a cold metal bar by the edge and pulled myself up.

Claire cranked the boat into a higher gear, piloting the wheel. "Sorry to test your abilities like that," she shouted over the *burr* of the motor. "We couldn't risk being on the ground in case of spies and waystations."

"It's okay," I said. "I should've practiced flying and landing more often at the farmhouse. I just thought I had more time."

"Didn't we all?" She smiled her gap-toothed smile.

"Whose boat is this?"

"Who cares? It's ours now. So, are you going to tell me where we're going, dear?"

I bit my lip. Medea had told me to keep it a secret. I didn't even now if she was still alive, but I thought I might need to keep mum on it a little longer, just in case. "South," I said, hoping that would do.

Claire shrugged. Her eyes grew large for a moment, but she drew a deep breath and nodded. "South, it is. Go see what you can do for Sarah."

On the other side of the deck, Sarah lay on her back. Her prairie dress was stained almost completely scarlet, and her pale face shone with a gleam of perspiration. I thought I could see her skull through her skin. All the healing they'd done for her along the way didn't appear to have helped much. She was restless, her breathing shallow and fast. Fern brushed the hair away from her head.

Maribeth held her ashen hand in her deep brown one. "What are we going to do?" she sniffed, her blood-shot eyes searching me. "None of us have enough energy to heal her. We spent everything on the flight here. This was a bad idea."

"What about more cat magic?" I asked. "Maybe there are some along the pier."

She shot me a withering look. "There aren't any near-by. I'd feel them. And now none of us have enough energy to fly back to the shore with an invisibility spell. We're stuck here." She glared at Fern. "We never should've tried to move her. We should've taken her to a hospital."

I hung my head in the thick silence. Her words seemed to imply Fern was at fault for Sarah's condition, but she was wrong, in a way. If it hadn't been for me, the demons wouldn't have hurt anyone. Something deep inside me compressed with remorse. We should've listened to her.

Fern's eyes pinched. "We couldn't have taken her to a hospital. How would we explain to the police how she got shot? Besides, you know as well as I that Hell has demons working at hospitals all over the place. We couldn't chance it. We might all be dead if we'd taken that route."

Tears coursed down Maribeth's cheeks, her mouth a grimace of sorrow. "Demons can't work in every hospital."

I shook my head. If only there was something I could do for Sarah.

Fern met my eyes for a moment. "See if you can find a medical kit on the boat."

I dashed off and looked around the deck, searching for anything that might have medical supplies. The only things I found were floatation devices and coils of rope. I opened the hatch and stared into the dark belly of the boat.

"Manus illumino lux."

My palm lit up the area a couple of feet in front of me — I was too weak to cast a wide light, but it was better than nothing. I walked down the rickety stairs, my other hand clutching the wooden bannister as waves rocked the boat.

To my left was a thimble-sized kitchen, with cupboards and a small stove. I pulled open the cold metal knobs. A few canned goods with faded labels looked back at me, but other than that and some dishes, the shelves and drawers were empty. To my right sat a closet of a bathroom. I opened the mirrored cabinet and looked below the sink. Everything but a half-empty bottle of vodka had been cleared out. There was no water on the boat at all. The desalination spell I'd written down from the cabin would be pretty useful, but there was no time to worry about that.

I lifted a Moroccan-print curtain that hung next to the kitchen and saw a wide room with several port windows on either side. Four metal bunk beds lined the walls, with gray mattresses and blankets nestled into the nooks. My nose twitched with a stale smell. This wasn't a luxury yacht, that was for sure. I rummaged around the bedding, but didn't find anything that would help Sarah.

"Come on!" I shouted to no one in particular.

It crossed my mind to pray to Donovan again, but I could barely think of his name before hopelessness came over me. *Where was he now? I needed him.* I leaned against the wall. Exhaustion was making me angry.

I took a steeling breath and opened the groaning door to the last room, at the prow of the boat. Inside nestled a bed and a triangular window-seat at the apex. I checked under the bed, but didn't find anything, and was about to leave when I noticed the window-seat cushion was crooked. I raised it and saw a plastic white box with a red cross lying in the hollow interior. A medical kit. I grabbed it, a flutter of hope in my belly, and ran upstairs.

On the deck, I flipped up the buckles of the kit and lifted the lid, gazing at a couple of bandages, three packets of iodine wipes, and a small roll of gauze. My shoulders sank. I had no medical knowledge, but I knew we needed more than that.

I wished Jane were here. She'd know what to do, what with her decades of hospital work. She'd have staunched the wound, rehydrated her, and treated what smelled like an infection. I didn't even know if Sarah was still alive. As it was, our feeble attempts to make her comfortable only seemed to emphasize her pain.

"Heal her again," Maribeth said to Fern. "I'm drained, and she's . . ."

She didn't finish her sentence. We all knew what she meant. It was obvious, from Sarah's waxen face to her limited movements.

"I'll help," I said.

Fern waved me toward her. "Repeat after me, but stop if it feels like you're going to pass out."

I knelt beside Sarah, determined to give her as much energy as I could, no matter what it cost. Maribeth smiled at me weakly with bloodshot eyes that seemed to say *thank you.*

"*Halvit anam. Sacra kolm mada.*"

We chanted the words over and over. After a couple of minutes, my vision started to cloud over. I felt so tired I could fall asleep right there. When my voice came out in barely a whisper, Fern touched my arm, her eyes telling me to stop. Even though my energy had faded so much, I still wanted to help more. I squeezed out everything else I had inside of me in one last push.

The eastern sky had lightened, and the red lip of the sun rose above the shimmering water, illuminating Sarah. Her face looked less sunken and her cheeks had a rosy blush. She stirred, her eyelids fluttering open. Her hand reached out. "Maribeth," she murmured.

She clasped her hand, gazing into her eyes. "Yes, I'm here."

"I don't want . . ." She breathed an uneven breath, her voice rattling. "Don't worry about me."

"What do you mean?" Maribeth blinked back tears.

"You're the best friend I've ever had."

"As are you." Maribeth tried to laugh, but it came out as a sob. "Don't worry! We'll keep healing you. You'll come out of this."

"No." Sarah's breaths came slower. Her lips trembled and she swallowed with tremendous effort. "I can't stay. I want to cross over . . . into the ether."

I leaned back a little, a lump rising in my throat. *No. I didn't want her to die.*

Sarah glanced at me, her cornflower-blue eyes glazed. "Belle."

My eyes darted to her. I took her hand and did my best to smile down at her, but all I really felt was a wide chasm opening up inside of me.

"You'll find a way," Sarah heaved a breath, "to make all this better."

I searched her eyes. The other witches gazed at me.

She turned her head to face the last remnants of the night sky. Stars still shone, though the rising sun was eradicating them one by one.

"The stars," Sarah said. "They're so . . . *beautiful*."

Maribeth's shoulders shook as she sniffed her tears back.

An indigo mist dissipated into the air from Sarah's mouth and trickled away from her, dancing over the sea toward the stars.

"No," Maribeth cried, lying down on her friend's chest and sobbing, rocking with the waves.

I looked back at Claire at the helm. She must've seen something in my eyes, because she winced and shook her head. The motor stopped.

Sarah's face looked different in death — less like Sarah, more like any other person. Her mouth lolled open, and her eyes, once so tense with pain, were calm and serene.

After a long moment, Fern closed Sarah's eyes with her palm. She placed a hand on Maribeth's shoulder. "It's time. We should let her go into the waters."

I shrank back, my eyes darting to the cold blue harbor below us. Surely, she couldn't mean . . .

"She's not even cold yet!" Maribeth said.

Fern touched her arm. "We all knew what we were signing up for when we agreed to help Belle. Sarah is
344

gone. We need to let her go."

With shaking hands, Maribeth removed Sarah's necklace, a tiny sparkling diamond, and put it over her head. She clutched Sarah's hand one last time and then stood, moving back toward the railing.

I looked around the bay. We were far away enough from land that we weren't surrounded by people any more, but someone could still see us dump a body overboard.

"Are you sure this is a good idea?" I asked Fern.

She nodded. "It's a natural death. We witches don't mind that. And it's not like she has a ghost hanging around this time to witness it. We get an extra life in Hell. That's more than most people get. *Camarquat heroses. Sutulerant,*" she murmured, holding her hands out.

A glow covered Sarah's body, then it raised in the air. The wind played with her long blonde hair one last time. Fern pushed her hands out gently, sending Sarah over the sea. Claire stood beside us, her arms weaving behind me and Maribeth, holding us as tears coursed down our cheeks. Maribeth choked back sobs.

"We release our sister Sarah to the waters today," Claire said. "But we go forward carrying her with us until the end of our days. Whenever I see stars shine, I'll think of her and the ultimate sacrifice she made for our cause."

I swallowed, gazing at Sarah's beautiful, peaceful face. Claire nodded to Fern, whose hands slowly lowered. Sarah's body floated down until it met the sea. She appeared to float for a moment before the waves overtook her, washing over her face and body. She slowly sank in the blue-green water until she was gone.

Maribeth stumbled away, keening, and went below deck.

The three of us stood there for some time. The warm sunlight on my face and the arcing, crying seagulls almost didn't feel real, as if I were watching a movie. I said a prayer. I knew it could be useless, but I wanted to anyway.

Fern sniffed back tears and glanced at me. "Belle, you need to rest."

I turned to leave, but a dark figure flying through the clouds caught my eye. I jerked my head toward it, watching with hope and fear.

Donovan?

As the speck came closer, I saw it was a witch on a broomstick. My heart soared as I recognized Iona's short brown hair and rosy cheeks. She flew close and landed on the boat, running, her broom clutched in one hand. Her eyes were red and her skin blotched. She dropped her broom and reached for us, then collapsed into our arms.

"They're all dead," she whispered.

CHAPTER THIRTY

I stood transfixed, staring at Iona. "What do you mean, they're all dead?"

She sniffed back tears. "The demons tore Hazel limb from limb. They ate Lovetta right before my eyes! Helga and I fought the demons — we killed several of them. And then I was the only one left in a field of bodies."

"What about Medea?" Fern asked, breathless.

Iona swallowed. "She was fighting Lucifer the last I saw her. But then I saw him leave with that skinny ugly demon."

"Mephistopheles?" Fern asked, a bitter scowl on her face.

Iona nodded, wiping her tears with the back of her hand. "They took one of those temporary waystations back to Hell."

Fern's brows rose. "If Lucifer didn't take Medea, she may have escaped."

"Maybe," she shrugged. "I didn't see her body anywhere. But there were so many, everywhere I looked, I saw more and more."

"What about my friend Jane?" I asked. "I saw a demon take her into the woods. You chased after them, remember?"

More tears streamed down her reddened cheeks. "Once I got into the woods, it was so dark, I couldn't find her. I did find a spider-beast. I'm afraid he might have gotten her."

I sat back. Poor Jane. Could she have made it out of there? She did have a weapon, though who was to say her meat cleaver was a match for the jackal that caught her, or the spider-beast?

"Are you injured?" Fern asked her.

Iona shook her head. "Not physically, except for a few scratches, but Fern, the fighting," she gasped, gazing at the sky. "I relived my death. Not just an echo, I was *there*. I was helpless all over again. All the strength I'd gained over the years was gone, and I was a mother fighting for her children." Her shoulders racked with sobs.

My heart ached for her. I put my arm around her shoulders, my tears starting up again. I didn't have any words, but I wanted to be there for her.

"Iona, why don't you go downstairs and rest?" Fern said. "Get your strength back. Belle, help her."

I helped Iona below deck and settled her into a bed,

drawing a moth-eaten wool blanket over her. Maribeth huddled in a bunk on the other side of the room.

"Iona, I'm so sorry about all of this." Tears fell from my eyes. "I never wanted people to die."

She gave me a quivering smile. "No, you don't understand. This fight — it isn't just about you. It's been happening for a long time. When you were imprisoned, that's when it reached a boiling point. People have died, and people will continue to die. Good people. But it's not your fault. This fight is bigger than you and me."

I searched her eyes, wanting to believe her. Lately, I'd felt our mission was a fool's errand. It was ridiculous, thinking my stupid idea about killing Lucifer could work. Too many of my friends had died for it.

Iona kissed my forehead and tucked my hair behind my ears. "Did Medea ever tell you about when she was Lucifer's mistress?"

I nodded.

"What they're calling Stockholm Syndrome nowadays never happened to her. She *never* fell in love with him, not even when he was kind, and yet, he kept her for *twenty years*. She went crazy in there, talked to inanimate objects, and thought she'd left her cell when she'd been locked away the whole time. That's just one of the monstrous things he's done. This fight is about more than what's fair, more than just right and wrong. It's about basic human rights and decency. We've had a few years of peace lately, but now, the beast's back, and we don't want to go back to the way things were."

"But we don't even know if my idea will work."

"I don't know what kind of weapon you and Medea hatched up," she placed a hand on my chest, "and you don't have to tell me, but here's the thing. We'll take any chance we can get. It only took one well-aimed stone to bring down Goliath, didn't it?"

My heart clenched. I put on a brave face. "Yes."

Her impish face smiled. "This is sort of like you trying out magic, isn't it? You thought it couldn't be done, and yet, look at you now. Casting spells left and right."

I laughed a little.

"That's more like the Belle I know. Keep your optimism. They hate it when we're hopeful. And we aren't alone. There are more who agree with us — pockets of them everywhere who want to see him go down for everything he's done. We all believe in you. And if we fail, we'll fail together. If this weapon doesn't work, we'll think up another one."

I nodded. It was a lot to take in, and I didn't know how I felt about everything. However, I was determined to not show her any more of my internal doubt.

She slumped beneath the blanket and her eyelids fluttered closed. I started to whisper a healing chant.

She held up a hand. "Save your energy. I'll be okay." Tears spilled through her eyelashes. "But thank you. I'm so glad you're among us."

On the deck, the air felt more damp, and salt-spray scented the air. A strong wind played with my skirt. Claire, now wearing a puffy orange safety vest, steered the boat at full speed, eyeing a black nest of clouds that boiled and spat lightning to the west.

"I'm trying to outrun it," she said, "but I don't know if we can. Do you still not know what element you are?"

"No. All that's left is fire and water, though."

"It's too bad you're not air. We need a weather witch. If only we had Medea." Her eyes looked out over the sea, stoic and distant.

"I hope she's okay." I held onto the rail as the boat slammed down into the trough of a giant wave. The wind had whipped up the sea, even though the storm was still far away.

Claire gritted her teeth as she steered. "Go lie down. You need your rest. And take the brooms with you. I'm afraid they'll blow off the deck."

By the time I walked downstairs, Iona was asleep in a bunk bed and Fern was huddled into another. I tiptoed past them to the bedroom at the far end and closed the door.

I had to know if Jane was still alive. It killed me to think she was out there, wandering the cold Swedish wilderness, alone and starving. I lie down on my stomach and dug the magic mirror out of the bottom of my satchel. My reflection gazed back at me for a few minutes. I looked at my tired eyes without Mephistopheles making an appearance. Where was he?

When I awoke, strong sunshine shone through the port windows, lighting up the barren room. I sat up and blinked. We must've outrun the storm after all. I felt better, but I was starving. But what was more disturbing was the fact that I only had one small vial of vapor with me. Did the others have any? What were we going to do near the 24-hour mark?

"Ahem," Mephistopheles' voice rang out.

I gasped and snatched the open mirror by my pillow, my hands trembling. I'd left it open.

Mephistopheles' gaunt face and cocky black eyes gazed back at me. "Belle, you're—"

"*Shh!*" I leaned close. "Whisper."

He laughed. "You're so cute when you sleep. Did you know you snore a little?" His gaze shifted around the mirror. "Where are you?"

"You won't be able to find me." I straightened my features. I didn't trust him. He was too inquisitive, too predatory. "I just called to make sure you found the love charm I left for you on the chimney."

He exhaled heavily. "You weren't worried I perished in the battle?"

I frowned and shook my head. His presumption disgusted me. "I wasn't worried about you."

He laughed. "Thank you for *finally* fulfilling your half of the deal. But it's funny — from what I hear, you weren't actually a witch when you were locked in the cell. But now you are. *Interesting.*" He put his hands behind his head and raised his brows, waiting for my answer.

For a second, my brave mask slipped. I flushed and felt my pulse ramp up. I didn't know what to say. I made my face neutral again. "So, you'll never tell Lucifer about my name, right?"

"Oh, I promise, I won't." A dirty smile played on his face. "But you have bigger things to worry about now. He's furious you escaped. He's a little mad about the forty-one dead demons too, but they're replaceable."

My chin jutted out. "I don't care if he's mad. Anyway, I heard you and Lucifer ran away from the battle once it started looking bad."

"Generals never go down with their armies," he sneered, his lips curling. "But I'm glad you called. I wanted to tell you about the price on your pretty little princess head."

I leaned in. "What price?"

"There's a reward for your capture. All karma debt cleared if anyone can bring you to Lucifer alive. For some, that means going to Heaven. For those of us who are evil, it means never having to work again. A life of luxury."

I froze. Of all the creepy things to do, this was taking it to the extreme. I'd always thought Lucifer would move onto the next pretty temp in Hell, but this was personal. "Does that mean every demon in Hell will be after me?"

"Yep, probably every single one. Except for me, of course. I'd let you go again." He smiled and popped his eyebrows. "And again, and again."

I cringed, stifling the urge to vomit. "Do you have Jane? Is she alive?"

The mirror went blank.

I stared at it for a second, willing him to come back. When he didn't return, I threw it on the bed, silently cursing. It hurt to think about it. Hundreds of thousands of demons would be on the lookout for us all over the world. At least we were at sea. No waystations existed here, and no means-stations could magically appear — they'd have to find us by boat or by plane. At least, we'd see them coming.

But that meant I needed to tell the witches what I learned so we could be prepared. I didn't know how they'd react to the mirror, but I doubted it'd be favorable, even though Mephistopheles had helped us by telling me about it.

I stood up and whimpered, looking out the round window at the deep green sea that stretched to the horizon. I sighed, trying to summon the strength to go on. I said a quick prayer for Jane and wished Donovan would come again, even though I knew he wouldn't.

Something purple passed over the window, darkening it completely. I ran to look out of another window and squinted at what looked like a tree trunk-sized lavender pole. Then a beast rose from the waters, its gaping maw open. It gazed onto the deck with completely black eyes, sending violet tentacles snaking around the hull.

A *kraken*.

My breath hitched. It had begun.

CHAPTER THIRTY-ONE

The boat rocked violently, the wood creaking under the pressure of several tentacles squeezing against it. My heartbeat clamored in my ears as I ran up the steps to the deck. I stared in horror at what looked like a grayish-purple island surfacing just a few feet from our boat. I recognized the kraken from last year's chili cook-off in Hell. It opened cold, pitiless black eyes and focused on me.

"BELLE!" it bellowed.

The sound shook my bones, and the smell of rotten fish almost knocked me over. Its mouth looked like an underwater cave, with rows of razor-sharp stalactites and stalagmites covered in slime.

A purple tentacle shot up from the water, serpentine, and extended toward me. Another wriggled toward Claire.

"Get below deck!" Claire blasted it with an orange

bolt of light, shut off the engine, and hobbled toward the cabin.

We ran downstairs. When I slammed the door shut, tentacles slapped against the door. I pushed the little slide lock, though I didn't know what good that would do against the creature. He obviously wanted the reward — never having to work again would tempt any demon. I wanted to tell the others about what I'd learned, but I didn't want to admit that I'd spoken with Mephistopheles. They wouldn't understand.

Iona held out her palms. "Join hands. We have to call on our allies. Come on, Belle! We don't have all day."

I grasped their hands and took a deep breath. The energy flowed between the five of us like a current, making the hair on my arms stand up. A cool energy rose inside of me, vibrating my insides, then a pulse knocked me back. A translucent blue ring shot out beyond our circle. Through the port window, I saw it race across the sea.

"I hope they get here soon." Maribeth ran a hand through her dark braids, her face tight.

"This kraken," Claire shook her head. "I recognize him from one of the office parties. He's a demon."

"Why's he attacking us?" Iona asked.

I bit my lip. Should I tell them?

Iona noticed, and opened her mouth to say something to me when the yacht walls bowed, contracting under the kraken's tentacles. Crunching noises came from all around.

The ship rocked hard to one side, and we were thrown against the bunk beds. My hands and forehead slammed against the steel frame. Gasping, I held my head, a sharp pain throbbing. At first I could only see a blinding whiteness. When my vision returned, blood covered my stinging, trembling fingers.

"Help!" Maribeth reached out from under a wooden beam. I got to my feet, unsteady, and rushed to her side.

The others helped me lift the beam, heaving. Maribeth scrambled out.

More dark tentacles covered the windows. The boat groaned, the wood creaking as if it'd give way at any moment. Ice-cold saltwater soaked the floor.

"I'm going to give this bastard a taste of earth magic." Fern threw open the door of the hatch and ran up the steps. She chanted spells in a deep, commanding voice, making green fire erupt from her palms. Claire followed, shooting purple streams of energy.

"Stay safe, Belle!" Iona leapt on her broom and flew out.

Maribeth winced, holding her arm at an odd angle.

"Can I help?" I asked. "I can do a healing spell."

She scowled. "I can heal my own arm."

"Maribeth . . ." I looked at her as she limped away. She'd been so distant since the battle at the cabin. She'd treated me like I was toxic, as if it were my fault Sarah had died. Even though I knew it wasn't my fault, I still sympathized with her losing her best friend. If a stranger had asked me to sacrifice everything, and Jane died because of it, I might be resentful too.

"What do you want?" Maribeth shouted.

I looked into her red-rimmed eyes. "I'm so sorry about Sarah — about everything. I never meant it to get this bad." I held back my tears, swallowing hard. "I never thought anyone besides me would get hurt. If you want to talk about it, I'm here for you. I lost my best friend, too."

She rolled her eyes and huffed. "Help them upstairs. I'll be up soon. I just need to repair the boat so we don't sink." With a mumbling chant, Maribeth waved her hand. The wood started rejoining into solid planks.

I ran up the stairs and whispered, "*camarquat heroses.*" Invisible, I stepped around a severed tentacle still twitching on the deck and made my way toward Fern at the captain's prow. The beast roared and swatted at Claire as she flew around it. Its black eyes followed her, as if trying to figure out if she was me.

"Steer the boat!" Fern yelled to me. She ran, tucked her broom under her, and streaked into the sky. As she spiraled up, she blasted the kraken's head.

The rear of the boat launched several feet into the air. I grabbed onto the smooth wood of the steering wheel and held tight. The boat fell back into the sea with a huge spray of water, drenching me. My eyes and the cut on my forehead stung like fire. I clung to the wheel.

Maribeth rocketed out from the cabin on her broom, firing golden bolts. The creature's skin became seared with fist-sized pockmarks, but he still fought. I wanted to join them in the fight, but I couldn't — I had to keep my karma on the good side.

A tentacle shot toward me. I dodged it, but it grasped the wheel of the boat, pulling it until the wood shattered and split with a ripping sound.

I backed away from it, my stomach dropping inside of me. If that was what it could do to wood, what could it do to me? And even though I was supposed to be brought back to Lucifer alive, I doubted the monster would play nice if we angered it. The tentacle wavered toward me.

On impulse, the words of the protection spell flew out of my mouth. "*Clemit pro sequious!*" The blue lights danced around me and formed a crystalline sphere. The tentacle bounced off my protection shell. At first, I thought it would leave me alone, but it returned to inspect it, prodding and poking it. I was safe for the moment, but it might not last long. I felt weak, my muscles tired. If only I'd eaten something.

"*Go away*," I whispered.

Upon seeing me, the creature swam closer and sent

another tentacle snaking my way.

I ran around the cabin, hiding from the beast. I couldn't fight, but I could try to stun it. When my protection bubble burst, I threw one leg over my broom, then rose into the air, around the beast's blind side. The back of its thick head looked like a mountain, with barnacles and sea plants growing on it.

Just as I was about to cast a spell, a wave shot up, engulfing me. I fell into the sea. Sheer panic raged through my nerves as I crashed into the chilly water. I broke the surface, lungs burning, and gasped for air, pawing at the water. I tucked the broom into place and tried to fly. Nothing happened.

The creature's tentacles slithered toward me like snakes.

Maribeth glanced at me from her broom, her face tense. "Hang on!"

I kicked hard, swimming toward the boat. My heart pattered as waves slapped against my face. Then, all was silent. The beast had disappeared. I looked around the sea and didn't see it anywhere. "Where did it go?" I shouted.

"Belle!" Maribeth pointed toward me, her eyes wide. "Down there!"

I tread water, my heart beating with a jagged rhythm, and looked down. Something dark appeared in the water below me. Then I saw the giant open mouth of the kraken. Its black eyes glistered in the dark sea water as it rose toward me. I wanted to scream. I couldn't take my eyes off it. I kept hearing Jane's scream echoing in my mind.

In that moment, I knew she couldn't have survived the battle. I'd known for quite some time, but I was just now admitting it to myself. She was gone. Part of me wanted to die too, to go down and give up the fight. But another part of me knew I had a mission. People were counting on me. I couldn't give up. I had to fight for what was right, or at least try. I spoke the words of the protection spell. It sparkled in the water, casting a globe around me.

The kraken's thick, sharp teeth beat against my bubble, making me shoot away from the yacht. The beast screamed, vibrating my toes, as its teeth tried to clamp onto me again. It only ever bumped me away from it. Tentacles bolted through the water at me, but they bounced off the sphere too. It tossed me across the sea, farther and farther from the boat.

"Hang on, Belle!" Fern yelled, swooping overhead and firing green lightning at the thing.

Several tentacles appeared near my bubble. They curled around it and blotted out the day with a tangle of suction cups and limbs. It managed to grasp my sphere and gathered me closer, toward its mouth.

"No!" I yelled, fists clenched.

Its maw full of jagged teeth appeared and grew closer,

then it bit into my sphere. This time, there was no place for the bubble to escape to. Too many tentacles held it. The air inside my bubble compressed. I screamed as it squeezed against my skin and face. My spell couldn't last much longer. The kraken's teeth threatened to pierce it by the second.

I cast another protection spell, expecting to see another sphere around me within the existing sphere, but it didn't work. There were no blue sparks, and no extra bubble to keep me safe when the other one popped. I started to feel weak. Either my magic was exhausting me or I didn't have enough oxygen. I slipped, helpless, as the kraken pressed in.

Then, the beast jerked back wards a few feet, its eyes bulging. It turned, bellowing. Its tentacles flowed away from me and toward something else. I stared, confused. Was it caught on something?

Then I saw creatures with fins and long, flowing hair darting around the monster. They pummeled the beast with slender arms and glinting silver weapons, their semi-human forms glimmering. I leaned closer, straining to see through the water. Could it be? *Mermaids?*

Claire cackled with glee as she swooped nearby and fired another shot at the beast.

Half-women half-fish creatures attacked the beast's tentacles just as my protective bubble broke. I fell into the cold seawater, swimming, darting back as a mermaid ripped into a tentacle with razor-sharp teeth right in front of me.

"Belle!" Fern held out a hand. I clasped it in mine. Never was I so glad to see anyone in my life. She struggled to pull me onto her broom.

"Thank you," I cried, dripping with saltwater.

She hovered above the deck and I managed to get down.

"I picked up your broom and put it below deck," she said, her eyes on the fight. "Are you okay?"

When I nodded, she flew off to fight again. I held onto the cold rail, chest heaving, and watched the battle. The kraken swatted at the witches and snaked its tentacles fast through the water. They wrapped around a mermaid's neck. She struggled against it, her hands clutching the thick appendage. It thrashed, knocking her about. She cried out, silent. A cloud of crimson followed her as she sank to the depths of the sea.

Other mermaids stabbed the creature, tridents flashing as their points pierced its flesh. It opened its giant maw and screamed. The sea grew turbulent and murky with blood.

Some of the mermaids encircled it with a golden net. It shook the net off with mighty thrusts, and ink spread in the water, making the sea even darker.

Mermaids darted around the kraken with the net again. They moved faster this time, and gathered the net tightly. The beast could only maneuver in tiny flails. It released another plume of ink, but the mermaids tightened the net even more, until it could barely move.

A mermaid near the kraken's face drove a trident into one of its black eyes. Another speared the other eye. The beast yelped and thrashed until it broke the net. It sped away, blindly retreating into the depths of the sea, leaving a cloudy crimson trail in its wake.

The mermaids surfaced and watched it leave. A huge sigh of relief escaped my lips as I collapsed against the wood of the deck. It was over.

CHAPTER THIRTY-TWO

The mermaids' fins rippled as they tread water. I thought their faces were wet with the sea, then I saw tears and realized they were crying. *Of course.* My heart compressed at the thought of the dead mermaid. I'd never forget her soundless scream, the way the kraken had tossed her body like it was a toy. She'd died for my crusade and because Lucifer was a bastard, offering such a reward.

I gripped the rail, anger burning in my heart. I expected to feel my dark inner coil throb, and my demonic features to take over, but this anger felt different. I felt the need to right this wrong, to end this injustice once and for all. No one else had to die because Lucifer wanted me. I took a deep breath. We'd be at the crater soon enough, and we'd make the weapon that would kill him. Then, I'd just have to find a way to use it. Until then, nothing else mattered.

"Sisters!" Iona flew out over the sea and then dove into the water like as gracefully as a duck. She embraced the women one by one, murmuring condolences.

I released my grip on the rail and turned, almost running into Claire.

She stacked her broom against the helm, her face weary and lined. "How are you feeling, Belle? Did you get hurt?"

"No. I'm starving, but I'm not injured. I feel like I have a guardian angel watching over me." I smiled weakly at her. Of course, I didn't. Donovan wouldn't hide from me. He'd reassure me if he were around. But it was a saying, and my escape from the kraken had felt like nothing short of a miracle.

"There are a few cans of soup in the cupboard. Why don't you warm some up for us? I'm exhausted."

"Sure." We walked down the stairs below deck. I opened a can of bean soup and warmed it over the stove while Claire washed her face in the bathroom.

"It hasn't been twenty-four hours yet," I shouted from the tiny stove, "but what about the vapors?"

She toweled off her face and sniffed the savory aroma of the soup warming in the pot. "I have a vial. Don't you?"

"Yes, but what about everyone else? We left the cabin in a hurry."

"We'll talk about that when Iona gets back. I don't

367

blame her for wanting to catch up — she never gets to see them."

I stirred the soup with a wooden spoon. "There was a lot of blood in the water. Do they have to worry about sharks?"

"I doubt it. They have agreements with sharks."

I dished the soups and handed a chipped bowl to Claire. We walked up to the deck again and sat on the edge of the boat, blowing on our soup and gazing at the sparkling water shining off the mermaids' fins. "Why aren't you and the others down there with them?"

"We're not water elementals." She shrugged, raising a mouthful to her lips. "The mermaids are nice enough to us, but they don't invite us to their parties."

"Belle!" Iona called out. "Get the bottle of vodka from the cupboard and jump in. We have a lot to talk about."

"Okay." My heartbeat drummed in excitement. "I'll be down in a minute!" Elation frothed up inside of me. I felt like laughing. To swim with real mermaids after everything I'd been through — it felt like a dream come true, or another reality.

"Why would they want to see me?" I asked Claire.

She shrugged. "Only one way to find out. Good luck." She patted my shoulder, lifted the curtain, and slid away.

My heart thrummed. If I was a water elemental, this would be the perfect initiation. I ate the soup as fast as I could, then ran below deck to grab the dusty old bottle.

The mermaids and Iona bobbed in the green seawater. I threw two red-and-white striped lifesavers overboard and clutched my broom in one hand. The swirling green seawater had to be at least ten feet below, but if Iona had flown overboard, I could too. I may not be as practiced, but jumping over wouldn't kill me.

I crouched over my broom, took a deep breath, and jumped overboard. For a second, I was certain I'd belly-flop, but I caught the wind. I sailed for a moment before landing with unexpected ease in the sea. It was my first decent landing, and I felt a rush of pride even as I shivered. I tread water until a mermaid swam a lifesaver toward me.

"Thank you."

She smiled, revealing sharp, fox-like teeth, before swimming to comfort a mermaid sniffing back tears.

The mermaids had dark green scales that ran over their backs and fins, but their bellies and chests glimmered pale, pearlescent, just like a fish. Some of them wore bikini tops of various colors, but others wore seaweed or nothing at all. Their large eyes seemed spectral, letting in more light than human eyes, illuminating their blue and green irises.

"*Calidus corpore*," I whispered. Warmth surrounded me, as if I were wearing a down coat. I passed the vodka bottle to Iona.

"Thanks, Belle." Iona uncorked it, wiped off the mouth, and held it high. "To your fallen sister. May she sleep in peace." She drank and passed it.

"Her name was Darya," a red-headed mermaid said, tears cascading down her face.

A mermaid with brown hair and wise green eyes wrapped an arm around her. "From the water to the water. As we are born, so shall we die."

We all bowed our heads. In the heavy silence, the bottle went around the circle.

The mermaids glanced at each other, then, without warning, half of them dove away, swimming in different directions. Their tails undulated in synchronous movements.

The six mermaids remaining were still crying. We were silent a moment longer. The sun broke free from the cloudcover, warming the water and playing on the sea like a million sparkling points of light. When the bottle came back to me, I drank, tears burning my eyes.

"So you're the one the Beast wants," said the brunette mermaid with the knowing green eyes. "We heard about the reward for your capture. I'm Attina. It's good to meet you, Belle." Hunks of blubbery purple flesh still hung from her trident.

I smiled and gave her a little curtsy, my insides contracting. Mephistopheles hadn't been lying — there was a reward.

"How did you hear about a reward?" Iona asked. "You're not a demon."

Attina inclined her head. "We're friends with a demon shark. The reward for her capture is all karma cleared off the work sentence — an instant release to Heaven or to live like a king in Hell." She gazed coolly at me. "But you're worth far more than that."

"Thank you." I released my breath slowly. "I appreciate your help with . . . that *thing*." I curtsied again and sniffed back tears.

Iona's brows rose. "Lucifer's cruelty knows no bounds, and he's set on having that poor girl."

A mermaid with tangled blonde hair adjusted her neon orange bikini top and glared at me. "I don't see what's so special about her."

"Hush, Sereia," Attina said. "You musn't be rude."

Sereia swallowed, her eyes red. "No. If Darya died, I want to know why. Why does Lucifer want you?"

All eyes wandered to me. I looked at their open faces. Even Iona didn't know what to say. "I'm not special." I glanced at the lapping water. "I don't know why he wants me."

Attina turned to her clan. "Belle is like any of us. That's why we must fight for her freedom — because it could've been you. Besides, none of us know what the future will hold. She may save your scales one day."

The mermaids tilted their heads in sympathy.

Iona trod water, eyeing Attina warmly. "We have a few things going for us. The demons don't know where we're going. Otherwise, we'd have seen a lot more of them."

I noticed Iona didn't mention anything about my idea for a weapon. Did her trust only extend so far? Or did she want to protect the mermaids against knowing too much?

Attina nodded. "Lucifer made an error — the reward is only for *one* demon. It doesn't help them to gang up on you. They'll fight you one at a time, while you can attack in numbers."

"About that reward," the blonde mermaid said. "Do you ever worry about the company you keep?"

I glanced at the horizon. I didn't know what to say. Kelsey's transformation still echoed in my head. I sighed. "Yes. We lost one sister from that kind of greed. We had a traitor in our midst, and we didn't even know it."

Several mermaids gasped or covered their mouths.

Iona nodded. "We also lost eight safehouses, a rendez-vous location, and who knows how many charms she gave them."

"I'm sorry to hear that," Attina said.

"It's in the past," Iona said. "But my sisters, thank you so much for all your help today. We wouldn't have survived it without you." She clasped her hand in prayer. "I don't want to keep you if you must go. We're about a day's journey to our location."

"Where are you headed?" Attina asked.

"The north shores of Poland," I said.

Iona smiled. "Of course, if you'd like to escort us there, we'd be even more in your debt."

The mermaids glanced at each other. A couple of them nodded.

Attina turned back to Iona. "We will accompany you, however, we must stop within a few kilometers of the shore. Our territory ends at that point. I trust you have other allies to call upon on land?"

Iona's mouth formed a thin, red line. "I certainly hope so."

"Very well. This reinforces our allegiance, though I must remind you that if we need you, we expect you to assist us as well."

"Thank you." Tears formed in Iona's eyes as she bowed her head. "You can rely upon the witches to assist you, should that time come. There's one more thing." She glanced at me sidelong. "Can you test Belle for the water element? I could do it, but—"

Attina nodded. "It would be our honor." She held out a two-toned arm to me, smiling.

"Go ahead, Belle," Iona said. "I'll hold your broom."

I swam toward her, my heart rising in my throat. This had to be it. I was certain I wasn't fire, and water was the only one left. My limbs tingled, anticipating what a water superpower would entail.

Attina held my hands and gazed at the water between us. "Push your power into the water."

I closed my eyes. Energy built up inside me, then I shot it out into the water. My eyelids fluttered open.

She gazed at me eagerly. "Did you do it yet?"

I sighed. I wanted to pull away from her, but she held my arms tight.

"Try again."

The look in her eyes convinced me to give it another go. I took another deep breath and commanded the depths of my power, from deep within. My breathing came hard and ragged as I pushed it out of me again.

After a minute, her wet hand touched my arm. "It's okay, Belle."

I nodded, but inside, part of me flared up in confusion. I couldn't be fire — I never resonated with it. There had to be a mistake.

"Even though you're not a water elemental," Attina glanced at Iona, "we want to offer you protection. If you ever need a place of refuge, you can join us. Now, or some time in the future."

I glanced at the faces surrounding me and felt buoyed. How kind — I'd never fit in, but they were willing to assist me.

Iona pulled me closer to her, her eyes squinting slightly. I could tell she was disappointed I hadn't passed the test. "Come on, Belle. Let's get to bed. We'll want to be rested for tomorrow."

My limbs felt heavy all of the sudden. Attempting to use my power like that had drained me. "Thank you for your offer. Goodnight."

I hauled myself onto my broom. The effort made my arms weak, but I launched into the air, murmuring the drying spell. I bungled the landing on the deck, but caught myself before falling on my face.

We walked toward the cabin. "Iona, I really wanted to be a water element."

"I suppose this means you're fire."

We walked down the stairs. She locked the door behind me and placed a hand on the counter. Her brown eyes seemed to pin me. "Why didn't you look surprised when Attina mentioned the reward?"

CHAPTER THIRTY-THREE

I bowed my head and sighed. I'd wanted to tell them about the reward, but the kraken had attacked. There'd been no time.

Iona tapped her foot.

Claire walked into the kitchen, glancing between me and Iona. "What's going on?"

Fern appeared from behind the curtain. "What is it, child? Spit it out." Her eyes were sharp and her arms were crossed.

I looked at the witches. I didn't want to tell them, to say it out loud, but I knew I had to. They deserved the truth. I swallowed and took a deep breath. "Someone told me about the reward. Someone I trust."

"Who, exactly?" Iona asked, her voice stern. "And how?! We're in the middle of nowhere!"

"Calm down," Claire said. "I'm sure there's a reasonable explanation. Go on, Belle."

I shook my head. She was only making it worse, but I had to get it out. "I have a two-way mirror with someone. I'm sorry I didn't tell you. I wanted to tell you about it sooner—"

Claire's eyes opened wide.

"Who is it?" Iona asked.

I shook my head. "It's no one."

Maribeth walked into the kitchen, her face livid. Her eyes looked sleepy, as if she'd just awoken. "Who has the other mirror?"

I shrugged. "He's a friend."

Fern threw out her hands. "Are you going to tell us who it is? You're putting us all at risk here."

I smiled helplessly. "It's just Mephistopheles. He's not that bad—"

"Are you kidding me?!" Maribeth yelled, her teeth bared.

Fern backed away from me, her eyes alarmed. "Belle, are you an idiot?"

Iona paled. "He could be tracking us!"

"No," I said. "He's helping us. He didn't have to tell me about the reward. Besides, he said he's not going to look for us."

Maribeth's lip curled back in disgust. "And you be-lieve him? He's one of Lucifer's demons. *He could've sent the kraken!*"

"Where's the mirror?" Fern held her hand out, her

face a mask. "Give it to me."

"I was thinking we'd keep it," I squeaked. "We can use it when—"

Iona shook her head. "No, Belle. Out of the question. Very much so. You should've told us about this."

With a tight chest, I trudged into the bedroom and retrieved my satchel. I clenched the cheap brown plastic mirror in my hand. I wanted to open it right there, to prove to them that he wasn't bad, but I knew they were right. It had to go.

From behind the curtain, I heard one of them murmur that the mirror could've led the demons to the safehouse. I shook my head. No, that'd been Kelsey. Why couldn't they see? But there was no reasoning with them. I knew that.

I walked back to the kitchen and placed the compact into Fern's outstretched hand. She dropped it on the floor, then stomped on it with her boot. The compact split, crushing the mirror.

My heart sank as I looked at the silvery, splintered dust on the floor. There'd be no more warnings or bargains, no more midnight talks. I'd never be able to contact him again.

Fern opened a port window and said some words that made the compact and the dust rise into the air and trickle out. She slammed it shut and faced us. "Now that we *can't be tracked*," she shot me a venomous look, "we might have a chance to escape with our lives."

My friends glared at me. I knew it hadn't been right to keep the mirror from them, but I didn't think it was that bad. I knew Mephistopheles wasn't entirely on my side, but he wasn't entirely on Lucifer's side, either.

"I don't think he was tracking us," I said.

Maribeth rolled her eyes. "We were lucky only one demon attacked us. Who knows how many more are out there? Maybe they're waiting for us on land!"

Claire held out her hand. "Let's not get ahead of ourselves, dear. We don't know that."

"Belle," Iona frowned. "This area we're going to — does it have any waystations?"

"No. I've used every waystation in the bank, and there's not one that leads directly to it. But, it is just a couple of kilometers from the waystations in a nearby city. Do we really have allies everywhere? In case we're attacked?"

Iona's mouth twitched down. "I certainly hope so. It's been a while since we called upon some of them, and we'll need all the help we can get. Not all of our enemies will be so easy to vanquish."

Easy? If she'd thought the kraken was easy, what did she think laid in store for us over land?

Claire fell forward onto the counter, her breathing constrained. She opened her mouth, but nothing came out but a ragged breath.

"The vapors!" I dug in my satchel and pulled out the vial.

Claire took a sip, then another, and corked it. Her breathing returned to normal.

"Are you okay?" Fern asked.

Claire put her hand up. "I'm okay now," she croaked, handing me the remains of the vial. "Thank you, Belle."

I looked at the greenish-yellow vapor pooling in the bottom of my vial. It was half-gone.

"Which brings us to our next point of concern." Fern looked around the room. "Does everyone have a vial?"

We all nodded except for Maribeth. She gazed dejectedly at the floor. "I didn't have time to get my purse. The demons attacked too quickly."

"It's okay," Fern said. "Someone will have to share."

"I'll share," Iona piped up, smiling sweetly.

"Bottoms up, everyone." Fern said.

I drank the remaining sips from the vial, the brimstone air tasting even worse than I'd remembered. My heart fluttering nervously as I peered at my empty vial. "Will we really be near land tomorrow?"

"Aye," Claire said, braiding her white hair. "But if we don't have any more vapor tomorrow night, it'll be bad. We only have three doses left."

"Don't think like that," Fern said. "We just need to come up with a plan. Maybe one of us can go back to Hell and fill the vials."

We gazed at each other. I knew I wouldn't be going back to Hell, not with the reward on my head. That meant one of them had to go.

The witches avoided each others' gaze, their eyes darting around the tiny kitchen. I felt sorry for them. We had no idea what Lucifer knew about our group — whom he saw, or who could be recognized. Going back could be a death sentence.

"We'll talk about it tomorrow," Iona said, walking toward the bedroom. "I'm peaked. Goodnight."

The other witches followed her into the bedroom.

I looked out the kitchen's porthole window and scanned the coral clouds on the horizon. I couldn't help but think about the magic mirror. Had it rung when Iona crushed it? Had Mephistopheles witnessed any of its destruction, or heard anything? Maybe he was staring at a snail on the bottom of the sea at this very moment.

When I climbed into bed, the sounds of mermaids singing a rapturous, interweaving harmony lulled me to sleep.

The next morning, Maribeth compelled silvery gray fish to leap out of the sea and onto the deck. "You'd better catch them!" she taunted me.

Between the five of us, we'd eaten all of the canned goods last night. All that was left was a salt shaker, some stale crackers, and a tin of old paprika. I grasped the squirming fish and carried it to the chopping block on deck, grumbling a little.

"Don't complain," Maribeth said. "It'll ruin your karma." She pointed to another fish bouncing down the deck. "That one's getting away."

After I filleted the fish and set them into the little oven to steam, I took the slop bucket to the side of the ship. The mermaids swam beside our boat or held onto one of the trailing ropes as we sailed. From time to time, their glimmering backsides flashed in the sunshine. Iona had mentioned the mermaids would eat the fish scraps, but I was doubtful. The bucket of guts, heads, and scales smelled too raw. I threw them over anyway, one piece at a time. The mermaids snatched them in the air and gnawed them. I smiled, knowing my karma was going down little by little.

I wondered what the mermaids' world was like. Where did they live, and what would my life be like if I went with them? They'd offered it to me so easily, without even knowing who I was. After all I'd been through, I was a little suspicious. Did they want me for the same reason as Lucifer did — for some nefarious purpose? Or did they want to protect me?

Claire steered the newly rebuilt wheel, thanks to either Fern or Maribeth None of the other witches could've reassembled it — we weren't earth elementals. I could still see the cracks from where it'd exploded into pieces, but it appeared to be working just fine.

"Hello, Claire," I said, breathing in the salty air.

She gazed out over the sea, her blue eyes distant. "Good morning, dear."

I looked out too for a moment, trying to find the words to apologize to her. The witches had been frosty to me since last night. I should've told them about the mirror — I should've trusted them as much as they'd trusted me. But they'd never understand that I had to protect myself from Lucifer any way I could, and that I trusted Mephistopheles enough to keep his promise. All I wanted was to make it right, to go back to the way things were.

"I'm sorry about the mirror," I said, casting my eyes down.

She smiled. "Supposedly," she croaked, pausing to looked at me with her weary blue eyes. "Fire elementals are very stubborn. It's been said they have a hard time apologizing. Would you agree with that?"

I fidgeted. "Well, if I really am a fire elemental, then yes, I'd have to agree."

She smiled a little. "Are you saying you're ready for your test?"

I nodded, but my chest felt full of shadows and light. What if I failed that test too? It'd be just my luck to be terrible at every element. And I'd really wanted to be anything but fire. Then again, I wanted to belong to a group more than anything else.

Claire reached in her pocket and pulled out a clear glass jar. Inside was a half-burned yellowish beeswax candle. She set it on the dashboard. "See if you can light this with your mind."

I looked at the candle and focused on the little black wick, willing it to catch fire. My eyes closed and I pushed the energy out from my core, just as I had with the other elements.

Something slipped inside of me — it was as if I'd travelled into a mental pocket. I saw a green flame, and then a dank cellar. I heard the whimpering of children, then the sound of horse hooves and chatter. I looked around and saw that I was on a wooden pavilion at dawn, at the place I'd died. The tall structures of the village rose around me, blocking any chance of escape. Surrounding me were the faces of the people from my village. I saw the swirl of the magistrates' black cloaks as they read from a book. The smell of hay and horse dung clouded the air.

"What is your name?" the old scribe asked.

I glanced at the crowd. My father and mother were huddled in the back, near the shops. Tears spilled from their eyes. Guards with spears stood near them, forcing them to watch.

"Babelin Gobel," I whispered. How long had it been since I'd last eaten? They'd starved me in that cell.

The old man dipped his quill in the pot of ink and wrote my name in a book.

"No," I said. "You misspelled it. It's—"

The scribe's crazed blue eyes flashed at me. "Did the devil teach you how to read?"

My mouth opened. My family had taught me — it was one of my favorite things to do. Was that why I was here?

Strong hands pressed on my shoulders, forcing me to kneel on the dry, red-stained wood. Before me was a blackened chopping block. The air was rife with the putrescent smell of old, rotten blood, and flies buzzed around me in a macabre dance. I almost gagged, but I was distracted by booming steps echoing on the planks. I glanced backwards at a muscled man wearing a black hood. He lugged a giant silver axe, then swung it around in the air. The jeers of the villagers rose. Some of them pointed fingers at me or made the sign of the cross.

I shook my head. "No. This is a mistake!" Someone pushed my neck down onto the block. It felt slick and cool beneath my ear. I swallowed hard. Then the old man said something I'd tried to blot out from memory, for centuries.

"May God have mercy on your soul," he said in a teetering voice.

Anger boiled inside of me. *"May God have mercy on yours!"*

The *chop* echoed in my ears.

I barely knew what happened next.

I was outside of my body, witnessing as a spirit, in denial. The executioner picked up my body and threw it onto a bonfire, which leapt high and crackled with thick logs. I watched as it caught fire and burned. The villagers covered their mouths with handkerchiefs. When the black smoke filled the square, they cleared out reluctantly. Only I remained, watching my flesh blacken and burn.

I felt the rock and sway of the boat skimming over the waves and smelled fish and saltwater. I sat up, feeling the wooden floor of the deck beneath my fingers.

Claire looked down at me from the wheel. "Are you alright, dear? You passed out."

I pressed against the floor to stand up. For centuries, I'd refused to look at the details of my death. Even though I saw the last part whenever I killed evil people, I'd shoved it down into my subconscious. Some part of me was still in denial, after all these centuries. I had to face facts. It had happened. I had been beheaded and burned as a witch. For whatever reason, it was time for me to look at it, and look well.

All of the sudden, my current battle didn't seem so out of place. I'd been facing injustices my whole life. I'd been fighting system after system, only now, I was stronger. I knew myself more. I trusted myself — my thoughts and intuition — over that of others. I knew what was best for me, not the magistrates, not Lucifer. And I knew what must be done.

Claire pointed up to the candle on the dashboard. "Look."

A vibrant orange flame flickered, a halo radiating from it like sunshine. I swallowed a lump in my throat. I'd finally passed a test. I belonged somewhere — I had a sisterhood within the sisterhood. The power of fire lived inside of me.

"Welcome to the fire clan." Claire smiled. "Don't listen to what Iona says about fire elementals. We're a fine lot, and if you hear otherwise, give them an earful."

I laughed a little.

"I'm sorry that I can't teach you any fire spells until your karma is lower. I hope you don't hate me for it. It must be a let down."

"No, of course not! I know my karma is still too close. I'm just happy to belong. I was afraid there was something wrong with me. I was so afraid of fire. I hadn't realized it was a part of me."

Her blue eyes focused on mine. "Your soul survived a burning, didn't it?"

I nodded, tears sparking in my eyelids. She clasped me in a hug. I lay my head against her shoulder, the fire coil inside me burning. It hurt until I took a deep breath and released everything I couldn't use for my mission. My eyes teared up as I thought of the village girl I used to be, of the life I could've led. I released that too — everything except for the present moment and the determination I felt.

"That's right," Claire cooed, patting my back. "Let it go."

After a moment, my inner coil quelled with something that felt like peace. That feeling inside me had been fire all along, and I hadn't realized it. I had pushed it down, afraid of it, just as I'd been afraid I wouldn't pass the tests. It took looking at my deepest fear and my lowest moment to realize how strong I was.

Maribeth popped her head downstairs. "Where's the fish? I'm starving."

I lifted my head from Claire's shoulder and wiped away my tears, going to tend to the fish in the oven.

"You'd better be careful." Claire wagged a finger at her. "Belle's a fire elemental."

Maribeth shrank back, her mouth twisting. "Great."

"Land ahoy!" Attina called out from the sea.

We all walked to the prow and looked at the tiny ridge

of land on the horizon. Seagulls wheeled overhead, crying out.

"This is where our territory ends," Attina said, treading water. "Belle, have you considered our offer?"

I drew in a slow breath, aware of the multitude of bright, sea-colored mermaid eyes on me. As much as I appreciated their proposal, I was resolved more than ever to see my mission through to the end. "Thank you, but I'm going to stay with the witches. Lucifer won't stop looking for me, and I can't put my friends in danger." When I saw Fern beaming at me from across the deck, I knew I'd made the right decision.

"As you wish," Attina bowed slightly. "We wish we could help you more, but it sounds like your journey is continuing on land."

"Thank you for everything, sisters," Iona said. "I always enjoy seeing you."

The mermaids sank beneath the waves and swam away, their fins shining through the sun-glinted waters.

After lunch, we huddled together on the deck and studied a map. The wind whipped at the edges, making a rattling noise. Claire placed her hands on the southern portion, and Fern touched the edge nearest to her, but the map still fluttered in the strong, salty wind.

I smoothed down the corner near me and gazed into their expectant eyes. "It's time I told you where we're going. I'm sorry I haven't said anything more than just 'south' — Medea asked me to keep it a secret. But now that we're the only ones remaining . . ." I bit my lip. I didn't have to finish my sentence. They knew what I meant. We were alone.

I pointed to a green spot, far inland on the map. "We're going to a crater southwest of the city of Ceské Budojovice. It's in the southern part of the Czech Republic."

Fern's mouth twisted. "What's there? Did you find something that can kill Lucifer? Or someone?"

I shook my head. "I never found anything about that. This is where he landed when he fell to earth."

"And what's the significance of that?" she asked.

"I think his angel wings crystalized, because that spot has crystals that aren't found anywhere else on earth. If I'm right, they might be able to pierce his skin. We just have to get there, extract the crystals from the earth, and forge a weapon. I'll take it from there."

"You make it sound so easy, Belle." Iona laughed. "I don't envy you the task after the weapon is made. Have you thought about how you're going to kill him?"

I shrugged. Despite how familiar I was with dispatching the scum of the earth, I'd been too distracted by everything else going on to figure out the best weapon for my sneak attack. Plus, we had to consider the nature of the crystals. If they were too brittle, the knife would break. "I thought we'd figure it out once we're there, working with the crystal."

"What about vapors?" Maribeth asked, her brows raised. "We don't have enough for all of us. We're going to run out in a few hours."

I reached across the map and pointed to a sprawling port city in Poland. "Gdansk is just a few kilometers away. It has a waystation near the stadium that lands near the far end of Death's Cross. Those hallways aren't used as much as the waystations near the office door."

Claire gave me a small smile. "Less chance of being seen by the guard."

"We need a volunteer." Fern looked at the faces around her. "Not Belle, obviously."

No one spoke up. I ducked my head, watching the wind play with the sails. I understood why no one wanted to go to Hell. It was dangerous. Whoever volunteered would be risking their life. It was possible Lucifer knew everyone in our little rebellion, or maybe the guards were watching the waystations closer than before.

After a long moment, Maribeth leaned forward. "I'll go. I was seen the least that night at the cabin."

"I just realized," Claire said. "We only have three doses of vapor. One of us needs to go with her."

"I'll go." Fern said.

"No, dear." Claire put her hand out. "We need an earth witch to stay, to help with the weapon if . . . something happens to Maribeth, Heaven forbid. You two are the only ones who can summon the crystals from the earth. I can go."

Iona pinned her blue cloak over her shoulders. "I dare say you'll need a fire elemental to make the weapon too — that means you're out, Claire. No offense, Belle, but as a novice fire elemental, you shouldn't have that kind of pressure. I'll accompany you down the waystation, Maribeth. If you'll have me, that is."

"Of course." Maribeth nodded.

My heart panged, watching Iona summon her broom and pack bottles into her brown leather purse. I didn't want her to leave. She was like a mother to me, more than Claire or Fern. If anything happened to her, I'd hate myself for it. But she was right. We needed everyone else to help with the weapon. I only hoped nothing happened to her.

Iona laughed at my expression. "Belle, don't worry so much. You'll be cooking my dinner again in no time." She kissed my forehead.

I smiled, and after a moment, nodded. "You're right. I do worry too much."

Maribeth appeared from below deck, holding her broom lightly. The vodka bottle was visible through her cross-strapped purse. She looked weary, like Sarah before she passed. Her once-bright eyes appeared sunken. I hoped it didn't mean anything bad would happen to her.

She had to make it, otherwise, we'd be short two more witches and out of vapors in twenty-four hours.

Claire strode toward Maribeth and Iona and clasped their hands in hers. Her white hair streaked across her grave expression. "Listen to me. As soon as you get near Death's Cross, cast an invisibility spell. No sense in showing your faces. Unplug the bottles, then cork them up, press the button, and fly back lickety-split."

Fern nodded. "We'll be waiting in the harbor. If we don't see you in an hour, we'll meet you at the crater."

"Be safe, Iona," I said, giving her a hug.

She hugged me, then patted me on my head. "Take care. I'll see you soon."

I handed Maribeth my empty vial. "Good luck, Maribeth, and thank you."

She took the vial, but glanced through me as if I weren't there. She and Iona situated their brooms, cast the invisibility spells, and flew into the blue sky.

Once they were specks, Fern turned to me and Claire. "We'll leave as soon as they return, so be ready to fly in an hour. We won't want to make the journey to the crater at dark."

I swallowed, watching the specks in the sky grow even smaller. Fern didn't have to say why flying at night would be bad. Demons came out at that time — by the thousands. And if they were all looking for us, we wouldn't last long.

CHAPTER THIRTY-FOUR

Claire turned off the motor. The boat drifted in the deep blue harbor before she threw the anchor overboard with a hefty *sploosh*.

I stood on the deck, fiddling with the strap of my satchel. My broom leaned against the helm. The sun sank lower, shining amber light on the rippling waves. Gulls wheeled in the late afternoon sun, crying out, and workers on the docks and shipyards went about their daily activities, but there was no sign of my friends.

Claire sidled up beside me and gazed at the coast, her eyes pinched. "They should be back by now."

"Maybe they got lost." I bit my lip. I should've been more descriptive when I told them the location of the waystation. What if it got decommissioned, and they had to find another one?

Fern walked onto the deck, her bag slung over her shoulder. "We can't wait any longer. Something must've happened to them." She hung her head. "Lucifer knows we need the vapor. He might be watching Death's Cross."

I trembled, my fingernails digging into my palms as I scanned the sky. I refused to accept they were gone. They had to come back. *They had to.* "Can we fly over the waystation?"

"No." Fern's eyes hardened. "If Maribeth and Iona were found, we can't be anywhere near there."

"But we could use the invisibility spell," I said. "Please?"

"I'd feel better if we looked for them too," Claire said.

"Fine, but drink up." Fern rolled her eyes. She passed me a half-filled vial of vapors. "I know it hasn't been twenty-four hours yet, but we can't risk a seizure while we're flying."

I tipped it back and drank, the thick sulfurous air clotting on my tongue before I swallowed it down.

We cast the invisibility spell and flew off the boat and over the sea. From our height, it looked like a rumpled cerulean carpet. We passed over the docks, over people loading fish and boxes, then we flew over the asphalt and concrete city. In the distance was the giant white ring of the stadium, but the cinderblock warehouse with the waystation next door was gone.

I searched the surrounding area, looking for another red door with hellfire, but didn't see one anywhere. "It's gone!" *What happened to them?*

Claire flew beside me. "Don't worry dear. There's not much we can do. They'll try to meet us at the crater."

"We have to get higher," Fern shouted, "before the invisibility spell breaks!"

"Should we cast another one?" I asked as we soared upward.

"No, we won't have enough energy to make it to your crater if we're invisible the whole time."

We ascended into the sky. There were no clouds to hide behind, so we climbed to the safe point — too high for humans to see.

Higher up, the sun warmed my back, and the air smelled rich with ozone. After spending so much time on the always-rocking seawater, it felt good to be in the air again. Soon, the cityscape petered out, and patches of forest and farmland were visible.

I glanced over at my friends. They'd followed me through so much, and trusted me, somewhat blindly. Or at least, they trusted Medea. I only hoped my plan worked, that all our trials and losses hadn't been for nothing.

Fern glanced over her shoulder, her brows close. "Can you fly any faster, Belle?"

I leaned forward, engaging my willpower, and accelerated a little.

She sped up to match my speed. "Claire, come beside

me. We should summon our allies."

Claire flew closer, her lined face puzzled. "What is it?"

"Maybe it's nothing," Fern said, "but I think I sense demons behind us."

My heartbeat raced. Fern was an earth witch. She had intuition when it came to creatures. If she was concerned, it didn't bode well for us. I peeked back, but I didn't see anything except the white and blue expanse of the horizon.

I held Fern's warm hand in mine and reached across her lap to hold Claire's. A surge of energy rocketed through me. A blue ring radiated out from us, racing in all directions and knocking me back. I sank a few feet, but pulled up before Fern had to reach a hand toward me. Her mouth twitched into a small smile.

I knew what she was thinking — I was becoming better at flying. What Sarah had said about my trying too hard was right. I'd learned it wasn't so much about trying to fly as it was *wishing to fly*. As long as my emotions weren't too heavy, I could empty my mind and become as light as a feather. I chuckled. Why hadn't I figured out I was a fire elemental before? They were known for being overly emotional. Maybe that was another reason why Kelsey hadn't liked me — because we were so similar in that regard. Even though she was cruel to me and had betrayed us, I still felt sorry for her. She'd been fooled by Lucifer's false promises. Did he make her perform the same rite and lock her in a cell too? Or did he just use her to get to me? I wished we could've saved her. She didn't have to go the route she did.

I accidentally dipped low in the air again. With a deep breath, I cleared my mind and leveled out with the other witches again. It was clear I couldn't let myself think about all the unsolvable problems of the world, even though I wanted to help.

Some of the trees in the forest below were crowned with yellow or fiery red, some splayed bare branches, and some were evergreen beauties. I longed to be on the ground, to feel the soil beneath my feet, and walk in the autumnal woods. I missed the smell of the earth.

I wondered what my karma score was. The whole time on the boat, we had no cell reception. I dug in my satchel and pulled out the burner phone from the cabin. After turning it on, I loaded the app.

```
Belle Dame: 95.4% bad, 4.6% good
```

I sighed. It was taking so long. I still couldn't harm anyone, not until it was time to dispatch Lucifer. Turning evil before that wasn't an option.

Fern checked behind us again, only this time, her head jerked forward and she sped ahead even faster. Her eyes strained across the horizon.

I turned and saw a few specks. When I squinted, I thought I saw gargantuan black wings and gangly red limbs, forked tails writhing. My breath caught in my throat.

"Are those fire imps?" I asked.

Fern searched the sky ahead of us. "I'm afraid so."

"How did they find us?"

She shook her head and frowned. "Who knows. Maybe they saw us, or maybe someone has been watching us, and now they know our allies are gone."

"But we called on new allies," I said. "They'll help us, right?"

Her eyes looked distant, faraway. "*If* they get here in time. And it's not always a guarantee that they'll help."

I shook my head. "What do you mean? The mermaids helped us."

"This is more work than taking down a bully. Anyone who signs up to help is asking to be targeted by Lucifer for the rest of their lives. You know how many demons there are in Hell at his command?"

My shoulders sank. We'd only been flying for three hours — we had another three to go before we reached the crater.

"Clouds ahead!" Fern called out. "Keep close!"

She nose-dived into the puffy thunderheads. Claire and I followed after. Fern jerked left. We followed, weaving a maze through the clouds. She steered down and popped out only to dive into another cloudy mass.

"*Camarquat heroses.*" Fern's voice was charged with determination.

Claire and I cast the invisibility spell too, just in time, as the clouds disappeared and a wide, cloudless horizon was visible again.

We flew for several minutes. I looked behind us and didn't see anything. When the invisibility spell broke, I felt safe enough to not cast it again. Besides, I needed to save my energy.

Squawk!

Five fire imps appeared directly behind us — giants, easily twice as big as I was. Their hulking black wings pumped, launching them through the air. The largest of the imps pointed a black-clawed, crimson finger at me. "That's the one he wants," he said in a gruff voice. He dove after me, his black eyes malicious.

"They must've uncloaked from an invisibility spell," Claire said, dodging an imp.

The leader reached for me. I spurred my broom faster, diving and dipping through the air.

The beast pumped his wings, pushing himself toward me — always at the straw of my broom, his hands grasping at the ends of my hair. The words of the invisibility spell were on my tongue when Claire called out.

"*Marmore indeficadus!*"

A golden-colored spell struck the creature as he reached for me. His motions stopped and he turned gray, then sank like a stone to the earth.

The other imps beat toward us, evading the spells the witches cast. They swooped, hands outstretched. I dodged them like a hummingbird, going down when two of them attacked, and zipping backwards when they blocked my way forward.

After evading them for a few minutes, I couldn't see Fern and Claire anymore. Where were they? I scanned the sky, not seeing anyone at all. Did the imps cast another invisibility spell? I sped ahead, knowing that if I hovered, I could be caught in an instant. But where were my sisters?

In a flash, the imps were visible again. Two of them wrestled with Fern and Claire. They fired spells at them, but the beasts were too fast, flying out of the way as the witches' bolts of light streamed over their shoulders or behind her backs.

I nearly jumped off my broom when two imps appeared at my backside.

"*Camarquardt heroses.*" The invisibility spell rattled off my tongue, then I plummeted into a cloud. After a moment, I caught my breath. I lost them. But where were my sisters?

A flock of birds flew in from the south in a V-formation. At first they looked like eagles, then I saw ivory faces and silky, chestnut hair where their heads were. My mouth went slack, watching in awe as *harpies* flew past me. I hadn't even known of their existence, but there they were, thrashing their umber wings and flexing their talons. There must've been a dozen of them. One by one, they twitched bird-like eyes to glance at me, even though I was invisible. In the middle of them, a woman with flaxen hair and a long black skirt rode a broomstick. My heart rose in my throat. "Medea!"

Her eyes lit up and she darted close to me. "Belle! Are you alone? Where are the others?"

"They're fighting fire imps. The imps are invisible."

Her black eyes hardened. "How many?"

"Four left."

The harpies tucked their wings close and dove, swooping and circling in the air, as fast as falcons. Four of them clustered in on an invisible imp, flapping hard and tearing it with their talons. The imp appeared a moment later, crying out as he lashed a clawed hand at them. The harpies fended him off and pecked at his flesh with gleaming white teeth.

Medea shot a red spiky ball that ripped a hole through his chest. The imp was bloody, and in pieces. His wings were nothing more than a skeleton. When the harpies released him, he sank like a stone to the earth, screaming.

Something caught me around the stomach. I clutched

my broomstick and looked down in horror at crimson arms encircling around my waist.

"Medea! Help!"

She appeared almost instantly and blasted it with purple light. It reared back and fell to the earth, clutching a wound on its belly.

The invisibility spell broke on the remaining imps, and they became visible again. Fern and Claire fought against an imp, their faces twisted with exhaustion as they fired spell after spell. Harpies dove close behind the imp, their talons tearing holes in its flesh and wings. Another imp attacked them, but the harpies clustered an attack.

The imps were outnumbered. Soon, the second-to-last imp fell. Everyone but me ganged up on the remaining one. He swatted at the harpies, and his massive hand struck one of them square in the face. She began to fall, head first.

I flashed back to the night at the cabin where Jane fell off Iona's broom. My mouth went dry. I couldn't have a repeat of that event. On reflex, I dove after the little harpy, racing through the sky toward her. I urged my broom faster. I sped closer and closer to a field of wheat, but still I charged on.

I reached out, my arms straining, and grasped the little creature with my fingers. My feet brushed against the spiky heads of wheat before I climbed into the sky again. My breath caught — I'd saved her. She felt so light in my arms, like a little pillow stuffed with air. As we rose, her limbs shivered. She blinked luminous green eyes at me before closing them and rolling into my chest, her cream-colored face creased in pain.

The harpies fought, tearing at the last imp until his body was marked with gouges and his wings were clipped. He fell, screeching, to the ground.

Medea flew toward me. "Is she okay?"

"I don't know." The little harpy was curled in a ball, twitching.

Everyone flew in to encircle us. Some of the harpies kept an eye out for more imps, but it was clear to me that other harpies were in no condition to do so. One of the harpy's legs twitched, her joint appearing to be dislocated. Yet another flapped with only one wing.

The witches hadn't escaped unharmed, either. A vermillion gash raced across Fern's cheek, and part of Claire's scalp had been ripped out near her temple. Blood streaked down her forehead and cheek. They each had scratches up their arms from the imps' claws.

Medea closed her eyes and held out her hands. *"Halvit anam. Sacra kolm mada."* White light poured from her hands into the injured.

I joined into the healing spell, sending them all the spare energy I had. A rush went out of me. After a minute, the harpy in my arms perked up and leapt into

404

the air, flapping to join her sisters. The other ones looked healed as well.

"That's enough." Fern held up a hand. "I feel better now."

"Me too," Claire croaked, though she looked close to tears. She turned her face away.

This had to be hard for her. The stress from the last few days would be enough to kill almost anyone, but knowing we had so much more to do must seem daunting. She'd been so strong the whole time I'd known her. Now, her frailty was starting to show. I hoped one day, we'd make it out of this alive and have time to reflect upon it. There was just so much between now and then that I could barely even think about the future.

"We're headed another two hours to the west," Medea said to the harpies. "Will you accompany us to our destination? We can talk there."

The harpies nodded. They flew around us in a broad V, their watchful eyes sweeping the skies. I glanced around too, wary of another attack. Who else might be out there, watching, waiting?

By the time we descended into the wide, grassy crater, the sun was setting in a multitude of magenta and orange clouds. The crater was edged by a forest of pine trees, with a somewhat higher elevation to the east. From my vantage point, I could see the impact Lucifer made when he fell, where his angel wings must have crystallized and shattered.

We cast invisibility spells and descended into the forest on the ridge. I managed to pull up on my broom and land with aplomb on the soft, pine-needled ground, surprising even myself.

A warmth burst through my body. We'd finally reached our destination. After all we'd been through, I was beginning to think we'd never make it.

The witches stacked their brooms against trees, then bowed low to the harpies. I bowed too, my limbs tingling with gratitude for their assistance. If they hadn't shown up . . . I barely dared to think what might've happened.

They nodded gravely in our direction.

I tried not to stare at their beautiful heads on eagle-like bodies, but it was hard. Unlike the witches and mermaids, who came in all ages and shades, the harpies looked nearly identical, with heart-shaped faces, ivory skin, and long sepia hair. They tilted their heads and rustled their feathers, teeth nibbling at their chests from time to time. But perhaps the most stunning thing about them were their eyes, which ranged from yellow to chocolate, from cobalt to electric purple.

A harpy with dark hair and gray-blue eyes leapt forward. "What news, sisters?" she asked us, her voice silky-smooth.

Medea curtsied. "Lucifer is after another woman —

this one." She pointed to me.

All heads swung in my direction. I blushed under their scrutiny.

The harpy hopped toward me, her sharp eyes watchful. "What will you do now?"

I glanced at Medea questioningly. Could we tell them about our plan? I wondered if she felt the same way I did, that we needed all the help we could get. She nodded.

I took a deep breath and faced the harpies. "We plan on fighting Lucifer."

"Truly?" she asked, her eyes doubtful. "How is that possible? In the battle several millennia ago, Lucifer defeated all of his attackers because no one could harm him, neither with blade nor magic. He destroyed more powerful witches, magicians, and creatures than you."

I frowned. At least she was honest. I didn't know what the customs were among harpies, but I respected her words, even though they sounded like an insult.

"Were you there, at the battle?" I leaned closer.

She nodded. "We helped the last lot of you, and it nearly destroyed us. We cannot risk a loss — we are all that's left of what was once hundreds of flocks. You see, we have no way of reproducing."

"I'm sorry to hear that. We have an idea on how to take him down. If you wish to join us—"

The harpy shook her head. "We cannot join in your

fight. We are a hunted species by demons, even more so than angels are."

"I understand." I smiled apologetically. "We are currently being hunted by demons and Lucifer, himself. We barely escaped several times, flying away with little more than our lives."

The harpy's eyes turned stony, even more bird-like. "The battlefield is no place for a harpy. A valkyrie, maybe. Perhaps you could call upon them."

I nodded, a numbness coming over me. I couldn't believe they didn't want to help us, but I should've expected it. It was a risk they couldn't take.

"Before you leave," I stumbled, trying to find the words. "Could you tell me what happened when the witches cast spells on Lucifer?"

"The spells did not harm him whatsoever. Their best magic was no more powerful than a strong wind against him. They were slaughtered. The ground ran red with blood."

I nodded. The other witches looked at me, their expressions bleak.

"Thank you." I bowed.

The leader bowed gravely again, then her wings arced wide, exposing tawny feathers. With an audible beat, she pushed herself into the air. The others followed suit until they flew above us, traveling south.

I watched them leave, my chest shrinking. Fern was

right. Our allies weren't with us to the end. I couldn't count on them to join in our crusade, but I had hoped we might have more than just the four of us.

Medea talked about where she'd been, how she'd looked for us and couldn't find us, but I couldn't focus on her words. I felt tired. My world got darker and my eyelids began to feel heavy.

"Whoa, Belle!" Claire held me up, fanning my face. "What's wrong?"

"I don't know," I whispered.

Medea gazed at me. "I think she needs more vapor. Does anyone have any?"

Fern shook her head. "She should be fine. We sipped the last of the vials before coming here."

A branch snapped from deep within the forest. Fern perked up as footsteps sounded.

I blinked at someone walking down a path, with short brown hair and a pallid, moon-like face. Relief lit me up like a yule tree to see Iona walking toward us, her midnight blue cloak tied around her neck.

Claire ran to her and pulled her into an embrace. "Iona, you made it! But where's Maribeth? Did you get any vapors?"

Iona's face wrinkled with an unreadable emotion and she backed away from Claire. She looked weary, as if her wellspring of energy had been sapped. "*Marmore indeficadus,*" she murmured sadly. Orange light sprang from her palms.

I halted, frozen in place. I tried to move, but my muscles wouldn't respond. "Wh–" I tried to speak, but no words came out of my mouth. I couldn't even move my head. *What was happening?*

More footsteps came from the woods. Short gray gargoyles with black eyes marched toward us, their grotesque features lit with animosity. They walked around us. Strong, clawed hands clamped down onto my wrists.

I tried to pull against the gargoyles, but I was stuck, immobile. Iona gazed on us with a sad expression.

Mephistopheles strolled down the path toward us. His lips curled into a sneer. "What? Aren't you happy to see me?"

I scowled at him. Whatever he wanted couldn't be good.

CHAPTER THIRTY-FIVE

I couldn't believe Mephistopheles had captured us, that he was the one behind the attack. And to think I'd trusted him!

When the stunning spell broke, Iona shouted, "*magnas perdetto!*"

Four black balls of energy flew through the air, landing on my throat and on the throats of the other witches. A silencing spell.

The gargoyle behind me kicked my knees in, forcing me to fall onto the hard forest floor. I heard the shuffle of the other witches falling to the ground too. Medea was forced to kneel beside me, her quiver of arrows rattling.

Another gargoyle marched someone down the path toward us. He held a knife to her throat. My heart leapt as I recognized Maribeth, looking haggard, but alive.

"Don't bother trying to talk," Mephistopheles said. "Iona took your voices away. It's just for a few minutes, I promise."

"I'm sorry!" Iona cried out to us. "He said he'd hurt Maribeth if I didn't help him! And Belle, you trust him, right?" Her eyes searched mine.

I glared at Mephistopheles, straining against the gargoyle holding my hands behind my back. My cheeks burned. What on earth was he doing?

Fern shot me a hard look that said, *'See? I told you he was garbage!'*

He sighed, pacing before us. "The reason I silenced you all is because I need you to listen without casting a spell on me. I've been turned into a frog before, and I *really* don't like it." He stood in front of Medea and gazed at her, transfixed, his eyes soft all of the sudden. "All I want to do is talk with you."

She tried to wrench her arms free from the gargoyle. Her slitted black eyes smoldered, wild and terrifying. She bared her teeth. I knew if she could, she'd curse him in an instant.

"I'm doing this for you, Medea."

She drew back, her mouth a grimace.

He crouched low in front of her, his eyes level to hers. "I have your memories, from before you were evil."

She froze, then glanced at me, her eyes questioning.

I shook my head furiously. She couldn't trust him. Was this some kind of sick game? Was he keeping us busy until Lucifer arrived? I recited the words of the stunning spell in my mind, ready to use it whenever I could speak again.

"Belle," he said. "I know you think I've lied about everything, but I haven't." He reached into his pocket and pulled out the topaz stone I'd enchanted with the love spell. The one I'd left on the chimney right before he'd pointed me out to Lucifer. He held it out to Medea, his arm outstretched. Even though it was dark, the pendant gleamed like a talisman.

I pulled against the gargoyle's grasp, trying to get her attention.

Mephistopheles jerked his thumb toward me. "Belle's probably trying to tell you to not touch it. She put a love spell on it for me."

Fern and Claire glanced at me, their lips flat and their nostrils flaring. I could feel the disappointment coming off them like steam. I bowed my head.

He dangled the pendant in front of Medea, leaning forward to hang it around her neck.

I launched myself between them. The necklace flew in the air before landing in the grass a couple of feet away. Medea's eyes went wild. She lunged after it, but the gargoyle held her back.

"Let her go," Mephistopheles said to the gargoyle holding her.

Medea ran to the area the pendant fell and searched for it. As soon as she touched it, her face contorted in a silent scream. She fell to the ground, clutching her head.

Mephistopheles gazed at her with sympathy. His eyes were wet with tears. "I've waited two millennia for this moment. I can't believe it's finally here."

I wrenched my wrists free from the gargoyle and ran toward Medea.

Her silent shrieks grew in agony, and her palms pressed against her head as if it would explode. I reached out a trembling hand and touched her shoulder. She flung me off, rocking in pain.

He watched her, his face clouded with mixed emotions. "Her memories are returning. After so long, it hurts."

I glared at him, a white-hot fury burning inside of me. How could I believe anything he said? What if he was killing her? I couldn't do anything hurtful to him without turning evil, but luckily, I knew other spells.

Suddenly, Medea's screams pierced my ears. Her cries sounded like she was being tortured.

"*Virtona sanctum!*" I shouted, firing the spell through both palms at him.

An orb of white light struck his mouth and traveled down his throat. He choked on it for a second, then it fell into his stomach, glowing like a lightning bug in a jar. He swallowed roughly, glaring at me. "A truth spell?" he rasped. "Really?"

"What did you do to Medea?!" I asked, my voice

hoarse.

His eyes were stony as he watched her writhe. "I . . . gave her a remembrance charm."

"Why? Why would you care about her?"

He faced me, his eyes tight. "Damn it, Belle. She was my wife. Before she was a demon, she was my wife."

My mouth opened. I studied his ashen face, uncertain whether I believed him or not.

His eyes filled with tears as he wept. "She was my queen. After several years of happy marriage, Lucifer appeared in the guise of a wealthy merchant. He invited her to tour his ship and the gems there. Of course, his motives were less than pure. He killed her guards and sailed away with her." He sniffed and swallowed hard. "I searched the ends of the earth for her. When I finally found the villa where he'd kept her, they were gone. I didn't dare believe what his manservant said, that Lucifer was the devil himself. Not until it was the only solution possible."

I drew away from him, evaluating his face. This wasn't the playboy monster I knew. He gulped back his tears, but they only flowed harder. I wondered how long he'd suppressed them.

"I was willing to do *anything* to get her back. Even go to Hell." He gave a mirthless laugh and paced the uneven ground. "I studied with the best necromancers and demonologists of my time. After weeks of hunting, we captured a demon. After we set him behind thick bars of steel, we forced him to tell us how a man becomes a demon. He'd seen her — he knew who she was, but said her name had been changed to Medea." He shrugged. "There was only one thing for me to do. As soon as we released the demon, I set plans into motion for an assassin to kill me."

My hands flew to my mouth. "You actually wanted to be a demon?"

"I wanted to do whatever it took to get my wife back." He gazed at Medea with affection. "After the assassin killed me, I spent over a year being a ghost, barely holding on to my sanity, resisting Heaven's beckoning light every single moment. But try as I might, I couldn't figure out how to kill my assassin." He glanced at me. "In that way, you were stronger than I ever was, Belle. But, I did manage to whisper unbearable regret into my assassin's ear. I whispered every day, every night, through his sleep and every meal. Every moment of every day, I persuaded him. *Kill yourself. End your wicked life.* Eventually, he did it — he killed himself. Demons brought me to Hell, just like the caged demon told me. It was the best day of my afterlife." He smiled. "Lucifer didn't recognize me, the fool, but I knew him instantly. He was the savage who'd stolen my wife. He asked for my name, and I gave it as Mephistopheles. It's Greek for '*against Lucifer*,' but he had no idea, the idiot."

He paced through the forest, his eyes flicking between me and Medea. "I didn't see her for years. She was locked up. I worked in the kitchens, where I prepared food for her and Lucifer and the archdemons. After a few months, I convinced a guard to skip his duties so I could bring her food. I made her favorite dish — pasta with a basil-almond sauce. The first time I saw her, crouching in her cell, her hair matted . . . my heart stopped. I dropped the tray to the floor seeing her in that condition. And you know what she did? She cursed at me. I had no idea that she would have forgotten me, or that she'd be so cruel."

Medea winced, running a hand tenderly over his. "I'm so sorry. I was evil — I didn't know any better."

"I realized that. Your eyes gave you away. All of Lucifer's guards were evil too. So, of course, I knew I had to turn evil to join his guard. But before I did, I wrote down my story to keep my memories intact. Lucifer made me kill an innocent, and I turned at the next full moon and forgot everything. But I read that damned book every night, not daring to believe that my chosen mission was to kill my lord, the Prince of Darkness. Over time, I got more comfortable with the idea. I worked my way back from being evil by saving people's lives, by convincing them to not commit suicide. That was my karma, Belle. You'd asked what it was when you were in the cell."

He glanced at the ground, shaking his head. "And whenever I could, I whispered in Lucifer's ear, convincing him that his archdemons couldn't be trusted, that the only demons who could be trusted were the ones with no power, like me. Eventually, he started to listen. His archdemons were in place by that time, and more wanted to join the ranks. He liked that I didn't want power or a title. He didn't know that the only thing I wanted was my true love back and revenge against the beast who'd stolen our lives. He never even realized I'd come back from the other side from being evil."

"That's right," I said, thinking back to the app. "When I looked you up, you were actually more good than evil. I thought it was an error."

He smiled. "Nope. I have better karma than you do, Belle."

"But how did you become Medea's guard?"

"I convinced Lucifer I was the only one he could trust with his prisoner. And at least then, I got to see her, even if she didn't know who I was."

She laughed. "I thought you were just a creep."

He crouched low and touched her chin, his thumb caressing her cheek. "Did the charm work? Do you remember me from when we were human?"

"Yes, I remember." She gazed lovingly at every detail of his face. Her hand folded into his. "We were so very happy. You were my wonderful Laus."

418

He smiled, and his ugly face didn't seem so revolting anymore. He looked statuesque — royal, even. "And you were my radiant Helene."

I drew a deep breath, my mouth falling open. "Wait. Medea . . . Are you *Helen of Troy?*"

"She is." A gleam twinkled in Mephistopheles' eyes. "And let me tell you, she launched more than just a thousand ships. She launched them all! I searched to the ends of the earth for her. I tried everything to get her back, but it wasn't just because she was the most beautiful woman in the world. She was my soul mate." He turned to the gargoyles. "Let the witches go, and be gone with you. The gold is in my office. You can have it all."

The gargoyles released the witches and launched into the air, their wings and shoulder muscles bulging as they flew. They flew until they were a cloud of darkness, their bleak cries echoing across the valley as they flew toward Ceské Budejovice.

The witches stood and rubbed their wrists. They were still in shock, as was I. I still couldn't believe that for over 2,000 years, Mephistopheles had been plotting, waiting for some break in his luck. It explained so much — how he knew about things, why he'd helped me, and why my charm had never worked on him. He'd sacrificed so much for his undying love, and his work had finally paid off. I glanced at the clear skies and sighed.

"But . . ." I said. "Why were you so scary when we

were on the run?"

He laughed. "I'd hoped you'd tell her about the love charm — that you'd show it to her and it'd work, that she'd remember me and come find me." He shrugged helplessly. "I tried *everything* to make you distrust me, Belle, but you still trusted me. I couldn't believe it!"

I laughed, a little embarrassed. He was right. His actions were deplorable, but something inside me had told me I could trust him. Looking at them nestled together, I knew I'd been right. His actions had all been for a good cause.

"So," I cocked my head. "When you showed up to the cabin in Sweden with Lucifer—"

"That was arranged by your friend Kelsey. I was ordered by Lucifer to come along. I'm sorry, but I had to point you out. He made me watch the chimney for you. I tried to give you a head start, but . . ." He made a face. "Are you any better at flying now?"

"Yes." I blushed, chagrined. "Were you the one who told the witches about my imprisonment?"

"Guilty." He threw up his hands.

Iona stepped forward, one finger to her mouth. "Wasn't Doctor Faustus obsessed with Helen of Troy— I mean Medea?"

He chuckled. "Dr. Faustus was gayer than a unicorn with a rainbow mane, prancing down a Pride Parade in San Francisco. But, when I wrote the book about him, I had to make it seem like he wanted to be with her to hide my desire to be reunited with her. He didn't mind. He needed a beard anyway."

Iona laughed. "Can't believe everything you read, I guess!"

"He was a good friend. We trained together to become magicians. He helped me test enchanted objects on myself to regain my memory. Do you know how many objects I've tried over the years? Dozens! Finally, a few years ago, we came up with the combination of a witch's love spell, a magician's synapse booster, and a personal belonging, and it worked. My memories came back. Everything was there, just as I'd written it. My longing became even more real, a force stronger than any I'd ever felt before. It made me more determined to obtain a strand of her hair. It took months, and by that time, Kelsey refused to help me make me a second love charm. I was stuck until you came along, Belle."

I laughed. "I had no idea you were a magician."

"Who do you think made my thought charm? By the way, Belle, didn't you ever wonder why Lucifer didn't hear your thoughts?"

"I was praying," I said, thinking back. But that couldn't be right. I wasn't praying all the time. I looked at his dark eyes questioningly.

"I enchanted your journal so he'd never hear you."

I leaned forward. "You protected me this whole

time?"

"Yes, and I'll continue to do so. No one should be a slave to Lucifer's whims and mercy." He grasped Medea's hands. "I've planned everything. I have a wonderful place for us, stocked with vapor. We never have to go back to Hell." He kissed her hand. "We'll be so happy again, just like before. I promise."

Medea stood rooted to the spot, shaking her head. "We can't leave. We came all this way because, well, we think we found a weapon that can pierce through Lucifer's skin.

Mephistopheles' calculating eyes scanned me, giving me a stunned look. "Really?"

I nodded. "We're not certain, but it could work."

"You crafty witch." He grinned.

I couldn't help but smile too. "I like that nickname better than *princess*."

"What do you say?" Medea cast hopeful eyes at him. "Are you in?"

His eyes grew flinty and he stroked his chin. "A chance to take down the bastard who stole my wife and caused me over two millennia of pain? You bet I'm in."

Medea smiled a wide, open smile. I realized that all this time, I'd never seen her smile like that. She was radiantly beautiful, but it wasn't because of her features. It was because she was in love. Mephistopheles held her close, and their lips touched in a tender kiss.

I turned away, blushing. Of all the things that could've happened, I never thought this would be possible. I'd thought Mephistopheles was just some weirdo, but everything he'd said made sense. The truth spell had brought it all out of him. He had his mission, just like I had mine. We both wanted something bigger than our little lives.

Iona embraced me, her laughter filling my ears. "Thank heavens! For a moment, I thought it was all going to go sideways! But I kept thinking about what you'd said about him, that you trusted him, and . . . you were right, Belle. I'm sorry I doubted you."

"It's okay." I smiled. "He really is an asshole sometimes."

Mephistopheles nodded from his embrace. "Yeah, I deserve that."

Fern stood up. "So, we made it to the valley where the meteorite landed. What's the plan for the weapon?"

Mephistopheles and Medea untangled from each other and joined the group.

"An earth witch will need to get the crystals out of the ground," I said. "They're an olive-colored glassy crystal called moldavite, and they're usually not bigger than a three centimeters. If you can summon them up from the earth, I'm hoping Claire can forge them into a weapon that can slice through him. I'm thinking a sword would be best."

"Then what?" Maribeth asked.

I bit my lip. "I'd thought I would go to Hell and use it to kill him, but now I'm not so sure. What if the guards take the weapon before I see him?"

"What are you saying?" Medea asked. "You don't have a plan?"

I looked at Mephistopheles' crystal pendant hanging from his neck. "I could just take my thought charm off. Lucifer will hear my thoughts and come after me. We'll be waiting with the weapon. We could fight him here, from the high ground. If we have enough moldavite, we can make several weapons. We could all fight."

"That could work," Claire nodded.

"Belle, have you breathed the vapors recently?" Mephistopheles looked over me, his eyes concerned.

"Do you have any?" I asked.

He pointed to the woods. "I brought a tank of vapor. It's just back in those woods. Fuel up, just in case. We don't know how this is all going to turn out."

"Let's go, Belle. I'll help you." Claire slung my arm over her shoulder and walked me up the ridge.

"Go ahead." Medea smiled at us. "I have some catching up to do." She took his hand in hers, and they walked into the woods in the opposite direction.

I watched them go, a warmth emanating from my chest. All this time, Medea had wanted to remember her past, and she finally had. I'd played a small part in it. I was so happy for her.

"So, tell me, dear." Claire limped up the hill beside me. Her white hair rustled in the slight breeze. "How did you know Mephistopheles was on our side? We all thought he worked for Lucifer."

"Well . . ." My mind raced through the possible answers. He told me he didn't like Lucifer, but sometimes his actions said the opposite. "My intuition told me I could trust him. It's something I've been working on lately — listening to my gut. It all started with a feeling I had about a target. I was supposed to torture him, but he wasn't really bad. I felt the same way about Mephistopheles — that he was actually good beneath it all."

We found the tank Mephistopheles mentioned. A hookah hose ran from one side. I breathed in the stinky vapor first, gazing into the dark green woods.

"What does your intuition say about this battle with Lucifer?" Claire sat beside me and took the mouthpiece.

"My gut says we're doing the right thing. He has to be stopped. I've been thinking about that prophecy in Revelations. Maybe Lucifer's obsession with the beautiful woman who'll bring about the 'end of days' will actually bring about the end of *his* days."

Claire let the mouthpiece fall from her hands. "I hope so. I'm worried, Belle. He's powerful. He might bring an army to try to capture you."

"We only have to take him out, not the whole army.

425

Don't worry. We won't summon him until we're ready. And when we do, we'll have planned it out so well, it'll go off without a hitch. It'll all be over soon."

She patted my leg and smiled. "You're so sweet, Belle. It's going to be so fun to teach you more about your fire element powers once this is all done."

"Yeah." I blinked, hoping I was right about the battle.

"Mind if we crash your party?" Fern walked into our group and crouched to pick up the mouthpiece. She drew a deep breath, then looked back at the valley. Maribeth followed her, her arms crossed.

Fern blinked hard, her brows locking together, then stood and pointed at the grass plain. "What the hell is that thing?"

I looked down at the dark valley. Hellfire blazed in a tall rectangle on the grassy lawn. The unmistakable clankings of a means-station rising from the depths of Hell rang out, coming closer by the second.

Someone was coming up.

CHAPTER THIRTY-SIX

Medea and Mephistopheles ran through the dark woods toward us. He pointed at the hellfire rectangle on the plain, his brow furrowed. "What the Hell is a means-station doing here?!"

"I don't know," Iona said. "How does anyone know we're here?"

"Is everyone wearing their thought charms?" Claire asked.

Everyone patted their pocket or touched a necklace and nodded.

Mephistopheles scowled. "It must be those damned gargoyles. They swore allegiance, but they must've told Lucifer. I'm so sorry."

Medea shook her head. "Maybe it's our fault — we fought some fire imps on the way here. I thought we destroyed them, but they could've survived the fall and reported back to Hell."

"We don't have time to blame anyone," I said. "We need the crystals, now!"

Maribeth and Fern spread their hands wide. Their fingers clenched, and the muscles in their arms strained. The earth trembled beneath my feet. I stumbled, reaching out to grasp the rough bark of a tree trunk to stabilize myself.

A giant spray of earth rose before me in a cloud. Fern and Maribeth's hands flew, sorting the dirt from the rocks and crystals. Soil and pebbles rained down to the ground in a staccato, leaving six dark green crystals hovering in the air. Maribeth summoned them into her hands and showed me. Each one was only a little bigger than one of my fingernails.

My heart sank. "That's not enough to make an centimeter of a sword, much less a knife. We need more, and fast!"

Fern clenched her hands again. Another spray of soil rose. Maribeth sifted through the clouds of dirt for the crystals. Fern raised another cloud, and another.

"Hold on." Medea shouted. "Stop!"

I glanced at the rattling means-station, my stomach hard with fear.

Ding!

We leaned forward, breath tight, watching the hellfire dancing in the shape of a doorway over a rectangular patch of open earth. My limbs trembled, and the sound of my heartbeat rushed in my ears.

From the shadows of the means-station, someone in an ink-dark suit pushed black hair behind enormous black horns on his head. His suit did little to hide the tension in his muscles or the fiery anger in his black eyes. He took massive, earth-quaking steps onto the plain, his ruddy crimson skin gleaming in the bright hellfire light. Five orcs stepped out after him, sniffing the air, their noses twitching.

"What are you waiting for?" Lucifer roared, shoving the nearest one. "They're here somewhere. Capture them!"

The orcs ran across the field, scrambling to find us.

I cursed under my breath.

"What are we going to do?" Maribeth asked.

Medea gazed at the orcs, her eyes wide. "We're up-wind of them, and I can keep it that way, but that won't keep us safe for long."

"Does the invisibility spell work against Lucifer?" I hissed.

"Yes, I've tried it out before."

"*Camarquardt herosis*," Fern whispered.

Once the sparkles floated around us, I began to breathe a little easier.

"We have eight more crystals." Maribeth held out the small stones in her dark hand, her face uncertain.

I rubbed my thumb into my temple. "This is going to

take forever."

Medea caught my arm. "If we don't have time to make a knife, we make an arrowhead. Or a couple of them. Can you forge one?" she asked Claire.

"Sure. I've done it before with steel. The crystal has a lower melting point."

"Do it." Medea nodded.

"But . . ." I gazed into her black eyes. "You know what could happen if you kill him. You could turn evil again. You'd forget who you are, all over again."

She looked down at me with confidence in her eyes. "You were willing to face the same consequences, and I didn't stand in your way."

I bit my lip. "But you just met the love of your life again."

They glanced at each other and nodded. "We're in agreement that Lucifer needs to die. It doesn't matter who does it. Whoever can take the shot should take it. But we need a distraction, something to keep their attention off of us while we work."

Iona stepped forward, broom in hand. "I guess this is where I come in handy." She gave me a half-hearted shrug. "I can't help with the weapon, so I might as well put myself to good use."

I gazed at her, biting my lip. "What are you going to do?"

She smiled a sad smile. "I'm going to do what I do

best. Fly."

I hugged her and tried to resist melting in her embrace. I didn't want her to take the risk. Losing Jane had been hard enough.

She backed away, her warm brown eyes leveling with mine. "I know what I'm getting into. We all do. We all believe in this cause."

I sniffed and drew back from her. She was right. We'd be found faster unless someone diverted the orcs while we worked.

Iona adjusted her midnight blue cloak, and threw a leg over her broom. "Time to fly." She grinned and launched into the air, traveling through the forest before emerging onto the open field. Once in the open, she blasted the orcs with electric blue bolts.

Gunshots rang out. Iona zoomed around them, cackling like a madwoman.

Medea cast another invisibility spell on us while Fern launched another cloud of dirt into the air, sorting through it desperately. Claire dug an arrowhead-shaped hole in the earth, compacting the soil around the edges. She set the crystals in and pushed her energy into it with all her might. Orange light blasted from her hands. The crystals lit up with a green fire, filling the air with the scent of scorched earth and minerals. She wiped her brow with her arm and waved the molten crystal arrowhead. "It needs time to cool."

Mephistopheles drew an arrow from Medea's quiver and ripped off its tip. "Are you still as good a shot as I remember?"

"Better." She smiled. "I learned from the best."

"Sweetheart," his black eyes crinkled. "You know, I could take the shot. I don't want to lose you again so soon."

"But we may only have one shot, and the sight on my bow is messed up." She laughed half-heartedly. "I don't know why I never fixed it. What I'm saying is it needs to be me."

He kissed her hand. "If you turn again, I'll do everything I can to help you, I promise."

I swallowed, my eyes sweeping the open field. Iona was out there all by herself, flying and casting. She was doing a good job of distracting them, but some of the orcs were starting to wander off. "We need another distraction."

Mephistopheles pulled Medea close. "Just in case." He kissed her.

They separated, and she gazed at him. "Knowing you again has been *so wonderful.*"

"The best." He grinned before running out into the forest. Once he ran onto the grassy plain, sprays of red light blasted from his palms, toppling over two orcs. They got back up and charged him again.

When another *ding* sounded through the crater and

ogres ran out, more adrenaline rocketed in my blood. The odds kept shifting against us. We had to end this, and fast. I glanced at the cooling moldavite arrowhead.

Maribeth situated her broom. "No sense in having two earth witches here when one'll do."

"Be careful," I said.

She smiled. "Those demons won't know what hit them." She rocketed out onto the grassy plain, firing yellowish-green spheres that exploded upon impact. One of the ogres was blasted across the field.

Lucifer roared. "BELLE! I know you're here! Come out of the woods!"

"Look!" Claire pointed in the sky, where a flock of harpies dive-bombed the demons, ripping into them with their talons. I gazed at their majestic wings and long hair, barely believing what I saw. They must've changed their minds. Maybe they saw the logic in our mission after all.

Claire handed Medea the arrowhead — a perfect green, glassy tip. She fitted it onto her arrow and wound catgut around it. My pulse pounded. We needed to shoot him, and fast.

On the field, Mephistopheles was knocked flat by an orc with a broadsword. He leapt up again and hit the orc in the chest with red fire.

Maribeth and Iona cast spells at the demons, arcing across the sky like bats. The orcs fired round after round at them, but they kept missing. I wondered if they had protection spells up too.

"Bring me the girl!" Lucifer commanded. "She has to be in the forest somewhere."

The orcs scattered, running toward the forest rimming the crater. One of them started up the hill toward us. His eyes lit up when he saw me.

I froze for a second, then turned to the group. "The invisibility spell must've broken!"

The orc broke into a run. "Over here!" he grunted.

Medea threw up her hands, blasting him with hurricane-strength winds. He was blown back, but his fingers clamped his gun. Bullets ripped through the woods, pocking the trees and making bark fly up.

"*Clemit pro sequious!*" I screamed, running in front of the other witches as they worked. The bullets hit my bubble and bounced back onto the orc with a higher velocity, denting his armor. He fell to the ground, clutching his neck. I gasped with fear for my karma until I remembered what Claire had said. The protection bubble would protect me and my karma too — I wouldn't turn evil for shielding myself from their attack.

Fern raised more crystals while Claire worked on forging another arrowhead. They didn't see the two orcs that ran toward our group through the forest, from the other direction. Even though they couldn't see us, the invisibility spell did nothing to hide our footprints on the ground or the cooling arrowhead. When I saw they had automatic rifles, every muscle in my body tensed. I ran, trying to block the witches with my protection sphere, but I wouldn't make it in time. I was too far away. The orcs raised their guns, fingers reaching for their triggers.

Behind them, a wall of fire erupted, stopping them in their tracks. The orcs writhed, falling to their knees and crying out in agony.

Mephistopheles walked around them and blasted them again with red fire from his palms. "You will not kill MY WIFE!" he shouted.

They fell to the ground, smoking and cooking in their armor.

"Hello, wife." Mephistopheles smiled lovingly at Medea.

Medea laughed. "Hello, husband."

Another loud *ding* rang out over the field.

I gasped, a sinking feeling in my belly. *Not more.*

A fresh batch of demons ran out of the means-station — cyclopses and ogres pounded the grass beneath them. Maribeth and Iona fired bolts at them and dodged their javelins and spears.

"I'll have the next arrowhead ready in a sec!" Claire yelled, blowing on it to cool it off. Medea pulled back the first moldavite-tipped arrow and scanned the ground below, trying to find a good shot.

"Take the first good shot you can," I yelled. "We need to end this."

She concentrated, looking through the sight on the bow, then let out a deep breath and released the arrow. It sailed through the air. We held our breaths, hoping against hope.

It flew just over Lucifer's shoulder and hit an ogre in the leg. The ogre went down, clutching his green shin with a yelp.

Lucifer turned toward us. "I'm getting tired of these games, Belle! Don't make me dissipate every last one of your friends. *You know I will!*"

I shook my head, doing my best to rise above my trembling emotions. "Keep those arrowheads coming! We just need one good shot."

Claire fired the third set of crystals in the earth. Iona and Maribeth swooped overhead, attacking the demons with all they had. But they had to watch out for the cyclopses. They threw spears with deadly accuracy. Twice, Iona dodged the spears with only a millimeter to spare.

My heart sank in my chest. It was like the cabin raid all over again — I'd wanted to help my sisters then, but I had to watch. Now might be my chance, maybe my last one. This time, I'd defend my friends. I knew I couldn't do anything actually harmful without turning evil, but I could do other spells.

"*Pelluminbestillia*," I shouted.

One of the ogres' leather armor turned into chipmunks. He kicked them off, furious and embarrassed.

I aimed a spell at a cyclops and shouted, *"karnicia jamais far heinke."* Long hair grew over his eye. He tripped and fell. Mephistopheles climbed onto his back and tied his hands together with a rope made of white energy.

"Calloy piscitum!" I aimed the spell at two orcs. In place of their knives, they held live fish in their hands. They dropped them, staring at the fish flapping on the ground in confusion.

"Belle!" Lucifer's voice carried through the crater. "I can see you're not going to come willingly. But you should know," a black light crackled in his palm. "You're not the only one with magic."

He launched the fireball from his palm and struck Iona. She shrieked and fell from the sky, landing hard on the ground.

I wanted to run to her, but a black ball of light whizzed toward me. I tried to dodge it, but it sliced my leg. Searing pain bit into my flesh. I looked down and saw a gaping wound on my shin, blood dripping from it. I spoke the words of the healing spell, but stopped after a second. I couldn't risk spending all my power on healing, not with everything else happening around me.

The witches behind me still worked, the words of their magic like a chant. Another red streak shot across the sky. I thought I saw Maribeth fall to the ground.

I ducked as Lucifer blasted more black, spiky balls of energy into the forest.

"Try another arrow now!" I said. "He's distracted."

Medea pulled back another arrow, her face constricting as she focused. She released it — it crossed the field in a whisper and struck Lucifer right in the heart.

I gasped, breathless, my mouth falling open.

He looked down at it incredulously, not comprehending what had happened. A rivulet of crimson spilled down his suit and ran onto the earth.

Medea laughed nervously.

"We did it!" I said. "It worked!"

"Wait," Medea pointed to him, eyes wide.

He clutched the shaft of the arrow and pulled on it, moving it back and forth. Blood spilled out of his flesh. After a second, he ripped it out of his chest. He looked in our direction with malice, his eyes burning red and black.

"Why didn't it kill him?" Medea asked, her voice frantic.

I shook my head, unable to speak. My heart beat so fast I felt as if it'd explode. I'd been nervous about this — it made sense that his crystallized feathers could pierce his skin, but I had no idea if he could actually be killed. He was once an archangel, after all. Were we doomed to fail, just as the others had before us? Would he exterminate us all?

Lucifer's horns extended even further, and black smoke curled from his red nostrils. "Belle, come to me!" He lifted his hands in the air.

I felt light, like I was flying, only my broom was lying against a tree trunk several feet away. My feet lifted off the ground. "Medea!"

When I looked at her, I saw the same thing was happening to her, too. She had a bewildered look on her face as she clutched her bow. Claire and Fern also rose with us.

Claire passed Medea the last arrowhead as we floated over the field of our friends battling against demons. Bursts of light clashed against clubs and armor.

"Hurry!" I shouted.

She bound the arrowhead to a shaft, winding the string around it, then extended her bow. She released her arrow. I watched, unable to breathe, as it soared over the field. It pierced Lucifer's neck, right in his carotid artery.

"Yes!" I shouted.

He roared, blasting everything in a ten foot radius of him to ash. He raised a hand to his wound, touching the place where a fresh torrent of blood ran down his white shirt and onto his suit.

We fell to the ground, some fifteen feet from him. My leg and my hands were bloody, but that was nothing compared to Lucifer's injury. He tried to wriggle the arrow out, but the arrow was lodged in. More blood poured from his veins. He finally pulled it out and threw it to the ground.

He glared at us, and a black mist shot out of his hands. I heard a choking noise. When I glanced at my friends, I saw them choking on a purple mist. It traveled out of their throats and into the air. Lucifer was dissipating them, just like he said he would.

"Stop!" I yelled, my stomach sinking.

Fern's breath rattled in her throat. She threw something at him. Countless jagged pieces of moldavite flew through the air, shooting into him like shrapnel.

He winced. Blood ran down his neck and arms.

My friends gasped for air. "Mephistopheles!" I screamed. I looked around for him, but he was defending himself against two cyclopses on the other side of the crater. He couldn't hear me.

Lucifer laughed. "Belle, did you really think these rocks and a stupid little demon could hurt me?" He flicked one of the stones off him. "Let's go. I need you to fulfill the prophecy. I'll deal with him later."

"No." Even with my friends struggling to breathe, I couldn't give into him. If I did, everything would be destroyed — the earth, Heaven — everything. I couldn't let the prophecy come true. "I'm not going with you. I'll *never* go with you."

"YOU'LL DO AS I SAY!" Lucifer ran toward me. His

eyes glowed black and red.

A silhouette leapt between me and Lucifer, stopping him in his tracks. He held a glowing white sword with trembling hands. His armor appeared to be made of steel. Donovan glanced over his wing at me, his blue eyes fearful.

I inhaled sharply. I hadn't known he'd come here! But what was he doing? His sword wouldn't hurt Lucifer. He could get killed!

Bright lights shone from the edge of the crater, blinding me. The sky lit up with what looked like the moon crash-landing to the earth. I blinked and held my hand over my brow. For a second, I couldn't see anything. Then I saw human forms flying, wings spread wide. Each of them wielded a sword blazing with white-hot light.

Angels — I nearly cried with relief. They charged toward the demons and clashed head-on, their armor deflecting the spears and swords.

Another *ding* rang out. Goblins ran out of the means-station. They attacked the angels, their monstrous features glaring in the light of the swords as they skirmished. The clank of metal on metal grew louder.

"Out of my way, cupid," Lucifer growled.

Donovan crouched in a fighting stance before me, his blazing sword ready. "If you want her, you'll have to go through me."

Lucifer seethed, two giant balls of black energy spinning in his palms. "So be it." He flicked the spheres toward him.

Donovan sliced clean through one of them with his sword, destroying it, but the other one nicked his ribs. His armor dissolved as if acid were eating away at it. He convulsed, clutching his side, and knelt, his knee hitting the ground.

I covered my mouth to keep from screaming. Why had he leapt in front of me? It hadn't accomplished anything, and now he was going to die!

Donovan stood upright again, breathing hard. He charged toward Lucifer, sword held high.

Lucifer threw up his arm, shielding himself. The sword sparked against it. Donovan leaned in closer, the sword close to Lucifer's head. With a mighty heave, Lucifer pushed him aside. Donovan flew through the air and landed in a heap twenty feet away, with a loud thud. He moaned. His angelic blue eyes blinked once before they went still.

My chest clenched. I wanted to run to him, but Lucifer walked toward me, arm outstretched, hand open as if to drag me to Hell.

I scrambled back from him. My gut convulsed with dread, but I always knew it'd come down to this. Me against him. I'd put everything on the line for this one chance to take him down, and I had to take it.

I stood up and summoned the only battle spell I knew

— the spiky red energy that Medea had used on Kelsey. "*Misanae volgam!*" It cracked in my hand, hot and ready. I blinked back tears, knowing it couldn't do anything more than knock him back a few centimeters.

"It's time to come with me," he said.

Then I saw it — the dying means-station, flickering with white and blue flames.

I gasped. There was another way. I ambled away from him, the red star fading in my hand as I lurched toward the dying means-station, every step hampered by the wound on my leg.

"BELLE!" Lucifer crossed the gap with angry, earth-quaking steps.

When I was near the means-station, I crouched and shouted, *"clemit pro sequious!"* A crystalline sphere shot into place around me, larger and stronger than any I'd ever cast before. I almost laughed. It was a blood spell. I may not be able to harm him, but I could certainly push him onto the means-station gate with my energy.

Lucifer reached a bloody arm out to snatch me up. I shifted, making his arm ricochet off my sphere. He fell backwards near the metal grate, his eyes wide with sur-prise.

I glanced around the field for Mephistopheles, but I could barely see anything except for a blur of angels clashing against demons. It was just me and the devil himself.

I walked toward Lucifer. With every step toward my greatest fear, the protective bubble pushed him onto the metal grate of the means-station. He resisted, but the sphere pushed back. He grasped it, growling at me. *If only he would step on the button.*

An arrow whizzed over my head and clattered on the gate, striking the red button. The little metal gate shot down, and with it, Lucifer. His fingers clawed at the air, but there was nothing to hold onto. He fell, vanishing from my sight.

I gasped, my eyes searching for him in the dark shaft, but he wasn't there. There was just the rectangular hole in the earth. *Could it be? Was he really gone?*

Across the field, Mephistopheles lowered Medea's bow, an amazed look on his face. He started to run toward me, his face breaking out into a smile.

Whooshing noises came from the flickering means-station. When I turned back to it, my chest clenched.

Lucifer flew up from the shaft, his giant bat wings beating hard. He roared, reaching clawed hands toward me.

Mephistopheles shot red bolts from his palms. "You bastard! You stole my true love away from me!" His eyes were wild with rage as he shot bolt after bolt at the winged beast. "You took her to Hell and turned her evil! And for what? For a few years of subservience?" He threw everything he had into thick cords of red lightning,

444

locking Lucifer just above the shaft. "I won't let you do the same thing with Belle!"

A mountain of dirt rose in the air all around me. When it fell, Maribeth faced Lucifer, her dark face livid. "This is for Sarah and everything you did to Medea and Belle!" Hundreds of crystals launched into the air and struck Lucifer, blasting into his body and tearing holes into his leathery wings.

Without the tension in his wings, he began to drop into the shaft. "No. NO!"

Maribeth gritted her teeth and summoned another mountain of dirt to rise. The crystals rotated to their sharpest point and fired at him, even harder than before.

As more holes appeared in his wings, his face contorted with fear, his eyes wide. He began to fall, and then disappeared. His cry echoed as he fell, down, through the earth.

CRUNCH! CRUNCH!

Stone and earth slammed together — the means-station was closing. The ground shook, bringing me to my hands and knees. Something screeched, like metal scraping against metal. I pressed my hands against my ears, trying to block out the scream.

CHAPTER THIRTY-SEVEN

The crunching noise rose to the surface, rumbling the ground, then all was silent. The means-station blipped out like a snuffed flame. Where it used to be was only black smoke and ripples of energy fading in dawn's early light. I stared at the rectangle of scorched, blackened earth and molten rock, breathless, my heart still pounding hard. After a second, grass appeared, covering the spot completely.

My protection bubble burst and I fell onto the grass. I shook my head. "He's gone. I can't believe we did it!"

Tears coursed down Maribeth's face. She laughed shakily.

Across the field, Medea, Claire, and Fern gasped for breath. Purple motes spun through the air and went back into their bodies.

Mephistopheles lowered his bow and ran to kneel by Medea, holding her hand as she breathed the purple motes of her soul back in. The shadow of a smile played on his face as he glanced at me and Maribeth. "What do you think happened to the old bastard?"

Maribeth's lips curled into a beautiful smile as she walked toward her friends. "We killed the beast! He's stuck in the middle of earth with the only thing that can kill him."

Her eyes met mine. She'd sacrificed so much — she'd done what no one else could have. She'd saved me from becoming evil too, at the risk of becoming evil herself. My heart rose in my throat. "I'm so sorry you had to do that, Maribeth."

"It's okay. I knew what I was doing, and it had to be me." She helped Claire up and patted her back as she coughed. "Anyway, I don't have any friends in Heaven. They're all right here on earth, but I can't say the same for you. I didn't want you to be barred from it forever, not if I could help it."

I gave her a sad smile. What she had done meant the world to me. She could come back from being evil, just as Medea had. It might take a while, but she had a coven full of friends to support her and remind her of who she was.

Mephistopheles had sacrificed everything too — he'd already been evil once, so he didn't lose out on Heaven. Only, if he turned evil, he'd lose the one thing he'd worked so hard for — he'd lose his memories again. Who knew how long he'd have to work to make up his karma before he could use a remembrance charm again? It could be decades. But the way he looked at Medea made me think it was all worth it. She smiled, tears dripping off her face. She met my eyes for a moment, and I felt myself break into a smile. I wondered if she felt the same thing I did — pure, exhausted relief at not having to worry about Lucifer ever again. We were free, at last.

On the smoldering battlefield, the remaining demons ran away from us. Their armor clinked as they scattered up the ridge toward the rising sun and the waystations in the city. The angels sheathed their glowing swords and attended to the wounded. White light burst from their hands in spectral orbs that glowed across the daybreaking field. Two angels approached the witches and enfolded them in their wings, healing them.

Then I remembered — Donovan had leapt in front of me. He'd saved me when no one else had been able to. I ran, limping to the last place I'd seen him, my eyes searching the grass desperately. I saw someone lying facedown, his shiny armor torn open, and dashed toward him. It was Donovan. One of his wings was cocked at a strange angle, and a dark red stain covered his side.

I darted toward him, forgetting my injury, then stumbled and crawled. Every step forward sent sharp pains from the gaping wound on my leg. But I had to get to him. When I reached him, I nudged his shoulder.

"Donovan?"

He didn't respond. Worse still, there was no buzz between us, no vibration at all. He hadn't moved since Lucifer had swatted him aside. I took a deep breath, resisting the panic rising within me. I pushed energy out of my center and chanted the healing spell. Spots swam before my eyes. I was weak — I had so little to give, but I wanted to give it all to him.

When I cracked my eyes, he was still, silent. "Donovan, wake up!" I shook him, barely able to think. Tears clogged my throat and ran from my eyes. He couldn't be dead. Not after everything we'd been through.

An angel with a pale, pointed child's face and long white-blonde hair pulled at my shoulders, drawing me away from him. "Miss, please," she said in a small voice. "You need healing."

"I'm fine." I swatted her hands off me. "Help him. Please!"

Her sad eyes evaluated me, then her wings opened wide, encompassing him. A light shone through her feathers.

I looked away, a sob stifling in my throat. I couldn't believe he was gone. I swallowed hard and said a prayer for him, even though nothing could be done if he was really dead. He'd be gone forever, just as he'd feared.

Something buzzed on my back, and my heart rocketed. Was he alive? Was he communicating to me from the other side? I peeked around the angel's wings, but he lay still, silent. Soft hands caressed my shoulder and arm again. I turned and saw an angel with ochre skin and short, curly hair. His white wings spread around and stroked my back.

"It'll be okay," he cooed.

I gazed into his kind eyes. I wanted to tell him it wouldn't be okay, that Donovan was either dead or close to dying, but I was too tired. I couldn't do anything.

"Listen to the sound of my voice," he said.

His words calmed me and the buzzing from his wings made me feel numb. I lay down on the grass, blinking at Donovan until my vision faded and went completely dark.

I slipped into another realm. It felt like a dream, only there was nothing but darkness. A tiny white dot appeared, floating like a milkweed seed in a breeze. It crackled with a soft blue light, as if it had some kind of electricity. The light grew bigger until it was the size of an egg, floating in the air around me, then it was the size of a baby, then it was as large as I was. The arcs of blue light grew thicker and branched out like a tree.

The light sparked onto me and spread all over my body. Instantly, a deep peace permeated my mind. The white field was all I could see, but I wasn't scared. I breathed it in and felt it trickle down my throat. The burning pain inside me quenched. The wound on my leg knitted itself whole again with a wet slurping noise. I was healed, whole again.

But Donovan wasn't.

My eyes flew open. "That's enough."

"I'm not done healing you." The angel's wings surrounded me in a pale cocoon.

I sat up, pushing him back with my hands. "Please, let me see him."

He nodded. "As you wish." His wings retreated from me, then he backed away and went toward a fallen harpy.

Donovan lie on his back, his eyes closed, his mouth partially open. His healer was gone. I looked, but didn't see her anywhere. My hand found his, but he didn't respond. There was no energy exchange, no buzzing. I studied his freckled cheekbones and willed him to wake up.

I sighed, my tears falling onto his chest. He didn't deserve this. He'd fought against Lucifer, had stood right in front of him when he was about to take me to Hell. He'd spared me from lifetimes of suffering. It wasn't right for him to die — it wasn't fair. What God would let him die?

Fingertips batted weakly against mine, then Donovan clasped my hand. He opened his eyes and gazed at me, a tired smile on his face. "Belle." His grasp strengthened. "We must've made it."

I laughed even as hot tears ran down my cheeks. I'd

been through so much — from torture and imprisonment to learning spells and fighting demons, and I'd finally come through the end battle, defeating the Prince of Darkness once and for all. And he was there with me.

"I can't believe it's really over," I said. "If you hadn't come . . ."

He smiled weakly. "I came as soon as I could. I heard your prayers, but I was rallying the army. I couldn't stop thinking about you. I'm so sorry I tried to stop you from fighting him. You were right. I was just afraid." He stared at me, his blue eyes welling. "I'm so glad you're alive."

"I'm so glad *you're* alive."

I was barely aware of the people limping off the battlefield and the light from the angels' healing. Something deep within me released, as if another healing was taking place, or as if some weight I'd been carrying all these centuries had finally fallen away. It hardly felt real, that we'd killed Lucifer, and my friends and I had made it out alive. Maybe it had all happened like this for a reason. Maybe all my years on this earth had a purpose I hadn't seen until now.

"I'm sorry," an angel called out. "This one didn't make it."

I turned toward the angel. His brown curly hair hung as he stood over a crumpled form wearing a blue cloak.

"Do you want to say last rites?" he asked me.

I broke away from Donovan and ran toward them.

"No. Not . . ." But even from the distance, I saw her short brown hair fluttering in the slight breeze.

Iona.

I fell to my knees before her, barely feeling the rocks as they cut into my flesh. I couldn't take my eyes off her beautiful round face. I placed my hands on her and murmured the healing spell.

The angel's gray eyes were mournful. "I'm sorry. There isn't anything more we can do. She's gone. Dissipated."

A sob choked me, stuck in my throat. It burst into a flood of searing pain. I couldn't respond, couldn't move. All I could do was stare at the figure on the ground. Iona was my teacher, my friend, and now she was gone, an open gash sliced through her heart, staining her blue cloak with crimson. I felt terrible. I hadn't realized she was injured so badly. I hadn't even seen her soul dissipate. I could've helped her, given her a healing spell.

Fern ran over and covered her mouth, gasping. Claire limped close behind her. When she saw Iona's crumpled body, she sighed heavily and her blue eyes became watery. In the distance, Mephistopheles and Medea gazed onward, holding each other.

Donovan hooked an arm around my shoulders. "I'm so sorry, Belle." His hand ran over my arm, smoothing it.

I gazed at Iona's body, still unable to comprehend that she was gone.

"She was brave," Donovan said.

I nodded, swallowing. "She knew we might not make it out alive, but she fought anyway." I gazed up at the sky, willing my tears to recede. Iona wouldn't want me to feel so sad, to feel so torn up, but I couldn't help it. Losing her was devastating. I wondered if she had been the tipping point. If she hadn't sacrificed herself, would Lucifer have taken me to Hell? Would he have gotten away with it? Maybe she had saved all of our lives.

Medea stepped forward. "Belle, would you do the honors for Iona?"

As much as I didn't want to, I knew it was the right thing to do. I swallowed hard and focused on the fire inside of my belly, feeling the raging sadness burn my throat and heart. I felt my pain so acutely that when I opened my eyes and saw Iona's body was in flames, I wasn't surprised.

Claire knelt on the other side of me. She looked deep into my eyes and sniffed back tears. When she spoke, her voice was heavy with emotion. "We release our sister Iona to the fire today, but we go forward carrying her with us until the end of our days. We will always remember her willingness to fight for our freedom, even against all odds."

Iona's body burned in a warm, dancing yellow flame. After a minute, it turned to a dark gray ash and trickled away in the breeze. I embraced Claire, a new stream of tears running down my cheeks.

The harpies flew over to us and dipped their heads in bows. They were less in number — I'd seen at least two of them go down in the battle. "We are sorry for your loss," the leader said.

"We are sorry for yours as well," I said. "I never thought you'd come."

A few of them cooed. "Your fight was honorable, but more than that, we wanted to support you in the fight of the millennia. This time, the witches got it right."

I smiled through my tears. "Thank you for your help."

"We thank you for your bravery and cunning. We must leave you now." The eight remaining harpies opened their chestnut wings and took flight.

I watched them leave for a second, wishing there was something I could do to help them and their dwindling numbers. Maybe I could make it my next area of research. I huffed — if I had any energy left in me after this, I'd certainly try.

The little blonde angel tugged at my skirt. "We burned the bodies left on the field. They should be ash in a few minutes."

The field was empty. Besides the ash, there was no evidence that the battle of the worlds had taken place. Humanity would never know what had happened, how close they might've been to having a dark overlord.

The angel continued. "We must leave, and I advise

you to do the same. The humans are coming."

The whine of a siren sounded from the road, far away.

I nodded. "Thank you for fighting with us."

She smiled. "Thank Donovan and his friend. They persuaded us to join. I hope to meet you again one day." Her wings opened, then she and the other angels flew up into the clouds.

"We should go too." Medea said, her hand nestled in Mephistopheles'. "We're going to one of his hideaways. We want to get to know each other in case he turns evil, and we don't have much time before the full moon."

"Meph, do you think you'll turn evil?" I asked.

He shrugged. "Been there. I still have the book I wrote that helped me come back from it. Although, I'll need to write a new chapter now." He squeezed Medea closer and smiled sadly.

Medea nodded gravely. "If he does turn evil, I'll help him find his way back. When the time comes that his karma is below 100% bad, I'll make another love charm spell. He already gave me the magician's half of the remembrance token — his wedding ring." She raised a golden band that hung on her necklace beside the topaz pendant, then flashed her happy black eyes at us. "I'll see you soon, my sisters."

The sirens came closer. Blue flashing lights strobed through the trees on the horizon.

Fern stood, wiping a tear. "As Iona always said, 'time

to fly.'" She summoned her broom and caught it.

Maribeth walked beside her. "Can we go to the safe-house in Austria?"

"Aye," Claire said. "That sounds like a right nice idea. I could use some mountains to look at." She gazed wistfully at me. "Coming, dear?"

Fern and Maribeth turned to me expectantly.

I was speechless. I hadn't thought about what would happen after the battle. If I were completely honest with myself, I never expected to survive it. This moment, and every moment after, were gifts, ones I was deeply grateful for. I'd never have to run from Lucifer again. I was free, finally.

Donovan faced me, his wings rustling in the breeze. "I know you've been through a lot today, but I can take you to see your parents now. If you want to go to Heaven, that is."

I gasped, drawing away from him. "But how? I'm not good enough. My karma . . ."

"Your karma isn't that bad now, and I'll vouch for you." He smiled. "Your friends can come too, if they want, except for . . ." He gazed at Medea and Mephistopheles and shrugged apologetically. "Sorry, except for you. Nothing personal."

"No worries." Mephistopheles laughed, his black eyes glinting. "I lost that option a long time ago." He kissed Medea's hand. "And I have no regrets."

Medea smiled at him. "I only regret I didn't remember you sooner. We could've had decades together."

"Yes, but we still have the rest of our afterlife."

Medea waved. Mephistopheles reached into his pocket and drew out a beige sphere. He popped it in that air. It spun around them until they vanished from sight.

"What about the vapors?" I asked Donovan.

He shrugged. "Heaven has its own atmosphere. The laws of Hell don't apply there."

"I think we'll pass on Heaven," Claire said, summoning her broom. "But what'll it be for you, Belle?"

Car engines sounded across the bend in the road. It was now or never.

I gazed into Donovan's cerulean eyes. The thought of seeing my parents after all this time made my heart take flight. I could barely conceive of what they would think, but I hoped they would remember me, that they would be happy to see me. And if not, I had a family here on earth. "Take me to Heaven, please." I turned to the witches. "Can we meet up later?"

"Of course, dear." Claire leapt up from the ground on her broom and hovered into the air before me. Her long white hair flowed in the wind, and her eyes twinkled. "You're always welcome at any of our safehouses."

"Thank you so much for everything. I'll be in touch, I promise."

The other witches flittered into the air.

"Take care, Belle," Maribeth nodded.

"Thank you for everything."

Her lips curled up, revealing a perfect smile. "It was all worth it."

Fern patted my arm. "It's not a 'goodbye,' Belle. We'll find each other again soon."

"Yes," I said, hoping it was true.

The witches glided off into the air, the invisibility spell sparkling around them as they flew higher and higher, until they were mere specks in the sky.

I summoned my broom from the woods, and for the first time, it worked. I caught it, the rough bark feeling marvelous against my palm. Looking down at it, I marveled at the magic that was so much a part of me, the magic that had helped to kill Lucifer.

Donovan and I were alone. I cast an invisibility spell around us and watched it sparkle.

"I'm glad I get to try this a second time." Donovan swept me off my feet. A pleasant pulsing ran up my arm to my chest. His wings spread wide. "I didn't get a chance to show you how it's done at that kitchen in New York."

I wrapped my hands around his neck, watching with bated breath as he pushed up into the air. The feathers of his wings beat, shivering with strength and grace. We flew over the trees and above the crater. For a moment, I forgot everything else. I found myself smiling like a child.

When I tried to stifle it, it came back, bigger than before. We rose through the clouds and kept climbing. My heart strained in my chest.

"What happens next?" I asked.

"I'll help you get your karma back. We can work together."

I made a face. "But I'm still mostly bad. Does that matter in Heaven?"

He gave me a small smile. "Not to me."

"But . . . I'll be a *beast* compared to everyone else up there."

His grin widened. "Does that make me the beauty?"

I laughed. "Don't push your luck."

He laughed too.

And to think I'd growled at him, had threatened and screamed at him when we'd first met! I shook my head. It was so long ago. Almost another lifetime. I'd grown so much since then. I'd learned to trust my intuition, had become more fully myself. This whole time, he'd seen who I was beneath all the layers.

Donovan's wings fluttered, and still, we rose through the clouds. Above them, another set of clouds glowed with a blue energy. As we rose higher, I saw a garden growing on top of the cloud. Cherry trees flowered beside a hedge of blooming red roses, more than I'd ever seen in all my travels. A wide grass lawn stretched out from a forest with sprawling old oak and yew trees. In the distance, a watermill spun by a stream and a stone cottage.

Donovan's wings spread out, then he set me down gently onto the garden grass. My toes sank a little — the ground felt firm and squishy at the same time.

He picked a rose and handed it to me. I clasped the prickly stem and inhaled, savoring the perfect scent. A fly buzzed near my rose. I swatted it away.

"You missed me again!" said a little voice near my ear.

I leapt back and stared with disbelief at the housefly dancing on the rose. It was McMillan — my old manager in Hell! He rubbed his little forelegs together.

"What're you doing here?" I asked. "You're a demon!"

"Nope! I'm just a fly who hitchhiked into Hell one day and got a job. For some reason, they all thought I was supposed to be there. I told them my paperwork got lost, and they believed it. Suckers!"

I laughed and shrugged. The filing system was pretty bad.

Donovan extended his forefinger and gave McMillan the fly-equivalent of a high-five. "McMillan is great. We never would've figured out the karma calculations if it hadn't been for him."

I turned to the little fly. "Really?!"

"Well, I had a little peek at Lucifer's books." He shrugged. "You know, I tried to warn you, Belle. I had an escape plan and everything."

I stared at him incredulously. I had no words whatsoever. All I could do was laugh and shake my head.

"I see it all worked out," he buzzed. "You're in Heaven, you dethroned the Prince of Darkness — I always said you did good work."

"I had no idea you were trying to help me," I said. "I thought you were just incompetent."

His fly head pivoted. "Not everything is as it seems. Take that Bible verse about the 'beautiful woman riding the beast,' for instance. Even Lucifer was fooled by that false prophecy."

"False prophecy?" I echoed him.

"It's true." Donovan nodded. "Once Lucifer started looking for a beautiful woman, we knew he was trying to overthrow Heaven. It lit a fire under us."

My mouth hung open. I couldn't believe McMillan had been in on it the whole time. I grimaced. "I'm sorry I called you incompetent."

"It's okay. I must be going," he droned, flying away. "See you around."

I glanced at Donovan and felt my cheeks flush. "Gosh, I feel really bad for calling him that."

"Don't feel bad," he grinned. "I heard he really was a bad manager."

I laughed. "He was the worst!"

We walked into the garden. Bluebells and daffodils waved by a stream, and pale pink cherry blossoms blew in the wind. It was like a dream I never wanted to wake from — it was everything I thought it might be, but somehow, even more beautiful.

"Hullo, Belle."

I turned around. Jane stood beneath a majestic old oak tree, smiling radiantly. She wore a beautiful black dress, and her hair was braided to one side.

I broke away from Donovan and ran toward her. She clasped me into a giant hug.

"You made it here?" I asked, laughter bubbling up from my belly. "But how? I thought you . . ."

She looked over my shoulder at Donovan. I glanced at him.

He smiled serenely. "I did what I could. I wasn't brave enough to fight at the cabin, but I was on the periphery of the battle. When I saw her soul dissipating, I collected it and took her back here."

My jaw dropped. "Really?"

"It's true," Jane huffed. "And not a moment too soon, either. I was nigh close to dissipating. I even saw the purple vapors for what seemed like an eternity before he swooped in. But yes, he brought me here, thank heavens!"

"I'm so glad to see you."

She leaned toward me, her eyebrows raised. "Did you do it, Belle? Did you kill the Beast?"

"Yes, we did it." I smiled, a calm satisfaction melting

over my heart. "He's gone for good. He'll never harm anyone else ever again."

"Yes! I knew you'd give him hell!" She laughed and nudged me with her elbow. "And didn't I tell you they'd let you into Heaven? I gave them a great talking-to about it. Told them they needed you more than they needed anyone else here, that you deserved it after all you've been through."

Donovan nodded. "After I brought her here, she convinced me to fight alongside you. She even rallied the army that came to fight against Lucifer. Without her, we might not have won the war."

I embraced her again, crushing my head against her shoulder. I could hardly believe my luck. She'd fought so hard for us, just as she'd wanted to, only from the other side. It made me wonder how many others were working behind the scenes. All this time, I'd thought my mission was mine alone with the witches, but Heaven had my back after all.

I sniffed and drew away from her to gaze into her warm brown eyes. "Thank you, Jane. That means so much to me." I glanced at Donovan, who was pulling a weed from the garden. "Thank you for saving her."

"Of course."

"Babelin?" A man's voice sounded from the direction of the cottage.

I turned, adrenaline spiking in my blood. "Father?"

My parents ran down the path toward me, their arms outstretched. My father smiled broadly as he ran. His hair had gone silver, but my mother's was still brown, just as I remembered it. Her cherry-pink cheeks and her cinnamon eyes were exactly as I remembered them. They wore the simple village clothing, just like the old days. I ran along the path, my heartbeat fluttering, and rushed into their arms. We embraced, and I laughed through my tears. They even smelled the same, like oatmeal and beeswax. I could barely believe it. My greatest wish had come true — I was with my family and my best friend in Heaven. I was home for the first time in centuries.

My father stared at me, his blue eyes lit up with joy. "But how . . . ? What are you doing in our garden?"

"I'll tell you all about it." I dashed the tears from my eyes. "I'm just so happy to be here. I've waited so long to see you. Everything I've done was to get back to both of you."

My mother smiled, sniffing back her tears. She held me tight with one arm, and with her free hand, she smoothed the flyaway hair from my face. "I don't care where you've been or what you've done. I'm over the moon to see you. I felt so bad about what happened. I thought about you every day." Sobs wracked her chest.

I held her hands and gazed into her eyes. "Mother, don't cry. We're together now. Maybe it had to happen this way." I shrugged.

She nodded, her brown eyes glistening before she hugged me again.

"Your daughter is a heroine," Donovan said. "She killed Lucifer and saved the world from eternal damnation. Some of the angels are saying they might make her a saint."

"Our daughter?" My father grinned at me. "I don't doubt it. You were always such a rebel. But how in the world did you manage that?"

I gazed at my family, my best friend, and my angel. I had no words. It was everything I'd ever wanted. My heart felt so full, I thought it might burst.

Donovan looked around the group. "You have a lot of catching up to do. How about we go to a teahouse? There's a great place on the sunrise cloudscapes. I hear they have a killer Earl Grey."

I smiled and slid my hand into Jane's. "There's nothing I'd like more."

~ the end ~

~ Afterward ~

This story was inspired by the poem *La Belle Dame Sans Merci* by Keats, part of which is in the introduction of the book; and also by the J. W. Waterhouse painting on the cover. I've loved the painting for a long time, and always imagined she held a knife in her hand, and yet, her facial expression is sweet. My imagination spun stories about what the knight had done to deserve such a death, and what Belle Dame had done to deserve a life of killing people. She looked like a good person trapped in a bad situation. Instead of a faery-child, as Keats thought of her, I imagined her as a demon who was forced to kill bad people to achieve her salvation. Of course, where there's a Belle, there's a Beast . . .

When I set out to rewrite my 'doomed circus' story in March 2016, ideas for Belle Dame wouldn't leave me alone. I jotted down the ideas and wrote the first chapter as a short story. But more inspiration came to me throughout the day and even in the middle of the night. I wrote down all the ideas, while straining to write the about the circus.

Eventually, Belle's story won out. I finished the first draft in 21 days during the April 2016 Camp National Novel Writing Month and kept going, using Critique

Circle to assist. By December 2016, the fourth round of editing was over, and by early March 2017, beta readers started giving me feedback. The first edition was published shortly thereafter.

The first printed version of *Beauty and the Beast* was *Le Belle et La Bete,* by Gabrielle-Suzanna Barbot de Villeneuve, published in 1740 and made into a film in 1946. Other variations of this story abound, including *Twilight* and *Fifty Shades of Gray.*

As a child, I loved the 1991 Disney version of *Beauty and the Beast* because Belle was the most literate Disney 'princess' at the time, and I was really into reading. However, something about the story always seemed wrong. Why didn't Belle have any friends? Why didn't the village do anything about Belle being kidnapped? And how on earth could Belle fall in love with someone who'd imprisoned her and treated her so cruelly?

Belle Dame Sans Merci is a very different version of *Beauty and the Beast.* I really enjoyed playing with the elements of the story while crafting something entirely new. I still plan of finishing the doomed circus story — really, I will. But for now, Belle has a special place in my heart. I love how strong her rebellion is. It inspires me to do more good in the world. I'm going to donate a percentage of the proceeds from this book to Safe Child

Africa, a registered non-profit charity who assists children in Africa accused of witchcraft. The fact that witch hunts are still happening and children are being outcast, starved, and killed means this world has a long way to go. This charity will help.

Thank you for sharing this adventure with me. Proceeds from this first edition will go toward getting the book properly copy-edited for wider distribution. Please let me know what you think and if you'd be interested in a prequel / sequel.

~ Acknowledgements ~

I'd like to thank several people who helped me with this book. First and foremost, I thank my husband Tim Krug, for all his brainstorms and his many skills. I owe a huge debt of gratitude to Kristl Chitty for being there every step of the way and for her problem-solving assistance. The three of us hurdled over those writers' blocks with such ease that I hardly ever felt stuck at all.

A humongous thank you to all my wonderfully helpful critique partners, especially Katie Tillwick, Beth Sanchez, Taylor Jones, Kathryn Heligman, and Mandi Oyster. Your feedback helped so much. I look forward to reading your exquisite stories and trading critiques with you again soon.

Thanks to my awesome bunch of fabulous friends and beta readers Holly Simpson, Susan Roper, Gretta Smak, Paris Alexander, Lulabelle, Victoria Ramga, Patricia Chalfant, Veronica Sorcher, Kare Pickett, and Robyn Winstead. This was my first time working with betas, and you were all so responsive and thorough. I appreciate your help so much.

A huge thanks to Tim Krug, Veronica Sorcher, and Judy VerValin for copy and line editing suggestions. This book is better because of your help.

Thanks also to all my other gloriously supportive family and friends who encouraged my strange writings, especially Kari and Jason Himes, Joelle, Heather Jones, Alex Straaik, Matthew Temple, Andrea and Chris Hutson, Keri Spec, Jay Cavender and Lisa Baber Cavender, Vic Mackunis, Judy and Dave VerValin, Leah, Jennifer Trent, Scott Stolsenberg, Rob Badger, Gary Glaser, Elizabeth Peters, Mary Burnside, and Laura Sextro, Ryan Osborne. You are true friends, and I am forever grateful for the chance to talk about my weird ideas with such supportive and kind people. Thanks also to my faery godmother Penny Goody and the rest of my magical family, including Shringara Hasya, Nicki Ojeda, Kimberly Thalia, Marcus McCarty Towers, David and Veronica Sorcher, Fantasy, Wildflower, and many more. Thanks also to Gail Lichtenfels, Lawrence Hammar, Leslie Williams, Maddie Smith, Tammy Ballinger, Dwayne Gross, Scott Glum, Pam Hull, Chuck Mellon, Greg Brown, Sydney Poole, Anthony Campbell, and anyone else who let me talk about this project.

A great big thank you goes out to the musicians who inspired the atmosphere of the story, especially Faith and the Muse, Switchblade Symphony, Dead Can Dance, Autumn's Gray Solace, Diva Destruction, Collide, Garbage, and Cocteau Twins. The gritty and beautiful music was crucial for me to capture the energy of this story. Thanks to Youngman Brown from the Your Creative Push podcast and Liz Gilbert from the Big Magic podcast for inspiring me to keep going when the road was rocky, uphill, and dark as fudge. I also would like to thank Clarissa Pinkola Estés. Her books have reinvigorated me many times throughout my life, and her inspirations on authentic, empowered living made me who I am today.

~ About the author ~

Astrea Taylor is the author of *House of Transformation* and *Belle Dame Sans Merci*. Her other writing projects include an unfinished novel about a doomed circus, and a non-fiction memoir about the triumphs and trials of fire dancing called *Trust Us, We're Fire Dancers*, expected late 2017. She's a co-leader of Soul Fire Tribe, a fire dance performance group, and she has two humongous cats, who keep her company when she's writing and inspired the cat-energy part of this book.

Please consider leaving a review for Belle Dame Sans Merci on Amazon and or Goodreads. The more ratings a book has, the more likely someone is to read it. Reviews especially help newer indie authors find readers for their strange stories. If you're interested in more content, look for videos on Youtube or read strange stories on the blog or newsletter, or follow her on Goodreads, Instagram, Twitter, or Facebook.

Printed in Great Britain
by Amazon

25098293R00274